ALSO BY TERRY ROW

Summer Capricorn (2006)

Untarnished Reputation (2009)

Honorable Mention,
Genre Category,
Hollywood Book Festival (2009)

Winner, Western Category,
National Indie Excellence Awards (2010)

Phyllis Marie

By

Terry Row

Clifton Edwin Publishing
SANTA BARBARA

CEP

Clifton Edwin Publishing
3463 State St., PMB 244
Santa Barbara, CA 93105
www.CliftonEdwin.com

Copyright © 2011 by Terry Row
Edited by Kathryn Lynn Davis
Book Design by Florbnine Plnickick
Cover Design by Michael Row
Technical and Military Advice by C. Russell Byers
Text set in Sabon LT
Manufactured in the United States of America

Publisher's Cataloging-in-Publication
(Provided by Quality Books, Inc.)

Row, Terry.
   Phyllis Marie / by Terry Row.
   p. cm.
   LCCN 2010915384
   ISBN-13: 978-0-9786036-7-0
   ISBN-10: 0-9786036-7-2

   1. Row, Perry V., 1918-1997--Family--Fiction.
2. World War, 1939-1945--England--Fiction. 3.
Historical fiction, American. 4. War stories,
American.   I. Title.

PS3618.O87257P49 2011   813'.6
                        QBI10-600213

DEDICATIONS

Perry Vancil Row
1918-1997

Irene Palmer
1902-2006

Corliss Caroline Row
1912-2006

Kenneth Stanton
1912-2007

Beverly Roberts
1941-2010

Gary Fuqua
1937-2010

Ann Fuqua
1939-2010

ROW FAMILY

Elijah Delvaine "Lige" Rowe (1860-1919)
Caroline Strong "Carrie" Roe Rowe (1870-1952)

1. Clifton Carnine Row (1890-1967)
2. Vancil Edward Row (1892-1946)

WHITAKER FAMILY

James Perry Whitaker (1854-1896)
Parilee Jane Perry Whitaker (1855-1897)

1. Adeline Whitaker (1878)
2. Ida Viola Whiteaker Wiley (1880-1972)
3. Ora Lee Whiteaker Bates (1883-1954)
4. Lena Sedalia "Betsy" Whitaker Crow (1886-1973)
5. Cora Augusta Whitaker Hunt (1887-1944)
6. Georgia Alice Whitaker Row (1890-1947)
7. James Stanley Whiteaker (1892-1979)
8. Beulah Jane Whitaker Fewel Little (1894-1983)
9. John Perry Whitaker (1895-1947)
10. Ernest P. Whiteaker (1897-1979)

Clifton Carnine Row (1890-1967)
Georgia Alice Whitaker (1890-1947)

1. Corliss Caroline Row (1912-2006)
2. Lois Whitaker Row Aley (1914-1996)
3. Perry Vancil Row (1918-1997)
4. Helen Loraine Row Allen Skinner (1921-2002)

STANTON FAMILY

William Salathiel Stanton (1852-1893)
Edith Bowles Stanton Worth (1854-1937)

1. Alva D. Stanton (1876-1968)
2. Irvin James Stanton (1880-1971)
3. Edwin M Stanton (1884-1948)
4. William Lester Stanton (1888-1982)

HILL FAMILY

John J. Hill (1849-1918)
Elizabeth Ann Allen Hill (1849-1932)

1. Josephine Grace Hill Outland (1871-1927)
2. Niota Belle Hill Rees (1874-1950)
3. Vervie May Hill (1876-1882)
4. Anna Edna Hill Chilson (1881-1945)
5. Ruby Delight Hill (1883-1887)
6. Hazel Helen Hill Stanton (1886-1974)

Edwin M Stanton (1884-1948)
Hazel Helen Hill Stanton (1886-1974)

1. Edwin LaMar Stanton (1907-1908)
2. Virginia Mae Stanton Roberts (1909-1962)
3. Kenneth E. Stanton (1912-2007)
4. Phyllis Marie Stanton Row (1919-)

Part 1

Prologue

The old woman watched as her husband sat motionless on the edge of the bed. He wore just his underpants, his baseball cap—the one with the fake ponytail sticking out the back, to make light of his recent hair loss—and one white sock. He seemed to be staring at a particular place on the floor. *What is he doing,* she wondered? He appeared even more tired than he had looked yesterday morning and certainly less dignified. *It's no wonder,* she thought. *He's endured half a dozen biopsies and two rounds of chemotherapy during the last eight months.* Every time they thought they had the cancer in check, it presented again with new symptoms in new locations. His bravery in the face of adversity had amazed her, and she had known his bravery for a very long time.

A moment later she realized what he was doing. He was contemplating whether he had the strength or flexibility to bend down and pick up the other sock from the floor where he had dropped it. She got up from her chair and went over to him.

"Can I help you with this?" she asked, bending over and retrieving the missing article. His response seemed less an affirmation and more a grunt. She kneeled down and lifted his bare foot up onto her thigh, pulling on the sock. *He's gotten so thin,* she thought, observing his legs.

"There you go," she said. He managed a weak smile before slowly hauling himself up on his feet and reaching for his pants that hung on the doorknob. She watched him, thinking that he may have shrunk as much as two inches from his adult height of six feet.

As he approached his eightieth birthday, the old man seemed to speak fewer and fewer words each day. Stoic, her father had called him, pointing out that it was not what he said but how he behaved that proved his measure as a man. He had always been the quiet type, having little to say unless speech became absolutely necessary. Today, she wondered how long it had been since she had actually heard him say something: a day?

He managed to get into his pants and shirt without help, and she would have let him put on his shoes unassisted if he wasn't already late for the doctor, so without asking, she retrieved his new loafers from under the bed—the ones that he could just step into—and put them in front of him, guiding each foot into place.

"Come on," she said. "I have your coat by the door. We've got to get going. Do you have your list?"

He nodded his assent and started his slow shuffle out the door and toward the car. He had his list in his pocket; the two of them had prepared it together the day before yesterday. It listed new symptoms to tell the doctor about, questions about his treatment plan, and comments about the side effects he had been experiencing from his medications.

She helped him into the car and drove him the four blocks to the Central Coast Cancer Center, parking in the handicapped zone out front, thankful that the spot was vacant. Why there was only one disabled parking place, she couldn't fathom.

By the time they settled into the waiting room, she saw that they were only five minutes late. *Not bad,* she thought, *but I'm going to have to start allowing more time in the mornings.* The door opened and the couple's older son arrived, taking a seat near his parents.

The nurse showed the three of them into the doctor's office where the doctor sat behind his desk, reading from a file. The woman waited for her husband to start the conversation, knowing that he would. He had always managed his relationships with health care providers on his own.

The old man unfolded his list. "The first thing I want to talk about is the nausea," he said. "I know you said to expect it, and I did, but it has gotten so I can't even look at a piece of dry toast without feeling it come over me like a wave."

The doctor took off his glasses and looked up at his patient. "Yes," he said. "I understand. We're going to take care of that."

"How?"

"I got your latest test results back last night," the doctor said, leaning back in his chair and staring at the ceiling for a moment before righting himself and sitting forward. "We're going to take you off all the medications."

"Do you have something new in mind?" the old man asked. "Because I read an article on the internet about a new drug trial in Minnesota and I—"

"We're going to take you off all the medications," the doctor repeated. "You can put your list away. At this point, we're just going to do everything we can to make you comfortable."

The old woman inhaled sharply. "Is that where we are?" she asked.

"Yes," the doctor said. "That's where we are. The cancer has reached his pericardium, the sheath that contains the heart. That, in combination with the tumor in his head—"

"You know, we've had over fifty-seven wonderful years together since we married. More than that, altogether."

"Yes, I know." The doctor looked again at his patient who sat studying his list. "Take him home and let him get some rest. Take him off all the medications. I'll call you tomorrow to explain our next course of action."

"How long?" she asked.

"I don't know, exactly," the doctor said. "Weeks?"

The four of them sat quietly for a minute before she turned to her son. "Will you call your brother?"

"I'll take care of it."

Back in the car on the way back to their apartment, the man turned to his wife and said, "Why didn't we go through the list? I had some questions on my list that we didn't cover."

"I know," she said. "He said to put away the list."

"Yes, but why? And why were you telling him about our fifty-seven years together? I didn't understand any of that."

"Because he just told me that the new goal is to make you comfortable. He just told me that I'm going to lose you," she said, trying not to cry.

Late in the night, the old woman heard a noise from the bedroom as her husband sat up in bed. She went to the door and looked in. "Do you need to use the bathroom?"

"Yes," he said. He had slept hard through the afternoon and evening and during that time, she had sat in the big chair in the living room, listening to soft music and staring at the ceiling fan as it went around and around.

"Okay," she said. She helped him to his feet and into his robe, following along behind him, hanging onto the robe's sash that she had tied around him.

In the bathroom, she suddenly felt him lose his balance. She had always believed that by holding the sash she could protect him from falling but now, in a sudden rush of terror, she realized she couldn't possibly keep him on his feet. In fact, if she didn't do something soon, he was going to drag her down with him.

She reached around his waist and pulled as hard as she could on the sash. If she could just rotate him a little, just ninety degrees, she might be able to prevent him from falling forward through the glass shower door. With one final tug, she sent him careening to the left and onto the toilet in a seated position.

It might have seemed funny under other circumstances, but not tonight.

"Are you okay?" she asked.

"Yes," he said. "You?"

"I'm all right." She helped him out of his clothes enough to allow him to use the toilet. While she waited, she looked back in the direction of the bed and estimated the distance at about eight feet. When he finished, she asked, "Are you going to be able to get back to the bed?"

He looked from the floor to the bed and back to the floor before answering. "I don't think so."

She tried to lift him, hooking her arms under his, but he felt like a sack of potatoes. He may have lost weight, but he still outweighed her two to one. He couldn't muster enough leg strength to allow her to help him. She relaxed her grip on him and made sure he was still balanced on the toilet.

"You rest there a minute," she said, walking to the edge of the bed and sitting down.

"Do you remember your promise?" he asked.

She felt her blood pulsing quickly through her head. The overwhelming truth came crashing in her ears, flashing in her eyes, until she thought she'd be deafened by the noise, blinded by the light. She remembered her promise, but she also realized that she couldn't move him back to the bed by herself. What was she to do now?

1

At twenty-two, Phyllis Marie stood slim, petite, and pretty, with stunning green eyes that became more emerald with each passing year, her porcelain-white skin turned rosy-cheeked from the cold Idaho wind. Beneath her heavy winter coat, she wore brown slacks she had tailored herself, with a green knit sweater that complimented her figure as well as her eyes. She rushed into her father's photography studio, her arms full of the morning mail, her brunette hair speckled white and wet from the unexpected morning snow.

Perry, her husband of twenty months, followed closely, his arms even more burdened with packages of developing solutions and photography paper. Not quite two years older than his wife, at six-feet-tall he towered over her. His ruddy complexion, wavy dark hair, and toothy grin contributed to his rugged good looks.

The two put their burdens and winter coats on the front desk before Perry wrapped one arm around Phyllis Marie's slender waist. She turned to him on tiptoe and returned the embrace, clasping her hands behind his neck before meeting his slow gentle kiss. She shivered slightly in response to the electric charge rippling down her spine.

"I love you," she said, during the kiss.

"I love you," he repeated.

Phyllis Marie's mother sang out from the back of the studio, "Here they are!"

"We've been found out," Phyllis Marie said, exhaling almost breathlessly.

Perry smiled and stared into her eyes. After one more kiss, the couple stepped though the curtain and into the large workroom.

Earlier that wintry Sunday morning in 1941, on the only day of the week when the business remained closed to customers, Edwin and Hazel Stanton had walked to his downtown

Caldwell studio in the dark, to get a head start on the backlog of holiday portraits. The Saturday after Thanksgiving had been the busiest day of the year, and the stream of people wanting family and single portraits had continued unabated. Edwin stood tall and gaunt, with thinning hair and an air of culture that belied both his rural upbringing and sense of humor. Under her faded blonde gray hair, Hazel carried a permanent expression of contentment and mischievousness in her crooked smile and pale blue eyes.

After working three hours, they had taken a break when the corner drugstore opened at seven, put on their winter overcoats and heavy boots, and walked down the block, knowing that Phyllis Marie and Perry would be leaving the house on Kimball shortly to join them. After a quick breakfast, they had rushed back to unlock again before the young couple arrived.

"I'm back here," Edwin called out from the re-touching booth behind the heavy curtains. The music that played on his radio steadied his hand and made the task flow more easily.

Each of them knew his role. Edwin remained in the booth, re-touching negatives, while Hazel perched on the tall swivel stool, where she tinted the portraits. Phyllis Marie moved directly to the darkroom in the back and started pouring and measuring the various developing solutions. Perry, who assisted in the studio during the holiday rush or whenever he didn't have other work, retrieved several dozen folders and dried portraits from under the weights, so he could start the process of gluing the finished portraits into the folders and mailers.

They chatted happily about this or that, listening to the music on the radio, keeping busy through the morning. Phyllis Marie emerged periodically, keeping one eye on her watch to time her films in the developing solution, while flirting with her husband.

Perry, grinning and returning his wife's attention, completed gluing a portrait into a folder and was about to ask if anyone was ready for lunch when suddenly, Edwin called out loudly.

"Listen to this!" He turned up the radio and emerged from the retouching booth.

The others stopped and listened: *"We interrupt this broadcast to bring you this important bulletin from American Press headquarters in Washington. Flash. The White House announced Japanese attack on Pearl Harbor one hour ago. Stay tuned to this frequency for more information as it unfolds."*

Edwin took his glasses off and pinched his nose between his eyes. Hazel swiveled on her stool and then sat very still, listening to the broadcast message, which continued to repeat, word for word.

Phyllis Marie felt her throat catch as she tried to find words, but there were none. She looked across the studio at Perry—in his scarlet letterman's sweater from Friends University with the gray Q she had sewn on the pocket for him. He scowled with indignation. Just thirty seconds ago, he had appeared the handsome boy of almost twenty-four with whom she had shared their marriage bed in the early sunrise light. Suddenly, he looked like a very serious man. Although no one spoke a word about the possibility, she knew at that moment that if there were to be a war, Perry would be going.

The next morning, Perry sat drinking coffee at the counter in Sally's Café watching the grey Idaho sky drop white snow, waiting for his buddy Paul English. He glanced at his watch. Yesterday, after the attack on Pearl Harbor, he had called Paul and asked him to meet him. If Paul didn't hurry, he would miss the speech.

"Sally, have you got the radio on the right station?" a man at one of the tables called out.

"Don't worry," she said. "It will be on all the stations."

"What time?" another man called. Perry noticed the place was starting to fill up. He put his hat and coat on the seat to his right.

"All morning, they've been saying ten-thirty. They aren't going to change it now," Sally said, then to Perry, "More coffee, honey? Another donut?"

"Sure," he said. "Just coffee, though."

"This seat taken, son?" Perry glanced over the man's shoulder to see the last table go, leaving only a few counter seats empty.

"Yes," Perry said. He could feel that the man was just an impulse away from taking the seat and crushing Perry's hat in the process when Paul came in.

"Here he is now," Perry said. The man nodded and moved away. Paul took Perry's hat and coat and hung them on the rack at the end of the counter with his own.

"Were you listening yesterday?" Paul asked as he sat down and pointed two fingers at the waitress. She brought him coffee and two donuts. "What time is it?" He grabbed Perry's arm and pulled it toward him to see his watch, just as the radio stopped playing music.

"Yes, I was working at my father-in-law's studio."

A hush settled over the café. Perry noticed that almost no one had ordered food, other than coffee and donuts.

"We take you now to the Capitol Building, Washington, DC, where the President is about to address the nation," a voice said.

After a few moments of seemingly dead air, the distinctive sound of a microphone crackled and hummed in a large chamber. A moment later, Franklin Roosevelt spoke.

"Mr. Vice President, Mr. Speaker, Members of the Senate, and of the House of Representatives,

"Yesterday, December 7th, 1941—a date which will live in infamy—the United States of America was suddenly and deliberately attacked by naval and air forces of the Empire of Japan.

"The United States was at peace with that nation and, at the solicitation of Japan, was still in conversation with its government and its Emperor looking toward the maintenance of peace in the Pacific.

"Indeed, one hour after Japanese air squadrons had commenced bombing in the American island of Oahu, the Japanese ambassador to the United States and his colleague

delivered to our Secretary of State a formal reply to a recent American message. And while this reply stated that it seemed useless to continue the existing diplomatic negotiations, it contained no threat or hint of war or of armed attack.

"It will be recorded that the distance of Hawaii from Japan makes it obvious that the attack was deliberately planned many days or even weeks ago. During the intervening time, the Japanese government has deliberately sought to deceive the United States by false statements and expressions of hope for continued peace.

"The attack yesterday on the Hawaiian islands has caused severe damage to American naval and military forces. I regret to tell you that very many American lives have been lost. In addition, American ships have been reported torpedoed on the high seas between San Francisco and Honolulu.

"Yesterday, the Japanese government also launched an attack against Malaya.

"Last night, Japanese forces attacked Hong Kong.

"Last night, Japanese forces attacked Guam.

"Last night, Japanese forces attacked the Philippine Islands.

"Last night, the Japanese attacked Wake Island.

"And this morning, the Japanese attacked Midway Island.

"Japan has, therefore, undertaken a surprise offensive extending throughout the Pacific area. The facts of yesterday and today speak for themselves. The people of the United States have already formed their opinions and well understand the implications to the very life and safety of our nation.

"As commander in chief of the Army and Navy, I have directed that all measures be taken for our defense. But always will our whole nation remember the character of the onslaught against us.

"No matter how long it may take us to overcome this premeditated invasion, the American people—in their righteous might—will win through to absolute victory.

"I believe that I interpret the will of the Congress and of

the people when I assert that we will not only defend ourselves to the uttermost, but will make it very certain that this form of treachery shall never again endanger us.

"Hostilities exist. There is no blinking at the fact that our people, our territory, and our interests are in grave danger.

"With confidence in our armed forces, with the unbounding determination of our people, we will gain the inevitable triumph -- so help us God.

"I ask that the Congress declare that since the unprovoked and dastardly attack by Japan on Sunday, December 7th, 1941, a state of war has existed between the United States and the Japanese empire."

2

Radio commentators began analyzing the President's speech, but no one at Sally's Café heard them, because every one started talking at once.

"Man, I'm glad I'm not in your shoes," Paul said.

"What do you mean?" Even as the words echoed back to him, Perry knew exactly what he meant. As far as Paul was concerned, Perry faced a big decision as a Quaker—whether to enlist or seek a draft deferment as a conscientious objector—but for Perry, the decision had been made a long time ago.

"Well, do you? Do you know what this means?"

Paul had continued talking, Perry realized. He looked his friend square in the eye. "Yes, I know. It means I have an opportunity to pilot the Boeing B-17 Flying Fortress."

Paul's jaw dropped. "You plan to enlist—to be a pilot? You know which airplane you want to fly?"

Perry continued. "That's right, I plan to enlist just as soon as I can figure out how to ensure that I get to fly the B-17. What Japan has done, invading the United States, it's criminal. They must be held accountable."

"I thought all you Quakers were pacifists," Paul said, "like 'Sergeant York.' "

"You've seen too many movies," Perry said, smiling just a bit, for the first time since before the attack. "Besides, Sergeant York wasn't a Quaker, he was a member of the Church of Christ."

"Okay, but what about it? I thought your religion was opposed to war."

"There really is no unified policy, other than the fact that I should follow my own heart, which tells me I've got to get in this thing, and if I can do it from the cockpit of a Flying Fortress, so much the better."

"Don't you want to be a fighter pilot?"

"No, bomber."

"Why?"

"I think I'm better suited to it."

"What does your family think?"

"I haven't talked to them yet, but I think they'll see it my way." Perry shifted in his seat. "My mother, Georgia, wasn't a member of the Friends until she was adopted by her aunt. My father, Clifton, served in The Great War, although he never left Kansas, so I don't think he would object. My grandmother approved of his decision and I think she would approve of mine."

"Perry, I meant the Stantons, actually, your wife and in-laws. They're the more conservative Quakers, aren't they? They still say 'thee' and 'thou' don't they? They're not going to like it one bit."

"You really should quit calling us Quakers. We belong to the Religious Society of Friends, even though Phyllis Marie and I married at the Presbyterian Church."

He took a sip of his coffee, now cold in the cup, before continuing.

"Friends don't necessarily oppose war. We believe in an individual's right to choose his own path, and as to approving the path I intend to choose, I think my in-laws will, and I know Phyllis Marie will. I think they know how important this thing is."

Paul shoved the last of his second donut into his mouth. "Let's go talk to the enlistment office out at Gowen Field, then. I'm going with you. I want to make sure we can fly the B-17."

At Gowen Field, Perry waited in line two hours to talk to an enlistment officer.

"That's a pretty specific goal—what was your name?"

"Row. Perry V. Row. It rhymes with 'now.' "

"That's a pretty specific goal, Mr. Row. Most of the young men I've talked with today just want to fly fighters."

"I can understand that, but I think my personality is right for piloting the B-17."

"How so?"

"I'm steady. I don't get rattled under pressure. I function best in a leadership role with a team. And, frankly, the B-17 is the most interesting new airplane to be manufactured in the last decade."

The enlistment officer consulted some documents on his desk for a minute before responding. "Here's what I recommend, Perry. You wait three months, while the Army Air Forces get mobilized in response to what happened yesterday, and then you come back and talk to me."

"But I want to get into this thing right away."

"Yes, and you want to pilot the B-17, but right now, there just aren't enough assignments and airplanes to go around, and you might not get to fly at all, but in three months, after some big production orders get started, you're going to have your pick of assignments. Trust me, son. I can see you're sincere about wanting to fly. Come see me in March, and we'll get you up in a Flying Fortress."

Back outside, Perry started the car as Paul climbed in. "How'd it go, Perry?"

"He said I'd have a better chance at getting what I want in March."

"That's what my guy said, too."

In the evening, after dinner with Hazel and Edwin, Perry and Phyllis Marie sat in the parlor of their half of the duplex they shared with her parents, listening to the radio, sharing the small divan, his arm around her shoulders.

"How did it go today?" she asked.

"What?"

"At the enlistment office. Didn't you go there?"

"How did you know that?"

"You and millions of other American boys—"

"I went to see about flying the B-17."

"What happened?"

"He said to come back in three months. If I enlist too soon, there won't be enough airplanes available, and I might miss out."

"So, you're going back."

"Yes."

"I never doubted it."

"Then you support my decision," he said, stating it rather than asking.

"Yes," she answered.

"I never doubted that, either."

They sat quietly for a half hour, holding hands, kissing one another gently, listening to the music, wondering what the future held for them, before going to bed. He held her closely in the dark until he thought she had fallen asleep. Then he fell asleep, too.

On March the second, Perry and his friend, Paul went back to Gowen Field. The enlistment officer remembered Perry and welcomed him into his office. "First you have to get past our mental exam tomorrow, and then our physical exam the next day. If you get that far, then we'll talk. Be here at oh-eight-hundred, eight o'clock in the morning tomorrow."

Forty men out of one hundred fifty failed the mental exam, but not Perry. He scored near the top of the list, although they didn't tell him that. After the physical exam the following day, another thirty men found themselves on the street, while Perry found himself sitting across the enlistment officer's desk.

"Congratulations, you made it," he said, filling out the paperwork. "What's your religion?"

"Religion?" Perry wondered suddenly if the issue of conscientious objection was going to follow him around like a dog at his heels.

"Catholic, Protestant, or Jewish? It's for your dog tags."

"Oh. Protestant."

"Is there a problem?"

"No."

"You'd better start a new habit now and get used to it."

"What habit?"

"Calling your superior officers 'sir.' "

"Yes, sir."

The enlistment officer finished filling out the form and looked up. "Here's what I can do. I can put you on the fast track from Basic Training to Cadet Training. After that, it's up to you. If you pass their tests, you can request Pre-Flight Training and probably get it. That's the best I can do for you. After that, it's up to you."

"Thank you, sir."

"Consider yourself on thirty-day furlough as of today. It will give you time to get your affairs straightened out. Here's your first month's pay—thirty dollars."

"Thank you, sir."

"You're welcome. Report back here on April twenty."

"April twenty, sir? That's more than thirty days, sir."

"Welcome to the Army Air Forces, son."

"Thank you, sir."

3

Edwin Stanton, who stood silently in the cold winter wind of northern Kansas, had turned nine years old just three weeks earlier. The freezing wind tore the tears from his face; he was stricken with terror for himself, his mother, Edith, and his three brothers. As he glared into the open grave, he could not see his father's coffin. Instead, he read the tombstone lying on the ground beside him—William Salathiel Stanton 1852 - 1893. *What will become of us now,* he wondered.

The man holding the Bible offered Edith a small shovel loaded with dirt. Rather than take it, she pushed the handle up with the back of her hand, spilling the dirt onto the coffin. Edwin thought the sound meek and hollow. His oldest brother, Alva, tall and lanky at seventeen, took the tool in his hands and shoveled in a load that exploded against the coffin lid and Edwin's ears. The next brother, thirteen-year-old Irvin, followed his brother's lead and then extended the handle toward Edwin.

Edwin stood transfixed, gazing into the grave, his ears filled with the Kansas earth drumming against the pine box. When he refused the shovel, one of the many mourners waited a respectful moment—to see if five-year-old William Lester was to be given a turn—before taking up the burden and throwing a load of dirt into the waiting grave.

"Mother?"

Edwin stood alone. All the others were gone. The tombstone now stood over a mound of earth where the open grave had been. In the distance, Edith stood next to the horse-drawn hearse, listening to the man with the Bible. Edwin's brothers sat in blankets in the carriage that had brought the family to the cemetery. Edwin reluctantly left his father's side and moved toward them.

"Whenever thee is ready, Edith Stanton," the man said. "All thee needs do is send word."

Edwin helped Edith into the carriage.

"What did he want, Mother?" Edwin asked, sitting down across from her.

She did not answer.

When Edith was twenty, she married William S. Stanton, a handsome and delicate young teacher, tall and thin, with long hands and slender fingers. They were in Indiana, where she had become a teacher and a preacher. She produced four sons, one in each Leap Year, while William took up farming and tried his best to provide for his family in the long cold winters of Bridgeport, but he was not cut out for hard work. After the birth of his third son, he became ill with the dreaded consumption. To Edith's disappointment William's condition required a milder climate. When he worsened in 1885, Edith and William decided to move near her parents in Kansas. She guided her failing husband, two older sons, and infant Edwin onto the train without complaint.

With the proceeds from the sale of the Bridgeport farm, William bought 240 acres near Northbranch, Kansas, but his health prevented him from ever working the new place. All the work fell to Edith and her sons. After the 1888 birth of William Lester, his fourth and last Leap Year son, and despite failing health, William turned his attention to his finest accomplishment, the improving of the education opportunities for the children of the Friends Community of Northbranch. As the president of the school board, he rode from one community to another in the hitch wagon, raising the money to build the Northbranch Friends Academy in 1889. When his health worsened, he retired from public life. After lingering a few years, William was dead.

After the funeral, Edith spent two days alone in the room she had shared with him. The boys managed the farm chores, tiptoed through the house, and generally fended for themselves. On the morning of the third day, Edwin found his parents' door standing open and the room vacant. He searched the house for his mother and found her standing in her nightgown, next to the open dining room window, staring at the chicken coop, her teeth chattering, her hair swirling in the wind.

"Mother?"

She watched without interest as he closed the window.

"Thee will catch thy death—" He meant only to repeat the words she used whenever he or one of his brothers jeopardized his health, but the last word—death—hung in the air like a herald. He thought she would weep from hearing it.

"I'm sorry," he said.

"The chickens are not laying," she said, through clenched teeth.

"Why not?"

"I do not know. I shall ask Father when he comes in." Edwin was unsure whether she meant her own father, Ephraim, or her late husband, William.

The Stantons bowed their heads in silent prayer before supper that evening. Alva had warmed something on the stove, one of the several somethings the women of the Monthly Meeting had brought in the last several days.

"Mother, will thee pass thy plate?" Alva asked. When she did not respond, Irvin reached in front of her for it.

"What is it?" Irvin asked about the large casserole.

"I do not know," Alva answered, "but we are going to eat up all these gifts before they go bad."

"Alva, Mother is worried about the chickens," Edwin said. "Is that not right, Mother?"

Edith looked up from her lap at her third son.

"She told me earlier today," he went on. "They are not laying."

"They do not lay when it is cold, do they, Mother?" Alva waited to see if his mother would respond.

"Mother," Alva asked, "what is the usual period of silence at the beginning of mourning?"

She looked as if she would cry again, although she resisted the urge with all her will.

"I was just wondering," Alva said, "because if thee plans to remain silent for the rest of thy life, perhaps we could work out some sort of code or something, so that we could tell certain things, such as, whether thee wants seconds at mealtime, or if thee has seen the bills in the hallway."

Edith stood and ascended the staircase to her room without a word.

"That did not go well at all," Alva said to his brothers.

"No," Irvin said. "I would have to agree."

"She is worried about the chickens," Edwin said.

"She is worried about a lot more than that," Alva said. "Eat thy dinner. If thee has any constructive suggestions about how to help her, let me know." Edwin ate his supper in silence.

The egg gathering and basket delivery to the kitchen had been Edwin's job, but it had fallen to William Lester—known simply as Lester—at his fifth birthday. Edwin decided that he would examine the situation for himself.

The following morning at breakfast, Edwin waited until Alva and Irvin finished and went out to the field before locating the notebook on egg production. He turned to the current page and saw that his mother had not made a single entry since Father had died.

"Lester," he said, turning to his younger brother, "has thee been gathering eggs as thee is supposed to do?"

"Yes," he said. "There have not been any."

"For how long?"

"I do not know," he said, his lower lip trembling. "Since Father died."

"Do not cry, Lester. Thee is not in trouble. Has Mother been writing in the notebook?"

"I do not know. I do not think so. There have not been any eggs to write down."

"I thank thee, Lester," he said, putting on his boots. "I will go to the chicken coop for thee today. Is that all right?"

"Yes," Lester said, "if thee wants to."

Edwin put on his coat, took down the egg basket from on top of the icebox, and set off along the path to the chicken coop. He opened the back entrance to the coop, the entrance that provided access to the nesting boxes, but not the chickens, and stepped in. His eyes burned with tears momentarily as he remembered building this newer and larger coop under his father's supervision. Would he really never see him again? One of the church ladies had said he would see him again in Heaven. Did she really believe that?

He reached into each nesting box and found no eggs. Going out the back and around to the front, he stepped into the coop with the chickens. They raised a ruckus since they weren't used to him, but they calmed down after a minute. He searched everywhere and again, found not one single egg. He checked for drafts, but decided the temperature was fine. It wasn't the cold that was preventing the chickens from laying. After feeding and watering them, Edwin returned to the house.

He took the notebook and turned back a few pages. Indeed, when there were no eggs, Edith had marked that day with a zero, but the marks stopped the day Father had died, and yet she knew that the chickens were not laying, even though she had emerged from her room only once since William's death.

If only I could do something, Edwin thought, *anything, to bring the chickens back to production, to stop Mother's silent crying, to take away this pain I feel from missing Father.*

Father owned a book about raising chickens that he kept in the kitchen with Edith's recipes. Edwin took it down from the shelf and started reading.

"Here is a suggestion," he said aloud. He closed the book and walked to the front room.

"Lester?"

"Yes?"

"Would it be all right with thee if I took over the chickens for awhile? Just long enough to get them laying again, I mean? And then it would be thy job again."

"I do not mind," he said.

Edwin changed the feed and feeding schedule, adjusted the amount of daylight the hens received, and meticulously logged his observations. On the fourth day, he found two eggs.

"Mother?" he called from outside her door. Alva and his other brothers stood behind him.

"Open it," Alva said.

"She might be asleep," Edwin said.

"She has been asleep for a week. Open it."

They entered the room and found Edith lying on the bed, her eyes open, her Bible in her right hand.

"Edwin found some eggs," Alva said.

The four boys stood beside the bed, waiting.

"The chickens are laying again," Edwin said.

Slowly, she raised herself and lowered her feet to the hook rug. Alva nudged her house shoes closer to her feet and she slipped them on. She looked into the faces of her sons, first one, then the next. For the first time since the funeral, she seemed to really see them.

4

When the first class of 350 completed their nine-week course at the Air Corps Replacement Training Center in Santa Ana, over 5,000 new cadets took their places, including Perry Row and Paul English. Before classes began, the center was re-christened the Santa Ana Army Air Base and the structure—previously arranged under the Army's infantry system into companies—received an overhaul into an organization of Wings, Groups, and Squadrons. The government recruited a large new faculty from among high schools and colleges all over the country, so the new base more closely resembled a large university, especially since it had no airplanes.

Perry learned that a cadet could expect to complete a classification procedure first. If he didn't wash out, he would be classified either for Preflight School (Pilot) or Preflight School (Navigator-Bombardier).

Perry and Paul's arrival three weeks earlier at the Basic Training Base at Vancouver Barracks, Washington had signaled the beginning of the most difficult and most dull three weeks of their lives. From daybreak until sundown and beyond, they had been challenged and tested—their abilities to run, climb, shoot, work, and think stretched to capacity.

On his second day in Santa Ana, Perry reported to the low-pressure chamber.

"Row?" The technician called.

"Yes, sir."

"You don't have to call me sir," he said. "I'm a civilian contractor."

"Okay."

"I'm going to place you in this airtight ball," he said, gesturing for Perry to step in, "and then I'm going to alter the pressure inside to simulate the atmospheric conditions you would experience at an extremely high altitude."

Perry stepped in and the technician strapped him into his

seat. "What's that for?"

"If you pass out, I don't want you falling and hitting your head. Taken a low-pressure chamber descent before?"

"No, sir, I mean—no."

"Just relax and take it how it comes. Put on your earphones there so you can hear me. Don't try to breathe any harder or any shallower than you think is necessary."

The technician closed the hatch and stepped over to the controls. Perry put the earphones on and sat waiting.

"Okay, can you hear me?"

"Yes."

"Fine. I'm just going to take you up a bit. If you're uncomfortable or think you're going to be sick, don't be a hero. Tell me about it."

"Okay."

"Here we go."

Perry felt his eardrums change. He thrust his lower jaw forward involuntarily.

"Feel it in your ears?"

"Yes."

"Did your jaw thrust make them pop?"

"Not yet."

"Keep trying, but gently."

Perry waited, gently thrusting his lower jaws, until finally he felt one ear and then the other seem to open up a little. The sound in the room changed.

"Ears okay now?"

"Yes," Perry answered.

"Okay, here we go, a little higher."

Perry felt the effects of the change, felt his heart rate increase slightly, and allowed himself to breathe a little deeper.

"You okay?"

"Fine."

"Any air sickness?"

"No."

"Shortness of breath?"

"No."

"But you're breathing a little more frequently," the technician insisted.

"Yes, but it's fine."

"Good. We're going to stay here for a while."

"Okay."

After fifteen minutes, Perry felt acclimatized, as if he had lived his whole life at this altitude.

"You okay?"

"Never better."

"Okay, we're coming down now, just a little bit at a time. Let me know if you feel any nausea or any other discomfort."

The technician brought Perry down steadily over the course of the next twenty minutes. By the time the test was over, Perry felt normal. The technician re-opened the hatch.

"How do you feel?"

"Fine."

"Can you stand up?"

"Sure."

"Okay, come on out."

Perry stood and stepped out of the chamber. "That's some toy you've got there."

"Yes, it is," the technician replied, checking Perry's eyes. "Okay, I need your signature here."

Perry signed and turned to go. For a brief moment he felt—something.

"You okay?"

"Fine," he said as that something passed, and he walked out of the room and into the daylight.

After a day off from tests, but still restricted to the base, Perry reported Friday night for his first stretch of guard duty. His orders were simple: to patrol a 200-yard stretch of fence, preventing anyone from entering or exiting the base. In the fifth hour of his assignment, he felt—something.

Get a hold of yourself, he said, drawing a breath, deeper than usual. Black spots appeared and tried to cross his fence, black spots, as if he were looking at someone, a man, with black spots where his elbows and knees should be, shoulders and ankles, but nothing else showed, halt who goes there, black spots, not on my watch.

White walls in dim light reached over him to form a canopy of white, but dull white, not really white, but not gray either. He heard his own voice call out. "Who goes there?"

"Quiet," a woman's voice in a white uniform said. "I don't want you waking everyone."

5

"Are you hungry?" Edith asked.

"Yes," her sons answered, although they had eaten recently, thanks to the ladies of the Monthly Meeting, who were as worried about Edith's condition as her sons were.

"I will fix something, then," she said, and stood up. Lester took her robe from the foot of the bed and held it up to her. Edwin believed he observed a gentle smile of relief on Alva's face.

The five of them sat at the table before plates Edith prepared of re-heated fried chicken and potatoes that a neighbor had dropped off at the door. They lowered their heads in silent prayer.

When the prayer ended, Alva said, "I thank thee for making dinner, Mother."

"Thee is welcome, dear," she said.

"I thank thee, Mother," his brothers echoed.

"You are all welcome, boys," she said, as they began to eat. "I am glad we are altogether," she said. "I have been wanting to talk to you."

"We have been wanting to talk to thee, as well," Alva said.

"What about, dear?"

"No, I just mean—go on."

"Well, now that Father is—gone, we are going to have to make some changes."

"Yes, Mother," they said.

"The Monthly Meeting has offered me a job," she said.

"Doing what?" Alva asked.

"Circuit preaching."

"Thee is the best preacher I know," he said.

"I thank thee, son. I preach what I know, as my father taught me. It would mean traveling, four days a week at first, perhaps more after while. Thee would have to take over operation of the farm, Alva."

"I have already done so, Mother."

"Irvin has his schooling at Northbranch Friends Academy, and the boys could travel with me, so they could keep up with their lessons. Is that not a great gift?"

The following week, Edith and her two younger sons struck out on their new adventure. Each day they drove their mule-team hitch wagon to a town that had no Monthly Meeting. On Mondays, they visited Burr Oak, where they visited in the home of the Perrys. Tuesdays meant the Cawkers in Jewell—the county seat. Wednesdays they drove all the way to Lebanon, and on Thursdays they stayed with friends of Edith's parents in Red Cloud, before returning home on Friday. In each town, Edith held a small service in someone's home, leading them in song and prayer, sometimes delivering a sermon, sometimes not, as the inspiration moved her, and all the Friends in the area attended. She and her boys spent the night as guests in the homes where she preached.

On one such night, in a home where the attic guestroom contained one large bed for Edith and her two sons to share, the family awoke to a strange sound, a wheezing sound, as if air were being forced through a small opening.

"Mother, what is that sound?" Edwin asked.

"I do not know," she said. "Let me light the lantern."

Edwin thought it sounded like a ghost, although he did not know what a ghost sounded like. "It sounds like the air moving through old Mr. Cawker's accordion when he does not hold down any keys," Edwin continued.

Edith lit the lantern and listened carefully. "One of you is making it," she said, "and I do not find it funny, not one bit."

Edwin started to protest, and then turned to see his younger brother, still asleep, apparently, looking strangely blue. "It is Lester," Edwin said.

Edith leaped across the room and onto the bed, taking Lester's limp body in her arms. She held her son upright and blew air into him. "Edwin, rub his wrists," she said. "Try to get the blood moving."

"Is he dying?"

"Wake Mrs. Cawker. Quickly!"

Edwin ran for the door and down the stairs.

"What is it?" Mrs. Cawker lumbered into the room.

"I do not know," Edith said. "He does not seem to be able to breathe. He was blue when I found him." She pinched his nose shut, covered his little mouth with hers, and forced a breath past his constricted airway. Suddenly he awakened and his color improved to purple.

"Let us get him downstairs," Mrs. Cawker said. "I will put the kettle on."

Edith and Edwin carried Lester, now awake and gasping for breath, two flights down the narrow staircase to the kitchen. She and Mrs. Cawker put the struggling boy in one chair, and as soon as it was ready, put a pan of hot water in another chair and pulled it up to him. Mrs. Cawker put a towel over his head.

"Breathe in the steam, boy," she said. "Nice and slow, but fill thy lungs."

"Relax, William Lester," Edith said. "Relax and breathe." She stroked his neck and back as she spoke. Within ten minutes or so, the crisis seemed to have passed. His color returned to normal, or a pinker shade of normal.

Edith glanced in the doorway to see Edwin, barefoot, scared, and shivering in the cold. "Get thee back in bed this minute," she said. "I will only allow one sick child at a time."

She spent the remainder of the night in the rocking chair in the Cawker's sitting room, Lester sleeping calmly again, upright in her arms.

The next morning, Mr. Cawker drove over to Burr Oak and fetched the doctor, who looked Lester over, but saw only a normal apparently healthy boy.

"From your story, it sounds like asthma to me," he said, after the exam.

"Asthma just comes and goes like that?" Edith asked.

"Be glad it went," he said.

"Could it have anything to do with his being born in Kansas? My other three sons were born in Indiana, and none of them have this trouble."

"Lots of people are born in Kansas and do not get asthma."

"What if this happens again? What can I do about it?"

"Just what thee did," he said. "If he has another attack, keep him upright. Blow some air into him if he turns blue. Get him over a pan of steam, just as thee did. If it gets worse, thee may have to move him where the weather is warmer."

"Where?"

"South of here, I expect." The doctor leaned in close to Edith and whispered his next comment. "Keep him out of dusty places, too, like Mrs. Cawker's attic." He packed his bag and left.

Over the next few years, Lester's condition worsened. Edith left him at home with Alva and Irvin, which seemed to help at first, but soon his breathing suffered there as well. Alva propped him up with pillows in Father's old chair in the sitting room and spent the night camped out on a daybed so that he could check on the boy. He kept a large pot of water simmering on the stove throughout the night.

Several different doctors examined the boy. They agreed that the Stantons were doing everything they could, short of moving him to a warmer climate, but when Edwin started having asthma attacks, too, Edith reevaluated her theory that Lester's Kansas birth was the cause. Perhaps, because of her experience coping with Lester's illness, Edwin's attacks seemed less serious.

By 1899, Lester's breathing crisis became a nightly event. His growth slowed, due to inactivity over the years, until his general condition was poor. At the summer solstice, Edith made a decision, waiting for the following Sunday evening supper to discuss it with her sons.

6

A few hours later, Perry opened his eyes to find Phyllis Marie sitting in a chair, bathed in bright morning light, looking at him. "Are you all right?" she asked.

"I've been better." He raised himself on one elbow. As always, the sight of her face cheered him, but he could not understand the expression in her green eyes. *Why aren't they smiling,* he wondered? "What happened?"

"You tell me."

"I don't know." Perry tried to think. What day is this?"

His wife regarded him closely, trying to hide her concern. "Saturday. Do you remember yesterday?"

"Sure, I had a day off."

"What about last night?" she added.

"I had guard duty."

"What happened on guard duty?"

He rubbed his temples. "I think I fainted."

"That's what the doctor thinks, too."

"This is bad."

"He doesn't think there's anything seriously wrong with you," Phyllis Marie insisted, winding her dark hair absently around her finger.

"I'm glad about that, but fainting on guard duty is not a good thing." He rested his head on his pillow. "Not if you're trying to make Pre-flight Pilot."

"No, I suppose not."

A doctor walked in holding a chart. "Good, you're awake. How do you feel?"

"Fine," Perry said.

"Can you sit up on the side of the bed?" He glanced at Phyllis Marie. "Family?"

"Wife."

"Good," he said, turning back to Perry. "Can you follow my finger? Good. Ever faint before?"

"Is that what happened, sir?"

The doctor took his pulse.

"I see you were in the low-pressure chamber yesterday."

"Yes, sir."

"Do you think that's why you fainted?"

"No, sir."

The doctor took his blood pressure.

"Did you have your knees locked standing at attention by any chance?"

"No, I don't think so."

"No? One of the guards saw you topple over and, from his description, it sounds like a case of good old fainting."

The doctor looked deeply into Perry's face. "If we can't rule out the low-pressure chamber, and you say you didn't lock your knees last night, we may have to run some tests."

Perry met the doctor's gaze.

"So I ask again. Ever faint before?"

"No, sir."

"Did you have your knees locked, standing at attention?"

"Yes, sir, I think I did."

"Mm-hmm." The doctor looked at Phyllis Marie. "What do you think?"

"I think he's fine."

He looked back at Perry for a moment before writing in the chart.

"Don't lock your knees while standing at attention in the future. You can get dressed. Report to Cadet Reception Headquarters for Runner Detail, on the double." The doctor left the room.

Phyllis Marie watched as Perry dressed quickly. "Are you sure you're okay?"

"Yes," he said, taking her in his arms briefly, giving her the lightest of hugs and the quickest of kisses. "You smell good." He breathed her in, along with the barest hint of relief. "I'm fine, really. I'll see you tomorrow, as planned."

They left the hospital arm in arm, but at the front steps, he gave her one last kiss and bolted across the quad at full speed.

"Cadet Row, reporting for Runner Detail, sir," he said to the man behind the desk.

"It's about time you got here," he said. "I've been stuck doing your job, which is to sit at this desk, take phone calls, and dispatch those runners on errands," he said, gesturing toward four cadets sitting on a waiting room bench.

"Yes, sir."

"Don't 'sir' me. I'm a cadet, too."

As he took the man's place, Perry thought to himself, this is not a good sign. I've been washed out of Pre-flight Pilot. I'm going to sit out this war behind a desk somewhere.

At the end of the day, a packet arrived with his name on it. When he opened it, he read that his 24-hour pass for the next day had been cancelled, and that he had been assigned to kitchen police.

He picked up the phone immediately and dialed Phyllis Marie.

"Hello?"

"It's Perry. I just have a minute."

"What's wrong?"

He could picture how her forehead was creasing with worry. "My pass is cancelled."

"Tomorrow?"

"Yes. What's worse, I have KP duty."

"Is that bad?"

"Yes. It's punishment for fainting on guard duty. It means I'm probably washed out of Pre-flight Pilot."

There was a moment of silence. "Isn't there anything you can do?"

"I don't know. I have to go for now. I'm still on Runner Detail."

"Call me when you can."

"I will."

After Perry's day on kitchen police, he had three days off, but no pass to leave the base. He cleaned his living space until it shined, talked to Phyllis Marie on the phone, read a book, walked around the grounds, and tried to sleep at night, when he wasn't worrying about the fact that he was certain he had missed his chance at piloting a B-17. He would end up working as a clerk in a supply room, he told his wife, or patrolling the grounds at a training base, guarding a bunch of cadets with a future.

The following day, June the first, Perry received four envelopes. The first letter ordered him to report for Fire Warden duty the following day. The second assigned him to classes, 43-B-23, Squadron 24, starting June eighth. The third told him how to acquire his cadet uniform, and the fourth said he had been classified for Pre-Flight (Pilot) Training. He was in.

7

Seven-year-old Clifton Rowe and his five-year-old brother Vancil had heard the bedtime story many times, but it was one of Clifton's favorites, so he listened closely while his mother told it again.

Clifton's father, Elijah Delvaine Rowe—Lige, to those who knew him—was a teacher, not a farmer. The thought of riding roughshod over six million acres of virgin Oklahoma prairie in a cutthroat competition with hundreds of thousands of rough-and-toughs, to claim a one-hundred-sixty-acre homestead, without guarantee that the land would even be fertile, did not appeal to his sensibilities, not at his advanced age of thirty-six. When he read in his weekly Larned Kansas Advance that President Grover Cleveland had designated September 16, 1893 as the date of the Cherokee Land Run, he took little notice.

Furthermore, Lige held the opinion that the land still belonged to the Cherokees. It was not a popular point of view, but he believed that back in 1828, when the federal government granted that land to the Cherokee Nation in perpetuity, they didn't get to take it back, just because some of the Cherokees fought on the side of General Lee and the Confederacy. It wasn't right.

Nevertheless, after the Civil War, the Cherokees themselves had leased their land to white cattlemen who wanted to feed their cattle on the Oklahoma prairies before driving them into Wichita or Dodge City. Eventually the Cherokee Nation had sold the land back to Congress, so if folks wanted to line up their wagons and horses on the Kansas state line and rush into Oklahoma Territory like a bunch of hooligans, they could have at it. Lige would not be a part of it, or so he told his friends and associates at the Larned Friends Academy and at Monthly Meeting on First Day.

Lige's attitude softened, however, after the date came and

went, and he read further in the Larned Kansas Advance that despite the raising of dozens of towns in a single day, there remained hundreds of potential homesteads unclaimed in the rougher terrain of the western end of the strip.

"Carrie," Lige had said to his young wife, "there are lands to be had for the sum of fourteen dollars, and all one has to do is ride a horse in there and say, 'This is mine.' "

Clifton sat up in bed, his face illuminated by the light from the fireplace. "And that is how Papa decided to come to Oklahoma and homestead the land we live on now."

"Yes," Carrie said.

"One hundred and sixty acres."

"Yes."

"And we have been here for four years, now."

"Yes. Now pull up the covers, you two, and go to sleep. We have a long day ahead of us tomorrow."

"Why, what happens tomorrow?" the younger, Vancil, asked.

"Tomorrow we hitch up the wagon and drive to Hunter. It is an all-day trip, over forty miles, so we need to rest now."

"Tell us another story, will you not?" Clifton pleaded.

"No, I will tell you more stories during the trip tomorrow. Get some sleep. God's blessings to you."

"God's blessings to you," the blond boys said in unison, lying back in their bed. Clifton kept still so his brother could sleep, but instead of sleeping, he watched the fire and told another story to himself, one he had also heard many times, but it was one of his favorites, so he listened closely while he told it again.

When Papa and Mom had traveled by train to Cornelius, Oregon in 1890, to attend the wedding of Mom's brother, Thaddeus, Carrie went into labor, and had no choice but to deliver the child with a doctor she had never met before, Dr. Carnine. Due to the premature birth, they had to stay in Oregon for two months before they could travel home to Larned.

His eyes drooped as the flames danced among the lengths

of firewood. *And that is why I was born in Oregon instead of Kansas like my brother, Vancil,* he thought. He thought he heard his mother say 'Yes, that is right.' His eyes closed, just for a moment. *And that is why my middle name is Carnine,* he thought, *after the doctor.* 'Yes, that is right,' he heard again, just before he fell asleep.

The next morning in deepest darkness, Lige awakened his sons. Clifton knew his task: to help his father hitch the horses to the wagon, and after finding his shoes, he sprang to his feet, threw on his coat, and raced out the back door. Inside the barn, Lige handed Clifton the kerosene lantern. They fetched the bridles and other tack from the storeroom; Clifton held the lamp high, allowing the light to fall where his father needed it.

By the time they finished, Carrie and Vancil emerged from the house with the luggage, bags of warm buckwheat cakes and dried fruit, two canteens of water, and the large quilts from their bed. Lige arranged a nest of quilts on the floor of the hitch wagon for his family before helping Carrie climb aboard.

"Come on, boys," Carrie said. "Take your boots off and leave them at the back of the wagon. Snuggle up with me and we will all stay warm together."

"What about Dad?" Vancil asked, climbing up next to his mother.

"Worry thee not about me," Lige said, pulling on his wide-brimmed hat. "I have my horse blanket up here."

Clifton handed two buckwheat cakes up to his father before settling in on the other side of his mother. "Now will you tell us a story?"

Lige slapped gently at the reins and the hitch wagon started to roll.

"Yes," Carrie said. "We are about to embark on an important journey, one we have made before, one we try to make once every three months, if we are able, to the Quarterly Meeting of the Religious Society of Friends. So I believe this would be a good time to talk about the eight foundations of a true social order."

"What is that, Mom?"

"What is what, honey? Do you want a buckwheat cake?"

"Yes, please. What is a social order?"

She handed one to Clifton and another to Vancil. The four of them—for Lige was participating in the meal and the lesson as well—bowed their heads in silent prayer.

Caroline Strong Roe—Carrie, to those who knew her— could re-trace—with the help of the extensive pages of notes inserted in her family Bible—her entire lineage for ten generations on both her mother's and father's sides. They stretched back in time from her birthplace in Illinois through early colonies in New York, Connecticut, and Massachusetts, to sixteenth century England and Scotland. Some of her Religious-Society-of-Friends ancestors had withstood religious persecution at Salem, fought in the American Revolution, served as the last Governor of the Plymouth colony, and sat on the judicial bench in Long Island.

Lige could only trace his family history back five generations, to Georg Friedrich Rau, born in Germany around 1723, who Anglicized his name to George Fredrick Row some time before he was killed by Indians in 1780 and buried in the Row Salem Church Cemetery in Penn Township, Pennsylvania. Later descendants changed the spelling to Rowe, in a poor attempt to reflect the correct pronunciation.

At their wedding on Leap Year Day of 1888, Carrie's family members teased the eighteen-year-old bride that she didn't need to change the spelling of her last name, because some time soon, his family would change it again, anyway. After the ceremony, the Roe elders brought out Carrie's family Bible and asked twenty-seven-year-old Lige to provide his family history. When they figured out that his mother, grandmother, great aunt, and great-grandmother all shared the family name Roush, everyone broke out in gales of laughter, and they started over on a clean sheet of paper.

"What was your question?"

"What is a social order?" Clifton asked again.

"Well, you know, that is a group of people, a society, living together. Honey, keep your hat on," she said to her younger son before continuing. "We do not see very many other folks out here on the homestead, but we are about to gather together with others of our social order, at the Meeting."

"I see," Clifton said, his mouth full of buckwheat cake.

"The first foundation of a true social order is that the Fatherhood of God, as revealed by Jesus Christ, should lead us toward a brotherhood which knows no restriction of race, sex, or social class. Do you understand what I just said?"

"I did, but I do not think Vancil did."

"Well, Vancil is a little young for this lesson yet, so worry not about him. We will talk about this again another time, when he is older, and he will come to understand, but do you really understand?"

"Yes, Vancil is my brother, and we should know no restrictions." Clifton smiled.

"Well, that is true, yes, but the brotherhood I am talking about extends far beyond just the two of you. All of us, all of God's children, should know no restriction of race, sex, or social class. That means that the Negroes who work in the fields like Old Mr. Beans should have no restrictions that your father does not have. It means that women like me should have no restrictions that you, your brother, or your father does not have. It means that you and me and Old Mr. Beans should have no restrictions that the President of the United States does not have."

"So, everyone is equal."

"They should be considered so."

"But it is not really like that."

"No, but it should be, and you must do your part in helping to change it."

"I see." He took another bite of his buckwheat cake. "What is the second—what are these again?"

"The eight foundations of a true social order."

"So, what is the second foundation of a true social order?"

Carrie smiled at her son and kissed the top of his blond head. "That this brotherhood should express itself in a social order which is directed, beyond all material ends, to the growth of personality truly related to God and man."

"What does that mean?"

"It means that in each day, in each action we take, we act not just for ourselves, but for our relationship to God."

"So when I feed the stock, it is not just for the—what is that word?"

"Which word?"

"For the good."

"Benefit?"

"Yes! It is not just for the benefit of the stock, but for the benefit of God, too?"

"Yes, and for your own benefit, too, in two ways, since the stock and the crops ultimately feed your body, but also because the actions you take benefit your relationship to God."

The boy looked perplexed.

"We should use our money and time," she continued, "in ways that make life better for ourselves and others."

"I see. It is like this buckwheat cake."

"How so, honey?"

"Well, the stock eats buckwheat, too, and we eat them, but also, we spread the manure from the stock, and more buckwheat grows. It is like a circle."

Lige smiled broadly. *Clever child,* he thought, *to see the circle of life for himself at such a tender age.* Carrie looked up at her husband and enjoyed seeing his smile.

"Let us continue then," she said. "The third foundation of a true social order is that the opportunity for full development, physical, moral and spiritual, should be assured to every member of the community—man, woman and child. The development of man's full personality should neither be hampered by unjust conditions nor crushed by economic pressure."

"Okay, that one is easy," Clifton said.

"Tell me."

"Well, like—"

"For example—"

"Well, for example, if I want to read better, then I should be able to."

"You should be afforded the opportunity to learn to read better, yes," Carrie said. "That does not mean you are going to learn to read better. It takes years of hard work to learn to read better. It is the opportunity, not the ability that you are assured. What you do with the opportunity is up to you."

He nodded. "Can I have another buckwheat cake?"

"Certainly." She reached for the bag. "Lige?"

"No, thank you, I am fine." He turned in his seat. "We just reached the main road and we are leaving the homestead."

"Vancil, are you still hungry?"

"No, mama," he said, gazing out of the hitch wagon at the open prairie vegetation covering red clay.

"Here you are, Clifton."

"Thank you."

Carrie took a buckwheat cake for herself, now that she knew there were enough to sustain them through the day.

"The fourth foundation," she continued, with a mouth full of buckwheat, "excuse me, of a true social order is that we should seek a way of living that frees us from the bondage of material things and mere conventions, raises no barrier between men, and puts no excessive burden of labor upon anyone by reason of our superfluous demands."

"I do not understand that one," Clifton said.

"It means several things," she elaborated. "It means that we should not live beyond our means, that we should not live in such a way that sets us apart, such as an elevated social order—remember, from the first foundation—and we should not be so greedy that others have to work too hard to take care of our excessive wants."

"I was going to ask for another buckwheat cake, but I do not think I need it now," the boy said.

"And what changed your mind?"

"Well, I have had two already, and I am the only one who has."

"So, you do not want to put an excessive burden of labor on your old Mom, huh?" She held her hand over her face to hide the grin she could feel bursting from the corners of her mouth.

"Yes, I think that is it."

"That is very good of you, honey." She stood up in the wagon, steadying herself with a hand on her husband's shoulder. "We shall end that lesson right there, I think, and finish the other four foundations later today."

Clifton smiled. "Yes, Mom."

Carrie turned to look out ahead at the dirt track stretching east into the glowing sky above the horizon. Lige patted the back of her hand.

The children slept off and on throughout the morning, kicking the quilts aside as the day warmed. When they passed through the brand new town of Stella, Carrie took the reins for the next two hours while Lige stretched out in the back, until she reined in the horses at the familiar watering hole, the last source of good water before setting out across the Great Salt Plains.

8

June 30, 1942,
Santa Ana, Calif.,
Dear Mother and Father,

I hardly see Perry these days, he is so busy. I watched him march in review for the first time last week, no, three weeks ago, has it really been that long? He went back on Guard Duty, making sure not to lock his knees at attention. We don't want a repeat of that episode!

His classes started the next day, in math, ground force, code, and air force, and he brought home a much welcome pay envelope that first week. Next, he had to take some tests in air force tactics, math, and airplane identification, passing with excellent grades.

This week, he was Sergeant of the first platoon. I watched again as he led them onto the field, through the review, and back off the field, looking very handsome in his cadet uniform. Wait until you see him. He has gotten a lot stronger and leaner. He looks like he has lost weight, but actually he is heavier, more muscular.

He took pistol practice the other day, and we got a rare treat when we went together to the beach and swam in the warm ocean together. The next day, he was caught in a surprise rifle inspection that really had him worried, but he passed anyway, in spite of his concern.

Yesterday, he started a course in physics and in the evening, the cadets put on a show, which was the funniest thing I've seen in months.

Uncle Oris and Aunt Niota send you God's blessings. More later,

Your loving daughter,
Phyllis Marie.

July 27, 1942,
Visalia, Calif.,
Dear Mother and Father,

So much has happened since my last letter, I hardly know where to begin. It is very hot here in my little motel room, not much more than a bed and a chair, and there is no telephone.

Perry finished up the latter half of Cadet Training in Santa Ana with courses in jiu-jitsu, more math classes, a Naval Identification Course, which he finished with a perfect score, 100%, also track and field, where he ran 75 yards in 9.1, 150 yards in 17.8, the same as his year at Friends University, he says, despite a 20 lb. increase.

He had to take some typhus and tetanus immunizations early in July, and then right after that, they gave him a surprise evacuation of his barracks, followed by a nine-mile walk. He slept all day when he met me at Aunt Niota's house the next day, but he seems to have weathered it okay.

He wrapped up his math classes with the third highest score in his class, and completed his code check test at twelve words per minute, which is a good score, but then he got his first demerit for leaving his collar unbuttoned. In his personal inspection, he wore too much belt (I'm not sure what that means. How do you wear too much belt?), which worried him for a day or two, but then he got his final grade, 92%, an A, so I guess the belt problem didn't take away too much from his score.

Now we are in Visalia, in the San Joaquin Valley of California, for the next phase, Pre-Flight Pilot Training, where he is finally going to get to step into an airplane. He was as excited as a little boy shortly before his departure by troop train, but the trip was hard on him. It took 12 hours for Paul and him to travel the 160 miles here, and even though Mary and I left after they did, by bus, we got here ahead of them. Perry's asleep now, but I have to wake him to go to the base, check in, and pick up his flight uniforms (he says they look like zoot suits). We'll only have tonight together before he has to report.

Mary and I will be home again soon, as this next training period will be a very intense one for the boys, and they will have little time off. They will be staying in barracks at the Visalia Air Field, and taking classes there each morning, but then they have to get into buses and drive out to various private airfields to get in their actual flying experiences in the afternoons.

God's blessings from Aunt Niota and Uncle Oris, whose home we left two days ago. You should have seen Perry's grandmother, Carrie, when she visited from Montebello, bursting at the seams with pride over her boy in uniform. Also, Mary's regards to Paul's mother, who returned to Caldwell last week. As soon as I know our bus schedule, I'll let you know when to expect us.

Your loving daughter,
Phyllis Marie

9

The Stantons bowed their heads in silent prayer at the Sunday supper table. Alva, now twenty-three, sat at the head of the table, still considered Father's place six years after his death. Gertrude Perry, Alva's young lady friend, sat to his right. Irvin, nineteen and nearly as tall as Alva, had fallen behind in his schooling from spending so much time helping Alva with the farm. Edwin, fifteen, continued to accompany Edith on her preaching circuit, which had grown to six communities in six days. Lester, eleven and sickly, hardly resembled his tall brothers.

"Roasted pork?" Alva asked. "What is the occasion?"

"The only occasion that I know of is that I slaughtered the last pig of the season last week." Irvin had the same deadpan expression, whether joking or reprimanding, but he almost smiled.

"No," Edith said, "there is more to it than that." An expectant silence fell. "There are several issues we face as a family, and I need to discuss them with you." She looked each son in the face to be sure he understood the seriousness of her comments. When she was satisfied, she continued. "First, Alva, thee is a good son, too good, perhaps, for thee has stayed by thy mother's side, caring for her and her other children, when thee ought to have been seeking thy own life."

"Mother, I—"

"Please let me continue," she interrupted. "Irvin, thee has stood beside thy brother in keeping this farm operating after the death of thy father, and sacrificed thy education in so doing."

Irvin said nothing.

"Edwin," she said, "thee has stayed by thy mother's side year after year, riding the circuit, keeping her safe on the road. Thee is approaching the age thee should enter the Academy, and thy health is suffering."

"Lester, thee has been stricken with illness, and thee has been brave in the face of it, and I am proud of thee for the way thee has withstood the trial."

"Edith," she said, turning her comments inward, "thee is a good mother. Thee has provided for thy children after the death of their father, and with the help of thy sons, thee has kept this farm operating in the black."

The four boys waited to see whom she would address next.

"But now we have some new opportunities. Autumn is coming just around the corner and winter shortly on its heels. My brother, your uncle, Lindley Bowles and his wife Janie have a place in Friendswood, Texas, where a boy with asthma can breathe, I am told, in the warm humid air of the Gulf of Mexico. There is a school there, and some loving members of the Society of Friends."

Lester's eyes teared and he swallowed hard.

"When I first heard of this opportunity, I said to myself that I could never send my dear Lester so far away from me, and that is the truth, dear son, who I love."

Lester smiled.

"Then the Lord presented another opportunity. There is another school, a new Friends Academy called Stella, in Oklahoma Territory. The climate is a bit warmer there, and many of our old friends are there. The staff is excellent, the standards are said to be very high, higher than the Academy here, and there are positions there for both thee, Irvin, for thee to finish thy schooling, possibly in a year, and for thee, Edwin, as an entering freshman."

Edwin frowned.

Irvin's countenance remained unchanged.

"Again, when I heard of this opportunity, I said to myself that I could never send my dear sons so far away from me, and that is the truth, dear sons."

A smile returned to Edwin's face.

"It was at this point that I took the bull by the horns and made my own opportunity. I wrote to the Quarterly Meeting in Oklahoma Territory in Oklahoma, to a woman named Crosha Lynes, and asked for a circuit preaching position there. I have her letter here. Shall I read it to you?"

"Of course!"

"Please!"

"Yes!"

"Yes!"

She removed the letter from her pocket, waved it with a flourish, and read aloud: "Dear Reverend Stanton, thy letter comes as a remarkable relief to us and thy name is well known to many Friends here. Thee can have thy pick of three circuits, but considering thy desire to enter two sons at Stella Friends Academy, I am guessing thee would prefer an assignment as Women's Matron there. There is a room for thee in the women's dormitory, and Stella Monthly Meeting owns a small homestead near Stella, which they could make available to thee and thy family on a temporary basis at no cost, since there is no men's dormitory yet. Further, I have inquired on thy behalf in Friendswood, Texas, and thee would be most welcome as an occasional guest preacher there, so thee could see thy youngest son. How soon can thee start?"

She turned to Lester. "This way, we shall not be too far removed from one another, and thee shall grow healthy and happy."

"Mother, if the Lord wants me to grow healthy and happy, then that is what I shall do, and I shall give myself to His service, in that case."

Tears ran down Edith's face. Lester rose from his chair and walked into her open arms.

"And what about the farm?" Alva asked.

"Did thee think I had forgotten thee?" Edith smiled.

"No, I know better than that," he smiled back.

"Thee has a choice," she said, looking at Gertrude, who kept her gaze on her lap. "Thee may stay, taking sole ownership. I think that would be a difficult and lonely path, but it may be thy preferred path."

"No," he said. "It is too much for Irvin and me, now."

"Then we shall sell it," she said. "Thee may accompany me, and try the homestead they offered, which is about two-thirds the size of this property, manageable for one young man, I am guessing."

Alva glanced at Gertrude, but said nothing.

"There is another way, son," she said. "Thee may find thy own way, if thee wish. I would miss thee, but that is what mothers do. They watch their sons grow to adulthood, and then they miss them."

"Mother, I see that this is the time to tell thee," he said. "I have been offered a teaching job in Washington and I've been considering whether to take it."

"So far away?"

"Washington, Kansas, Mother," he said, "which didn't seem so far away from the family until I heard thy news."

"I think thee should take it, Alva," she said.

"Mother, there is more. I have asked the Perrys for Gertrude's hand. They have consented, and Gertrude has accepted."

Gertrude looked up with tears in her eyes, first at Alva, then at Edith.

"My dears, I hoped for nothing less," Edith said. "God's blessings to you both."

In the spring of 1899, after Edith and Lester departed for Texas by train, the two brothers Irvin and Edwin loaded two hitch wagons, one full with oats, the other with those possessions deemed necessary for Edith, Irvin, and Edwin to live in Oklahoma. They put their faith in two teams of horses, including Fred and Charley, and began the same journey most of their friends and neighbors in Northbranch had made six years earlier. They headed due south, across the width of the state of Kansas, bound for the southern border of the United States and into Oklahoma Territory and the town of Stella—three hundred thirty miles away.

The first night, the boys stopped at the Perry home in Burr Oak, where they joined up with two other families—a total of eight people, five wagons, fourteen horses, and three dogs.

In the morning, they set off before sunrise.

Traveling between county seats—because the roads were better—they saw something they had never seen before: whole towns illuminated by electricity against the night sky.

The March wind blew cold. Edwin, driving the second team in the wagon train, discovered that the horses required no direction from him to follow the lead team, giving half the road every time the lead team met a passer-by. So to keep warm, he walked in the field, parallel to the wagon track, carrying the single barrel shot gun and shooting rabbits for the evening stews.

In making camp at night, the drivers slanted each wagon tongue toward the road and tied the horses in back, so the teams would be hidden. They mounted feed boxes on the wagons and filled them with oats, and put hay on the ground. Each horse drew a full horse blanket.

On the side opposite the horses, the women built campfires in sheet iron cook stoves that stood on the ground. The pilgrims kept pots, kettles, pans, and groceries in box-like cupboards built on the sides of the wagons.

After their supper under the stars, the drivers placed the harnesses and other tack under the wagon to keep them dry and made beds mounted on overjets in the wagons, with lanterns hung from the center of the middle bow.

One night Edwin awoke to a noise down on the ground on the hand brake side. He raised up and put his face down to the slot where the brake came through the overjet and came face to face with one of the dogs, putting his nose up through the slot, evidently in pursuit of food. Their shouts and barks upon discovering one another awoke the entire campsite.

As they passed through various Kansas towns, their five wagons attracted a lot of attention. Storekeepers and customers alike stepped out of stores and homes and shouted, "Going to Oklahoma?"

Upon arrival on the ninth morning, Irvin inquired at Stella Friends Academy and found a former neighbor, Martha Woods.

"Young Mr. Stanton," she said, taking both of Irvin's hands in hers, "God's blessings on thee! How good it is to see thee!"

"God's blessings on thee!" Irvin almost smiled.

"I can take thee to thy new home," Martha said.

"Yes, that would be fine."

"The women's dormitory is there," she said, pointing to a large two-story wood frame house. "Thy mother's quarters shall be downstairs on the far end. This end is the dining hall, and the kitchen is in the middle."

Martha—on horseback, to the amazement of the boys—led the two hitch wagons to a small farmhouse a mile north of town.

10

Perry and Paul rose and dressed quickly at the sound of Reveille. If Perry slept at all during his first night in the Visalia barracks, he didn't remember it. Today marked the first day of classes and he ached to fly. Would he be allowed inside an airplane, finally, today, or would this be another day of tests and questions, forms to fill out, equipment to receive?

Dust filled the air as they crossed from the mess hall to the large hangar where their first class would begin in ten minutes. Perry took in the dry musty scent of the desert-like San Joaquin Valley, already hot though it appeared deceptively green on all the maps he had ever seen. He could put up with anything, he thought to himself, if only they would let him fly today.

"Up there," Perry said to Paul, indicating two chairs in the front row of the impromptu lecture hall, set up in one corner of the empty hangar. The remaining four-hundred chairs behind them filled up quickly just as an Army Air Forces Colonel stepped to the front of the assembly and exchanged formalities with the new class of 43-B-23, before he began pacing slowly from left to right and back again.

"At ease," he said. "Be seated."

He paused long enough for the men to take their seats before continuing.

"Do you know what a dodo is? Anyone?"

A few hands rose among the group, but the Colonel chose to ignore them, pacing slowly.

"*Raphus cucullatus?*"

Half of the raised hands lowered.

"Perhaps I should say what a dodo was, because they are now extinct," he said.

Realizing that the Colonel didn't want an answer from class 43-B-23, those men with their hands still raised brought them down into their laps.

"The dodo was a flightless bird that lived east of Madagascar until it became extinct in the seventeenth century."

Looking out at his audience for the first time he noticed many of the men writing in their pads.

"Don't take notes, son," he said, rather scornfully, although his comment was not directed to any individual. "The fact that this bird is extinct is immaterial. What matters is, the bird did not know how to fly, which means he had a lot in common with you."

He paused again to see if anyone laughed, but no one did. He began to pace again.

"There are four hundred dodos sitting here in front of me today. I will not call you gentlemen, I will not call you cadets, and I will not call you students."

He stopped and turned toward the class.

"Two months from now, half of you will continue on to Basic Flying Training. You won't be pilots yet, but you won't be dodos anymore, either."

He started pacing again.

"The rest of you—"

He paused again, dramatically.

"Well, the rest of you won't be dodos, either, but you won't be pilots. You will be re-classified. I want you to think long and hard about whether you are going to survive my school, or if you are going to be part of the fifty percent looking for another way to serve in this war."

He spun on his heels, went to a blackboard and picked up a piece of chalk.

"I am Colonel Randall," he said, writing his name as he spoke, "and I'm your instructor for today's introductory lecture. Once I'm through with you today, you will not have to suffer through my comments again, except half of you, who will see me at your graduation exercise."

Placing the chalk back in the tray below the blackboard and turning back to the class, he said, "This would be the time to start taking notes. The Ryan PT-22 Recruit is not my airplane of choice for a fun flight on a Sunday afternoon.

That airplane would be the PT-22's predecessor, the Ryan ST, the sweetest little ship you ever saw. It's so sweet, all you have to do is think about what you want to do, and your thoughts travel right down your arm to the stick in your hand, and you're performing spins and stalls to take your little girlfriends' breath away down there on the ground where she's having a picnic watching you."

The men chuckled a little.

"It's okay to laugh. Go ahead. You won't be laughing when you have to fly the PT-22 Recruit."

The men quieted down. The Colonel resumed his pacing. "But I digress. I was telling you about the ST. They have these nice little four-cylinder Menasco engines, ninety-five horsepower, that sing like the Sirens tempting Ulysses, and when you take off, she just runs halfway down and lifts away as if she had no obligation to earth's gravity at all."

To a man, the class sat listening with smiles on their faces, imagining themselves in the skies described by the Colonel.

"Everything I've said about the ST, you can forget about. Tear those pages out of your notebook, crumple them in your fists, and throw them on the floor."

He stood quietly and watched as the men glared at him in disbelief.

"Go on," he shouted, "that's an order!"

Four hundred wads of paper hit the floor of the hangar at once.

"The PT-22 Recruit is a pig," he said, continuing to strut from right to left and back again. "They took the sweetest little airplane and ripped out its heart, replacing those fragile Menascos with these muscular air-cooled Kinner R-540-1 radial engines, five cylinders in line that make you think you're inside a concrete mixer, that put out one-hundred-sixty horsepower at eighteen fifty RPMs—are you getting all this? Because there will be a test. They put ball-bearing assemblies in where hinges used to reside, increased the cockpit to allow full parachute packs, widened the landing gear, and moved the fuselage stringer extrusions outboard, turning the sweet little ST into a pig that is difficult to take off, difficult to put in a spin, difficult to stall, difficult to recover from a spin or a stall, and difficult to land. Why did they do this, you may ask? Was it done to make these airplane more robust, so we could utilize them longer, to train more pilots for the future? While that was the intent, the happy result of all this re-designing for you dodos, is that you get to learn to fly under these adverse conditions. Once you learn how to fly my nasty little bathtubs, you will be able to fly anything."

The Colonel stopped pacing and looked out on a sea of gaping mouths.

"Good, I have your attention, I see."

He resumed his walk, saying, "Do you remember what percentage of you I said would continue to Basic Flying Training? Half? The best part is that half of the washouts— one quarter of the men sitting here—won't even have to get bad grades to washout, because they'll throw up on my airplane, an automatic washout. That is a statistic you can take to the bank."

The Colonel stopped pacing and turned to face the men once again.

"There is another statistic I want to share. I don't want to, but in all honesty, I must. In all likelihood, at least one of you will crash during the next two months. Remember to follow all safety regulations. If your flight instructor tells you to bail out, then, by God, bail out. I only have two hundred airplanes, but I'd rather lose an empty airplane than a manned one. Now report to your squadron leaders on the flight deck, meet your flight instructors, and take your first hop in one of my planes. Dismissed."

11

Stella Friends Academy grew out of a concern for education that burned in the souls of the Oskaloosa families of Friends that had migrated to Oklahoma from Northbranch. They built the first elementary school out of sod within six months of their arrival, at a time when they were still living in dugouts. Stella Howard taught the children through the eighth grade, and her name stuck to the school and the settlement.

The growing number of high school age children soon presented itself as a problem. The cost of sending these children back to Oskaloosa or Northbranch was deemed prohibitive, so the community pledged six hundred dollars, bought lumber from the new community of Alva, Oklahoma and from Kiowa, Kansas, each about twenty miles from Stella, and built the school house with volunteer labor. In 1897, Stella Friends Academy opened in a tent, because the building was not completed in time.

The day after the Stanton boys' arrival, Martha Woods drove Edith from the train station to their new home in a small wagon.

Irvin homesteaded 160 acres of land covered with prairie. He and Edwin burned off the high grass, staked out their proposed buildings, built a sod house with a board floor, and plastered the walls inside with white clay. They broke up as much ground as they could that summer and planted broom corn, Kaffir corn, sorghum, and watermelons.

The following September, Irvin and Edwin started school along with another hundred students. Irvin joined the staff of the school newspaper and Edwin enjoyed Latin, his first exposure to a foreign language. Edith settled into her new duties as Women's Matron, watching over seventeen girls, preparing menus, supervising the cooking staff, and teaching the fineries of making lace and other sewing tasks so necessary to the young modern woman of the late nineteenth century.

Several months after her arrival, Edith received an invitation to preach at the upcoming Quarterly Meeting in Hunter, Oklahoma. When she arrived by wagon train, the number of people who refrained from using the plain speech surprised her. At first, she considered raising the issue in her sermon, but she decided not to. She felt self-conscious about it, something she had never experienced before. She felt old-fashioned.

She preached at the Saturday morning worship, reuniting with a number of old friends from Northbranch and meeting some new friends, including Crosha Lynes and her adopted children. Entrusting the care of Irvin and Edwin to the returning wagon train, she departed from Hunter with a family headed home to Enid, in order to take the train to Houston, Texas, to see Lester, recuperating from asthma at Friendswood.

After one year of schooling, Irvin graduated from Stella and entered Friends University in Wichita with the money he made from homesteading. He excelled in English Literature, Creative Writing, and Journalism. There was no school newspaper available to him as an outlet, so he saved the money he earned managing paper routes from the morning and evening Wichita newspapers. At the end of his first year in college he purchased a small foot-powered flatbed cylinder press from a professor and student who had lost interest. With that equipment, he started a small monthly school paper, the University Life.

In the late summer of 1900, Alva married Gertrude in her family's home in Burr Oak. He took a teaching position in Washington, eighty miles east of Northbranch, and the newlyweds settled in.

Meanwhile Edwin thrived at Stella Friends Academy. He moved onto campus with his mother, sharing her quarters in the women's dormitory. His teachers loved him, despite— or because of—his sense of humor. He always knew the material for class and always presented it with a unique and wry perspective. His classmates loved him, too, for he brought warmth to his friendships and a loyalty that seemed unshakable.

On the first day of school in Edwin's third year at Stella, he entered the main hall to attend the inaugural chapel and assembly.

"Welcome, students," a faculty member shouted. "Please be seated." The students settled in for the Invocation and announcement of new students.

"Hollie Ernest Crow," the faculty member called out, and a few students snickered. The tall young man stood and said, "I'm here, sir. Please call me Ernest."

Later during the front lawn picnic, Edwin saw Ernest and a new girl, and approached them. Though it was early autumn, the sun was shining, and the grass smelled sweet. "Welcome to Stella," he said. "Edwin M. Stanton."

"Ernest Crow," the boy said, offering his hand. "This is Lena Whitaker."

"Are you related to Lincoln's Secretary of War?" the girl asked.

"I don't know," Edwin pretended to think, running his fingers through his thin sandy hair. "What was his name?"

Ernest laughed.

"Seriously," Edwin went on, "I am not."

"You must be named for him, then," she insisted.

"No."

"What does the 'M.' stand for?"

"Nothing. It is just an initial."

"But that was the case with the Secretary, too."

"I know," Edwin said. "I cannot explain it any better than that, which is how my mother explains it. You can ask her yourself, Lena. She's right over there."

She wrinkled her freckled nose in distaste. "Please don't call me Lena."

Ernest turned and looked at her. "But that's your name, isn't it?"

"Yes, but I hate it."

"Why?" Ernest looked perplexed.

"What do you mean asking me that? You obviously don't care for your first name."

"No, I don't," Ernest replied, "although I have nothing against the plant. It makes a nice decoration at Christmas, but someone always laughs when I'm introduced that way. I much prefer Ernest."

"But that does not answer the question, Lena," Edwin said. "Oh, sorry. Why does thee hate thy first name?"

"I knew someone named Lena, once, someone I disliked. You must know what it's like to dislike your first name, and you can't even fall back on a middle name the way Ernest can. We can't go around calling you 'M' can we?"

"No, but I like my name," Edwin said.

"Well, I don't like mine," she repeated stubbornly.

Ernest frowned. "What is your middle name?"

"Sedalia."

"What? That's even worse than having only an initial!" Edwin laughed.

"I'll give you a name, then," Ernest said. "What shall it be?"

"Anything but Lena," she said.

"Betsy," he announced.

"Why Betsy?" she asked.

"Why not? Did you know a Betsy that you disliked, too?"

"No," she said. "Betsy is nice."

"I think so, too," Ernest replied.

She smiled up at him.

In his fourth year, Edwin attended an assembly where a guest speaker presented his photograph collection. It ranged from vast landscapes of the Colorado Rockies to single portraits of tiny flowers no bigger than a thumbnail. Edwin saw studio portraits and candid images of people who had not known they were being photographed.

"Did thee take all of these yourself?" Edwin asked the man after the assembly.

"Yes, I did."

"How does thee achieve such close-ups?"

"I use a different lens," he said, showing Edwin his camera, several lenses, and other equipment. He explained the concept of depth of field and the delicate balance between shutter speed and lens aperture to alter it. Edwin stood mesmerized.

It took him six months of work—painting the buildings and cleaning the yards at Stella—to save enough money and order a camera from the Eastman Company. From that day forward, no event went undocumented by the tall and handsome young man from Indiana by way of Northbranch.

Upon Edwin's graduation from Stella in 1902, Edith resigned her position at Stella Friends Academy, and together with her sons Edwin, and the newly arrived Lester, she loaded up the covered wagon, hitched it to the same two horses, Fred and Charley, that had brought them from Northbranch a decade earlier, and started for Wichita.

She bought a house in Wichita where she lived once again with her three sons, Irvin, Edwin, and Lester. Alva and Gertrude visited them from Washington, Kansas. Irvin, now a graduate, worked in the university basement in the print shop he had established. Edwin entered Friends University as a freshman.

12

Reaching his area, complete with his assigned PT-22, a table, and five chairs, the flight instructor held up his identifying cardboard sign and began to call out, "Squadron 24, over here. Squadron 24!"

Perry and Paul were the first to join him.

"Perry V. Row, sir, twenty-three, from Caldwell, Idaho," Perry answered, when prompted by the instructor.

"Paul W. English, sir, twenty-two, from Caldwell, Idaho."

"You two must have enlisted together."

"Yes, sir," they answered together.

Shortly, two other men approached them.

"I'm Mac B. Bradley, sir, twenty-two, from Seattle," the first man said. "I was working as a box boy when the Japs hit Pearl. I decided I wanted to get into this thing right away, but I had to wait for my sister to graduate high school, so she could get a job. My father, he don't work, see?" Blond, broad-shouldered and towering over the others, Mac seemed a nice enough chap, Perry thought.

"How about you, son?" The instructor turned to the other man.

"Rich Angel, sir."

"Middle initial?"

"J."

"What's your age?"

"Eighteen, sir."

"And where are you from?"

"Los Angeles, sir."

Looking neither rich nor angelic, he appeared angry or resentful to Perry. Rich stood an inch shorter than Perry, with black hair and black eyes that didn't seem to meet anyone's gaze.

"That makes four," the instructor said. "Let's step over to

the airplane."

Perry listened attentively as the instructor pointed out the various features of the PT-22 Recruit, but in truth, Perry already knew everything he could about the model without actually flying it, having read every book and magazine article he could find on it.

Finishing his orientation presentation, the instructor turned to his squadron and asked, "Who wants to go up first?"

Perry jumped on the answer, spitting quickly, "I do, sir!"

"Fine," he said. "Got your flying suit? Packed parachute?"

"Yes, sir."

"Did you pack it yourself?"

"Yes, sir."

After dressing, as he shrugged into the heavy pack, Perry listened attentively to the instructions, including the part about how tomorrow, each man would get to pilot for the first time.

"Today, you're just a passenger."

"Yes, sir."

"If you touch any control other than the headset, it's an automatic washout."

"Yes, sir," Perry answered.

He climbed up onto the wing of the two-seater and into the pilot seat in the rear, followed by the instructor, who stood on the wing and pointed out the various controls, before climbing into the front seat.

The instructor taxied the PT-22 Recruit out to the line of waiting airplanes. Perry marveled at how well he could hear through the headset, over the noise of the Kinner engines, throbbing in disharmony.

Finally, it was their turn to take off. The instructor turned, came to a complete stop, waited one extra second, and then pulled back on the stick. Perry felt only a small increase in prop wash in his face, but the volume of noise seemed to drill into his ear canals. *Come on, buddy,* he thought as the airplane rumbled down the runway. *You're never going to*

lift this thing off the ground if you don't give it more juice.
At what felt like the last possible moment, the ship lifted off
the runway, to Perry's surprise, reducing the vibrations by
seventy-five percent. He flew, for the very first time.

The instructor climbed to five thousand feet in nine
minutes—about as fast as the PT-22 is able—but to Perry,
the climb lasted all afternoon. He wanted to fly still higher,
but they leveled off and flew a straight course. The sensations
washed over his body, starting in his toes and flooding
through and out the top of his scalp. *This is flying,* he said
to himself, over and over. *This is what it feels like to be free
to move in three dimensions.* The sunlight glistening off the
aluminum and chrome parts of the airplane, Perry observed,
felt strangely chilly in these winds, brightness that ought
to feel hot, chilly winds that ought not be bright. *Strange
sensation,* he reflected.

"Are you game for a roll?" The instructor's voice crackled
over the headset.

"You bet! I mean, yes, sir!"

"Here we go, then," the instructor said as the right wing
dropped ninety degrees so it pointed straight down, leaving
Perry's head sticking out toward the horizon.

"That's fantastic, sir!" Perry shouted.

"Let's go back the other way, then," the instructor called
out, rolling back to level and then continuing to roll until the
left wing pointed straight down.

"Now, the best part," the man said, and continued the
left roll another ninety degrees, so the ship was completely
upside down.

"Still with me?" he asked.

"Yes, sir."

"Good. I lose more students that way!"

"Not me, sir."

"No, I see that." The instructor rolled right again, one
hundred eighty degrees, leveling off. "This time, we'll bank
instead of rolling, and head back to base. I've seen enough."

He rolled slightly left, adjusting the ailerons, and banked

the ship left, turning completely around, making a giant U-turn in the sky. Perry watched the sun shift from his left to his right, and observed as the chilly air and bright reflections shifted with it.

Paul and the other two men ran to meet the airplane as it taxied back into the instructor's spot. As soon as the ship came to a stop, Paul, already wearing his flying suit and parachute, climbed up on the wing.

"How was it?" he shouted, as Perry stood up.

"Fantastic!"

"Everything you'd hoped for?"

"More!"

"Are you next?" the instructor shouted, standing in his seat.

"Yes, sir!"

"Let's go, then."

Perry climbed down, giving his spot to Paul and allowing the ground crewman to ensure Paul's safety.

What is that incredible feeling I have, Perry wondered? Why do I feel so fulfilled? Is the power of achievement so strong in me? And after all, what have I achieved? I witnessed a fantastic experience, a thirty-minute flight over central California, with lovely scenery, which, frankly, I nearly forgot to observe. No, it wasn't the scenery, incredible as it was. I think it's just the pure joy I feel, the joy of flying, of moving through three dimensions at once, not just two. I have always imagined the sensation. I knew I would love it.

The other two members of the squadron, Mac and Rich, hung back, watching Perry from a distance. Suddenly he understood sadly, without knowing why, that they would be the washouts, the fifty percent, while he and Paul would go on to Basic Flying School.

During the next three weeks, life settled into a routine. Morning classes included the theory of flight, coordination exercises, navigation, aerodynamics, and airplane structure. Perry aced his theory of flight test, but got only 64% on his navigation test. Afternoon flying lessons consisted of airplane inspection, banking turns, inverted flight, holding a spin for two complete turns and recovering, and other aerial acrobatics. There was an occasional surprise navigation test, where the flight instructor allowed Perry to fly freely, performing maneuvers over a forty mile course from base, and then asked him to take them home. Fortunately, Perry had knuckled down and studied navigation after his dismal classroom showing and succeeded in getting the instructor and himself back on the flight deck in one piece.

By mid-August, with nearly ten hours of flying in his log book, Perry stepped out of the PT-22 feeling a strange combination of elation, queasiness, and apprehension. He stumbled a bit, coming off the wing and back onto solid ground as he pulled off his headgear. The instructor took him by the elbow and spun him around. Perry had to put his hand forward, thinking he might fall.

"Dizzy?" the instructor asked.

"No," Perry lied.

"Fever?" the instructor put the back of his hand against Perry's forehead without waiting for an answer.

"I'm fine."

The instructor put a thumb under Perry's left eye and peered closely. Perry pulled back a little. "Hold still."

After a moment, he took away his hand. "Report to the Base Medic," he said. "I'm going to need something from him in writing before you can fly again."

"What?" Perry protested. "I'm fine!"

"I don't really think so, but if the Medic says so, that's okay by me. Who's next?"

Rich Angel stepped forward, ready to fly. The instructor abandoned Perry on the flight deck. A new wave of dizziness washed over him as he struggled out of his flight suit.

"Come on, Perry," a voice said. "I've already flown today. Let's get you over to the Base Medic."

Perry looked up into the face of Mac Bradley. "I'm fine," he repeated, but this time, he didn't believe it either. He started walking in response to Mac's hand on his elbow, pulling him.

At the Base Hospital, an older man in white took one look at the two airmen walking into the Reception Room.

"Get him into that bed," he barked aloud to no one, but two nurses appeared from behind curtains and led Perry to a dressing area, stripping him quickly of his equipment and uniform, tying a gown on him, and pushing him back onto the bed in a seated position. One read his dog tags and made some notations on a chart while the other pushed a thermometer under his tongue.

"Take this," a third nurse said, handing him a pill and some water.

"You don't even know what's wrong with me," Perry said.

"Yes, we do. Keep your mouth closed for three minutes. I'll come back and explain later. Just rest for now."

After the second nurse removed the thermometer, Perry took the pill and leaned back against the pillow. The room began to swirl.

"Use this if you need to," the first nurse said, pushing a shiny metal bedpan into his arms. "Got someone I can call for you?"

"Phyllis Marie," he said, as the color of the room changed to a gray charcoal. He closed his eyes to prevent the color from changing to black, but it was no use.

13

After watering the horses and refilling the canteens, Lige and Carrie Rowe tied translucent muslin screens around the heads of their sons, their horses, and themselves to protect their eyes against the white-hot glare of the sunlight reflected off the Great Salt Plain. They wore wide-brimmed hats to hold the screens in place.

Shortly after starting out, Clifton felt the salt crust crunching beneath the horses' hooves and wagon wheels.

"I cannot see anything," he complained.

"Keep your screens on, boys," Lige said. "There is nothing to see, other than mirages. Time was, the great buffalo herds migrated here for the salt, but that was fifty years ago, before the hunters destroyed them."

Everyone sat very still as they crossed the salt plains, wanting to look out across the white shimmering mirages like shallow seas, expecting to see something, anything: a buffalo, another wagon, or even a sailing ship, but they worried that if they looked into the brightness for too long they might damage their eyes.

"The fact is, no animals can live out here," Lige said. "Have you noticed? There are no flies, no insects at all, and no plants."

Two hours later, at the eastern edge of the salt plains, Lige stopped the hitch wagon and stepped out on the salt-encrusted earth with a loud crunch. "Come down, sons," he said. "I want to show you something. Keep your screens on."

Clifton stepped out carefully, so carefully that his weight did not break through the salt crust. Not until he lifted his brother out of the wagon did the crust yield under his boots.

"Look here," Lige said. He took his knife from its sheath on his belt, and cut away a part of an outcrop of limestone, to show his sons the thick stratum of red clay slate underneath. Clifton crumbled a piece of it between his thumb and fingers.

"What makes this?" Clifton asked.

"I do not really know," Lige answered. "Perhaps it was an ocean that dried up. It may have been a hot springs, or a volcano, where the salt comes up from below the surface. However it was formed, I think it has been this way for a very long time."

"How much more is there?"

"We are almost through it."

"Good," Clifton said. "I find it strange out here."

When the wagon crossed out of the Great Salt Plain and they felt the salt crust under the wheels give way to the red Oklahoma clay, everyone sighed with relief and removed their muslin screens.

Late in the day, as the hitch wagon turned south onto a wider dirt track, the red sun dropped below the flat horizon to the west and Carrie completed the lesson of the eight foundations of a true social order. Clifton sat upright with his back against the wall of the wagon, facing the dimming sky, while his brother rested his head against Carrie's breast.

"The fifth foundation," she said, "is that the spiritual force of righteousness, loving-kindness, and trust is mighty, because of the appeal it makes to the best in every man."

"I see," Clifton said.

"Do you?"

"Yes."

"Can you explain it to me?"

"Well, it says that being good feels good."

Carrie smiled. "That is a very simple way to look at it, honey. I like it. There is a little more to it than that, but that will do just fine for now." She stroked her younger son's hair as she talked.

"What is the next one?" Clifton asked.

"The sixth foundation is a tough one to understand," she said. "It is that our rejection of the methods of outward domination, and of the appeal to force, applies not only to international affairs, but to the whole problem of industrial control. Not through antagonism, but through cooperation and goodwill, can the best be obtained for each and all."

"You are right," Clifton said, "I do not understand."

"Do you remember we have talked about war?"

"Yes."

"War is a very good example of outward domination, the appeal to force," she said.

"Yes, I remember."

"Do you remember last week when the dogs got into a fight over the food we gave them?"

"Yes."

"That was another example of appealing to force."

"Yes."

"As Friends—some people call us Quakers—as Friends, we reject war. We reject the appeal to force, and this rejection applies not only to whole nations, but also to the work we do. We can obtain the best for each and all through cooperation and goodwill, not through antagonism, like the dogs fighting over a scrap of meat on a bone."

"I see."

"On the other hand, you do not want to stand there and let some bully beat you into the ground, do you? Turning the other cheek only goes so far. Eventually a man runs out of cheeks."

Lige turned to look at her, but said nothing.

"I see," Clifton repeated.

Carrie was not convinced that he fully understood this last point, but she knew he was thinking about it, trying to grasp it for himself, and to her, that was the goal of the lesson, so she was satisfied.

She struggled with the concept herself. Her proud membership in the Daughters of the American Revolution stood in direct opposition to her proud membership in the pacifistic Religious Society of Friends.

Lige, on the other hand, believed in true Pacifism, objecting to any form of aggression, based on the belief that the willful taking of human life is wrong. This disagreement had festered between them since before their wedding.

Vancil's breathing slowed and his body suddenly weighed a few more pounds, it seemed to Carrie, as he relaxed into sleep.

"Shall we move on to the seventh foundation?"

"Yes," Clifton said, his mind still whirring over the inconceivable notion of two nations at war.

"The seventh foundation of a true social order is that mutual service should be the principle upon which life is organized. Service, not private gain, should be the motive of all work."

"God is first, others are second, and I am third, right Mom?"

"Right."

So, we are ready for the eighth foundation of a true social order," he beamed into the brightening evening star.

"So be it," Carrie said. "The eighth foundation is that the ownership of material things, such as land and capital, should be so regulated as best to minister to the need and development of man."

"What is capital?" Clifton yawned.

"Well, money, for example, but other things, too, like this hitch wagon and the horses, things that have monetary value, things that can be bought or sold or traded."

"And what is regulated?"

"You know that word," she said.

"I do?" Clifton slouched down onto the floor of the wagon.

"Yes, you helped your Dad install a regulator for the well, do you remember?"

"Oh, it regulates the water."

"Yes," she answered.

"So, money and capital should be regulated, too, made regular, like water." Clifton yawned again.

"If the water was not regulated," she said, "to continue with your example, some parts of the wheat fields would get too much water and other parts would be too dry."

"And we are like the wheat fields," he said. "We must have regular money and capital to minister to our needs and our—"

"Development," she said, finishing his sentence. It was too dark to see his eyes, so she waited to hear his breathing change as he fell asleep. "God's blessings to you," she whispered to both her sleeping sons. A rising half moon guided Lige and his sleeping family the rest of the way to the Lynes' ranch near Hunter, southwest of Pond Creek.

Crosha Whitaker was born in Texas in 1865, the same year her future husband, Henry Lynes, turned thirty while fighting with his Iowa cavalry regiment in the Civil War. Marrying when she turned seventeen and he forty-seven, they moved first to Kansas, where they joined the Society of Friends, and then ran in the Oklahoma land rush—Henry on horseback and Crosha in their wagon, to double their chances. They both succeeded, so they ended up with a house in the township that became Pond Creek and a ranch outside of Hunter. Now thirty-four, Crosha operated a school she had started in her barn and hosted the only Monthly and Quarterly Meeting in the L and O counties area.

"God's blessings to you, boy."

Clifton opened his eyes, startled awake by the salutation.

"God's blessings to you," he answered, without knowing to whom he responded. When he saw that he was alone in the back of the hitch wagon, he sat up to see Crosha Lynes smiling at him.

"Time to rise and shine, boy," she said. "You will find breakfast in the kitchen."

Clifton dropped down to the dust among a half-dozen or more hitch wagons of various sizes and looked through the open barn doors. He watched as several men and women, including Lige and Carrie carried and stacked bales of hay into an impromptu gallery of pews, in two columns, one for the men and the other for the women. Most of the men wore the same plain coat, wool or denim pants, and wide-brimmed hat as his dad. Most of the women wore the same plain cotton dress and bonnet as his mom. A few of them, the ones tossing hay bales down from the loft, wore overalls.

"Clifton," his mother called, "go on and get something to eat, then join the other children. They are having a class in the yard on the other side of the house."

The kitchen bloomed with the smell of pork bacon and coffee, but no one was there, and Clifton didn't see any food anywhere. He walked through the house to the front and saw his brother sitting with half a dozen children with plates of food in their laps.

"Clifton?" A pretty girl of seventeen called to him.

"Yes?"

"I have a plate for you here."

He walked over to her. She smelled of orange blossoms and bacon when he took the plate she offered him.

"Thank you—"

"Ida Whitaker," she said.

"Thank you, Ida Whitaker."

"You're welcome, Clifton," she answered. "Come and sit here, beside your brother." As he did so, she introduced the other children. "These are my sisters, Georgia and Lena," she said.

"How do you do?" Clifton said, standing again and bowing at the waist.

"Lena is eleven," she said, "and Georgia is seven, like you, and this is my brother, Jim. He's five, like your brother, Vancil. The baby on the quilt is John Perry, and he just turned two. We just call him Perry."

"And how old are you, Ida?" Clifton asked with the unabashed directness of a child raised within the Society of Friends. The other children giggled a bit, nervously.

"Well, Clifton, I am seventeen," she answered, smiling.

"Are your parents in the barn?" he asked.

No one giggled at this question. In fact, Clifton observed a marked change in his new acquaintances. Georgia put her fork down and stopped eating. She put her hands in her lap and stared at them. Lena and Ida gazed at one another in distress.

"No, Clifton," she said, in a softer voice. "Our parents died recently."

"Oh," he said, feeling a tug of emotion. He watched Georgia fight back tears. "I am sorry to hear that," he said, reaching out and touching her hand and directing his comment to her.

She looked up and smiled bravely at him as one tear escaped her right eye.

"Clifton," Ida said, "we asked Vancil how your last name is spelled, but he didn't know."

"Well, he's only five, so you must make allowances for him," Clifton said.

Ida grinned. "Then, you can tell us."

"Sure," he said. "It's R-O-W-E, and it rhymes with 'now' not 'grow,' like growing corn."

"Well, we were wondering about that."

"Yes, I guess a lot of people do."

Ida sat quietly for a minute or two, allowing Clifton to finish eating, and then started a short lesson on the purpose of the Quarterly Meeting. She outlined the schedule for the weekend and explained that the first session, starting later that morning, would be a silent meeting for worship, the second session would be a business meeting, during which the children could play, and that the Sunday morning session would be another silent meeting for worship.

"Of course, silent worship does not mean no one talks," she explained. "Aunt Crosha says it is just the opposite, that everyone talks, that is, anyone that wants, talks."

"Then, why do they call it silent?" Georgia asked.

"Because there is no sermon, no preacher," Ida answered.

Clifton looked at the other children. "Is this your first Meeting?"

"Not for me," Georgia answered. "I have been before when visiting Aunt Crosha, but for the others it is. We went to the Church of Christ back home."

"I see," Clifton said. He wondered where 'back home'

might be, but he remained quiet, not wanting to ask any questions that might give Georgia further cause for tears.

Clifton and Vancil remained in Ida's care for the rest of the day, along with her siblings and twenty more children who arrived with their parents. Ida brought all the children to the barn for Silent Meeting and brought them back to the yard in front of the house to eat lunch and play while the adults attended Business Meeting. At times there were loud discussions emanating from the barn and at other times the children could have been the only people on the wide Oklahoma prairie, the Meeting was so quiet.

The boys saw Lige and Carrie again when the four of them slept together in the hitch wagon Saturday night. On Sunday morning, they attended Silent Meeting, sitting with Lige while Carrie sat across the hay-strewn aisle with the other women. The boys played with the other children, again under Ida's care, for the remainder of the day, said their goodbyes to Georgia and her siblings, and went to sleep in the hitch wagon with their parents.

Early Monday morning, Lige and Carrie guided the wagon through the darkness and out onto the westward road without awakening their sleeping sons.

For the next seven years, Clifton continued to learn and grow under the careful guidance of his mother. During the cold winter months, when the winds blew rain and snow across their Oklahoma prairie homestead, Carrie pasted layers of Lige's newspapers on the inside walls around Clifton's bed, both to keep him warm and to foster his intense desire to read.

Every time they attended the Quarterly Meeting, Carrie returned the books she had borrowed previously from the school, and gathered up a new armload for her sons to study, and every time they attended the Quarterly Meeting, Clifton sought the company of Crosha's niece, Georgia Whitaker, the girl he had consoled.

14

Perry opened his eyes. The green-colored walls seemed vaguely familiar, military, not unlike walls he had painted somewhere, perhaps in the rain. All he could remember about it was the fact that the paint wouldn't dry and they had to repeat the job the following week. The memory of smearing that pea-green paint over those damp and clammy boards again made his stomach writhe.

"Perry?"

He turned his head in the direction of the voice. He recognized it; it belonged to his wife, Phyllis Marie.

"What are you doing here?"

She smiled; she couldn't help herself. "I'm waiting for you to wake up."

"Have I been asleep long?"

"Off and on for a few days."

He started to sit up, but his joints ached and he settled for a slightly raised position on one elbow. "Three days? What have I got?"

"Valley Fever."

He felt a knot form in his stomach. "That's not very good, is it?"

"You've been very sick." With an effort she kept her voice calm and her expression serene.

"I seem to recall reading something about six men dying from it recently."

"Yes." She sighed, but he thought it was with relief. "The doctors tell me it affects different races differently."

"Were those six men white?"

"No."

Perry lowered his head back to the pillow. "Then I'm going to be okay."

"They think so, but you need some rest and I'm here to see that you get it."

"Yes, sir." He glared at the ceiling.

"What are you thinking about?"

"My training."

Nodding in compassion, she leaned toward him. "I thought so. You'll have to drop back a class. I've already talked to the base commander about that—"

"You have? Randall?"

"Yes, that's him, Colonel Randall. He's a love."

"A love?"

"Yes, he said that no one washes out from being sick, and that you'd get to receive a rare pleasure."

"What's that?"

"You'd get to hear his dodo lecture again." She smiled but Perry could not quite make his lips turn upward.

The hospital discharged him on a Wednesday in early September, two weeks after his admittance. When he thought about it carefully, Perry realized he remembered only the last three days of his visit.

In the meantime, Phyllis Marie had rented a back guest house in Visalia for two weeks, from a nice older couple whose son had renovated the place, using rat traps mounted to the walls as clothes hangers. A moose head filled the space over the bed, and the bathroom featured a full-sized green traffic light attached to the toilet—something Perry called the GO light. She brought her husband home with the help of a three-day pass and a military ambulance and ordered him to rest while she started dinner.

Upon the expiration of his pass, Phyllis Marie returned to Idaho and Perry reported for duty to the Base Medic.

"Felling better?"

"Yes, sir."

"You look better."

Perry waited patiently while the same three nurses huddled around him, drawing his blood for testing, checking his temperature again, and taking his blood pressure.

"So, how did you know I had Valley Fever?" he asked the doctor.

"We've had dozens of cases. When they built the new runway, they stirred up all the dust where the fungus grows."

"So, the antibiotics caught it, huh?"

"No, not really, as I mentioned, it's a fungus, not a bacteria," he said. "We gave you antibiotics to prevent any secondary infections. The only real treatment for Coccidioidomycosis is bed rest, and plenty of it, which I ordered your wife to provide."

The doctor made a note in the chart. "I'm putting you on restricted duty. No flying, not yet. Come back in five days. Meanwhile, continue to take it easy. You're one of the lucky ones, you know. I lost six patients, right after they built the runway."

A week later, Perry flew the Ryan PT-22 Recruit again, with a new instructor, Captain John Hammer. Known to his students as Jack, he arrived on the flight deck just ahead of Perry.

"Are you the guy left back because of illness?"

"Yes, sir."

"Okay, let's see what you've got."

Forty-two, with sandy red hair, standing all of five-foot-seven, Jack knew he wouldn't see action in this war, but with his flying experience—over France in the Great War, and then barnstorming throughout the south as an aerial acrobat and crop duster—he knew that the best way to contribute to this war was to train the new pilots. Any fool could see this war would be won in the air, he told his wife as he left their home in Memphis.

'What a thrill it is,' Perry wrote to Phyllis Marie, 'to soar around overhead again. I hadn't forgotten as much as I had anticipated and my new instructor, Jack, approved of my flying almost to the point of praise.' Within a week, Perry flew solo for the first time, passing his twenty-hour check ride, and resuming classes, without having to re-visit Colonel Randall's orientation lecture.

After cramming for a week, he took all the final tests right along with his own class, with passing grades, and appeared before Jack when summoned.

"I wish I could just go ahead and graduate you with your class," he said, "but you must have sixty hours flying time, and you're twenty hours short."

Perry felt suddenly compelled to focus on several photographs of old airplanes on the wall before responding. "Yes, sir. I understand, sir."

Jack looked up. "I know you're disappointed, son, but, as good as you are, you haven't been rated on some of the maneuvers. I've given this a lot of consideration, and I have to hold you back. I'm sorry."

"Yes, sir."

"The good news is, since you've passed the course work, you can get the flying done within the month, and there is a new Basic Flying Class starting November in Lemoore. I've put your name in for it already."

"Yes, sir. Thank you, sir."

"And I'm adding you to an open spot in my squadron, where a man has already washed out."

"I appreciate that, sir."

"Meanwhile, there's someone here to see you."

Jack opened the door to reveal Paul English standing in the hall.

"Paul!" Perry stepped out into the hall. Jack returned to his office and closed the door.

"How are you, Perry?"

"I'm fine, really."

"I heard from Mary about how sick you were. I feel awful about moving on to Chico without you."

"It'll be okay, don't worry. What became of the rest of the squadron?"

"Mac washed out. He just couldn't take the stress of it, I think. He's going to go to Mechanic's School in Alabama, stay on the ground, he says."

"And Rich?"

"He passed. He and I ship out in an hour."

"Well, you and Rich—I didn't have it figured that way."

"Remember Perry, you didn't wash out."

Perry glanced at the floor. "No, I guess not, really, on a technicality."

"However you want to put it, you're not a washout. You're the one with real talent. Don't forget that."

Perry smiled, grateful for his friend's encouragement. He took Paul's hand and shook it warmly. "I'll see you soon."

Paul grinned. "You bet."

Perry worked hard in October of 1942, when the weather permitted flying, making up the lessons he had missed. When the day came for him to demonstrate the maneuvers for certification, the slow rolls, half rolls, snap rolls, and loops, he gave Jack a good ride.

In his sixtieth and final qualifying hour of flight, Perry climbed to ten thousand five hundred feet for the first time. He was exultant when, after the Graduation Dance at the Visalia Elks Club, he carried all his belongings, his graduation certificate, and his thirty-four-and-a-half-hour pass onto a bus to downtown Lemoore, California and met Phyllis Marie at a small hotel.

She threw her arms around him and they whirled around the room in their own private celebration.

15

As a young man of eighteen, Edwin Stanton affected different people in different ways. Some of his classmates thought he was restless or dissatisfied or flighty, when in fact, he was simply searching for a better way to do things, a better way to understand things, or a better way to be. He was neither a clown nor a buffoon, as the more conservative University elders thought, although he was capable of great mirth, and liked nothing better than a good laugh, when it didn't come at the expense of another. Nor was he the somber and serious student dedicated only to his books, his devotion, and the science of learning, as the University librarians supposed, though he spent long hours poring over each new title, whether the subject was photography, comparative religion, or poultry farming. On the contrary, Edwin was an extraordinarily contented young man, living completely at ease in the here and the now, so that people painted him with the colors they chose to see, without realizing they were seeing themselves in him, as they would in a mirror.

Upon securing a job in a Wichita photography studio during his third year of college, he looked for a better way, experimenting constantly with apertures, lighting, exposure times, and development solutions, seeking the proper balance of light and shadow, emphasizing the cheekbone in one subject's portrait, hiding the prominent jaw in another, and taking satisfaction in the process as much as the result.

He always looked for a better way to do things. He kept his eyes open to all possibilities, the opportunities that might present themselves, so when Hazel Hill and her family approached the lower entrance of Friends University to attend Monthly Meeting in the basement recreation center on a crisp September Sunday morning in 1904, he reached for the door, stood to one side, and greeted her with a broad smile.

Hazel's father, John Hill, carefully selected a pew on the

women's side for his wife, Elizabeth, and three of his four daughters—Josephine, Edna and Hazel—before turning to join Josephine's fiancé—George Outland—in an opposite pew on the men's side. He noticed two young men, obviously brothers, seated in the pew in front of him. One of them was Edwin Stanton, the tall young man who had held the door and smiled at his youngest daughter.

The Meeting rose to its feet and sang as one:

Hearken to the solemn voice,
The awful midnight cry.
Waiting souls, rejoice, rejoice,
And see the Bridegroom nigh.
Lo! He comes to keep His Word,
Light and joy His looks impart.
Go ye forth to meet your Lord,
And meet Him in your heart.

Edith also noticed her son's interest in the new girl. After Monthly Meeting, when she rejoined her sons on the sidewalk outside the University building, she traced Edwin's eyes to the new family as they ascended from the church.

"Good morning," she said to John and Elizabeth Hill as they approached. "I am Edith Bowles Stanton, and these are my sons, Irvin and Edwin." There was nothing forward or extraordinary about such introductions, not among Friends, for they eschewed titles, and held that men and women stood on equal ground. Further, in her capacity as a church elder and circuit preacher, it was perfectly ordinary for Edith Stanton to greet newcomers. John Hill introduced his wife and each of his daughters. Edith listened, taking care to note the name of the youngest girl, the one Edwin could not refrain from watching.

The Hills had arrived in Wichita only a few days earlier, in time for Hazel's enrollment as a freshman at Friends University. She was a loving and concerned daughter and sister, devoted and sensitive to the needs of others, and capable of enormous tolerance. Her family also knew what Edwin Stanton would soon discover: Hazel was an unrestrained and unmitigated prankster.

"Will thee come to tea?" Hazel asked Edith, her gloved hand still clasped in a gracious handshake with Edwin. "In an hour?"

"We would be delighted," Edith replied.

The Stantons had walked the entire four blocks to their Hiram Street home before realizing that the Hill's address had not been provided. Edith and her boys stood on the front porch, looking at one another, eyes wide, mouths open, before finally breaking into laughter.

The next day at school, Edwin thought about the new girl, wondering, had she really played a joke, as he imagined, or was it simply that she forgot to give them the address? He worried that perhaps the Hill girls had prepared tea, coffee, little cakes, any number of snacks and refreshments, and then had been disappointed by the Stantons' failure to appear. Perhaps Hazel had been offended. He didn't even know where to send an apology!

He was too busy with his new classes Tuesday and his work at the Larson Photography Studio Wednesday to worry about it, but then on Thursday, he thought he saw her across the University quadrangle, walking with two other girls, but before he could cross the short distance, she disappeared into a sea of white dresses and dark suits.

By Saturday, Edwin's mind was twisted into knots. One minute he considered running away to the circus in Wisconsin, the next he agonized over which of his three suits to wear to Monthly Meeting the following day.

Sunday morning he left the house for church fifteen minutes ahead of his mother and brother, arriving to a locked door and an empty basement. He sat under the archway of the broad main staircase, until it occurred to him that he didn't want to appear to be waiting for her. He walked the University grounds and athletic field, and by the time he returned, people were arriving, but he did not see the Hill family. He paced back and forth at the entrance, but finally the doors began to close and he rushed inside, only to see he had missed his opportunity. There she sat in the third pew, between her mother and one of her sisters. Edwin slipped into the back pew on the men's side and tried not to look out of breath or out of balance, tried not to feel his heart pounding uncomfortably beneath his shirt and coat. He didn't know whether to apologize for missing their appointment or to seek redress for the trick she might have played.

After the meeting, when the women rejoined the men on the sidewalk, she approached him directly. "South Hall for Women," she said, smiling. "My parents are the dormitory parents. In an hour?"

He fumbled nervously with a few coins in his pocket until she noticed and glanced down, maintaining her sweetly innocent smile. "We'll be there," he said, meekly.

She and her three sisters walked quickly to their new home, South Hall, outpacing their parents' leisurely stroll down Hiram Street and refraining from giggling until they reached the porch.

Inside, Hazel took her sewing basket and fell upon the task she had set for herself—the dining room table—while her sisters helped with the preparation of tea and cookies in the kitchen. First, she draped the table with a lace tablecloth, not the nicest in the hutch, but a very special tablecloth, one that had been used for her intended purpose on several occasions before. She set eight places with small plates, cups, saucers, and spoons. Carefully deciding on one of the places, she sat and placed her sewing basket in her lap. Threading her needle with the special thread—the light gray thread that matched the color of the silverware—she carefully sewed the spoon to the lace tablecloth, using just two tight stitches at the thinnest part of the spoon, just where the supporting stem meets the small bowl-shaped receptacle. After completing her task, she put her sewing basket away and entered the kitchen to help her sisters with the tea.

"It isn't too hot, is it?" she asked.

The Stantons arrived and Edwin knocked gently on the screen door. Hazel appeared, smiling. "Won't you come in?" she asked. "Reverend Stanton, won't thee take this place at the head of the table? Mother, Josephine, Edna, over here, please," she continued, "no father, not there, please. Here, yes, I thank thee. Irvin, next to him, and Edwin here, please."

She quickly poured the tea while she talked. "That was a lovely service, I thought, much nicer than we had in Guthrie, didn't thee think so, Mother?"

Her mother, Elizabeth started to answer, but Hazel kept talking. *What is she up to now,* Elizabeth wondered. She looked at her other daughters, but if they were in on whatever Hazel had cooked up, they were not letting it show in their faces.

"I think it is so interesting that the Monthly Meeting is held in the basement of the school," she prattled on, not letting anyone get a word in edgewise, until she had poured the tea all around, offered sugar, milk, and lemon, and sat down. Edwin did not take any of the offered condiments.

Suddenly the room was silent. Rather than wait for the hostess to lift her cup first, as was customary, Edwin started to reach for his, but before he could, Hazel reached for the sugar tongs, grasped two cubes, and plopped them into his cup.

"Hazel!" her mother admonished.

"Oh, I'm sorry, I thought you wanted sugar," she said. "I'll get you another cup," she said, standing up.

"No, that's quite all right," he said. "I'll take it this way."

Edith leaned forward. "Thee never take sugar in thy tea," she said.

"It's perfectly fine, Mother," he said.

"Is thee sure?" Hazel asked, her doe-eyes as wide and innocent as she could make them.

"Yes," Edwin said. "Please, I'm fine."

Hazel resumed her place and lifted her tea to her lips.

In the next moment, as the hot tea glowed against her

face, Hazel froze in breathless anticipation as she watched Edwin reach for his spoon. The action seemed to take forever. As his arm came forward, his celluloid shirt cuff extended from under his coat sleeve. His mouth opened as he started to speak again, just as he picked up the spoon.

Crash! His teacup and saucer tumbled into his lap as the tablecloth pulled up from the table along with the spoon, so carefully stitched together.

The Hills grinned and the Stantons marveled as Hazel leaped upon Edwin, wiping at him with a napkin and admonishing him. "Thee must be more careful, Mr. Stanton."

Edwin tugged at the spoon again, causing the entire table setting to go flying—tea, milk, lemon wedges, and cookies. The Hill family burst into laughter. Edith gaped, astonished, until Edwin plucked gently at the spoon, demonstrating that he was not the culprit. The Stanton boys broke into laughter at the look on Edith's face.

For one tense moment, Hazel feared she had offended the Reverend Stanton, until she, too, began to laugh.

16

"Are you Roe?"

Perry had just stepped over the threshold of the newly alphabetically assigned semi-private barracks at Lemoore Air field in California. His uniform still hung loosely on his six-foot frame after the weight he'd lost from the illness, but the ruddiness had returned to his skin.

"Row," Perry said. "It rhymes with 'now.' Are you Rupert?"

"I flipped a coin and took the bunk nearer the bathroom, leaving you the window. I hope that's Jake with you."

Perry glanced around. It looked like every other barracks with its line of bunk beds and institutional green paint. He threw his duffle on his new bunk and turned back to the outdoors, looking at the documents the base command office provided in lieu of an orientation lecture. "Obviously, these are the cadet quarters," he said, grinning.

"Where's the mess hall?" Rupert asked.

"This way," Perry said as he started walking. "Where are you from?"

"I'm a local boy. Can you imagine enlisting to see the world and five months later, winding up in the town you were born and raised?"

"You must have seen some other bases in between."

"Yeah, and I'll see some other ones, I'm sure. What about you?"

"Caldwell, Idaho, now. I was born in Kansas and lived some in Oklahoma, too."

"You married?"

"Yes, you?"

"No. I've got a girl here, or did. I told her to see other guys when I enlisted, never imagining she would, or that I'd end up back here, but she did, and I did, and now it's a big mess of my own making."

"Gee, that's rough. Here's the PX. Want to go in?"

"No, that's where she works."

"Really? Here?"

"Yeah. What's next on the tour?"

"Let's go see the main attraction."

"The movie theatre?"

"No, the flight deck."

"Oh, okay. You really go for this, huh, the airplanes?"

"It's why I joined."

They walked around to the other side of the two large hangars and ran smack into a line of several dozen two-seater tandems, some of them in silver fuselages, with red engine cowls and red-and-white horizontal-striped rudders, others in blue fuselages with yellow wings and tails. Some of the silver planes had silver engine cowls and some of the blue planes had red-and-white horizontal-striped rudders. Perry thought they looked like flowers in the sunshine.

"Man, are these babies gorgeous!" Perry called out.

"Is this what we're going to fly?"

"Yep," Perry replied, grinning. "Vultee BT 13A Valiant. It's a single-engine all-metal low-wing monoplane with fixed landing gear, twice as heavy, eight feet longer, twelve feet wider in wingspan, fifty percent faster, and it has twice the range of the PT-22 I've been flying. These babies would blow their doors off."

"How do you know all that?"

"I have a magazine article about it."

Rupert looked into Perry's clean-shaven face. "You really give a damn about the flying, huh?"

"Don't you?"

The air was very still and Perry's hazel eyes were piercing. "Well, not like you do, I can see that."

Perry was perplexed. "Why did you join, then?"

"To get away from home."

"And yet, here you are."

"I guess you never know how things are going to work out."

They found themselves in the same squadron the next day, assigned to flight instructor Warren Fox, another civilian instructor with a background in acrobatics and crop dusting.

"Row, you're first up," he said. "You've got a hell of a recommendation from your last instructor. Let me show you what this thing can do."

Perry climbed onto the wing, heading for the aft cockpit, when Fox asked, "Are you expecting to puke?"

"No, sir."

"Then get in front. You ain't a dodo no more."

Excited by the prospect, Perry obeyed and climbed into the forward cockpit. When he saw that no grounds crewman was going to strap him in, he reached for the harness himself. He placed the headset over his ears and heard Fox behind him. "Got some new instrumentation. Can you find the electric starter?"

"Yes, sir."

"Give it a go."

Perry hit the switch and the propeller sputtered to a noisy start.

"Think you can taxi it on out to the runway?"

"Yes, sir."

No more baby-sitting, Perry thought. *I get to fly this thing from the beginning.* He wanted to shout with joy, but remained respectfully silent. Fox provided only the necessary information, just as it became necessary, a teaching technique Perry appreciated, especially since he had already done his homework on this bird.

"It's a great little airplane," Perry told Phyllis Marie when she visited the base at the end of his training period, for the New Year's holidays after Christmas. "I flew in formation with twenty other BT-13s yesterday, and this morning, before you got here, I flew ten straight rolls. That completed my certificate requirements. Now it's on to Advance Flying School."

Smiling at his enthusiasm, his wife snuggled closer, seeking his warmth. "Does that mean you want to fly fighters now?"

"No, certainly not." He was shocked.

"I just wondered. You seem so fond of this airplane."

"It's not just the airplane. It's the fact that I can do so much with it. It's a demanding ship, but you can make it do what you want it to do."

"What about the Link Trainer? You don't seem as fond of that as this Valiant."

"No, I'm not, but that isn't an airplane."

Phyllis Marie wrinkled her nose in curiosity. "What is it, then?"

Perry had forgotten how much he loved it when she did that. "Come, on," he said. "I'll show you."

They walked hand in hand across the quad and into one of the large classrooms.

Phyllis Marie laughed when she stepped inside. "What is this, a funhouse?" She saw ten little make-believe airplanes, blue and yellow, looking for the entire world like some kind of carousel attraction. Then she saw that each little plane had a large black desk associated with it, with panels of dials and switches.

"Do you want to sit in one?"

"Good heavens! This is what you've been talking about?"

He nodded, pleased by her surprise.

"Well, sure, I'm game, if you think it's safe."

"It's safe. They aren't even turned on."

"No, I mean, if it doesn't break some top secret rule or something."

He put an arm around her and kissed her lightly. "Oh, no, it's open post day today and tomorrow, and there's no one around to mind. It's a holiday and the new class doesn't come it until next week."

She took the hand he offered, steadying herself with her other hand on his shoulder, and stepped onto the platform, taking her place in the cockpit of the Link Trainer.

"Well, this is cozy," she said. "What do you fly next? I

mean, in Roswell?"

"A couple of larger airplanes, advanced trainers, both twin-engine jobs."

"Does that make a difference?"

"Two engines? Yes, a huge difference, or so I've read. It's a real step up."

"Does this Link Trainer really help?"

"Oh, yeah, it does. It's great for learning to fly blind. But the BT-13 Valiant is a lot more fun. I got to experience two-way radio communications with the ground for the first time, and the Valiant has a two-position variable pitch propeller. Of course, you have to operate the flaps with a crank, because there's no hydraulics, and the landing gear isn't retractable, but they say that once you master flying the Valiant, fighters are easy to learn, and it's just another small leap to the bombers."

Phyllis Marie folded her hands in her lap. "So you aren't going to fly fighters."

"No, I'm going to fly AT class airplanes, Advanced Trainers."

"And you're still on track to become a B-17 pilot?"

"Yes, I am, more so than ever."

"As long as you're getting to do what you want to do," she said. "That's what matters." Her green eyes sparkled and she smiled warmly.

He leaned down and kissed her. He could always count on Phyllis Marie to support him, and it made the process that much more satisfying.

After attending a live Fibber McGee and Molly radio show the next day, Perry and Phyllis Marie took a transport bus chartered by the military for personnel and their wives, to Roswell, New Mexico, the next step toward his goal.

17

James Perry Whitaker cast a tall and lean shadow as he entered the Rising Star Mercantile Company. Forty-two and as handsome as the sun is bright, his piercing hazel eyes and broad dark moustaches turned a lot of women's heads in town until they learned that he was happily married. He had just picked up a new ten-pound sack of flour and flung it over his left shoulder when he heard a disagreeable and familiar voice.

"Hey, you!" Georgie Carnegie shouted from the threshold. It was a hot October Texas day and the sweaty little man had followed Whitaker into the store, itching for a fight.

Whitaker froze in his tracks while the shopkeeper behind the counter looked up and shouted, "We don't want no trouble here, Georgie!"

Carnegie ignored him. "I'm talking to you, Populist!"

"What did you call me?" Whitaker said, turning slowly to face him.

"I'll call you worse than that, you bi-metallist, you soft-money inflationist!" Carnegie stepped into the store and out of the doorway. He didn't want his dark silhouette against the bright sunlight outdoors creating an easy target in case the newspaperman should pull a gun.

"You Republicans are all alike." Whitaker checked Carnegie's hands for a gun before looking him in the eye. "You have no grasp of late nineteenth-century economics as they apply to rural Texas, you think industrialization and mechanization are going to solve all of this country's problems, and you don't care that the farmers can't sell their crops for a profit any more."

"It's called over-production, you sod-buster sympathizer. Stop living in the past! I read that last article of yours."

"Which one? The one where I pointed out that the price of cotton has dropped so low that your friends and neighbors would be better off leaving it in the field to rot, rather than spend the money to harvest it? The one where I explained the insanity of limiting currency to gold while Western silver mines are producing tons of equally acceptable metal for currency?"

Carnegie glared at him. "Don't you know what that would do to the banking industry?" The sweat on his brow trickled into his eyes. "But I'm talking about your article that said that Republicans should abandon their beliefs and vote for the Populist—"

"Peoples' Party, you ignorant, gold-standard deflationist!"

"Whatever you want to call it, Mr. Paper Money, your third party is taking votes away from the Republican ticket, the only ticket that has a chance to unseat the Democrats in 1896!"

"If you Republicans would bother to educate yourselves on the issues, instead of spending all your energy calling people names, you'd see that our platform is a better fit to your agenda than your own!" Whitaker waited to see what Carnegie's response would be, but there was none. "I've wasted enough time on you," Whitaker said. "My wife is waiting for this flour."

Whitaker reached into his right pocket. The shopkeeper dropped down behind his counter.

"Hey!" Carnegie shouted. He pulled his gun fast and fired twice, hitting Whitaker in the belly with both shots.

Parilee Whitaker waited in the rocking chair on the front porch, her abdomen only a little extended by the baby growing inside her. It was her tenth pregnancy in about two decades but you wouldn't know it to look at her—curvaceous and attractive at forty with large maternal breasts, her blonde hair falling around her face in wisps. She heard the two shots from the direction of Main Street but thought little of it. Hooligans and rabble-rousers, she thought. They're probably killing each other over the upcoming election. She felt a sharp pain low in her gut. That's the second time this week, she thought.

She closed her eyes. Just for a few minutes, she thought, until Jim gets here with the flour.

She jumped awake at the sound of someone's voice. "Missus Whitaker," it said. "It's your husband. He's hurt bad."

Five men carried Jim, one holding each limb and another pressing three shirts, soaked red with blood, against his abdomen.

"Good Lord," she cried. "Bring him this way."

They followed her into the house, into the downstairs bedroom she and Jim had shared since arriving in Rising Star, and laid him gently on the bed. She put the back of her hand against his forehead. His face appeared whiter than the sheets that reddened with his blood. He was not conscious.

Doc Hamilton appeared with two women Parilee did not know. "Let me in," he said, elbowing his way past the men standing there, gaping at the blood. No one knew his true age, though they thought he was old because of his white hair and spectacles, but the vigor with which he pushed the men away showed no hint of aging or weakness. "Thanks for bringing him. Now get out!"

"Honey, where are your sheets?" one woman asked.

When Parilee pointed to the bed without speaking, the woman started searching the house for material to make bandages. The other woman went to the kitchen, moved the kettle of water forward on the stove and stoked the fire underneath. "It's a good thing you've already got hot water," she said to no one.

Parilee leaned on the doorframe to hide her trembling. "What happened?" she asked the doctor.

"Gunshot," he said, "twice."

"Who did it?" she turned to look at the men still lingering in the hall.

"It was Georgie Carnegie," the tall, heavy one said. "He come looking for an argument."

"Who's he?" she asked.

"Don't you know, Missus? He's Jim's biggest rival. He runs

the newspaper over there in Cross Plains, except his point of view is somewhat different from Jim's."

"Somewhat?" His slender companion jeered. "It couldn't be more different. Georgie's a gold standard man."

"I told you men to get out!" the doctor shouted. "Where are those bandages?"

Parilee turned back to her husband just in time to see the doctor pull a long surgical tool and a bullet out of Jim's belly. The wound gushed red with blood and the doctor pushed his finger deep inside to contain it. When she fainted, the men caught her and carried her to the divan in the small parlor.

"Missus Whitaker, can you hear me?" The doctor stood over her, his hands clean and dripping wet.

"Yes," she said. "How is he?"

"He's bad off. I got both bullets out of him, but he's—"

With an effort, she sat up. "He's what?"

"He was shot twice, Parilee, and he's going to need a lot of attention. I don't think you're up to it, what with your condition."

"No, you may be right," she said, remembering the sharp pain she had felt before they brought Jim home. She did not like it, but what was she supposed to do? She glanced helplessly around the bright parlor. The eyelet curtains suddenly seemed frilly and ridiculous.

"Have you had any more pains?"

"No," she lied. Had he seen the memory in her face? Why else had he asked?

"I sent Emma Ball down to the school—"

"Who?" Parilee rubbed her eyes in confusion.

"One of the women that was here, Emma, I sent her down to the school and she's arranged different places for all your kids to sleep tonight."

"Yes," she said, though she was not used to being ordered about in her own home. She sat up straight and glanced toward the bedroom.

"Now, the other woman, she's a pretty good nurse," the doctor continued, "and she's going to stay the night in there, so I want you to go sleep in one of the children's beds."

"Is he awake?"

"No," he said. "I gave him something to knock the tar out of him. I don't want him rolling around and tearing up my stitches."

The sharp pain returned and she tried not to wince. If the doctor saw it, he made no comment.

"Get some rest," he said. "I plan to. If the nurse needs me, she'll send her husband. He's already asleep on your porch."

She shook her head in surprise. "Is it that late?"

"It's a bit after midnight."

Parilee shivered. All at once, the house that usually felt so comfortable and cozy felt cold and empty. Though her husband was sleeping downstairs with a nurse at his side, Parilee felt all alone as she climbed the stairs to the chilly room her older daughters shared.

The following morning, she awakened to the sound of her daughter Georgia screaming. "What is it?" she called as she ran down the stairs and into the bedroom. The seven-year-old stood five feet away from the bed, staring at the blood-soaked bandages around her father's middle. The nurse was not there.

"Come here," Parilee said, covering the girl's eyes and dragging her out of the room. Another sharp pain stabbed at her insides, the worst one yet. She clutched wildly for the back of the divan with one hand, trying not to let go of Georgia with the other, but fell to the floor, doubled up in pain, pulling her child on top of her.

"Quiet, child," she whispered in her weeping daughter's ear. "You just be quiet now." She wrapped her arms tightly around the child and waited for the pain to go away.

"Missus Whitaker?"

She looked up to see Doc Hamilton standing over her again. She was in her daughter Ida's bed with the covers pulled up to her chin.

"How did I get here?" She blinked to clear her blurred vision.

"I carried you," he said. "Are you in any pain now?"

"No," she said, and meant it.

"No, I should think not. I gave you something, not a lot, but enough to quiet it down."

"Where's Georgia?"

"She's fine," he said. "I had her taken back to your brother-in-law's place. Cora's there, too, and Lena."

Frowning, Parilee tried to make sense of it. "What about the others?"

"Ida's down at the office. She says she's not going to let this stop the newspaper. She and Ora are going to look after the three little ones down there."

Parilee's heartbeat slowed and she tried to focus on the quilt pattern. "Not let what?" she asked quietly.

The doctor turned away and looked out the window.

"Not let what?" Parilee repeated.

"Missus Whitaker, I did all I could for Jim, but his fever rose and I couldn't do anything to bring it down."

"Where is he?"

"He's gone. I'm sorry."

Maybe it was the drug—the little something the doctor had given her. She didn't know, but she didn't cry. She felt nothing.

"Parilee, there's more," he said, pulling up a chair and sitting down.

She waited.

"It's about the baby."

Tracing the faded diamond shape on the covers, she murmured, "It's all right, isn't it?"

"Yes, for now, but to keep it safe, you have to stay in bed for the rest of your term."

"The rest of my term? You're talking about six months."

"If we're lucky, you'll go six months," he said. "It may come sooner, but we want to do everything we can to prevent that."

She finally understood. "Are you afraid I could lose it?"

"When I saw you on the floor two days ago—"

"Two days?" Parilee was shocked

"When I saw you, I thought you had already miscarried."
She stared at him helplessly.

"Jim died yesterday morning," Doc explained gently.
"The service was this morning. Your children were all there,
along with the whole town, your brother and his wife, Jim's
sister, Crosha, and her husband. She's downstairs now with
the children."

"I want to see them."

"Tomorrow," he said. "I told them you'd be ready to
see them tomorrow, but they'll be coming to you, do you
understand? You're not to leave this bed."

"What about the man who shot my husband?"

"He's in the jail down at the Sheriff's office."

"Why did he do it?" She felt bewildered.

The doctor sighed. "The store keeper says they were
arguing about the upcoming election. Georgie says he thought
Jim was going for his gun."

"Jim doesn't own a gun," she said.

"I know." The doctor looked away toward the window
again. "I think, as far as I can piece together, Jim was reaching
for his pipe, and when the store keeper leaned over to pick
something up, the other fellow thought he was trying to get
out of harm's way."

Later that month, Georgie Carnegie stood trial for first-
degree murder.

"Ladies and gentlemen of the jury," the judge said, "have
you reached a verdict?"

"No, your honor, we want to ask a question."

"Go ahead."

"Are we allowed to consider reduced charges?"

"What do you mean by reduced charges?"

"Well, one of us was on a trial this other time, where the
judge said if they couldn't convict on the highest charge, they
could consider a reduced charge, and that's what they did.
They couldn't all agree on the top charge, but they could
agree on a reduced charge."

"No, in this case, because the defendant is accused of shooting twice, and because the victim wasn't armed, the People of the State of Texas are required to charge him with first-degree murder and no less. Now go back and deliberate some more."

Crosha walked from the courthouse to the newspaper office where her niece Ida was waiting for her.

"Is it done?"

"Not yet," she said. "They went back into deliberations. I'm afraid they might not convict him."

"Why not?"

"The judge says it has to be all or nothing," Crosha said. "They seem like they'd convict him of second-degree murder if they could, but I don't think they've got it in 'em to go all the way."

"He shot Dad dead, standing there, defenseless, with a sack of flour on his shoulder, and he admitted it. There was a witness."

"I know."

One of the paperboys poked his head in the door. "Jury's back again," he said.

Crosha and Ida ran back to the courthouse together, entering the back of the room as the jury sat down.

"How about it, Mr. Foreman," the judge said. "Do you have a verdict?"

"Yes, your honor."

"Give it to the Sheriff," he said. "The defendant will rise."

The Sheriff took the slip of paper and handed it to the judge. He read it and handed it back to the Sheriff, who returned it to the jury foreman.

"Go ahead," the judge said.

"Not guilty," the foreman said.

"God damn it, Wallace!" the judge said. "Do you want to explain yourself?"

"Well, your honor, we just don't think it's right to convict him of first degree murder, and you won't let us consider a reduced charge."

"So you agree with the defense that it was an accident, that Mr. Carnegie thought Jim was going for his gun, and he thought that the shopkeeper knew Jim was going for his gun, and that was why he bent down behind the counter, so Mr. Carnegie drew and fired in self-defense."

"Yes, sir."

"Well, I think it's a miscarriage of justice, but I have no choice but to set you free, Georgie Carnegie, but if you have the nerve to come into my town again after killing our newspaper man, you had better leave your guns at home."

"Is that a threat, your honor?" the defense attorney asked.

"Court is dismissed," the judge said.

Parilee felt another sharp pain low in her gut and cried out. The pains had become frequent by now and she tried not to scream, so as not to wake Jim and the children, but occasionally, one slipped out. She heard voices in the distance and wondered who they were. Dim shadows seemed to come and go from her room, but they never seemed to say anything important, or do anything to stop the pain.

"He's a fine looking boy," one of them said, but Parilee didn't know whom he meant. Someone answered for her, though, using her voice, but she didn't hear. *What was everyone saying? Why would no one answer her?*

She wished she could get up and go for a walk down by the Mobile River, where it empties into the bay. Someone said it aloud, using her voice again, about the river, as if she only had to think it, and the dim shadows knew her thoughts, and said them for her. *It's so warm today. I want to go to the river to cool off. Maybe Jim will be waiting for me by the river.*

18

After putting Phyllis Marie on her bus in Roswell, Perry stepped onto the military shuttle to the base. They had spent one free night together, not enough, as usual, and to suppress the sting of her departure, to get his head right for the next stage of his training, Perry concentrated on his goals. He knew that this would be the final competition, the final winnowing of six hundred men into two categories: pilots and co-pilots. My first goal, he thought, is the mastery of these two airplanes, the Cessna AT-19 Bobcat, and the Curtiss AT-9 Fledgling. Although both boasted top speeds just shy of two-hundred miles an hour, he had a keener interest in the Cessna, because of its ties to Wichita, whereas the Jeep—as the Curtiss was known—had a reputation of being difficult to fly, or at least, difficult to enjoy flying.

More than that though, Perry knew he had to ace his classroom tests. He didn't know how the brass made their decisions, how they chose a man to be a pilot or co-pilot, but he felt certain that he had to excel in every aspect. Then he could assure his assignment as pilot.

When his bus arrived, he and two dozen other men lined their way into the main lobby of the headquarters, filled out forms, drew supplies, applied for their commissions, and signed the oath of office.

"Where to next?" Perry asked the clerk who took his papers.

"A physical examination, sir."

Yet another physical, Perry thought, as he picked up his things and followed along.

For the first time since his flying training started, he noticed that clerks and nurses started calling him 'sir,' even though his status had not changed. He was still an aviation cadet, but he expected to receive his pilot wings and lieutenant bars at the end of this ten-week course.

After passing his physical, he received his school and flying equipment, including fur-lined flying boots, a leather jacket, sunglasses, winter flying gloves, and a radio headset.

On his third day in Roswell, he settled into the same routine as the other training camps: classes in the morning and flying in the afternoon. He caught up with Rupert, his former roommate at Lemoore, and the two of them went over the curriculum, waiting for their squadron instructor.

"This is quite a list, Perry: airplane identification, air forces, ordinance, airplane electrical systems and radio, airplane maintenance, machine gunnery and skeet shooting."

"The flying lessons include formation, instrument, night, and cross country."

"Cadets!" a man growled at them from the window of a Cessna AT-19 Bobcat, "are you in my squadron or not?"

Perry and Rupert double-timed it over to the airplane, where three other students were already waiting. The man that had growled at them reminded Perry of a small bear, somehow.

"Thank you for joining us," he said sarcastically as they climbed into the airplane and took the two empty seats in the rear. The instructor sat in the right hand seat next to the student pilot, while the three student observers sat behind them. "You can take off now," he said.

Perry and Rupert glanced at each other, chagrined at missing the meeting point. They didn't know and didn't care to ask, but they felt as if they were in the doghouse unjustly.

"Take her up to eight thousand feet and set a course for due north." The instructor said little else, except to direct the student pilot to vacate the seat in mid-flight after half an hour, and direct another student into the hot seat. The instructor flew while the students exchanged places.

"Let's see you bank to the left ninety degrees and then fly level," he said. He gave the next two men just as little instruction. Finally, after everyone else had his turn, Perry got to fly.

"Bank left, ninety, and take us back," he said.

After two and a half hours of rather dull flying, Perry set the Bobcat down a little too hard. He taxied back to the position on the flight deck where he had climbed on board and shut the engines off. The instructor got out and walked away without a word.

Rupert waited until the man was out of earshot before speaking. "Well, what was that?"

"Can he do anything other than bank left?"

The next several days, flying lessons continued with little variation, except each man got a chance at take offs and landings over the course of the week. For the first time since his enlistment, Perry found less enjoyment in flying and more enjoyment in his morning classes.

On Thursday of the following week, dust and wind cancelled all afternoon flights. Perry and Rupert window-shopped for uniforms at the PX and went bowling in downtown Roswell. The next day, Perry awoke with a swollen eye.

"That looks infected," Rupert said. "Come on, I'll walk you down to the Infirmary."

"That's the last thing I need."

At the Registration Desk, the nurse asked a series of routine questions. "Have you had Valley Fever in the last year?"

"What?"

"Have you—"

"No, I heard you, I was just surprised. Yes, I have."

"Wait over here, please." She directed him to an empty waiting area but when Rupert started to follow along, she stopped him. "Not you," she said. "You run along."

Perry waited a half an hour before a doctor came to him, examined his eye, and treated him with some drops.

"If you have more trouble beyond tomorrow, you come right back here to this waiting area."

"Yes, sir. Can I go?"

"Yes. Don't fly today or tomorrow."

That night Perry dreamed of a large twin-engine spider that chased him across the flight deck, biting him with its pincers. In the morning, his face, neck, and shoulders felt funny. Looking in the mirror, Perry saw that hives covered his body.

"What's all this?" the doctor asked, seeing him again at the Infirmary.

"I was hoping you could tell me."

"Let's get you into a bed."

"Is that necessary?"

"I don't know yet. I'd rather err on the side of caution. Do you have any allergies?"

"Penicillin."

The doctor stared at Perry's chart. "I don't see that here."

"You'd better add it, then."

"As long as you're going to be our guest for a couple of days, let's take care of those wisdom teeth, shall we? No, wait. Tomorrow's your birthday!"

"That's okay, I might as well get it over with."

Upon his release—with a clear eye, no hives, and no wisdom teeth—Perry reported to the flight deck to find his squadron members standing around looking bored.

"Where's the bear?" he asked.

"Mr. Bank Left? He's gone," Rupert said.

"What do you mean, gone?"

"I wish I knew."

One of the other students spoke up. "He was just waiting for a transfer he wanted to Texas. That's where his family is, I think."

"Well, good riddance, I say," Rupert said.

Perry thought the same thing, but didn't voice his opinion in front of the others. After waiting another half hour to see if another instructor would show up, the students scattered.

The following morning in class, a runner from the office walked in and handed that instructor a note.

"Row?" the instructor asked.

"Here, sir."

"Go with this lad, please."

"Yes, sir."

Perry walked into the lobby to see his squadron mates

seated in the waiting area.

"What is this about?"

"I don't know," they chorused.

Rupert arrived at the same time a man stepped around the corner. The man carried a clipboard and bundle of files that Perry recognized as the squadron's flying file. He stood, and the others joined him.

"Ah, good," the man said. "At ease. My name is Cochrane and I'm guessing you're my new squadron. Row? Rupert? Shanks? Smith? Spitzer? Good. No, you needn't salute me, I'm a civilian."

He stood six feet even and looked about forty years old to Perry. He wore a red plaid shirt and black work-trousers with suspenders. As he called out the men's names, he re-sorted the individual folders according to some criteria Perry could not discern.

"You've had a bit of a bad patch, I see, but I'm here to change that. I know your previous instructor has not provided you with the kind of instruction you deserve and I'm sorry to read about that. We're going to have to make up a lot of work that your previous instructor seems to have ignored. Are you ready for it?"

"Yes, sir," they chorused.

"Fine," he said, smiling. "I'll see you on the flight deck at thirteen hundred and we'll take our first lesson."

He looked from man to man from a moment. "You're Row, right?"

"Yes, sir, I mean, yes."

"I know it's a hard habit to break once you've acquired it."

"Yes, sir," Perry grinned.

"Feeling one hundred percent?"

"Yes, I'm fine."

"Okay. See you all later."

On the flight deck, he passed out forms, asking the squadron members to evaluate their training so far. The members were horrified to see just how far behind the other squadrons they were. Not only had they not flown in formation yet, they had not taken a cross-country flight, something all the other squadrons had done.

The men flew every day from thirteen hundred hours until twenty-three hundred hours, each man taking two hours in the pilot seat, returning to base for re-fueling each evening. They combined cross-country flying with night flying, flew instruments for the first time under actual instrument conditions, and learned every aspect of the Cessna AT-19 and the Curtiss AT-9 under Cochrane's caring tutelage.

"Look at that." Perry spoke over the headset from the pilot's seat on a cross-country night flight. "Ten o'clock, high."

When the other members of the squadron turned they saw the shadow of the earth slowly engulfing the disc of the moon.

"Lunar eclipse," Cochrane said. "It's a good sign for this squadron, I think."

On the day the assignments came out, Perry felt that he and the rest of the squadron had done everything they could to recover from their bad start.

The men stood in the lobby and waited for the assignments to be posted to the bulletin board. When Perry saw his name, his jaw dropped.

'Row, Perry V., Co-Pilot'

19

When Hazel was a little girl, her mother taught her that all people are children of God and that each person is given a measure of loving Light to use in the world. In accordance with the Society of Friends, Hazel believed that using the Light strengthened the Light, that loving strengthened love. She further believed that if she waited silently upon God, there would be times when He would speak to her in her heart. Among Friends, this is known as the Inward Journey.

Once someone has been so moved, it becomes his responsibility to carry God's message to the people around him. It is this inspiration that has caused so many members of the Society of Friends to enter missionary work, become active in local politics, reform the penal system in America, found schools, and oppose preparations for war. This is known as the Outward Journey.

The sermon-less Meeting of Friends became, for Hazel, the sacrament of communion with God during which she opened herself to the leading of the Spirit. She took care of those around her. She paid heed to the needs of others.

Outsiders called them Quakers, from a story about the seventeenth-century English founder of the Society of Friends, George Fox, who, during his first trial for blasphemy, bade his court magistrates that they should quake and tremble at the word of the Lord. One of the judges mocked him, calling him a Quaker. The Friends didn't argue very strenuously against the epithet—it wasn't their way—so the name stuck.

Of course, it was never Fox's intention to start a new sect. Instead, he sought a return to the fundamental Christianity of the Apostles, when all men and women of all races and classes thrived, equally bestowed upon by God and surrounded by love: a time prior to the organized oppressions of Orthodox, Catholic, and Protestant.

Love God and thy neighbor as thyself. This outlook suited

Hazel perfectly. Even if she had known another way to live, which she did not, she would have chosen the Inward and Outward Journey of the Friends.

John and Elizabeth Hill had grown up in the very embodiment of the Religious Society of Friends in America, each of them only a single generation removed from the original colonies, he from Virginia and her family from North Carolina and Pennsylvania. They met and married in the bosom of the Yearly Meeting in Indiana and settled into a comfortable life on his dependable income as an insurance salesman and adjuster, until, like so many others of their generation, they sought more space for their growing families and decided to run for land in the newly opening Oklahoma Territory.

John went alone on horseback, running in the Guthrie land rush, the first Oklahoma land rush, in April of 1889. He homesteaded a parcel just a mile outside of Guthrie, the city that would become the first capital of the state of Oklahoma.

Elizabeth followed later with her four surviving daughters of six. The two older girls, Josephine and Niota, were eighteen and fifteen, and they spent as much time as their mother caring for the other two, eight-year-old Anna Edna and three-year-old Hazel.

20

Phyllis Marie stepped down from the bus to the concrete parkway at the Roswell station. From the second she saw Perry she knew something was wrong. He had that look she had known for years, that crestfallen face that meant trouble. As soon as he spotted her, he grinned as broadly as he could, but it was too late. He could not hide his feelings from her.

"It's so good to see you," he said, holding her in a long embrace.

"Is it?"

"Of course! Why?"

"Well, something's wrong."

"It is? What?"

"You tell me."

Without answering, he picked up her bag in his left hand, extending his right elbow for her to take, and escorted her down the street to the hotel where he had made reservations for her and for his parents.

"So, are you going to tell me now or make me wait?"

He grinned again, except for his eyes. "I passed all my exams. The last one was this morning."

"Yes, I know. I'm here for your graduation ceremony, remember?"

"And I got my pilot's rating."

"Yes, I know that, too."

They stepped into the hotel and crossed the lobby to the elevator. On the third floor, Perry led her down the hall to their room and unlocked the door. She went inside and sat on the edge of the bed.

"What haven't you told me yet?"

Perry put her bag on the luggage rack. He stood there facing the wall for several seconds before finally turning toward her and leaning back against the desk.

"I've been assigned as a co-pilot."

"Oh, my!" she said, unsure how to respond. "Is there—?" She peered into his face. "What are you going to do?"

"I don't have a choice, as far as I can see. I'm going to be a co-pilot."

"Oh, Perry! I know you're disappointed."

"Yes, I am." He walked over to the closet and pulled out a uniform. "This is a co-pilot uniform," he said. "Will you pin my wings on for me?"

"Of course." She could hardly bear to look into his eyes; his distress was so deep and raw. But she swore to herself that she would smile and be a good wife, and together they would get through this.

His parents arrived later that day. At dinner that evening and at the graduation ceremony the next morning, he gave no hint of his disappointment, smiling for pictures, shaking hands, and receiving his discharge papers as an aviation cadet, his diploma and appointment to the Officers Reserve as a Second Lieutenant, and his orders to report to Salt Lake City for active duty.

"Why do they do it that way?" his mother Georgia asked. "It seems so peculiar."

"Do what, Mom?"

"Appoint you to the reserves with one handshake and order you to report for active duty with another?"

"Because I have no Commanding Officer on this base. I have to go where someone has authority to give me orders. Salt Lake City is a Replacement Depot. Someone there will tell me where to report next."

She looked at Phyllis Marie and knew that whatever discontent Perry was trying to hide continued to trouble him. She took a step toward him and put her arms around his waist. When he bent down to kiss the top of her head, she arched her back to bring her lips closer to his ear.

"This is the time, son, during adversity, to be your bravest." She kissed his cheek and started to step back, but he took her more deeply in his arms and wouldn't let her go for another moment.

In Salt Lake City, Perry spent more time at the local movie theatre than anywhere else.

"Come on, Rupert," he said. "Let's see a movie."

"Again? We saw 'Hitler's Children' yesterday."

"What a nightmare!"

"And 'Star Spangled Rhythm' last night. Can't we go bowling or play some pool or something?"

"Sure, we can do that, too, but I've been wanting to see 'Random Harvest.' I missed it at Christmastime. Phyllis Marie says it's good."

"Okay, whatever you want. I just want to get an assignment."

They stepped out of their chilly Replacement Depot quarters and into the falling snow. Perry scooped up a handful and flung it at Rupert. It didn't stick enough to make a snowball.

"I talked to a gal down there at the Replacement Depot yesterday," Perry said, "because I wanted to put my name in for a B-17 assignment, and she told me that the best way to get the assignment you want is to go back to the field where you enlisted."

"What?"

"That's what she said, so she says she'll fix it for me to go back to Gowen Field."

Rupert looked skeptical. "In exchange for what?"

"In exchange for nothing. Because I'm a nice guy!"

"Well, your mood is better, I'll give you that."

"Yeah, well, we may have been assigned as co-pilots, but I don't plan to stay a co-pilot," Perry said emphatically.

"How are you going to arrange that?"

"When I figure it out, you'll be the first to know."

Two days later, Rupert shipped out for Lemoore, bemoaning the fact that he would be seeing his former girlfriend again, after having escaped to Roswell. He and Perry made their goodbyes.

"Maybe they send everyone home from here."

"Which means that gal you talked to was just pulling your

leg."

"Maybe. Good luck to you."

"You, too, Perry."

Perry shipped out to Gowen Field at Boise, Idaho the following day. For the first time in a year, he slept in his own bed in Caldwell, although Phyllis Marie wasn't there; she had accompanied his parents home to Wichita from Roswell.

"Happy third wedding anniversary, sweetheart," Perry said to her on the telephone the next morning. "Guess where I am."

"Where?"

"I'm having breakfast at home with Mother and Father in their kitchen."

"What?"

"Can you hurry back? I have a five-day pass."

"I'll catch the next bus."

Perry entered the Enlistment office the following day. The same enlistment officer stood and saluted when he walked in. Perry returned his salute. "At ease, Sergeant," he said. "You recruited me."

"I remember, sir," he said, extending his hand. The two men shook hands and took their places across the desk.

"Row, Perry V. Am I right, sir?"

"I'm flattered you remember."

"Of course I remember. I never met a recruit, before or since, with a clearer goal, to pilot the B-17." He looked at Perry's uniform. "I see you're part way there."

"Yes, partway," he said. "If there's anything you can do to see that I get sent to a B-17 base and not a B-24 base, I'd be most grateful."

"I thought you were going to ask me if I could help you move up from co-pilot to pilot, sir."

"I didn't imagine you could help with that."

"No, sir, you're right. I can give you some advice about it, though, sir."

"Please do."

"Be the best damn co-pilot you can, sir."

"Yes, I will."

"As to the other matter, I can write a letter. Are you on your five-day pass, sir?"

"Yes."

"You'd better go over and put my recommendation in your file right away. They may be making a decision about you any day. Hold on, sir."

The enlistment officer turned to his typewriter and banged out a letter in record time. "Take this over and ask for Sergeant Collins. He's a file clerk over there and a friend of mine. He can get it into your file right away, sir."

"Thank you," Perry said, rising. "I appreciate your help."

"Thank you for coming in and showing me I was right about you, sir."

Phyllis Marie arrived the next day. She and Perry enjoyed the privileges of home, as Perry put it, for three days, until the call came.

"Sir, your orders have come through," the voice on the other end of the telephone said. "The Adjutant requests you pick them up no later than oh-nine hundred tomorrow, sir."

"Thank you," he said, hanging up and looking at Phyllis Marie. "My orders are ready. I have to go to the base in the morning."

"And then where?"

"I don't know."

21

Oklahoma disappointed the Hill family. There were too many rough characters who ignored the church, and not enough of a Friends community to sustain their faith. They stuck it out for fifteen years, but when Hazel was old enough to start college, they turned to the large Friends community of Wichita, Kansas, with an eye toward improving Edna and Hazel's education.

The family was in luck. Friends University needed a stable family to take over as dormitory parents for their South Hall for Women. John Hill found a job with one of the downtown Wichita insurance companies. They sold their homesteaded farm for a pretty profit, packed their belongings, and moved to Wichita in the spring of 1904.

After Hazel's tea party prank on Edwin Stanton, she only saw him occasionally at a distance at Monthly Meeting, or going about his business on the campus. They nodded and smiled, or waved cordially, but as far as Hazel was concerned, she had more important things to consider, especially the impending wedding of her oldest sister, Josephine.

Whereas Niota, the second daughter, had married at twenty-one and had already brought two daughters into the world, Josephine had stayed with her parents and younger siblings throughout the years in Guthrie and the move to Wichita. Now in her early thirties, at an age when she had begun to imagine she would never marry, she had been struck dumb in love with George Outland, a younger man by three years, who returned her love with equal ardor. They planned a May wedding.

On the appointed day, Hazel—nineteen, pretty, charming, and innocent—entered the front room carrying the bridal bouquet. There was only an hour until the ceremony, yet there were so many details left to arrange.

"Psst!" she heard just as she was about to ascend the

staircase.

She turned to see Edwin Stanton standing in the doorway. "What is thee doing here?"

"I came to see my friend George marry your sister," he said.

"How does thee know George?"

"He's a photographer like me," Edwin said. "In fact, George and I have been talking about opening a studio together. Outland and Stanton, how does that sound? He is older, after all, and alphabetically—"

"I can't talk right now," she interrupted, turning back toward the stairs.

"Wait," he said, taking a step forward. "I have something for thee."

He reached up and carefully pierced the cloth of her shoulder sleeve with a hatpin. Mounted at the top was a cut stone of pale blue.

"What on earth—"

Edwin grinned. He nearly blushed, but quickly wiped his face with the back of his hand in an attempt to look more serious. "I've been thinking about thee," he said, "and now, during thy sister's wedding, thee shall be thinking about me, too."

Hazel smiled at him and blushed. She turned quickly and dashed up the steps and into a room with a bang of the door.

"Goodness!" her mother Elizabeth said, down on her knees, her mouth full of pins, making last minute adjustments to the hem of Josephine's wedding dress. "What has gotten into thee?"

"A hatpin," Hazel chirped. "Ouch!"

Josephine and her other sisters started to giggle. "What?" Hazel showed them her left sleeve.

"Where did that come from?" Josephine asked, straining to see what all the fuss was.

"Stand still, dear," Elizabeth said.

Whether Edwin had thought of the idea spontaneously, or

planned it for weeks, Hazel did not know, but she did know that it worked. She could think of no one else throughout the ceremony.

Within days, Edwin and Hazel were inseparable. In the summer evenings, they sat on the front porch of the Outlands' new home—just a few doors down from South Hall and within a stone's throw of Friends University—listening to the crickets, watching the fireflies, and drinking lemonade. On First Day morning, they strolled up Hiram Street to University Avenue together to attend Monthly Meeting, and during the week, Edwin became a fixture at the Hill's supper table.

Upon Edwin's graduation from Friends University, George Outland invited him to join him in a photography studio, which they promptly named Outland and Stanton.

After another year, Edwin and Hazel married. For a wedding gift, Edwin gave Hazel a brand new cedar chest with brass fittings. The hinged lid opened to reveal a large enough space for blankets and quilts, and a drawer below held sheets, pillowcases, and towels. Hazel gave Edwin an opal ring.

Hazel's sister, Edna, married a devout young man, Arthur Chilson, and together they became missionaries of the Religious Society of Friends and departed for the dark continent of Africa.

By the end of 1907 Edwin and Hazel had a son, LaMar, but after six months he was lost to them, dead from a bowel blockage. A few years later, they had a daughter, Virginia, and settled into contentment once again. The studio thrived, thanks in part to the advertisements they placed in Irvin Stanton's monthly newspaper, University Life. When Irvin bought the Fowler Hustler and turned over University Life to his young protégé from Oklahoma, Clifton Row, Outland and Stanton continued to advertise with the young man. The administration, faculty, and students of Friends University represented a fair percentage of their business, but George Outland was bored.

22

In the early daylight hour, frogs croaked and plopped about, maneuvering amidst the unthinking hooves of a dozen perplexed cows. There had been fresh grass there the day before—they were sure of it—but that had been before a construction crew covered it over with runway two. Second Lieutenant Perry V. Row found himself feeling just as out of place as the only other living being standing in that wet and muddy field, the flight deck at Walla Walla Army Airfield, where he had been ordered to report. Without an aircrew or an airplane to fly, Perry walked over to the tower, which was operational, but still under construction.

Two days earlier, he had stood holding the envelope that contained his orders, but he had not opened it. *This is the moment,* he thought. *This is when I finally find out what I'm going to fly.* Breaking the seal and removing the contents, he read the papers inside.

The Stanton Photography Studio phone rang, five minutes later. Phyllis Marie answered. "Where? Day after tomorrow? I'll be there."

Edwin and Hazel stood next to their daughter, waiting. "What did he say?" Edwin asked.

"He said he got it. The B-17 Flying Fortress. He's going to Walla Walla, Washington for Crew Flight Training."

The three of them had stood quietly, not knowing whether to celebrate or not.

"I don't care how you do it," barked an irate officer into the telephone. "Just get those cows off my runway. How am I supposed to provide these men with heavy bomber training under these conditions?" The officer took a moment to return Perry's salute. "About two dozen. I know they used to graze there. Yes, before tomorrow morning. Goodbye."

The man turned to Perry and took his papers without comment. "Your crew is over in the hangar taking a lecture on the Sperry gun sight. You can get some Link Trainer hours in, too, if you're so inclined. I hope to be able to put you in the air the day after tomorrow. Got a girl in town?

"Yes, sir, my wife."

"Good. There's a formal dance tomorrow night at the Officer's Club. Attendance is mandatory so you can get to know your pilot and the other officers. Dismissed."

"Thank you, sir."

While Perry shot skeet the next morning, Phyllis Marie located the only dress shop in town.

"Good morning," she said. "My name is Phyllis Row. I called earlier about a formal gown for a dance at the Officer's Club tonight. Do you have anything at all?"

"Yes, Mrs. Row," the saleslady said. "We have several. After the first class of flyers graduated last month, several of the wives sold their gowns back to us. We decided it would be easier if we rented them out each month. Size six?"

"Let's start there."

"Excuse me," a tall, dark-haired woman said as the saleslady went into the back of the store. "Did I hear right, that you're Mrs. Row?"

"Yes, that's right."

"Mrs. Perry V. Row?"

"Yes."

"I'm Mrs. Balckman," she said, with great satisfaction.

"How do you do." Phyllis Marie felt she was missing something, but she was, as always, unfailingly polite.

The woman raised one elegantly plucked eyebrow. "You don't recognize the name?"

"No, I'm sorry. Should I?"

"My husband is Wallace Balckman."

"Oh?"

"Lieutenant Wallace Balckman. Well for goodness sake! Your husband is my husband's co-pilot."

Phyllis Marie shook her head at the confusion. "Oh, I see."

"Yes," she continued. "You and I are going to be good

friends, dear."

"Are you going to the dance, tonight, then?"

"Certainly. Each set of officers and their wives share a table at this shindig. Have you been fitted yet?" She looked Phyllis Marie up and down, envying her slim waist and green eyes.

"Fitted? I was just going to get something that's close enough and take it home. If I need to, I can alter it."

Mrs. Balckman looked appalled. "Oh, no, my dear, that won't do at all. Cigarette?"

"No, thank you. I don't smoke." Phyllis Marie barely managed to keep from wrinkling her nose in distaste.

"Do you know a hairdresser in town yet?"

"Oh, I'll just put it in curlers this—"

"You planned to alter your own dress and put up your own hair, and you don't smoke? We're going to have to work on you, I can see. What's your name, dear?"

"Phyllis Marie." She wasn't sure she liked the sound of Mrs. Balckman's plans for her.

"I'm Eve. Have you met Nancy and Beth yet?"

"No, who are they?"

"They're the other Officer's wives from Wallace's crew."

"Oh, I see."

"Yes, dear, you're starting to."

The saleslady brought a powder blue dress for Phyllis Marie to try. "This ought to fit you. Would you like to try it on?"

"Yes."

"Right this way."

Eve smiled. "I'll be right here, dear. You can come with me to my hair appointment. I'm sure they can squeeze you in, considering it's an emergency."

Phyllis Marie was not sure it was a good idea, but she found it difficult to say no to Eve, who seemed very determined. Besides, she didn't want to embarrass Perry. For now, she would follow Eve's advice.

Perry walked into the Married Officers Quarters he

shared with Phyllis Marie. Now that he was an officer, she no longer had to stay in hotels. Although she planned to return to Caldwell and work in her father's studio once Perry was assigned to a Theatre of Operations, for now, she could stay near him without an extra expense.

Perry looked at the powder blue gown hanging from a hook next to his dress uniform.

"Wow! Where did you find that on such short notice?"

"In town," Phyllis Marie called from the bedroom, where she sat in front of a dressing table and mirror, applying her lipstick. "Do you like it?"

"It's great," he said.

"I met someone interesting today."

"Who?"

"Mrs. Balckman."

"Really? The pilot's wife?"

"Yes." She touched up the two-dollar permanent wave Eve had insisted upon and walked to the doorway in her slip and brassiere. This is the moment of truth, she thought to herself, and pushed the door open so her husband could see her. "Like it?"

"Wow! Did you do that?"

"No, Eve's hairdresser did it. You didn't answer me."

"Yes, I love it."

He took her in his arms and started to kiss her, but she resisted gently.

"Now, now. I just got my hair and make-up all done." Good, she thought to herself. It hasn't occurred to him what this must have cost. "You need to get moving if we're going to get to this big event on time."

"Okay," he said, releasing her after a gentle squeeze and heading for the shower.

Half an hour later they made their grand entrance to the Officers' Club, thinking no one had noticed them, but a voice called out from a table to their left.

"Phyllis Marie, dear, we're over here."

Three officers dressed exactly like Perry stood up from the

table for eight, while their three gowned and coiffed wives remained seated.

"Wallace Balckman, may I present my wife, Phyllis Marie Row. Phyllis Marie, this is my pilot." If there was a glimmer of resentment or envy in Perry's voice, it went undetected, but Phyllis Marie knew that such an introduction must hurt somewhere deep inside him.

"Phyllis Marie, it's a pleasure," Balckman said. "You've met my wife Eve earlier. This is our Navigator, Everett Davidson, and his wife, Nancy."

"My pleasure," Davidson said, before Balckman continued.

"And our Bombardier, Ramsey Fifer, and his wife, Beth."

"Glad to meet you," Fifer said.

"So, finally we all meet," Balckman said, as Perry held Phyllis Marie's chair and the other men took their seats. "I think this calls for a toast, and the champagne is already poured." He lifted his glass, waiting for the other seven members of the party to follow suit. "First, to our wives— looking lovely tonight, one and all, and second, to my new officers: may we get over there, do our jobs, and get back safely to our wives, who will be waiting for us."

As the group drank, Phyllis Marie looked around the room at all the tables of four men each in their spotless uniforms, and wondered what percentage of them would be able to get over, do their jobs, and get back safely to the women seated next to them.

"Phyllis Marie," Balckman said. "May I have the first dance? With your permission of course, Perry."

"Of course," Perry said, "and Mrs. Balckman, may I return the compliment?"

"Oh, heavens," she said. "You mustn't stand on ceremony. Call me Eve."

As the two couples moved toward the dance floor, both women walking backwards, beckoning the men they did not know, Phyllis Marie could see the same ritual being played out among all the officers at the other tables in the room. *Do they read this in a manual somewhere,* she wondered, *how to be an officer and a gentlemen at the first dance of the first bomber training class? Will three-quarters of them still be alive in a year? Half of them?*

23

"Come on children," Crosha said, "it's time to go."

"Where are we going again?" Little Georgia Alice Whitaker, seven years old, stood in her Sunday dress, looking up curiously. "Why aren't Mom and Dad coming with us?"

"We are going to have our picture taken," Crosha explained. "You have a brand new baby brother, and we are all going to be in the picture together." *One portrait,* she thought, *before the family is torn completely apart. How does one separate nine children without at least one family portrait?*

After the murder of her father and the death of her mother in childbirth, Georgia found herself removed from her brothers and sisters, taken in by a family that had been close to her parents. Two sisters went with an uncle to Cameron. Another two sisters and two brothers went with Crosha to her farm near Hunter, Oklahoma. Another family took one sister, leaving only the fate of the newborn, Ernest, undecided, before the doctor voiced his opinion.

"Missus Lynes," he said to Crosha, "the child is too delicate to travel. I'd rather he stay here under my care, so I would like to suggest a nice couple here, friends of your brother, who have offered to raise him. I think you have your hands full adopting three, even with Ida to help you." Crosha had to agree it was for the best.

A few months after getting her new brood settled in at the ranch, Crosha received a letter from the family that had taken Georgia:

Dear Mrs. Lynes,

We fear that our best intentions may not be working out for little Georgia Alice. She is so despondent and cries all the time for her father, mother, brothers, and sisters. She is not paying attention in school, not doing her chores, not saying her prayers, not eating, and not sleeping at night. We took her to Cameron to see the other children there, which perked her up a bit, but, as you know, they are in no position to take another child. She pines most especially for little Jim, and we wonder if it wouldn't be better to re-unite her with you and her other siblings. Please write to me and advise me,

Sincerely, et cetera.

Crosha wrote back.

Of course, we will take Georgia here. I have arranged for her uncle to take her to the train station in Fort Worth and put her on the train to Pond Creek, where I will meet her. Don't blame yourself. Georgia is a tenderhearted girl, and the loss of her parents may have been hardest of all on her.

God's blessings on thee.

Crosha's friend Althea arrived at the Pond Creek station and approached the ticket counter. "Has the train come in from Fort Worth yet?"

"Ten minutes yet," he said.

"I'm asking because I'm meeting my friend's niece," she said. "I've never met the girl."

"Are you Crosha Lynes' friend?"

"Yes, did she speak to you about me? She's going to be a few minutes late, so I agreed to wait with the girl."

"Yes, she did," he said. "It should be in soon." He walked away toward the baggage room.

When the train arrived, Althea watched as the passengers disembarked, but there was only one little girl who matched Crosha's description, Althea thought, and she was with a dark woman, perhaps a gypsy, or her nanny. Still, the child had the light hair Crosha had described and seemed the right age, but the child went right along with the dark woman, clutching her hand, as if she belonged to her.

What now? Althea felt panic rise in her throat. She ran up to the conductor, keeping one eye on the dark woman, who walked toward the exit without picking up luggage, without looking left or right.

"Was another girl on the train besides that one?" she pointed. "One traveling alone?"

"No, only that one," he said, looking over his glasses at the departing pair.

Althea ran after the pair as they disappeared around the corner. She reached the corner just as the dark woman entered a store. Althea ran faster than she ever had in her life.

"Do you know this girl?" she asked the dark woman as she burst into the store.

"Of course I do," she said.

"Are you Georgia Alice Whitaker?" she asked the girl.

"Yes, I am. Where is Aunt Crosha?"

"Come with me, Georgia," Althea said, taking Georgia's hand out of the other woman's. "Aunt Crosha wants you to stay with me until she gets here. I think maybe she's at the station now."

The shopkeeper looked up. Althea turned and left the store with Georgia in hand. The dark woman started to follow, but the shopkeeper blocked and closed the door. "What were you doing with that child?" he asked.

"I was helping her find her aunt," the woman said. "She wasn't at the station."

"You thought you'd find her here, a block away?"

The door opened and a man forced his way in. He, too, was dark-skinned, and wore a gold earring in one ear. "What's the trouble here?" he asked.

The dark woman spat a few words at him in a language the shopkeeper did not understand.

"It just so happens I know Crosha Lynes," the shopkeeper said, retreating to his counter. "You two get out of here."

The man took a step toward him, but the shopkeeper produced a pistol. "Out, I said."

Althea and Georgia, still carrying her little valise, returned to the train station, where a frantic Crosha and Henry Lynes had just arrived and spoken to the stationmaster.

"There they are," the stationmaster said, and walked away.

Georgia ran into the open arms of her Aunt Crosha.

"What happened?" Crosha asked.

"A woman tried to take her."

"What woman? Show me."

The four of them returned to the shop.

"Where is she?" Althea asked.

"She had an accomplice," the shopkeeper said. "You're lucky you got here when you did. I ran them both off."

Crosha turned to Georgia. "Who was that woman, honey?"

"I don't know," she said. "She told me she was going to help me find you at the station, but then we left the station, and she said she was going to buy me some candy and a red dress."

"They were gypsies, I tell you," the shopkeeper said, "and that little girl is mighty lucky."

24

Perry met his new instructor, Captain Datsch, the next morning on the flight deck, along with a flight engineer and a ground crew of four men. None of the other officers joined them.

"All right, if you're ready, we'll begin with the external inspection of this B-17 Flying Fortress," Datsch said. "This is the responsibility of the pilot, but as co-pilot, you need to know the routine as well, so you can perform the inspection when your pilot requests it."

"Yes, sir."

"I always start here, outside the right-hand landing gear."

"Just like Arthur Kennedy's training film, sir."

"Yes. Make the checklist a habit, he says, and I have. First the tires, to be sure there hasn't been any slippage on the rim, to see that the tread is adequate, and to look for cuts or other damage." He took a step back. "What do you think?"

"It looks fine to me, sir."

"Good. Next comes the outboard brake line for signs of oil leakage."

Perry looked at him and saw that he expected Perry's opinion again.

"Clean and secure, sir."

"Wheel chocks?"

"In place."

"Inboard brake line?" He did not move inboard, waiting for Perry to prove he knew where to look.

Perry moved inside the gear. "Clean and secure, sir."

"Nose gear olio?"

"One and a half inches of shiny filament showing, sir."

"Whip antenna?"

"In place, sir."

"Good," Datsch said. "Where shall we go next?

"The other landing gear, sir."

The two of them moved under the nose of the plane together. Datsch said, "You tell me now."

"Very well, sir. Perry squatted down next to the gear. "Tires show no slippage, adequate tread, no cuts or damage. Outboard brake line is clean and secure, wheel chocks in place, inboard brake line, clean and secure, and the left olio shows one point five shiny, sir."

"Fine," Datsch nodded, agreeing. "And now?"

"Engine two, sir." Perry stood and took a few steps back, mindful of the propeller. "Turbo wheel—" He reached up and turned the turbo wheel with his thumb. "No cracks, three thirty-seconds of an inch clearance, linkage is clear, cowling is intact, no damage, and no oil leaks."

He inspected the three propeller blades, pulling each propeller through, in order to access the next. "No damage, prop governor appears sound, nothing wedged between the pins, sir."

After inspecting engine one the same way and checking the de-icer boot, the two men walked together under the wing. Perry kept his eyes open for access and inspection doors out of place, checked the fabric on the aileron, and confirmed that the aileron trim path felt tight. He approached the ball turret and squatted beside it, confirming that the door was secure and that the guns were horizontal and pointed toward the rear.

"Okay, Lieutenant, one point off. You can turn it into half a point if you can tell me now what you missed."

Perry turned and looked back along the ball turret door to the wing, then back to the top of the fuselage. "The antennae, sir."

"Yes, that's right. Most guys miss that on their first inspection. I don't know why. I bet you never do again."

"Yes, sir."

"Okay, where to from here?"

The inspection continued to the tail of the airplane and around to the other side, with Perry noting the anchored trailing antenna, the undamaged marker beacon antenna, the de-icer boot on the stabilizer, the covering on the elevator and its trim path, the rudder covering and trim path, the elevator downspring on the elevator control arm—by opening the tail gunner hatch—and a repeat inspection of the right wing and engines three and four.

"Except there is no trim tab on the aileron, sir."

"Very good. You caught that downspring. A lot of guys miss that, too."

"Thank you, sir."

"Okay, we've circled this bird. Let's get inside."

"Yes, sir." Perry, Captain Datsch, and the flight engineer pulled themselves in through the rear entrance door as the ground crew began the laborious task of pulling the propellers through in order to rotate the engines and bring the cold oil up from the oil pans. With each engine requiring five to ten full rotations, it took three men from four to eight minutes to complete the procedure.

"What do you want to check first, Lieutenant?"

"The tail olio, sir, showing two and a half inches of shiny cylinder."

"Good."

"The ball turret is locked and immobile for take-off, the control cables are free of any debris, the hand cranks for the bomb bay doors, landing gear, and flaps are all in place, the hatch is secure, and the locking dogs are in position."

Perry took a quick sweeping glance around before turning toward the notebooks and slide rule computer mounted on the bulkhead.

"What was that look?"

"Checking for loose equipment, sir."

"Why didn't you say it out loud?"

"I didn't see any, sir."

"All right, but again, make your checklist a habit. Don't leave out a step because you are accustomed to thinking that step to yourself.

"Yes, sir."

"Now, what?"

"Loaded weight and C.G., sir, center of gravity."

"Which you, as the co-pilot, will have computed in advance for your pilot."

"Yes, sir."

"Has it been computed?"

"Yes, sir, by me."

"When did you do that?"

"Before you arrived, sir."

"Good. Next?"

"Fire extinguisher one in place," he said, pointing, "bomb bay free of bombs, free of extra fuel, emergency bomb release, leather in place, fire extinguisher two in place, and—" he raised himself up onto the platform leading to the cabin, stood, and stepped into the right seat, the co-pilot seat. Glancing out the starboard side window, he continued, "access doors closed on top of the right wing."

Datsch, following, stepped into the left seat and said, "Access doors closed on top of the left wing. Good. Are you ready for your first ride in this thing?"

"Yes, sir!"

After following the steps of the checklist, starting the engines, and taxiing into position, Captain Datsch and Perry accelerated down the runway. Perry felt his heart leap. *Keep a cool cucumber, man,* Perry thought. *This isn't Old Man Persons' model airplane field. Wouldn't the old man be thrilled to see this, to be inside this bird?* Perry couldn't help it. His heart pounded underneath his officer's blouse and his hands began to sweat as he played the role he had memorized for himself, performing the co-pilot steps by rote. Another self, another aspect of himself, sat back in the seat and watched and experienced his first ride in the Boeing B-17 Flying Fortress, the airplane of his choice from the beginning.

They banked left out of the air field and continued to climb, spiraling to one thousand feet, one self following the script, listening to the comments and instructions Datsch provided—three thousand feet—while the other self reveled in simply being inside the airplane—five thousand feet—feeling the pure joy of flight—seven thousand feet—the exhilaration of the experience—nine thousand feet—oxygen masks on, the unusual sensation as they reached the ten thousand feet mark and leveled off.

This is fantastic! What is that? The two thoughts occurred simultaneously. Suddenly his two selves slammed together, occupying the same space within his body. *This is disconcerting,* he thought. *I'm really not going to be airsick am I, after all the training I've been through so far without it, in front of this instructor, who is sitting in the left seat, the seat I think I deserve, in front of this flight engineer? This isn't going to happen, is it?*

He breathed. He waited. He resisted. He knew that if he could just give it a few more seconds of breathing deeply—

"You okay, Lieutenant?" Datsch's voice came into his ears through the interphone.

Great, Perry thought. *Tell everyone.*

"Don't throw up in your oxygen mask," Datsch said, handing Perry a non-regulation plastic-lined paper bag he had brought on board for such events. Just seeing the precaution Datsch had taken was the last straw. Perry pulled off his mask and emptied his stomach into the bag.

25

Perry raised himself up onto the platform leading to the cabin like he had done nearly a dozen times before, stood, stepped into the co-pilot seat, and glanced out the starboard side window. "Access doors closed on top of the starboard wing," he said, buckling his seat belt and removing the checklist from its pocket to his right.

Balckman followed, stepping into the pilot seat. "Access doors closed on top of the port wing."

"Pilot's Preflight," Perry called out, reading from the checklist.

"Complete," Balckman responded.

"Form 1 A,"

"Checked."

"Controls And Seats,"

"Checked."

"Fuel Transfer Valves and Switch,"

"Off."

"Intercoolers—" Perry reached his right hand down next to his calf, "cold. Gyros,"

"Uncaged."

"Fuel Shut-Off Switches,"

"Open."

"Gear Switch,"

"Neutral."

"Cowl Flaps—" Perry glanced out the starboard side window again, "open right,"

"Open left,"

Perry checked the cowl flaps switch. "Locked. Turbos," he continued.

"Off."

"Idle Cut-Off,"

"Checked."

"Throttles,"

"Closed."

"High RPM,"

"Checked."

"Autopilot,"

"Off."

"De-icers and Anti-icers, Wing and Prop,"

"Off."

"Cabin Heat,"

"Off."

"Generators,"

"Off."

Meanwhile, the ground crew, having run the propellers through, stood by their positions, one with a fire extinguisher at engine one, another out front, in view of the pilot.

"Fireguard," Perry called.

"Prop clear!" Balckman shouted out the side window at the ground crew.

"All clear!" the ground crew chief shouted back.

"All clear," Balckman repeated to Perry.

"Master and ignition switches," Perry said.

"On."

"Batteries and inverters,"

Balckman turned on the number one battery and the familiar whine started in Perry's ears. After checking two and three independently, Balckman turned on all three batteries at once and looked at the voltage meter. "Twenty-six volts."

"Check."

He switched the inverter to normal and re-checked. "Twenty-six volts."

"Check."

Balckman leaned out the window and punched his left fist into his open right hand. The ground chief started and connected the external generator to the B-17.

"Parking Brakes and Hydraulic Check—" Perry said, then continued, "brakes on. Pressure,"

"Just under eight hundred."

"Check. Booster pumps and pressure,"

Balckman set four switches and said, "On and checked."

"Carburetor Filters—on. Fuel quantity, tanks one, two, three, and four, right and left, all full."

Balckman extended his finger out the side window and rotated it in the air, signaling the ground crew to start engine one. The fireguard moved into position behind engine one and the ground chief signaled back to Balckman.

"Okay," Balckman said to Perry. "Adjusting throttle." He opened the throttle locks and re-closed them before setting them up about an inch.

Perry depressed the starter switch with his left hand and started counting to fifteen. With his right hand, he set the hand primer to the number one engine and pumped a few times, bleeding the air out of the primer line.

Balckman unlocked the mixture control, put his hand on mixture control one, and waited.

Perry depressed the mesh switch and pumped the primer. Engine one kicked up with a belch of smoke and Balckman pulled back on the mixture control. As the engine revved up over a thousand RPMs, Balckman watched the oil pressure gauge, knowing that if the pressure didn't rise in thirty seconds, he would have to shut down the engine and initiate an investigation. When the oil pressure rose, Balckman adjusted his number one throttle lock and brought engine one down to a thousand.

Balckman set his vacuum selector switch to left, in order to check that the vacuum pump delivers immediately with two engines. "Starting number two," Balckman said, rotating two fingers out the window. "Okay," he said to Perry.

Perry set the hand primer to engine two, depressed the starter switch and mesh switch, and pumped the primer. Engine two came alive and Balckman set the mixture control, checked the oil pressure, and adjusted the number two throttle lock to a thousand.

After confirming that the vacuum pump was operational, the team of men started engines three and four, turned on the radio and interphone, and checked their instruments.

"Fuel pressure,"

"Fifteen pounds."

"Wing flap indicator. Waist gunner from co-pilot, over."

Co-pilot from waist gunner, over."

"Flaps clear?"

"Flaps clear, sir."

Perry lowered the flaps. "Flaps down?"

"Flaps down, sir."

Perry raised them again. "Zero flaps?"

"Zero flaps, sir."

"Compass card,"

"Free."

"Hydraulic pressure,"

"Eight hundred."

"Suction gauge,"

"Four."

"Right vacuum pump, suction gauge,"

"Four. Re-setting left,"

"Check. Oxygen,"

"Three hundred fifty pounds each."

After confirming each crewmember's oxygen equipment tests, Perry turned back to Balckman. "Warning lights,"

"Checked."

"Checked. Filters on." Perry raised his left hand to the radio control. "Walla Walla tower, Walla Walla tower, this is 230223, over."

The tower voice crackled in the radio, "223 this is Walla Walla tower, over."

Walla Walla tower, this is 223, request taxi instructions for four-hour local flight, pilot Balckman, over."

"223, cleared to runway one zero to the northwest, over."

"223, roger, out."

Balckman dropped his throttles back and signaled out the window to the ground crew before reporting to Perry, "External power removed," and "wheel chocks clear."

"Check."

Balckman gave the orders, "brakes off,"

"Brakes off," Perry responded.

Balckman taxied onto the runway and set the airplane at an angle.

"Tail wheel locked," Perry called.

"Brakes," Balckman answered.

"Brakes set. Trim tabs,"

"Set. Oil temperature, fifty degrees." Balckman began the task of exercising the turbos, advancing the throttles to circulate warm oil through the turbos, and repeating the props. He checked his generators and turned them off. He boosted the manifold pressure on engine one, throttled up, and applied full turbo. Setting the lock, he checked the RPMs, looked out the window at the engine, and then turned, nodding to Perry.

"Check," Perry said, watching Balckman repeat the five-minute exercise procedure on each of engines two, three and four.

After hearing Perry call the tower for take-off clearance, Balckman taxied into position.

"Tail wheel locked," Perry called. "Gyro,"

"Gyro set."

"Generators,"

Balckman raised two pairs of switches and responded, "Generators on."

Each man closed his side window. Balckman pushed the throttles to twenty-five inches and released the brakes.

The B-17 rolled down the runway. Balckman felt the rudder kick in by the time they were going fifty miles an hour. At a hundred, the bird lifted off the ground in a perfect three-point takeoff. Balckman touched the brakes to stop the wheels from spinning and retracted the landing gear. After he reduced the manifold pressure and RPMs, Perry trailed the cowl flaps.

"Up left," Balckman called out, checking the landing gear.

"Up right," Perry called. "Nice work."

"Thanks. You, too."

Balckman leveled off the B-17 at ten thousand feet, reduced his manifold pressure and RPMs, and auto-leaned his fuel mixtures. Perry closed the cowl flaps.

They had flown about an hour before banking into their course for today's practice bomb run, when Perry saw the manifold pressure. The engine two gauge showed a reading about an inch above the other three. He glanced over at Balckman, expecting him to pull the number two throttle back.

"How's that number two?" he asked.

Balckman didn't answer. Perry waited a few seconds more, but still, Balckman didn't seem to be aware of the problem. Perry pointed his thumb up and first finger out, his other fingers folded under, like a kid pretending his hand held a pistol, and pointed at the manifold pressure gauge. "Are you looking at number two?"

By now, the engine two gauge approached nearly two inches too high. Still, Balckman did not react, although he appeared to be looking right at the manifold pressure.

"Wallace!" Perry said.

"I see it."

"What are you going to do about it?"

"What's your recommendation?"

"Throttle back before it becomes a serious problem."

"I can't do that, I'll lose airspeed."

"You'll lose engine two pretty soon."

Suddenly the needle climbed to forty inches on its way to pegging out.

"Throttle back, number two!" Perry called. "Feather."

Balckman responded, pulling the throttle back for number two engine and feathering, disengaging the propeller from the engine. "Throttle back. Feathered."

"Mixture and Fuel Booster,"

Balckman turned his eyes without moving his head and stared over his shoulder at Perry.

"Come on, Captain," Perry droned into the interphone,

"we've run this drill a dozen times. Mixture and Fuel Booster,"

"Off," Balckman said, reaching for the switch.

"Turbo,"

"Off."

"Prop,"

"Low RPM."

"Ignition,"

"Off."

"Generator,"

"Off.

"Fuel Valve,"

"Off."

The two of them sat in silence, each man staring out his side window for a moment—probably no more than four seconds—before aborting the practice bomb run and returning to base.

"What happened up there?" Captain Datsch and Perry sat across from each other, alone at the de-briefing table.

"We had a runaway supercharger on engine number two, sir."

"And?"

"Lieutenant Balckman throttled back and I initiated the feathering checklist, sir."

"Is that all you have to say to me?"

"That's all that happened, sir."

26

One year, the governing of the children at the Quarterly Meeting fell to fourteen-year-old Georgia.

"God's blessings to you, Clifton," she sang in a lilting tone, her formerly blonde hair darkened to chestnut. He thought she looked fully six inches taller than the last time he had seen her.

"God's blessings to you, Georgia," he sang back in his adolescent voice, no longer a tenor, dropping into a mellow baritone. His chest swelled, bursting with happiness to see her, and with pride in his latest achievement. "Dad let me drive the wagon through the salt plains this time," he said.

"Is it as bad as they say?" she asked. "Could you really go blind from looking at it?"

"In the summer is the worst," he said, scowling with great authority. "You have to be sure to wear a screen over your face to protect your eyes."

They stood quietly in front of the open barn doors for a moment, each trying to think of something else to say to the other.

"We dropped the 'E,' you know," he said.

"I beg your pardon?"

"We dropped the 'E,' from our last name."

"Oh," she said, unsure how to respond.

A few more moments of awkward silence passed.

"We still pronounce it the same, though," he added. "Row—it still rhymes with 'now.' "

He looked down and kicked at the dirt.

She followed suit, digging her toe into the red clay.

"I'm going to Stella in the fall term," she said. "I guess I'll find out for myself, then, about the salt plains, I mean."

"You are?" he shouted. "Why, that's marvelous! I'll be there, too!"

"Yes, I know." She smiled.

Carrie watched them from Crosha's kitchen window. Crosha turned away from her piecrust and saw the worried look on her face.

"They've become close friends over the years," Crosha said.

"Yes," Carrie answered.

"Is something troubling thee?"

"Oh," Carrie said, wiping her hands on her apron. "No, not about them."

"What, then?"

"I'm worried about Clifton. He wants so much to attend Stella Friends Academy."

"It's a good school, honey," Crosha said. "They have an excellent reputation, and rightly so. They have a first-rate staff, with high standards, a demanding curriculum."

"Yes, I know."

"Their mathematics and literature courses are among the best of the Friends Academies. They require four years of Latin. I've sent two of my girls through there, and on to Friends University in Wichita, and Georgia will be the third."

"Yes, I know," Carrie said again. "It's not the school."

"What, then?"

"Well—"

"Is it the money?" Crosha asked. "I know it's a lot."

"Partly it's the money, yes," Carrie confessed. "I don't have any trouble about the seven dollars per term. It's worth it, I know that."

"So, it's the cost of boarding him."

"Yes," Carrie sighed. "We can't afford to board him privately, and I don't want him staying in that third-story dormitory with no outside fire escapes."

"I know, believe me," Crosha said.

Throughout his first term, Carrie continued to worry that her son would be trapped in a fire on the third floor. When Lige visited the campus at the end of the term, Clifton presented a possible solution.

"Look out there, Dad," Clifton said, standing on the front steps. "See those huts across the way?"

"Yes," Lige said.

"Some of the boys live in them. I've got an older chum, says I can show his to you. Come on."

"Are they sanctioned by the school?" Lige asked, stepping off the bottom step and following his son.

"Yes, they call it self-boarding. It costs fifty cents a month, and I could still eat the meals in the dining room."

The shack stood just a hair under six feet, not enough for Clifton to stand up inside, Lige noticed, but it had a bed and some bookshelves, and decent sod insulation, like the first dugout house Lige had built on the homestead, twenty miles to the northwest.

"What do you think?" Clifton asked.

"I think we should build you one," he said, "but we can do better than this, don't you think?"

"I think that would be marvelous!" Clifton refrained from jumping for joy, lest he push a hole through his friend's roof.

Lige and Clifton brought a load of lumber and an old stove from the homestead to the campus at the beginning of the second term and built a sturdy shack out of lumber and sod, complete with a ventilated stove, a shingled roof, newspaper-insulated walls, just like home, and Clifton's cat, to keep the rodents at bay.

"If you pay attention to the condition of the roof," Lige said to his son, "and don't bring any food in here, you should be able to keep this place livable until you graduate."

In his third year, Clifton won the Literary Prize for his short story, "Deep Water," about the short and tragic life of an Indian brave. In his fourth, the staff chose him as one of two class orators for his graduation ceremony.

After the ceremony, Carrie, now thirty-seven, approached her son with tears in her eyes. A great deal was changing for all of them that day. "I'm proud of you, son," she said.

Lige and Vancil stood apart while she put her arms around her tall and handsome son's neck.

Lige had begun to gray at the temples. He smiled solemnly and shook hands with the new graduate. "Congratulations," he said. Vancil followed suit.

"Your brother and I brought two wagons down," Lige said. "I figured we'd need them both to bring all your things up to Wichita."

"Are you all moved out of the homestead?" Clifton asked.

"Yes, I signed the transfer last March. We hauled some of the things to Wichita for your mother and Vancil and the rest to Kiowa for me."

"Things won't be the same with you and Mom separated," Clifton said.

"They never are, honey," Carrie said through her tears, "but your father and I agree it's best this way. We disagree about so many things—politics, money, prohibition, religion, education—that we've decided to stay married but live apart."

The following September, in the year 1907, Clifton entered the Registrar's office at Friends University and presented his documents.

"What is your major?" the clerk asked.

"I haven't decided yet between English Literature and Languages."

"Literature? Are you interested in printing at all?"

Clifton loved books, loved the printed page, but had never considered the process of creating them. "Well, yes," he said.

"Were you planning to work while you go to school?"

Clifton didn't answer. Of course he was planning to work, he thought. One cannot get good grades without working hard.

"The reason I ask," the clerk continued, removing his glasses, "there is an opening in the University print shop in the basement." He wrote a name and room number on a slip of paper. "Why don't you go see this man?"

"Do you mean for wages?"

"Of course for wages."

What an interesting idea, Clifton thought. *I rather like it.* "Very well," he said. "Thank you."

The clerk handed him a new stack of papers. "Just don't let it interfere with your class work."

"No, I won't. Where is the—"

"One flight down, stairs on the right."

The print shop turned out to be something less than an office and more than a closet. An empty desk and chair stood in one corner. A man kneeled on a stack of paper beside a bucket of soapy water and scrubbed at a large rectangular grimy patch in another. He wore a large dirty canvas apron and rubber gloves over his worsted wool suit trousers, linen dress shirt, celluloid collar and silk tie. His matching coat hung on a rack in another corner. He scrubbed vigorously at the floor with a bulky brush, held in two hands. When he paused to rinse the blackness from the brush, Clifton tapped on the open door.

"Thee is early," the man said, without looking up.

"I can see that," Clifton answered.

The man turned his head and gazed at the young man. He dropped the brush carefully into the bucket and brought his left knee up, carefully placing his foot behind the stack of paper, and slowly rose, unfolding himself to his very full height, easily six-foot-five.

"Irvin Stanton," he said, wiping his enormous right hand on his apron and thrusting it out.

"Clifton Row."

"I was expecting a delivery."

"I can see that, too. I thought there was a print shop here."

"There is, or there will be again, as soon as the new equipment arrives. I expect them at three, and I need to get this corner cleaned up before they arrive."

"Have you an extra brush?"

Irvin almost smiled. "Thee is here for the job."

"Yes."

"Does thee have any experience in printing?"

"No."

"So far, thee is the most experienced candidate I have interviewed," Irvin said, lowering his six-foot-five frame back down onto the stack of papers. "Thee is the only candidate I have interviewed. Thee will find an apron and more paper next door. I recommend at least two inches to protect thy trousers."

Clifton found another pair of gloves and a brush as well, and after joining Irvin on the floor, asked, "What happened to the old printing equipment?"

"I took it," Irvin said, without missing a beat. "That's because I bought it in the first place. Thee is getting an old foot-powered flatbed cylinder press the University found at auction in Kansas City. It may not be as nice as mine, but at least it's older." Irvin almost smiled again.

"How much older?"

"Does thee remember Abraham Lincoln?"

Clifton applied more weight to his brush. *What have I gotten myself into,* he wondered. "And where are you taking your equipment?"

"Fowler, Kansas," Irvin said. "I just bought a newspaper. I don't like the name, though, The Fowler Hustler. I shall have to change that. Anyway, I only graduated nine years ago, so it may be premature to leave the nest. I promised to stay and arrange the purchase of the new press and hire someone to operate it, so let me be the first to congratulate thee on thy new position as head of the University print shop."

"I don't know anything about how to run a flatbed cylinder press."

"Fear not," Irvin said, holding back a grin. "Neither did I."

By seven o'clock in the evening, Clifton and Irvin, with the assistance of the two teamsters who arrived from Kansas City, completed the installation of the press.

"Tell me thy schedule for the next week," Irvin said.

"Well, of course, I start all my classes."

"When are thy free times?"

"Saturdays."

"I shall return on Saturday morning and we shall give this beast a thorough cleaning and lubrication."

"Very well," Clifton said, wiping his hands. "I'll see you then."

Soon after meeting, Clifton and Irvin discovered they shared the same alma mater, Stella Friends Academy, and had probably attended Quarterly Meeting together at Crosha Lyne's ranch outside of Hunter, Oklahoma. They became friends, despite the ten-year difference in their ages.

Over the course of the next year, Irvin mentored Clifton frequently, either in the basement print shop at Friends University or at the office of Stanton's newspaper, renamed the Fowler Gazette. The distance from Wichita to Fowler exceeded what Clifton could drive comfortably in a day in the hitch wagon Lige provided, so he took the train or borrowed a school friend's automobile, until, in 1909, he bought his own Model T Ford Touring Car, with money saved from his print shop wages.

Prior to 1909, Clifton and Irvin would, on occasion, attend Monthly Meeting together in Wichita or at the new Meeting House next door to Fowler Friends Academy, but after Irvin started courting the lovely Mary Sullins, newly arrived from Missouri and a dyed-in-the-wool Baptist, Irvin's interests led him in a different direction altogether.

In 1910, The University stopped funding the print shop, but an enterprising Professor realized there was a community to be served and money to be made, so he took over ownership. Under his financial umbrella, Clifton founded and edited the new weekly version of University Life, a departure from the former monthly school magazine, and published the Talisman—the school annual—sending the print bills to the University. He took in more print work on the side, from students, faculty, and the West Side merchant community. He was so busy, he had to find help, and it arrived in the form of a new freshman interested in Journalism, named Carlton

Dimsdale. With Dimsdale's assistance, Clifton soon found himself on the brink of expulsion from the school.

27

Perry and Phyllis Marie entered the Officers' Club three nights after the supercharger disaster. Balckman and Perry and the crew had flown a practice bomb run and two routine high-altitude missions without a hitch in the intervening days, and as far as Perry could tell, the incident was a closed chapter. *I never want to be that close to an air disaster again,* he thought after they reached the ground that day, but he never mentioned the event to Phyllis Marie, and he never discussed it with Balckman. It wasn't the way things were done among pilots. If you get through it, you put it past you.

"Yoo-hoo, darlings!" Eve called to them from one of the tables closest to the bandstand.

"There they are," Phyllis Marie said, making a beeline toward Eve. Perry trailed behind her.

"Hello, darling," Eve shouted, grasping both of Phyllis Marie's hands in hers.

"How are you, Eve?" Phyllis Marie asked, taking the chair into which Eve guided her.

"Me? I'm fine, dear. Can I borrow your husband for a dance?"

"Of course," Phyllis Marie said, "but where's Wallace?"

"He's at the bar, getting a round for all of us. Do you mind? We'll be right back." She stood and swept past Phyllis Marie, taking Perry by the hand and leading him onto the dance floor. Phyllis Marie seated herself at the empty table.

"So, how is everything with you?" she asked.

"Just fine, Eve. You?"

"I'm fine, dear, but I just had to ask you something."

"Go ahead," Perry said.

"What happened the other day?"

"When?"

"You know perfectly well 'when.' On your mission the other day, what was it, Sunday?"

"Eve, you know I can't talk about any training missions with you or anyone else."

"Well, Wally does, or usually, but not that one, which is why I hoped to worm it out of you or Phyllis Marie."

"She doesn't know anything."

"So there is something to know," she said, smiling. "I thought so."

Balckman appeared and tapped Perry's shoulder. "May I cut in?"

"Of course," Perry said, backing away from Eve and handing her to her husband. Perry retreated to the table, where Phyllis Marie guarded four martinis, up.

"What people see in these," she said, tilting her head toward the drinks, "I'll never know."

Perry took his seat with a smile.

"No comment from the peanut gallery?" she asked.

"I'd rather have a beer."

"No, I mean—"

"You wanted to know what Eve wanted."

"Yes."

"She wanted me to talk about something I'm prohibited from talking about."

"Oh, well, she doesn't know you very well then, does she?"

"No, but you do." He leaned toward her and kissed her.

Balckman's crew had no mission the next day. On the following day, they flew a very routine flight, seemingly without purpose, and returned to base. When Perry got home, he found a new set of orders waiting for him, to report to Redmond, Oregon for a week of maintenance training.

"This is odd, isn't it?" Phyllis Marie said, after he handed her two round-trip overnight train tickets.

"Yes," he said, "very."

The next morning, Perry entered the Redmond Lecture Hall lobby at nine o'clock. "Lieutenant Row, reporting for maintenance lecture, sir," he said, saluting the man at the table with a clipboard.

The man didn't look up. "I am not an officer, Lieutenant. You may put your arm down, you needn't call me 'sir'; you may call me Sampson. Please fill out this form and when you're done, take a seat in that area." Sampson jerked his head to Perry's right. "There is no talking whatsoever to anyone but me for the next hour. Is that clear?"

"Yes, thank you," Perry said, writing his name, rank, serial number, and base commander on the sheet of paper. Then he took a seat among another two-dozen Second Lieutenants in the lobby.

More young officers drifted in. One of them spoke to Perry, asking, "Is this seat taken?"

Perry ignored him, and the man took the seat.

At exactly nine o'clock, the man with the clipboard stood from his table and came over to where the men sat waiting.

"Gentlemen, you are about to hear the first in a series of five lectures on the proper care and maintenance of the Boeing B-17 Flying Fortress. I encourage you to take copious notes because there will be a test—"

The outside door opened and another Second Lieutenant entered the lobby. Sampson turned to him and repeated the speech about him not being an officer, filling out the form, and not talking. The young officer put his arm down and took the last available seat. Perry noted that the latecomer brought the count to exactly thirty.

When the latecomer handed Sampson his sheet, Sampson repeated his speech.

"Gentlemen, you are about to hear the first in a series of five lectures on the proper care and maintenance of the Boeing B-17 Flying Fortress. I encourage you to take copious notes because there will be a test. Remember, there is no talking whatsoever, except to me. Please follow me into the Lecture Hall."

He led the men through a door and ushered them wordlessly into the last two rows on the right side of the Lecture Hall, a large room that could hold two hundred people.

The room was dim. A slide projector stood in the middle

of the room, throwing light on a white screen on the stage. An operator sat in a chair next to the slide projector. An empty lectern stood on stage to the left of the screen, on the far opposite side from where the officers sat.

A man in a white coat entered from backstage, walked to the lectern, turned on a small lamp there, gestured to the slide projector operator—who slid the first slide of the series into place—and the lecturer began to speak. He did not have a microphone, and he spoke in a quiet voice. If he said what his name was, Perry didn't catch it.

All the young officers took out notebooks immediately and started trying to take notes.

This is ridiculous, Perry thought. *I can't hear the man at all.* He looked at his fellow officers, all struggling to hear, scratching furiously with pencils and notepads, and then looked at Sampson, who stood watching the lecture.

Perry stood. He waved at Sampson, who glanced at him, then resumed watching the lecture. *This really is ridiculous,* Perry thought and left his position in the row and walked to the center aisle. When he reached it, he turned to see all the other officers watching him, but Sampson acted as if nothing were happening except the lecture.

Perry walked down the aisle and took a seat in the front row, situating himself equally between the screen and lecturer, who continued speaking in his natural voice.

Soon afterwards, all the other officers left their seats and joined Perry in the first or second row on the same side of the room as the lecturer. As soon as the last one seated himself, the lights came up, the lecturer left the stage, and the operator turned off the projector.

As Sampson approached the officers, one of them turned to an officer next to him and said, "What is this, some kind of joke?"

Sampson passed out a set of papers. "One to a customer, please. Take one and pass it along. Thank you."

Perry looked at his form. There were only three questions:

Why did you leave your seat? Did you disobey any orders? Is there anything you would do differently if the same circumstances were to occur again? He answered, 'To see and hear the lecture better,' 'No,' and 'No.'

Sampson gathered the papers and excused the men, with a reminder to report for another lecture the following morning at nine o'clock.

That evening, after Perry and Phyllis Marie went to dinner and a show in town at the 86 Club, the Barracks Master At Arms handed him an envelope. "Lieutenant Row, sir" he said, "you're excused from the lecture tomorrow. There's a twenty-four pass in there. Be back by this time tomorrow."

"I don't get it. What did I do to deserve this?"

"Sir, if you don't want it, I'll take it."

"No, I want it."

Perry and Phyllis Marie spent the day together, renting a canoe and picnicking on the Deschutes River before seeing 'The Pride of the Yankees' at the downtown theatre.

That evening, Perry phoned the Barracks Master at Arms. "Anything for me?"

"Yes, sir, new orders," he said. "You're to report to Walla Walla Army Air Field the day after tomorrow."

"That's where I came from three days ago!"

"Welcome to the Army, sir."

28

Dr. Sampson opened his briefcase and removed the folder of evaluation forms from the recent B-17 maintenance lecture. Thirty officers had started the program. One washed out before the program even started by arriving late, although he never knew that, because Sampson didn't want the other men to know. So the man sat blithely through the entire experiment, oblivious to the fact that his fate had been determined at precisely nine o'clock the first day. Another two washed out the first day when they spoke to other officers.

One man advanced in the first round by taking the initiative to move closer to the lecturer. *Where was his form? Yes, Lieutenant Perry V. Row.* Furthermore, Lieutenant Row had answered all three questions correctly.

Ten other men had answered the three questions correctly, but unlike Lieutenant Row, they had not taken the initiative to move. That meant they got to stay in the hunt for the next round. The remaining sixteen men that day answered that they had moved because someone else had moved. They were sheep, and Sampson was not interested in sheep. They, like the latecomer, sat through the remainder of the experiment, helping Sampson eventually identify two other men for re-assignment. Sampson was interested in men who took initiative, men like Lieutenant Perry V. Row.

Perry and Phyllis Marie arrived at their Married Officers Quarters to find Second Lieutenant Balckman sitting on the ground with his back to their door. "I've been waiting for you," he said. "May I come in?"

"Of course," Perry said. "I've got new orders. I have to pick them up in the morning."

"I know," Balckman said, standing up. "I recommended you."

Perry turned to Phyllis Marie, but before he could say anything, she took the hint. "You boys will excuse me, won't you?" she said, and took her overnight bag to the bedroom.

"What's this all about, Balckman?"

"I can't do it. I realized it last Sunday. I don't have that steel, or whatever it is, that nerve to face those kinds of decisions."

"It was one mistake."

"One mistake that could have cost ten men their lives, and I can't do it."

Perry looked at him. "If you're here for me to talk you out of some decision you've made, you can forget it. You're the only one who can know."

"No, I'm not here for that. I wanted you to know, I requested re-assignment. I'm going to be a flight instructor. Eve is as mad as hell about it, but I think I can help the war effort better by training others to fly, and maybe weeding out the few that aren't meant to sit in the left seat, like me. You've been re-assigned as a pilot."

For a moment Perry couldn't find his voice. Then he managed, "I don't know what to say."

"Datsch told me the only catch is, you have to start over with new officers and a new crew at a different base. The crew here, they'll get new pilots, so that's the down side of it. I'm sorry about that. Here are your orders. You're going to repeat Crew Flight Training—from the left seat, where you belong—at Ephrata Army Airfield." Balckman extended both hands, Perry's orders in his left and a handshake in his right.

While he spoke, Perry had gotten his breath and excited heartbeat back under control. He had wanted this for so long, fought for it, and now it was being handed to him—but a at another man's expense. He knew Balckman was right, if he did not have the steel in him, it was best to step away now. But it took guts—a very particular kind of courage. "Goodbye," Perry said, taking the orders and shaking the man's hand firmly. "Good luck to you."

"You, too." Balckman stepped outside, appearing to Perry to be an inch taller than when he had arrived.

Three days later Perry entered the Group Operations

building at Ephrata and gave his name to the enlisted man sitting behind the desk.

"Yes, sir," he said, "Captain Moon is waiting. You can go right in," but before he had the chance, Moon came through the door.

"Captain this is Lieutenant Row."

"Excellent! Come right in," he said. "You're the first, did you know that?"

"First what, sir?"

"The first officer assigned to this new transitional school. Don't worry, though. We'll be getting several dozen more shortly, and you'll have first priority at picking a crew. Here, sit down." He gestured toward the chair opposite his desk. "How many hours do you have in the Flying Fortress?"

"About a hundred, sir."

"That's great. We'll get you through this and caught up as soon as we can, so we can get you over there. What do you say?"

"Sounds fine, sir."

"While you're waiting, say, a week, I want you to take my jeep, relax, see the town, spend time with your wife. She's along, right?"

"Yes, sir. I situated her in the Married Officers' Quarters before coming over here."

"You had your choice of apartments, I'll bet."

"The place was empty."

"Good. It'll fill up, soon enough. This is a transitional school, made up of officers and crew who, for whatever reason, didn't come together as a crew on the first try. You've got some great recommendations in your file, and we're going to do everything in our power to get you a good set of boys and get you back on track." He stood up and fished a key out of his pocket. "Here's the key to the jeep. It's that one," he said, pointing out the window.

"Thank you, sir," Perry said. He intended to take the Captain at his word.

The following week, Perry sat in Captain Moon's office

again, going over personnel files.

"Here's one," Moon said. "a bombardier, had a good record at Redmond, but the pilot crashed his plane on a landing and washed out. No one hurt, but it means I have some more men to transition. His radio operator would be a good choice, too."

"They look fine, sir," Perry said, reading their files. "That leaves a Navigator and a co-pilot."

"We're getting some more pilots and co-pilots next week. You won't get a navigator yet. Whoever he is, he's still in school."

"Yes, sir."

"Is Sergeant Bennett waiting out there?" Moon asked into his desk intercom.

"Yes, sir."

"Send him in."

Bennett entered the room with a salute, which Moon returned. "At ease. This is Lieutenant Row, Perry V., and your new pilot. Perry this is your Flight Engineer, Sergeant Bennett, Eric E."

"Yes, sir," Bennett said in a smooth Georgia drawl. "Pleased to meet you, sir."

"Glad to meet you," Perry said.

"What do you say we go for a spin?" Captain Moon said. "I've got a Fort standing by, along with your other crewmen."

"Yes, sir," Perry grinned. He hadn't flown a B-17 in nine days.

The first crewmember Perry had chosen was Louis Kiss, the tail gunner, because of his exemplary record. Kiss was from New York and talked in a loud bass voice, but underneath that eastern seaboard bluster, Perry realized, he was rather shy.

"Are we going up, sir?" Kiss called out when he saw Perry and Captain Moon approaching. The other men stood at attention.

"How about it?" Perry called back.

"I'm game, sir," another man said. Arthur Dix hailed from Milwaukee. He preferred to be called Art. Perry had chosen him for the Ball Turret position because of his skill on the gunnery range, but also because of his piloting skills. All crewmembers on the B-17 Flying Fortress trained as pilots, in case both men in the cabin became incapacitated.

"This is our new Flight Engineer, Eric Bennett, boys," Perry announced. "Make him feel at home. Captain Moon's going to be our co-pilot today."

"Yes, sir."

Two days later, Perry met two new crew members, his Radio Operator, Sergeant Mathias Biehl—"Just call me Matt," he said, and his Co-Pilot, Lieutenant Poythress.

"My name," he drawled, "is Whitney Fulton Poythress, Jr., sir, but call me Billy. Everyone does." His gentle brown eyes gave him an innocent look, almost boyish. He seemed slight, although he stood a full six feet. Perry liked him right away.

"Billy? Why do they call you Billy when your name is Whitney Fulton?"

"That's a good question," Billy said, scratching his head and drawing out his words. "I'll have to ask my father. They call him Bill."

Perry laughed. "His name is Whitney Fulton as well? And they call him Bill?"

"That's right. I guess they call me Billy because 'Bill' was already taken."

Perry grinned at his new co-pilot. "Well, come on, Billy. Let's go flying."

Although the mission was a practice bomb run, Perry took the opportunity to check Billy out on procedures and teach him the AFCE, the Automated Flight Control Equipment. This was also Perry's first flight without Captain Moon along as Flight Instructor. Everything went along normally until the bomb run. Before reaching the correct moment over the practice target, the bombardier released the bombs.

"Bombardier from Pilot, over," Perry called on his

interphone.

"Pilot from Bombardier, over."

"What happened? Over."

"I released the bombs, sir, over."

"You were early, over."

"Sir, what difference would it make in combat? Over."

After landing, Perry reported to Captain Moon's office.

"What happened, Lieutenant? You missed the target by miles. You must have been some ten to fifteen seconds early."

"That guy released the bombs early, sir."

"What did he have to say?"

"He asked, 'what difference did it make?' sir."

"I presume you want him bumped from your crew."

"Yes, sir, I do."

"Say no more," Moon said. "I'll have him cleaning latrines tomorrow morning."

In mid-May, Perry and Billy got a new gunner, Sergeant Walter Byrne. Walt hailed from Brooklyn and they liked him right away.

The crew spent the next five weeks making practice runs, flying in formation with other airplanes, making cross-country flights, and generally becoming familiar with each other and with the airplane. Perry and Billy spent every waking minute together, including many evenings on the town with their wives, Phyllis Marie and Fran.

"Yes," Billy said, one night at dinner, "Mr. Montjoy— that's Fran's father—he owns the local A & P there in Chapel Hill, and I worked there after school."

"Billy was so shy," Fran said. "You should have seen him. I tried to get him to take me to the movies half a dozen times before he finally caught the hint."

"We went all through grammar school and high school together," Billy said.

"Do you have any brothers and sisters, Billy?" Phyllis Marie sat forward.

"I have two sisters I need to buy something for," Billy

said, looking down in his lap. "I'm late with both their birthdays."

"Phyllis Marie," Fran said, "What do you say? Shall we try to find something suitable for them together?"

"Of course," she said.

Fran looked across at Perry. "How's Billy doin', Perry?"

"What do you mean?"

"Is he doin' right by you, you being a more experienced pilot and all?"

Phyllis Marie knew Perry wouldn't comment on anything to do with their flying, or thought so, and was very surprised when he finally spoke.

"Billy's one of the best pilots on base, Fran, and I'll tell you something else I haven't told him until now. I feel toward him just as if he were the brother I never had."

29

"California," George Outland said one night at dinner with his wife, Josephine, and the Stantons.

"What about California?" Edwin asked.

"Father and Mother Hill are going there," he said, "to homestead."

"Yes, in the Mohave desert," Edwin said.

"We should go there, too, open a studio," he said.

"There won't be many customers in the Mohave desert," Edwin said.

"I'm not talking about the desert. Why, do you know how much bigger the city of Los Angeles has become since 1911, since the Christie-Nestor Studio started last year? Now the Universal Film Manufacturing Company and Independent Motion Picture Studio are there, too." He reached across the table and took the glass water pitcher by the handle. "Next year they are going to open the first motion picture palace in New York City—The Regent—with a capacity of nearly two thousand people."

"George's sister wrote to us last week from Pasadena," Josephine said. "The climate is wonderful, it's summertime all year around, and it's warm."

"And there are a lot more people there now," George continued. "More customers means more opportunities for us, and there are more things to see and do, more things to photograph."

"Thee sounds as if thee is ready to go today," Hazel said.

Josephine looked across the table at her little sister, fifteen years her junior. Josephine couldn't be blamed if she thought of Hazel more as her own child. "We wouldn't dream of going without thee and Edwin, and think of how much better the climate would be for little Virginia, and we would be closer to Mother."

George sat forward in his chair and pointed with his fork.

"I have to tell thee, Edwin, I think that if I have to take one more portrait of some stuffy couple that still thinks they cannot smile for a portrait, like the Beaumonts last week, or—"

"Or the Higganbothams!" Edwin interrupted and laughed out loud. "Could they look any more miserable if they tried?"

"Edwin!" Hazel said. "The Higganbothams are perfectly lovely people."

"Indeed they are," he answered, "but when seated before a camera they become store mannequins."

"I had a couple last week who reminded me of frozen fish," George said. Edwin and Hazel laughed.

Josephine sat quietly eating her dinner. "Frozen fish, indeed," she said. The others turned and looked at her. When she looked up, three sets of eyes met her gaze at once. "If this is what George wants, then I say let us pack our bags."

In the spring of 1911, the Outlands and Stantons—with two-year-old Virginia in tow—packed up all their belongings and took the train from Newton to Pasadena. They bought a house on Signal Hill in Long Beach and established their new studio.

When the time came the following year for Hazel to deliver a new son, Kenneth, everyone agreed that Long Beach lacked the necessary medical care, so Edwin and Hazel left Virginia in Josephine's care and took the Red Car of the Pacific Electric Railway from Long Beach to Pasadena—twelve cents each, including the Los Angeles transfer. Mother Hill made the long journey down from their homestead in the Mohave Desert.

Kenneth was a sick child. The doctors called it asthma, nothing new to Edwin, who had watched his brother Lester gasp for air back in Northbranch, and he had suffered with it himself as a boy. Hazel washed their home free of dust every day. She kept the baby indoors when the Pacific Ocean let loose its volume of fog during the summers. She simmered a large pot of water on the cook stove all night, so she could provide his tiny lungs with steam when his attacks came.

The family met other difficulties. The Hills grew weary of the amount of work necessary to maintain the desert homestead. John, now sixty-seven, complained that he spent half his day transporting water with the mule-driven wagon and the other half giving the same water to the mules.

The photography business did not flourish the way George hoped it would. Long Beach was a long way from the newly forming film industry in an area west of Los Angeles called Hollywood.

Finally, the doctors advised the Stantons to take their child to a dryer climate, away from the ocean. George's brother John, a surgeon in Kansas City, Missouri, owned property near Fowler, Colorado and he needed someone to manage it, so the three couples decided it was time for another change. The Hills decided to buy a small home within the town, while the Stantons and Outlands agreed to farm the property to the north, on the other side of the river.

30

"Gentlemen of the Redmond, Oregon City Housing Authority," Phyllis Marie read from her typewritten notes, "I stand before you today with these five women, six wives of officers from the sixth squadron of the Combat Flight Training School, to tell you something you already know. There is a profound housing shortage in this city."

If Phyllis Marie was nervous, if her hands were shaking and her feet were cold despite the June sunshine that day, she refused to show it. She and Fran and four other women—picked up along the way in the search for a place to live for a week, ever since their husbands had completed Crew Flight Training in Ephrata—had learned that there was no housing available. But they had determined that with a little pushing, housing could be made.

Their first week in town had been fraught with disaster, not just because of the housing shortage, but because of the runway accident many of their husbands had experienced on their first day.

"You look as pale as a sheet," Phyllis Marie had said when Perry got back to their over-priced hotel room. "What happened?"

"The instructor pilot was going to take a few of us up, show us the mountains and the flight training area, but on take off, a wheel began vibrating, so he pulled back on the throttle, but the tire blew, and we swerved off the runway."

"Oh, no! Was anyone hurt?"

"Everett Davidson. Remember Everett and Nancy from Walla Walla?"

"Sure."

"Everett was in the navigator desk, and he hit his head getting out. The plane is pretty busted up. The landing gear crumpled, and we ground looped."

"What does that mean?"

"We spun out."

"Where were you?"

"I was in the co-pilot seat. I hope that's the last B-17 accident I see."

"We are here to petition the Housing Authority," Phyllis Marie continued, "to rescind its order of condemnation of the old Fifth Street Hospital and Clinic building. It may be true that the building is no longer suitable as a hospital, but it contains six rooms, suitable for bedrooms, along a short hallway, a kitchen at one end, and a bathroom at the other. The place only needs a bit of a clean-up, which we could give it, and then, after that, surely the City of Redmond could use another revenue stream from the rental of this property to the parade of Officers' wives coming through town in two-month shifts."

The old men looked up from their papers at her.

"Gentlemen, there is no reason for you to refuse," she said, lightly stamping her foot. "It's a win for the city and for the officers and their wives."

Phyllis Marie, Fran, Nancy, and the other women waited in the corridor while the board voted. After a fifteen-minute wait, the door opened and a clerk emerged.

"Petitioners Row, et al?"

"Over here," Phyllis Marie said.

"Your petition has been approved."

The two women lost no time in collecting their things and making their way to the old hospital. They thought they were the first to move in, when they heard noises coming from the kitchen. They walked in to find Nancy on her hands and knees, scrubbing the floor.

"Oh my," Fran said. "What on earth are you doing?"

"It's called cleaning, dear," she grinned, winking at Phyllis Marie. "I gather you've never had to do it yourself."

"Oh my, no," Fran said.

Phyllis Marie spied the wringer washing machine in the corner and winked back at Nancy. "Well, Fran," she said, "you said you had Billy's laundry, and we're not going to have a live-in maid here, so let me show you how to run the washing machine."

"Oh, that's fine, yes, please."

Nancy stood up from her floor washing and followed Phyllis Marie and Fran to the corner.

"Now, what do we have here?" Phyllis Marie asked.

"Billy's underwear."

"Have you ever washed clothes before?"

"No, Phyllis Marie, not a lick."

"Well, men's underwear has special needs."

"Does it?"

"Yes, you have to add a lot of starch."

One morning Perry and Billy reported to the flight deck together, expecting to meet two new officers. Instead, a familiar face greeted them.

"Captain Moon, sir!" Perry said saluting, Billy falling in beside him until Moon returned their salute.

"Surprised to see me?" Moon asked.

"Yes, sir!"

"Well, it turns out that transition crews need to learn how to fly, too, so here I am. I have your new officers, too. Gentlemen?"

Two men turned and faced Perry and Billy.

"Gentlemen, meet your pilot, Lieutenant Row, Perry V., and your co-pilot, Lieutenant Poythress, W. F. Jr. Call him Billy, but don't ask him why. Lieutenant Row, this is your new Bombardier, Lieutenant Fitzsimmons, James—don't call him Fitz, and don't ask why—and your new Navigator, Lieutenant Boettcher, L., rhymes with 'betchyer,' right Les?"

"Yes, sir," he said, smiling. "I betchyer wondering why."

Everyone shook hands all around.

"All right," Perry said. "I'll bite. Why?"

"Because that was my father's name, of course!"

Groaning laughter did not dissuade Perry from feeling a sense of satisfaction at adding these two officers to his crew, now a complete set of four.

Billy adjusted the starched shorts under his pants without

anyone noticing.

In the afternoon, at the old hospital, the six girls cleaned the kitchen together. At least some of them cleaned while the others watched, chatting and smoking, fulfilling their obligation to the Housing Authority.

"Phyllis Marie, don't you smoke?" Nancy asked.

"I tried it," she said, scrubbing the rust stain out of the large porcelain sink, "but I didn't like it. I know it's the hep thing to do, but I just don't care for it. Someone hand me that sponge, won't you?"

Fran took her the sponge. "I just can't believe how hard some of you Yankee girls work."

"Darling Fran," Phyllis Marie said, "some of us weren't raised with maids and butlers and nannies to fulfill our every need."

"That reminds me," Fran said. "I gave those shorts to Billy the last time he was here. He gave me a queer look, I must say."

"He's just not accustomed to you doing anything so domestic," Nancy said.

"Yes, that must be it," Phyllis Marie said. Some of the other girls laughed, including Nancy, Everett Davidson's wife, who Phyllis Marie had met back in Walla Walla.

Suddenly the front door opened and in walked Perry.

"What are you doing here?" Phyllis Marie asked, stepping into his embrace.

"Twenty-four hour pass," he said. "The others are right behind me."

When the men arrived, the old hospital changed. What had been an open-door dormitory of six young women—living in mutual support, knowing they had only weeks before their men would be shipped into combat—became a block of six isolated chambers, where six couples behind closed doors held a new and urgent purpose: to spend as much time as possible in pursuit of mutual pleasure.

In the course of a month of flying, a group of men gets to know each other very well: their habits, their ways of doing things. If they are lucky, their habits and ways of doing things are complementary, and something special happens. Perry noticed it shortly after picking up his ninth and tenth crewmembers, Sergeant McCormick, Robert J., or as everyone immediately called him, Mack, and Sergeant Byrnes, Walter, both Waist Gunners. These two completed his crew.

"So you two are both from New York City?" Perry asked.

"Well, yes, sir, and no, sir," Walter said. "I'm from Brooklyn."

"And I'm from Manhattan, sir."

"Aren't those both parts of New York?"

"Well, yes, sir, but—" Mack said.

"Haven't you ever been there, sir?" Byrnes said.

"No, I haven't."

"If we're ever there together, sir, we'll show you around."

In mid-June, after a particularly grueling cross country flight over the Pacific at high altitude, followed by a practice bombing mission with live rounds, Perry gathered his crew together in the hangar.

"As you know, after four weeks, we're at the midpoint of our Combat Flight Training, and I must say I think we're ready now. In short, gentlemen, your work today was outstanding."

"Thank you, sir," several murmured.

"I have good news from the front office," he continued. "We each have a ten-day pass with travel orders home. This is Uncle Sam's way of telling us that when we come back from this pass, after completing the last month of training, we'll be going over there. I want you to make the most of the time you have with your families and report back here, safe and sound, and ready to step up to the next level."

After salutes and handshakes all around, he passed out the orders and dismissed his crew, three officers and six enlisted men, and caught a ride into town to pick up Phyllis Marie. The two of them took the bus that evening for Idaho.

Perry and Phyllis Marie tried to squeeze a lifetime into

ten days: dinners with their parents, Hazel and Edwin, other evenings with their friends, Hugh and Mary, a USO dance, cherry picking out at the Symm's place, a Claudette Colbert movie with his sister, and a Kiwanis meeting where Edwin Stanton, bursting with pride, introduced his son-in-law, the pilot.

Although they shared their days with family and friends, they reserved their nights for each other. Each night, they locked the door, closed the drapes, turned out the lights, and undressed each other in the living room through long, dark kisses. His hands ran up and down her torso and thighs while she unbuttoned his blouse and unbuckled his trousers. As the clothing fell away, he lifted her; as she wrapped her legs around him, he carried her to their bed. They allowed their bodies to merge into one, prolonging the act of love for hours, until finally, exhausted and satisfied, they fell asleep in one another's arms.

After a final grand dinner party with Edwin and Hazel, Edwin's brother Alva and his wife, Gertrude, their children and their grandchildren, Perry and Phyllis Marie packed their bags and took a taxi to the bus station for their return to Redmond. No one spoke the dreadful words, that from there he would be going somewhere far away, although the hugs and kisses were longer than they might have been under different circumstances.

July became an endless parade of high-altitude formations, cross country flights, and practice bombings. The afternoons were for movies, window-shopping, bowling, and boating expeditions on the pond. Most importantly, nights were spent in the old hospital, cloistered behind closed doors.

On the first of August, Perry addressed his crew on the flight deck before takeoff. "Gentlemen, this is a big day. We are flying to Walla Walla."

Everyone knew what that meant, that they were about to pick up a brand new airplane, their airplane, the one in which they would fly to their combat assignment.

"Sir, we know it's the pilot's right to name the plane. Have

you thought of a name for her yet?" Kiss asked. The enlisted
men knew they could count on him to cross the line, ask the
pilot what they wanted to know.

"Yes, I have," Perry said, just a hint of a grin showing
below his flared nostrils. "We're going to throw a christening
party when we get back, but first, I want to talk to you about
something. We've all worked hard to learn all the proper
protocols, 'pilot from bombardier, over,' et cetera, and I'm
here to tell you something important. From now on, we're
dropping the formal protocol."

"Why, sir?"

"Because when we're in the middle of an air battle, we
don't have time for it."

"Then why did they teach it to us in the first place?"

"To instill proper discipline, to get us accustomed to
working together, but from now on, we're going to work out
our own shorthand protocol, and we're going to do it before
we ship out."

The crew nodded solemnly.

A week later, after the new airplane passed its 25-hour
inspection, the crew and their wives held a small ceremony.
After all the crew members had escorted their wives,
girlfriends, fathers and mothers through the plane, Perry
stood on a mobile platform at the nose of the plane and spoke
to those gathered below him.

"I'd like to ask my wife to come up here, please."

The twenty-some people applauded as Phyllis Marie
ascended the rollaway staircase.

Handing her a bottle of champagne, he pointed to the
nose of the airplane and said, "Hit it downward, right there
on that thick metal part."

Taking the bottle by the neck, she said, "I christen thee the
Phyllis Marie!" Swinging hard, she broke the bottle on her
first try, splattering champagne and broken glass all over the
flight deck, to the cheers of the gathered throng.

"Don't worry," Perry said to the crowd. "We have some
for drinking, too." Perry and Billy cleaned up the broken

glass after the party.

The following day, Perry took the Phyllis Marie out for her maiden voyage, leading and delivering a formation of thirteen planes to Vancouver British Columbia, and intercepting an escort of Canadian Supermarine Spitfires for the return to American air space. After the escort, Perry flew another three hours out over the ocean. On his return over Seattle, he was intercepted and escorted by P-38s and Grumman Wildcats, concluding a marathon joy ride that lasted over eight hours.

Phyllis Marie and Fran heard the news first, at the laundromat in town, having abandoned the wringer washer in the hospital after Fran's starch experience.

"You haven't heard?" A woman asked.

"Heard what?" Phyllis Marie asked.

"All the second-month crews are done. They're being assigned. Aren't your husbands second month?"

"Yes, they are. Where?" Phyllis Marie asked. "When?"

"I don't know where yet, but they're supposed to fly to Scott Field, Illinois, on August the tenth."

"That's only two days from now!"

"Scott Field," Fran said. "That means they're going to Europe."

"We need train tickets right away."

31

Perry arrived at the old hospital ahead of the other five officers to find all six women waiting for him.

"Is it true?" Phyllis Marie asked.

"Is what true?" The other women hung on his every word.

"Are you flying to Scott Field on the tenth?"

"Who told you that?"

"Oh," Phyllis Marie said. "I don't know her name. She's an officer's wife. She was at the laundromat. Is it true?"

He looked at the sea of womanhood before him. "Come on," he said, taking her elbow. "We need some privacy."

"Oh, no," the other wives chorused.

"Wait for your husbands," he said.

Once behind the closed door of Phyllis Marie's room, he sat on the bed. She quickly sat next to him, wrapping her hands around his forearm. "It is true, isn't it?"

"It's Scott Field for Billy and me, and my crew, yes. I don't know about the others. I've got your traveling arrangements here, but you can't discuss them with the other women."

"How am I going to be able to know where you are?"

"I've been thinking about that," Perry said. "How about this?" He reached for a pencil and a piece of paper. "I'll write you a letter that starts off, 'Dear Wife,' instead of 'Dear Phyllis Marie,' and that means this letter contains my location."

"I knew you'd think of a way."

"And then, you circle the first letter of the second word of every sentence, and put them together."

"Oh, that's great!"

"But don't tell anyone."

"No, I won't."

"Not even your family. Promise me."

"I promise." She turned her face toward his, wanting to kiss him, wanting even more for him to kiss her, which he did.

"I have something for you," she said. She walked to the dresser and pulled open a drawer, taking out a gift, wrapped in red paper. "Here," she said, returning to his side. "Open it."

"What is it?" he asked, as he started tearing at one corner.

She didn't answer, waiting instead until he unwrapped and opened the box, finding a toy, a plastic figure of a boy, wearing red.

"He's cute," Perry said.

"He's more than that." She held in a tear that started to form in the corner of her eye. "He's a new promise, the promise of the family we've talked about starting, the family we've delayed, because of this war."

"He's our son, Mickey, then," Perry said.

"Yes, he's our son, Mickey. I want you to take him with you, and bring him home safe to me."

"I will."

"Do you promise?"

"I promise."

On August the ninth, Perry and Billy took Phyllis Marie and Fran to the train, bound for St. Louis, Missouri, the big city just twenty five miles west of Scott Field. "Here are your tickets," Perry said to Phyllis Marie. "When you get to Portland, you have to transfer to Oakland."

"We'll be just fine," she said. "Isn't there a song? 'Meet me in St. Louis?' We'll meet you there."

"At the Mayfair."

They kissed one last time, and when the train started to pull away, Perry lifted her onto the bottom step.

"Come on," he said to Billy. "We have a lot of work to do and only twelve hours to do it."

Perry and Billy packed their gear and headed for the flight deck, finding that the mess hall had complied with his special request and supplied two large Thermos flasks of coffee and ten cups. They poured two cups and together, walked the inspection circle around the Phyllis Marie, noting every single detail, in spite of the fact that the ground chief assured them that he had already done it.

"Rookie pilots," the ground chief muttered, out of hearing range.

By this time the bombardier Fitzsimmons had trained everyone to call him Bud, as a defense against being called Fitz, while the navigator, Boettcher seemed to enjoy being called 'betchyer'.

"Bud, Boettcher," Perry said as they arrived, "there's coffee over there. Won't you have some and join us on the inspection?"

Together, along with Billy, they had started to refer to themselves, the officers, and sometimes the whole crew, enlisted men, too, as Row's Rowdies, a nickname Perry didn't mind at all since the pronunciation rhymed, and it was correct.

The enlisted men arrived in pairs, first Sergeants Biehl and Bennett, the radio man, Matt, and the Engineer, Eric, or as Billy called him, 'E.'

"Every thing squared away, boys?" Perry asked, casually returning their salutes.

"Yes, sir," they replied.

"It's going to be a long flight. Get some coffee, over there, if you want it."

"Thank you, sir," they said.

The United States Army Air Forces had strict rules against fraternization between officers and enlisted men, a rule that some may have considered broken by the christening party, but Perry felt that the morale and teamwork of the crew was more important, a fact his crew noticed.

"Democratic sort of fellow, isn't he?" E said.

"Quite down to earth, I'd say," Matt smiled.

Sergeants Walter Byrne and Robert McCormack, Byrne and Mac, the New Yorker waist gunners arrived next, and received the same offer of coffee from their captain.

"I think I'm going to like this war," Byrne said.

Last to arrive, Sergeants Arthur Dix and Louis Kiss, Art and Kiss, the ball turret gunner and the tail gunner reacted the most to Perry's accommodations.

"Sir, yes, sir, coffee! Thank you, sir!" Kiss said.

Art almost laughed out loud.

"Don't mention it," Perry said, grinning. "We've got a long flight ahead of us."

"Sir, can I ask a question?" Kiss asked.

"Shoot."

"How did you wind up with so many New Yorkers?"

"Just good luck I guess."

The men all laughed.

Perry looked into the bottom of his coffee cup and at the empty Thermos flasks.

"Gentlemen, I propose we get started."

After take-off, Perry made a request. "Boettcher, he said, abandoning the protocol as he had promised he would, "Can you set a course for Caldwell, Idaho?"

"Yes, Captain."

"One last look?" Billy asked.

"I thought so, maybe, yeah."

"That's nice. North Carolina's too far off course, so I'll say goodbye to your hometown with you, if that's all right."

"Sure."

About half an hour later, as they reached the coordinates, Perry looked out over the moonlit countryside, but had trouble spotting the town.

"I forgot about the blackouts," Perry said. "We must be about over it now."

"Next time," Billy said.

"Yeah, next time, he said.

"Boettcher," he called. "Your hometown is in Nebraska, right, over?"

"Columbus, Captain."

"Set a course for it will you?"

"Will do, and thank you."

"It'll be light by the time we get there," Perry said to

Billy.

"Yes, he'll be able to see it."

The Phyllis Marie and her crew flew on through the dark without incident, until the sun rose beyond Nebraska, blinding Perry and Billy, who quickly located their Ray-Ban sunglasses.

"Where's your house, Boettcher?"

"East end of town. Follow the highway and it's one of those red roof jobs."

"Are you going to buzz them?" Billy asked.

"That should be quite an event, don't you think?"

Perry dropped to two hundred feet above the flight deck and followed the highway all the way through town, waggling his wings back and forth.

"Boettcher, you can call them after we get into Scott Field and let them know you were in the B-17 that woke up the town this morning."

"Thank you, that will mean a lot."

Phyllis Marie and Fran sat waiting in Phyllis Marie's hotel room at the Mayfair, the door to Fran's adjoining room open, the radios in both rooms on and tuned to the same station.

"Phyllis Marie, I just have to say that I know Billy is in good hands with Perry."

"That's nice of you to say."

"No, I mean it. I don't think I've ever met a man as solid and trustworthy as your husband. You find him so, don't you?"

"Absolutely," Phyllis Marie said, smiling. "He's dependable."

"That's good. They've become so close, like brothers."

"Perry doesn't have a brother, you know. He has three sisters, whom he adores, but Billy has become very important to Perry."

"Billy hasn't a brother, either, and like Perry, he adores his two sisters, but I've never seen Billy look up to anyone quite the way he looks up to Perry."

"They make a good team."

Both Phyllis Marie's and Fran's doors echoed loud knockings.

"They're here," Phyllis Marie said, rising, as Fran ran through the adjoining door, closing it behind her. Phyllis Marie opened hers and Perry walked in, taking her around the waist with his arms. After a long embrace, he stepped back into the hall, retrieved two large duffels, and dragged them inside.

"What's all that?"

"Equipment for overseas duty."

"Do you know where you're going yet?"

"Scotland. That's all I know so far." He took off his coat and sat on the bed, crossed his leg, and began untying one shoe.

"When?"

"Tomorrow."

"So this is it." She sat down on the bed next to him.

"This is what?"

"Our last night."

"No, it certainly is not," he said removing his other shoe and turning to face her. "We're going to have thousands of more nights. I don't want any crying, understand?"

She turned her face away to hide her tears.

"We need to talk about something before I leave tomorrow," he said. "If I don't come back—"

"Don't say that!"

"Listen to me," he said gently. "This very important to me." He waited until she turned back to him. "If I don't come back, don't waste your money on a funeral. The Army will pay for that."

"What are you asking, then?"

"Take the money and go to Wichita. Spend it on a party with our families and friends. Spend it on a celebration of what my life meant. Promise me you won't waste your time crying."

"Yes," she said. "I promise." She wiped at the corner of her eye with her sleeve. "Tell me what else you want."

"I want you," he said.

Phyllis Marie felt her heart pound suddenly, one extra beat, as Perry took her in his arms and pulled her toward him. He kissed her, gently at first, but as his breathing suddenly increased, and his hands roamed across her back, sending shivering sparks down her spine, his kiss became firmer, harder, and she returned it with delight. They undressed each other, interrupting the kiss only when necessary, to pull off her sweater, his undershirt, until they sat naked together. He stood and pulled her up into his arms for another long kiss, before pulling down the bedclothes and turning off the light.

32

"Are you Dimsdale?" Clifton Row asked, knowing he was, having learned his class schedule and intercepted him outside his English class.

"Yes."

"Are you interested in printing at all?" Clifton's question echoed the clerk in the Registrar's office three years earlier.

"Well, yes," he said.

"Were you planning to work while you go to school?"

"Do you mean for wages?"

"Of course for wages."

"Yes, I was."

"The reason I ask, there is an opening in the University print shop in the basement. Why don't you come see me about it?"

"I will. Thank you."

"Just don't let it interfere with your class work."

"No, I won't. Where is the—"

"One flight down, stairs on the right."

With Dimsdale taking over editorship of University Life, Clifton gained enough time to bring up his neglected grades, take in more outside project work, and earn some money for the future. He also found time to visit his father, living alone in Kiowa, Kansas, just a stone's throw across the Oklahoma border from the old homestead.

For his oration class, Clifton participated in a mock trial as the defendant in an arson case. Dimsdale was his attorney. Alas, Clifton was found guilty and sentenced to six years in the penitentiary.

Within a month of his hiring date, Dimsdale came to Clifton with an idea.

Wichita boasted two daily newspapers of significance, one in the morning and one in the evening. The competition between these sheets burned fiercely, and it had little to do with news and everything to do with the trains. The simple fact was, the morning paper reached their subscribers—a hundredfold greater than the evening paper—in a timely manner and the evening paper did not.

Until, in a stunning reversal, a new owner purchased the evening paper and changed the production schedule to match the trains. At the same time, he browbeat the local authorities into enforcing the previously relaxed Prohibition laws. Suddenly the evening subscription swelled to something close to competitive. In response to the challenge, the morning paper started a campaign against the alleged graft in City Hall, reporting on a so-called Hidden Room, where unnamed devious crimes occurred. The evening paper fought back with a blistering attack on the family that owned the morning paper, and the morning paper retaliated with an exposé of the current leader of Wichita's Irish mob, a mid-level trafficker in dope and liquor who greased the palms of local politicians and police before turning over a healthy percentage of his profits to his superiors in Chicago.

Sensationalism was king. The readers ate it up like spoon bread in hot milk with butter. For the first time in anyone's memory, Wichitans started subscribing to both papers in an effort to keep up with all the mucky gossip.

"Here's my idea," Dimsdale said. "We put out a yellow number, a hoax, that pokes fun at the yellow journalism in our local newspapers, casting the University faculty, administrators, and students as the City of Wichita criminals and politicians."

Clifton was intrigued. "Go on."

"I figured we could cast ourselves as the heroes of the stories: the University Life editors who fought bravely to bring the criminals to justice."

"What do you mean, 'we?' You're the editor now," Clifton said.

"Well, I know, but your name is still on the masthead."

"I think it's a funny idea," Clifton said, "but you're right, my name is on the masthead as editor. So put your own name there for this edition, and I'll help you where I can."

Dimsdale spent a disproportionate amount of time on the yellow number, organizing photographs of faculty members, writing fictitious stories to match them, and staging photographs of students, without being too specific about his intent. Row and Dimsdale posed for one such photo, playing cards and being interrupted by a policeman.

Some of the headlines included: 'Hidden Room In Basement: Shameful Condition Uncovered; Prominent Persons Implicated, Dump a Disgrace to Friends University: Used to Conceal Crimes, Ponies, and Old Clothes, Mysterious Disappearance of Textbooks and Innocent Freshmen Accounted for, Toughs Surprised at Card Game.'

Each story ran with photographs of the students' favorite faculty members, who were blamed for all the heinous crimes.

When Dimsdale was ready, Clifton assisted with the typesetting and they published the issue on the regular weekly schedule, passing out subscription copies and selling singles to all takers at the end of morning chapel, as usual. The issue deviated from the usual format only in the color of the paper upon which it was printed. Dimsdale had assured Clifton that by printing the hoax edition of University Life on yellow paper, they would be nodding and winking to their readers, telling them not to take it seriously, that this edition was a joke.

The administration was not amused. Neither was Clifton's mother, Carrie.

All semblances of order and discipline collapsed on that chilly autumn morning. No one attended class. Students sprawled in hallways, classrooms, under trees, and on the grand staircase of University Hall. Their laughter filled the enormous building as they read the absurd stories and observed the humorous images of the victims of the grandest practical joke in the history of the school.

Within an hour, Clifton Row and Carlton Dimsdale were summoned to a closed-door faculty meeting in the President's office.

"Sit." Two chairs stood in the center of the room, surrounded by professors and administrators in their caps and gowns. There being no alternative, the young men complied.

"Who is responsible for—" the President held a copy of the yellow number by its corner, using as little of his thumb and forefinger as possible "—this?"

Clifton started to speak, but Dimsdale beat him to it.

"I am, sir."

Each of the twenty professors turned his gaze on Clifton.

"Look at the masthead, sir," Dimsdale said.

Twenty bespectacled and balding heads turned downward. After a long minute, the President looked up and spoke. "Mr. Row," he said, "please wait outside."

Clifton withdrew, and dutifully sat in the anteroom. After an hour passed, the Professor who owned the print shop emerged. "Go on," he said. "You're dismissed."

Classes resumed the following day. Rumors spread throughout the campus that Carlton Dimsdale or Clifton Row, or both, were to be suspended, that they were to be expelled, that they were to be fired from their positions as print shop manager and Editor pro tem. Petitions circulated and committees formed, with the intent of organizing protest meetings and student strikes, in the event that the administration took any negative action. The faculty held another meeting to discuss the problem. No word issued from the President's office or anyone else. Another day went by and the faculty held a third meeting, still without any announced outcome.

Just when it seemed the dust would settle, the campus community learned that one rural family of a lampooned student—reported to have flung himself from the clock tower in a state of depression over a failed love affair—had believed the article. Since they did not have a telephone, it took them two days to ascertain that their son was still alive.

That new wrinkle brought the Board of Trustees into the fray. Another closed-door meeting in the President's office came and went, and still no word came from on high regarding possible repercussions.

The Wichita morning paper took up the cause with an article about the yellow hoax edition and the turmoil it had caused for the University, which, according to the morning paper, ought to give their freshman editor a raise and a promotion to Director of Advertising.

Finally, Dimsdale was summoned to the President's office. When he returned to the print shop, his face betrayed no clue.

"What happened?" Clifton asked.

"Nothing," he said.

"Meaning what?"

"Meaning I've been cleared, as have you. No expulsion, no suspension, no termination."

Clifton was surprised to find he felt a little let down.

A year later, Clifton said goodbye to Friends University and the print shop. Without graduating, he married his long time sweetheart, Georgia Whitaker, and after a year with Irvin Stanton at the Fowler Gazette and the birth of his first daughter, Corliss, he accepted a position as a printer with Jett & Wood Mercantile Company in Wichita.

Blanketed in isolationism, America hardly noticed the events leading up to the outbreak of the Great War. The average American didn't give a whit about Europe's problems, and the average Kansan felt likewise disinterested in America's problems, both foreign and domestic: the former being 'over there,' and the latter being 'back there,' in Washington. Kansans struggled with the issues of a man's right to drink—banned in the state for over thirty years—and a woman's right to vote, finally delivered in 1912.

The far greater concerns among most Americans that year were for a stable money supply, new legislation to prohibit unfair business practices, the rights of the individual, and the rights of the states versus a growing federal government. In response to President Taft's perceived incompetence and Theodore Roosevelt's challenge to it, the voters compromised and elected former college professor Woodrow Wilson as President, a man with only two years of experience as Governor of New Jersey, although, to his credit, he had served as the President of Princeton University for ten years before that. In his first term, Wilson created the Fair Trade Commission, passed the Federal Reserve Act, outlawed child labor, and created the first eight-hour workday. Despite Germany's 1915 sinking of the Lusitania and Wilson's strong warning—or feeble response, depending on one's political party—and with the help of a clever campaign slogan—"He kept us out of war"—Wilson squeaked into his second term by an electoral vote margin of only twenty-three.

Even Kansans noticed when Germany thumbed its nose at President Wilson in January of 1917 and announced they would resume unrestricted submarine warfare in the Atlantic. By the spring, most Americans favored entering the war, proclaiming, in Wilson's words, "the world must be made safe for democracy." Congress declared war in April and passed the Selective Service Act in May.

Part 2

1

Carrie took a moment away from her preparations to glance out the kitchen window of her estranged husband's Kiowa home. She recognized Clifton's Model T Ford Touring car approaching from three blocks away. With one mind she thought, *No, I'm not ready for them yet,* while with another she thought, *It's about time they got here.*

"They're here," she called out as she ran to the door, but Lige was already on the front porch acting nonchalant and pretending to look after the flowerbed.

"Papa!" five-year-old Corliss shrieked, jumping from the car just seconds after Clifton set the brake. Clifton assisted his younger daughter, Lois, not quite three, down to the running board and to the ground before extending a hand to his wife, Georgia, who descended the steps into the waiting arms of her mother-in-law.

"I'm roasting two chickens," Carrie said, "and I've shelled the peas, but I could use some help with the potatoes." The two women disappeared into the house, followed by everyone else.

"I got a letter," Clifton said at the dinner table, finally raising the question on everyone's mind. "It's from the Selective Service, telling me to register."

"Register?" Carrie asked. "I thought you drove up here today to tell us you had enlisted."

Lige looked up from his plate. "I don't want him to enlist," he said. "I oppose this war, like all war. Besides, he has a family to protect now."

"Exactly," Carrie said, "and the way to protect it is to put on the uniform and serve his country, the way his ancestors did."

"How is he going to protect his wife and babies if he puts on a uniform and goes over there?" Lige asked. "Besides, he is a birthright member, and the Religious Society of Friends teaches us that there is that of God in every one, which makes each person too precious to damage or destroy."

"It does," Carrie said, but before she could respond, Lige went on.

"No end could ever justify such means," he said. "I read the other day that Friends, as well as Mennonites and some others, are declaring themselves Conscientious Objectors. That's what he needs to do."

Suddenly, as if prompted by some silent cue, the two of them turned to look at Clifton, who had remained silent throughout the debate. He sat with his knife and fork still poised in the same position it had been at his first mention of the subject.

"I got a letter," Clifton repeated. "It's from the Selective Service, telling me to register. Because I have two children and I am older than twenty-five, I am to receive a one-year deferment."

"They say the war will be over by Christmas," Lige said.

"If that's true," Clifton said, "then there will be nothing to discuss one year from now."

The year of 1917 continued, during which the Great War devolved into the great stalemate. Men dug into trenches within rifle range of the enemy. Both sides rotated troops in and out of the frontline to combat the extraordinary stress. The newspapers reported that more than a million men died at the Battle of Verdun, another million at Sommes, and another half million at the Third Battle of Ypres. Rumors spread that the rules regarding deferment and conscientious objection were about to change.

Clifton did not want to go to war, and he did not want to dishonor his country by avoiding service. After the birth of Perry, his first son and third child, an opportunity presented itself, disguised as a customer with a job request in his print shop at Jett & Wood Mercantile.

"Can I help you?" Clifton said.

"I need a hundred copies of this document form," he said. "Can you help me?"

"What is it?" Clifton asked.

"Honorable discharge papers for the Kansas State Guard," he said. "I've got a group mustering out next month."

Clifton looked it over. "I can supply you with a better Kansas State Seal than this one," he said. "Does this qualify as a deferment against military service?"

"Yes, it does," the man answered. "Are you a Quaker?"

"Religious Society of Friends, actually."

"That's the same thing, isn't it?"

"Sure." Clifton said, deciding not to belabor the point.

"Captain Hansen," the man said, extending his hand.

"Clifton Row."

"I've got a lot of Quakers in my outfit. You've got to learn how to shoot a rifle at Basic Training, but after that, I don't think Kaiser Bill will be invading Kansas none too soon. Can you cook?"

"I'm an excellent cook," Clifton stretched the truth a little.

"I need a new Mess Sergeant," he said. "You'd have to give me three days a week. You can stay in Wichita, except for a two-week training period every six months, and you'd be expected to stay with the outfit for two years or until six months after the war ends. What do you say?"

"Let me speak to my employer," Clifton said. "I think I can work that out."

"Law says they have to let you go part-time for militia service if you want to, and they don't get to give your job away, neither. Got kids?"

"Three."

"Extra pay in the pocket isn't so bad, neither."

On his lunch break, Clifton took the trolley west to Friends University and entered the library.

"God's blessings to thee, Mr. Row," the clerk chirped. "How is thee today?"

"Good day, sir, I'm well, thank you. I need a book on cooking for very large groups of people."

"How large?"

"I'm not sure," he said. "At least a hundred."

The clerk found only one title, Gourmet Banquet Preparation, which Clifton studied from cover to cover, but fortunately for the soldiers of Company B, Third Battalion of the Kansas State Guard, the mess tent equipment and supplies included an official Mess Sergeant's manual, complete with recipes.

Clifton settled into his new routine without too much difficulty. Lige expressed relief at this compromise, but Carrie kept herself back, possibly because she held both conflicting opinions.

The highlight of Clifton's tour of duty came in the summer of 1918 when Company B furnished an escort to Colonel Theodore Roosevelt on his visit to Wichita in aid of the fourth Liberty loan drive. Clifton's attendance was not required, nor even expected in his role as Mess Sergeant, but his comrades found a spot for him in the ranks. When Captain Hansen noticed him, he simply waved.

Colonel Roosevelt died the following winter, just a few weeks before Perry's first birthday, and to the great surprise of his wife and two daughters, Clifton wept at the dinner table.

In November, Armistice was declared, and in May of 1919, Clifton mustered out of service, just a month before the signing of the Treaty of Versailles. The war killed eight and a half million soldiers, but after the signing of the Treaty, celebrants rang bells throughout the world. Even before the clanging faded, scholars studied the one-sided Treaty and concluded that the harsh terms imposed on the former Central Powers, especially Germany, sowed the seeds of another war, a greater war than the Great War, if that were possible, perhaps within two decades.

One night about five weeks after Versailles, Lige fell asleep, alone in his Kiowa home, never to awaken. He was fifty-nine.

2

"Sergeant, where the hell is my crew?" Lieutenant Perry Row felt dizzy, cranky, and mean all at once. He thought his head would split open from the headache raging inside, induced, no doubt, by the sudden change in time zones. The journey had taken six days to cross land and sea from Scott Field near St. Louis, Missouri to Prestwick, Scotland, when it should have taken two, and when he arrived, the powers that be had taken away his enlisted men.

An effeminate RAF clerk in the Prestwick office explained. "Your men are going to gunnery school, Lieutenant, while you and your officers attend ground school. You'll see them again at your assignment."

True, there had been some high points to the flight across, such as buzzing Youngstown, Ohio, so Bud Fitzsimmons could practice his bombing technique by dropping a handkerchief parachute with a note for his mother, and the amazing sight of the aurora borealis, the northern lights, as they flew between Presque Isle, Maine and Gander, Newfoundland, the last jumping off point before crossing the Atlantic.

But then came rain, thunder, and lightning. Perry and the Phyllis Marie stood waiting around the Gander Air Field for two days before receiving clearance to take off.

When he discovered his airplane was missing as well, he wanted an answer.

"Sergeant, where is my airplane?" he asked in a gentler tone as the ground crewman stood blinking at him.

"Just a moment, sir," he said. "Let me get someone who can help you, sir."

"Fine." Perry looked over at his three officers, asleep on a pile of mailbags and envied them their rest.

The sergeant returned with a Captain in tow. Perry snapped to attention and saluted.

"You were asking about your airplane?"

"Yes, sir."

"I'm sorry to be the one to break it to you, but that wasn't your airplane. That airplane belongs to the Army Air Forces, and it's gone."

"Sir?"

"I don't know what they told you stateside, but the ships they give crews to fly over here aren't the ships they get assigned in combat."

Perry's jaw dropped.

"Think about it, son. We don't know where you're going yet, but we know where that ship is going, and it has to get serviced after your flight over here, and painted in the livery of the bomb group to which it's assigned, with its group code on its tail."

"Yes, sir, I see."

"Who knows? You could actually end up with the same ship, but it's a one-in-a-million shot, so just relax. When you get to your assigned base and your group commander assigns you a new ship, you get to re-name it and paint its name on the nose."

"Yes, sir, thank you."

"Now, you and your officers get going. There's a troop train headed to CCRC at oh eleven hundred, and your names are on the list."

"Yes, sir."

The troop train the Captain had mentioned turned out to be an eastbound connection to the famous Flying Scotsman, the southbound train to London, the most luxurious accommodations Perry and his officers had ever seen.

"Look at this," Billy said, seated across from Perry in the dining car. "There's a place here in the table that perfectly fits my glass."

"Did you see the fine linens on every table?" Perry asked. "The crystal water glasses? What's a guy supposed to do with all these spoons?"

"I thought these people were at war!"

Perry and his officers disembarked before London, at

Hemel Hempstead, and shared a large cab to the Combat Crew Replacement Center at Bovingdon for ground school. As soon as they reached their shared quarters, Perry composed a V-letter to Phyllis Marie, encoding his location into the first letter of the second word of each sentence, knowing that the letter he wrote would be photographed and reduced to the size of a thumbnail onto microfilm. Phyllis Marie would receive a one-quarter-scale facsimile on lightweight photo paper, so he used short sentences and a large script, only as many letters as necessary to encode Hemel Hempstead.

Because of perceived low morale—due to the rookie Fortress flyers finding out about the high mortality rate—the CCRC put on an air show using P-38 Lightnings and P-47 Thunderbolts.

"They want to show us that the fighters can protect us," Perry said to his officers. "Let's go see what they can do."

The planes flew in formation just above the flight deck, followed by two squadrons of three B-17s. They made several passes, flying quite safely and conservatively. The rookie flyers cheered wildly each time, including Perry's group.

"What did you think?" Billy asked.

"I'd rather have escorts than not, that's for sure."

Perry found the ground instruction a dull, albeit necessary routine. He wanted to get on with it, but he tried not to let the other officers see how he felt. The brass was right. Low morale prevailed at CCRC and Perry knew why. These boys had been tightly wound and now they had to wait and endure lectures about how to fly as guests of the British.

Everyone assigned at CCRC had a bicycle. Perry had never seen so many in one place before. He soon found himself trying to borrow one whenever he could, in part, because he saw it as a necessary part of life, and in part to entertain his officers. Eventually he bought one for six pounds ten, about thirty dollars, even though he knew he might not be able to transport it to the assignment. It didn't matter. The fun it brought his officers was worth the price.

The very next day, his orders came through.

"What's it say?" Billy asked.

"It says we're to report to the three-hundred-ninetieth Bombardment Group (Heavy), five-hundred-sixty-eighth Squadron at Framlingham near Ipswich-by-the-sea. Here are the train tickets." He handed the tickets to Billy, who quickly opened them.

"We go tonight, y'all."

"Let's get packed," Perry said.

"What about your bicycle?"

"I'm taking it, of course, as far as they let me."

After a bewildering change of trains somewhere in London, Perry and his officers arrived in Ipswich and discovered an American military bus waiting to take them to Framlingham airfield, not actually situated within the boundary of Framlingham parish, but rather closer to the village of Parham.

The driver took them directly to their assigned RAF Nissen hut made of corrugated sheet metal and resembling a half-sunken keg on its side.

"Where does the tap go?" Billy asked the driver.

"It's better than it looks, sir. You're lucky, sir, because the latrine is next door, but the washroom is about three city blocks down that way," he said, motioning with his arm. "It's a good thing you've got a bicycle, sir," he said to Perry. "The rest of you would be advised to get some, too, sirs."

"At least we have some room to spread out," Perry said, approaching the door, but when he opened it, he saw four occupied bunks on one side and four unoccupied bunks on the other. No one was home.

"All right," he said, as his three officers came in behind him and realized they were sharing these quarters with another crew of officers. "You didn't think we had it all to ourselves, did you?" He dropped one of his duffels onto the nearest bunk, under a window. "Billy, you take that one next to me, Bud, the third one, and Boettcher on the end."

Perry sat down on his bunk and started his first order of business, a V-letter to Phyllis Marie with the word Ipswich encoded. Framlingham is too long, he said to himself, and besides that, I'd rather she didn't know the exact name of the airfield—just in case.

Perry's enlisted men arrived, the six sergeants as they were now calling themselves, or was it the sick sergeants? Perry thought his officers had low morale, but he soon concluded that these guys were seriously down in the dumps.

"How was it?" he asked at the informal reunion, when they located the officers at their hut.

"Better than a sharp stick in the eye," Kiss answered.

"Was it that bad? Tell me."

"It was gunnery practice," Byrne said. "Non-stop shooting and lectures about the nasty Nazis who want to drop us out of the sky. It got a bit tiresome."

"How about you, Mack? Did you get to pilot much?"

"Yeah, some. I'm just glad to be getting on with the business at hand."

"Me, too," Art said.

"How about you, Matt? Was it all gunnery for you, or was there some new radio training for you?"

"They had some new tricks up their sleeves for me."

"E?"

"I spent less time shooting and more time on pilot and co-pilot emergency procedures, engine operation, fuel consumption, and the operation of all equipment, including the oxygen system, radio equipment, bomb racks, and armaments."

"Well, gentlemen, there's a bit of bad news. I hate to break it to you. I know I was pretty surprised when it happened."

"Now what?" Kiss asked.

"They took the Phyllis Marie away from me, said it was never mine to begin with, and that the numbskulls stateside should never have let us believe otherwise."

He watched their expressions droop.

"But the good news is, we're going to get another airplane, and we get to christen her all over again. But gentlemen, I want to put it to a vote. I had my shot at it. I named one airplane. I want to know what you fellows think the name should be."

He'd warned his three officers that he intended to make this announcement, and that he wanted them to remain silent on the point, to see how the enlisted men reacted.

"Phyllis Marie," the six sergeants said as a chorus.

"We don't want to change it," Kiss said.

"Neither do we," Billy said, speaking for the officers.

"Very well. Phyllis Marie it is. Thank you, gentlemen, you will have made my wife very happy when she learns of your decision."

"How is she?" Kiss asked. Billy resisted the urge to shush the talkative tail gunner.

"I haven't heard from her yet." *And I miss her,* he added silently.

3

Having failed to prosper in California, the Stantons, along with the Hills and Outlands, moved to Fowler, Colorado in 1918.

Josephine became ill. The doctors told her she had a tumor on her spine. George's brother John agreed to operate, so she and George took the train to Kansas City. The surgery left her paralyzed and wheelchair-bound for the rest of her life.

John Hill did not live to see his oldest daughter return. He slipped away quietly in the night.

After the Armistice and the signing of the Treaty of Versailles, travel suddenly became easier. Hazel's sister Edna brought her husband Arthur Chilson to visit on a six-month furlough from their mission in Ruanda-Urundi. They also brought exotic gifts, unbelievable stories of their adventures, and their two daughters, Rachel and Esther.

"Have I told thee the tale of the snake?" Arthur asked the family, gathered together around the roaring fireplace in the Outland house.

"How big a snake?" Kenneth asked. Now seven years old, his breathing had eased and he was thriving in the arid Colorado altitude.

"Oh," Arthur continued, "it had to be twenty feet long."

Virginia squealed uncharacteristically. She was usually so sedate and calm that even at the age of ten, her schoolmates teased her, referring to her as a school marm, or a granny.

"I was trekking through the jungle," Arthur said, "when I came upon it. Its head was the size of my fist and it widened in the middle until it was as big as Kenneth here."

"No snake is that big," Kenneth said.

"They are in Africa," Esther said to her younger cousin. "I've seen them."

"So, young Kenneth, I understand thy skepticism," Arthur said, "and the reason this snake was so large in the middle was that it had just eaten something large."

"What was it?"

"I wondered, too." Arthur reached around behind him and pulled a large knife out from its sheath on his belt. "I pulled out my knife—"

Virginia shrieked. Hazel felt something stir within her belly. She reached over to Josephine, seated in her wheelchair, took her hand, and silently placed it on her own abdomen. Edna smiled from across the room.

"I pulled out my knife and I slit that snake open," Arthur continued his story, "and do you know what happened?"

"No!" Kenneth and Virginia shouted.

"A goat kid stood up from inside the belly of that snake and ran away into the jungle."

"You saved it!" Virginia shouted.

Kenneth jumped up and ran across the room to his mother. "Mother has something inside her," he said. "But it isn't a goat. It's a baby. Mother said I should pray for a baby, and my prayers have been answered."

It was true that, in an effort to restore Kenneth's faith after the loss of his grandfather, and knowing she was pregnant, Hazel had taken the opportunity to tell him that if he prayed for a little brother or sister, his prayer would be answered.

On a hot September day in 1919, the four cousins walked from their country schoolhouse to the farm to discover several of the adults—grandmother, aunts, and uncles—sitting in the parlor together talking quickly and acting very oddly, as if something important had happened.

"Where's Mother?" Kenneth asked. "Where's Father?"

Edwin came halfway down the stairs, grinning widely. "I'm here," he said.

"Where's Mother?"

"She's upstairs," he said. "There is a new sister in the house."

"I want to see her!" Kenneth shouted.

"Just a minute," Edwin said. "As soon as thy mother is ready, thee and the other children can visit."

Kenneth tried to run up the stairs, but Edwin caught him as he tried to run past. "I want to see her!"

"Calm down, son," Edwin said, patiently. "Thee shall see her soon enough."

"Edwin?" Hazel called from upstairs.

"Stay downstairs," he said to the boy and ascended the staircase. He stepped into the room.

Hazel sat upright in bed, her dressing gown in place, her hair combed, and her infant in her arms. "I'm ready for them," she said.

Edwin turned back to the staircase. "Children, you must be quiet, do you understand?"

"Yes, sir," came the answer.

"Very quietly and very slowly, you may come upstairs."

The girls came at once, barely containing their excitement, but doing their best to behave. Kenneth followed. As soon as the girls reached Hazel's bed, Kenneth elbowed his way to the front of the pack.

"She's mine," he said. "I prayed for her."

"Children," Hazel said, pulling the blanket away to reveal a small pink face and tiny hand, "meet Phyllis Marie."

4

"So, are you going to sit around moping?" Billy asked Perry as they sat alone together in their hut. "I haven't gotten a letter from Fran yet, either."

"Is that supposed to be some comfort? Besides, I'm not moping." Perry took a bite of a Hershey's bar from his rations.

"What are you doing, then?"

"Relaxing."

"Uh huh."

"We haven't got an airplane of our own yet."

"Is that what's eating you? I thought you missed Phyllis Marie. No, we haven't got an airplane, but we can fly one when we want, as long as we don't interrupt combat missions."

"I want to get into this thing," Perry said, ignoring Billy's comment. "I feel like a spectator." In truth, he missed Phyllis Marie terribly, as if a piece of him had been removed, and he could find no way to fill that void.

"Yeah," Billy drawled. "I hear that. Come on. Let's go over to the mess hall. There's a show there, some French fellow."

"Adolphe Menjou? He's not French. He's from Pittsburgh or Cleveland, I forget which. Didn't you see him in 'A Star Is Born?' 'Stage Door?' 'Golden Boy?' "

"No."

"Well, come on, then. We need to expand your horizons."

Perry and Billy attended the Red Cross show before dropping in on the Officers' Club.

"Now you recognize him, don't you?" Perry asked.

"Sure, I've seen him in lots of movies, only I didn't remember his name."

"Who's that?" a second lieutenant next to them at the bar asked.

"Adolphe Menjou," Billy said.

"Oh, that's right, he was here. I missed it. I just got back from escorting a mission."

"You fly fighters?" Perry asked.

"P-47 Thunderbolt. You?"

"Forts, only we haven't started yet."

"Oh, rookies, huh? Say, how'd you like to take me for a ride? I've been wanting to see what it's like."

"Yeah?" Perry grinned. "Maybe we could trade rides. I haven't seen the inside of a Thunderbolt yet."

"Sure. You get yourself a Fort and meet me on the flight deck tomorrow morning, say oh-eight hundred, after the mission tomorrow takes off."

The next day, Perry and the other officers signed out one of the spare B-17s and looked for the fighter pilot from the night before.

"There he is," Billy said. "Come on, fellas." He gestured toward Row's Rowdies, standing by waiting.

Perry took him up and Billy let him sit in the right-hand seat after the take-off.

"Man, this thing is big," he said. "I want one at home. I'd park it in my back yard!"

Once back on the ground, Perry asked, "Okay, where's your fighter?"

"Oh, sorry fellas," he said. "It's against regulations to take up a passenger that isn't rated for P-47s."

"What?" Billy said, in the loudest voice Perry had heard from him yet, though that was still not very loud.

"Sorry. That's the way it is."

"You knew that last night when we struck our bargain," Perry said, face flushed.

"Bye fellas."

Perry and Billy returned to the hut in an even fouler mood to find a full house. The other quartet of officers sat on their bunks chatting. One of them, obviously the pilot said, "Are you Row?"

"Yes, sir," Perry said, noting the man's rank as First Lieutenant.

"At ease. I'm Worthington. Maybe you've heard of me."

"Can't say that I have."

"Oh, well, you will." He grinned at his three officers. "I hear you got taken for a ride, or rather, didn't get taken for a ride, by a fighter pilot."

"I guess that's so."

"Well, he's not a fighter pilot at all. He's a ground crew man, and he plays that prank on all the rookie pilots. You've been had, old man."

Worthington's officers howled as Perry's ears turned crimson. Perry laughed, too, rather than look a complete fool, but Billy could see that his mood had not improved since yesterday, but rather, had reached a new low.

The next day, Perry and his full crew checked out another B-17 and reported for a practice bomb run. After gaining clearance from the tower to taxi, Perry began to wheel into position, but when he applied the brakes, nothing happened. The airplane kept on rolling beyond the taxi strip and the front nose gear sank two feet into the mud. The last time he saw it, several ground crews were trying to dig it out.

When Worthington returned from his mission and heard about it, he howled with laughter. "Hard cheese, old man," he said to Perry. "I say, we're having a little formation practice this afternoon. Would you and yours like to join us? Show us you really know how to fly B-17s? We keep a nice tight formation here in the three-ninetieth, and I'd like to know whether you can keep up."

Perry kept his voice even with an effort. "Give us the when and where and we'll be there."

"Good."

Meanwhile, Perry had done some asking around. George Joseph Worthington III had been a senior at Stanford when Pearl Harbor was attacked. He immediately quit school and enlisted as an aviation cadet, against the wishes of his father, a high official in the American Embassy to France, until the invasion of Paris in June of 1940. Worthington was among the original pilots of the three-ninetieth, which had arrived at

Framlingham in July. If he was a cocky son of a bitch, Perry decided, he had a right to be.

Worthington led the group formation of eighteen B-17s, three elements of six, spiraling to ten thousand feet, and flying north for four hours before returning to base. Perry flew left hind tit, the outside position of the low squadron, tucked in close, right where he belonged throughout the flight.

Back on the flight deck, Perry groaned silently when he saw Worthington walking toward him.

"Well done, old man." Worthington spoke quietly, giving Perry a quick pat on the back before walking away.

"Why does he call you that?" Billy asked. "He's no more than a year or two older than us, don't you think?"

Perry put his arm around his naïve co-pilot's shoulders and grinned. "He's just being ironic, old man."

Phyllis Marie's twenty-fourth birthday fell on the twelfth of September. To celebrate, Perry received a brand new Boeing B-17F Flying Fortress, wrapped like a birthday present, her two-tone fuselage in olive green above and drab gray below, sporting the newly modified national insignia—a white star and crossbar against a blue field—on both sides. On the tail, above her serial number—230713 in yellow, to match the rudder—she carried the three-ninetieth insignia, a black J against a white Square.

When Perry finally returned from admiring his new ship, he found four letters on his bunk—three from Phyllis Marie and one from the base commander. Because of his recent infractions, Lt. Row, Perry V. was hereby suspended for five days without pay. Perry wondered if the infractions stemmed from driving a B-17 into the mud or letting a ground crew man talk him into a joy ride. He decided not to ask and sat down on his bunk to read the letters from his wife.

5

"Good morning, good morning," Hazel sang as she and her sister Edna maneuvered Josephine's empty wheelchair down the steps toward the arriving car. "Everyone's here this morning!"

"I decided to come help, too," Elizabeth Hill answered. "I can wash the windows on the inside, or any other job thee wants me to do."

"Good morning, mother," Hazel said. "Blessings on thee. Good morning, George. Good morning, Josephine. Edwin and Arthur are just finishing breakfast."

The two older Stanton children, Virginia and Kenneth, and the Chilson daughters, Esther and Rachel came down the steps in a crash. "Good morning, Grandmother, Auntie, Uncle George!" they called as they ran past the car and down the road toward the next to the last day of the 1921 school year before summer vacation. "Goodbye, Mother!"

Edwin arrived just in time to help George lift Josephine out of the Model T and into the wheelchair. "Ready?" he asked. They had performed the task enough times that it had become second nature to them. As they placed her in the chair, a baby began to wail from inside the house.

"Did thee leave Phyllis Marie in her high chair?" Hazel asked, although she knew the answer. She wiped her hands on her apron and turned back toward the steps.

"Yes, she wasn't ready to get down."

The two men lifted the chair with Josephine in it, carried it up the steps, and onto the porch, as Elizabeth followed. "It feels like rain," she said.

Josephine wheeled herself through the living room into the dining room where Hazel lifted her youngest child out of her high chair, before starting to clean up the mess left from breakfast.

"Let me have her," Josephine said. Hazel complied with a

smile. "Go for a ride?"

The child grinned at the prospect of a ride in Auntie's wheelchair.

"What can I do?" Elizabeth asked.

"Where are the men?" Hazel looked out the window to see the three men already halfway to the granary.

"Edwin!" she called out the window. "Are you men coming back for lunch?"

"Yes," he shouted back and waved. "At three!"

The four women set to their appointed tasks. Hazel and Edna washed the windows on the outside of the house, working their way around the wrap-around porch, while their mother washed the windows on the inside. Josephine played with Phyllis Marie, giving her rides in her chair, reading stories, cuddling with her, and finally, holding her while she napped.

Next, they tackled the laundry, washing all the spare sheets for the expected guests, Alva and Gertrude, arriving Saturday by train from Boise, Idaho. Hazel arranged for her son, Kenneth to sleep on the divan in the living room, giving his room to his aunt and uncle. Virginia had already given up her room to the four Chilsons, on furlough again from Africa. By the time the women had thoroughly wrung out all the sheets and hung them on the lines, it was two o'clock. Hazel had one hour to prepare lunch for all the workers, eight men on this particular day.

"What can I do?" Elizabeth asked.

"Will thee slice the bread?" she answered. "I need to finish the stew."

After lunch, the men went back to the fields and the women moved the window-washing chore upstairs. Four hours of daylight remained.

Hazel took the outside, climbing out onto the roof and shutting each window behind her, while Edna and Elizabeth washed the inside surfaces. They moved from room to room, their work interrupted occasionally by the need to go downstairs and change Phyllis Marie, a task Josephine did not undertake, having no children of her own.

The following day, Hazel awoke to the sound of rain.

"My windows!"

"Don't worry," Edwin said, consolingly. "Alva won't notice."

"Won't notice? Dear heart, we worked for hours on those windows."

"I'm sorry. Yes you did, and they were beautiful."

The Outlands and Elizabeth Hill arrived again, as they had the previous day. The women cleaned every room in the house, dusting, sweeping, shaking out and straightening the antimacassar on Edwin's new Morris chair, laying out the good silver and china, and putting out the good dresser scarves from the cedar chest. The men spent the day checking the irrigation ditches and making sure the storm water diverted properly, moving from the upper fields to the lower, before draining off the property into the creek that eventually found its way to the Arkansas River.

At four o'clock, the rain increased. George decided it would be wise to get across the bridge to Fowler before darkness, so the three of them left without dinner. The Chilsons followed in their car. They planned to clean at the Outlands in the morning, before going to the train station in the afternoon to pick up Edwin's brother, Alva and his wife, Gertrude.

The heavy rain continued through the night and into Saturday morning. Hazel rose at her usual time, but she let her husband and the older children sleep. *The children will be disappointed,* she thought, *stuck in the house on the first Saturday of summer vacation, and Edwin cannot not make much progress outside in this storm.* She took Phyllis Marie from her crib and crept down the stairs.

"Good morning, little one," she whispered. "God's blessings on thee."

The pretty girl smiled and cooed at her mother. "Apoo," she said.

"Let us get thee in thy high chair first, shall we?" Hazel lowered the child down. "Does thee want some applesauce?"

She opened a new jar from the pantry, from a batch she had put up the previous fall.

"Apoo!"

Hazel loved the rain. She watched it falling as she fed her baby, one spoonful at a time. Peaceful mornings such as this one appealed to her sense of living in the here and the now, living for the moment. In this moment, there was only rain, heavy rain, and feeding her baby.

Hazel stoked the fire in the stove, ladled hot water from the big kettle into a pot, and started a batch of oatmeal. One by one, her sleepy-headed family appeared, first Virginia, then Edwin, and last, Kenneth.

"Aw, it's still raining." The boy had hoped to go down by the creek to look for his old frog friends from last summer, but he knew his mother wouldn't hear of it in this weather.

Suddenly the back door swung open with a bang against the wall. The neighbor from the east stood there in a yellow slicker and rubber boots.

"My clean floor!" Hazel said.

"Begging your pardon, Missus Stanton, Mister Stanton, the river's rising! Got to move your stock up!" He ran out as quickly as he arrived.

"What? How much time?" Edwin shouted out the back door at the retreating man's back, but if he heard the questions over the roar of the rain, he did not show it. Edwin threw on his own rain slicker and boots and ran out the door. Stopping at the barn for some tools, he ran as fast as he could in the mud to the far fence of the pasture.

"Children, sit down and eat," Hazel said, serving the oatmeal before it was ready. As she dished the cereal, she watched her husband in the distance as he started cutting the fence wires. "He's freeing the cows and horses," she said.

The back door swung open again; this time it was the son of the neighbor to the west. "Missus Stanton, can you drive your automobile?" he asked.

"Yes, why?"

"My Pa says we all got to get out of here, now."

Out in the field at that same moment, Edwin heard a sound, something louder than the steady pour of heavy rain. He stopped and turned toward it.

A fall of water two stories high broke over the levee bank behind the west house. It spilled into the field with a crash and widened left and right.

He dropped his tools.

He started to run—slog—through the mud toward the garage, his boots sticking in the ankle deep mud, slowing him to a crawl.

Hazel grabbed up the baby in one arm and as many rain slickers as she could carry in the other. "Come on, children," she said. "Right now!" She and the neighbor boy stepped out on the porch and froze for a moment as they watched the wall of water slam into the boy's house. His home crumpled into boards, becoming a part of the rolling wall.

"Where are thy parents?"

"They said they'd meet up on the road," he said.

"Good."

Edwin reached the garage first. He threw open the doors to each side, leapt into the driver's seat, and started the car. *If I still had the old car,* I'd be cranking for five minutes, *he thought.* He drove the car out, intending to drive to the front porch, but Hazel and the children arrived at that moment.

"Get in," he shouted, unnecessarily. No one hesitated. He pushed down hard on the pedal, but the back tires slipped and as the car pulled out of the garage, it drifted left almost ninety degrees.

"Too much mud for that," he said, and put the car in second gear.

"Go, Father!" Kenneth shouted, but Edwin took his time, made sure his tires had some traction, and then let the clutch out carefully. The tires grabbed.

"We must take this little hill slowly and cautiously, or we won't get out at all," he said. He rolled forward carefully, picking up speed. Hazel grabbed at the window frame. Kenneth and Virginia sat up in the back, watching their father maneuver through the mud. When the car reached fifteen miles an hour, Edwin pushed the pedal to the floor, and the car flew up the muddy embankment onto the main road.

"There's Ma and Pa," the boy called out. Edwin stopped cautiously, so as not to let the tires dig in.

"Come on," he said.

Now carrying eight people, he started ahead again judiciously, heading east on the road, but he turned in time to see the wall of water smash into his house. The water came at him from behind on the road, a wall over ten feet high, with timber floating in it—logs and lumber, furniture, boards that had been torn from houses, and animals—some of them swimming, some of them dead. The water slapped the back wheels of the car, pushing it off course as he accelerated away from it. Slowly, he regained control and pulled away from the danger. Everyone in the car sighed.

"We're not through it," Edwin said. "Where the road turns, we have to get there ahead of the water." He drove on as quickly as he dared.

"Stop!" Hazel shouted. Edwin passed another neighbor couple walking along the road. He stomped on the brakes, sliding in the mud. The couple ran to the car and crawled in.

As the road turned left, everyone in the car could see the wall of water running like a river beside the car.

"Faster," the west neighbor called out.

"Not too fast," said the east neighbor.

"Please," Edwin said, driving the only way that made any sense—away from the water and toward higher ground.

6

September 17, 1943,
Dear Phyllis Marie,

I was delighted to receive my first three letters from you, one from St. Louis and two from Wichita. I guess it takes a while for the Army to catch up. I am back on operational status now having served my suspension. Byrne and E (Bennett's new nickname) have already flown once with other crews, and Dix has gone twice. We have not flown a mission as a crew yet, although we were briefed and ready to go on our first, but it was called off. The food here is pretty poor. If not for our weekly rations, I think a lot of guys wouldn't get enough. I trade away my cigarettes (Camel, Lucky Strike and Chesterfield are the most common brands) to smokers for their chocolate bars and Life Savers, but I sure would like it if you would send me some of that candy I like. I keep thinking of the icebox at home, the steak Mother Hazel fixed for me when I came home in March, and the Swiss steak you and I had when we were home last summer. Maybe it isn't hunger, but just the emptiness I feel inside because you aren't near. We have been chopping wood and laying it in for winter. The hut we live in looks more like a woodshed than sleeping quarters. Bathing is a challenge. We take bicycles to the bathhouse a mile away, and there are only tubs, no showers. This reminds me, the government issued bicycles to all the pilots, so I sold mine to E. The government bike is a massive English-built thing. I was lucky and got a new one. Billy's is a little older and smaller and the tires go soft on him. I have noticed that all the airplane commanders are First Lieutenants, so I expect a promotion as soon as we fly. I'm running out of paper. Love, Perry

7

Thirteen-year-old Ped's favorite part of the bicycle ride out to Old Man Persons' field stretched for about four hundred yards, just after the road curved northwest and dropped about fifty feet, a significant elevation change in the northern plains of Oklahoma. The boy liked it even more when the wind came out of the northwest, blowing right into his face, which was almost always. Today, the winds were particularly strong. He didn't cut school that often, but this morning, when he saw the strong wind, he knew today would be a landmark day—a day he could not miss.

"Ladies and gentlemen, Lucky Lindbergh is taking off!" he shouted as he pedaled harder, stretching his arms out parallel to the ground, feeling the lift, wondering, as he had wondered so many times before, what it would feel like to fly.

It was a subtle pleasure, one he had tried to share with his school chums, but they didn't get it. They didn't feel the lift, they couldn't stretch their imaginations far enough to see that with just a little more thrust, ten to twenty times more, perhaps, and with improvements making their arms into wings to reduce drag, they could fly, too.

The ride ended too quickly, as usual, at the bottom of the closest thing to a hill on this side of Ponca City. Ped knew of some other routes around town with elevation changes, but none of them had the right wind conditions, or they didn't have the right directional. This one suited him best, plus it had the added benefit of being on the way to Old Man Persons' field.

The old man shared Ped's interest in flight. Persons owned four model aeroplanes, one of which—his new Cleveland one-sixteenth scale SF-1 rubber-powered Great Lakes 2T-1 Sport Trainer—appeared ready for its maiden voyage. Ped had watched the Old Man put it together in his shop over a period of only two weeks, much faster than his previous model aeroplanes, because this kit offered something new for 1931, an all-balsawood construction instead of the heavier pine and bamboo kits of the past. The design called for glue instead of nails and thread-wrapped joints.

Ped left the road and headed west across the south end of Old Man Persons' field to where he saw the man hunched over his new model.

"Hey, boy," he said, "you're just in time for some tests."

"Can I see it?"

Persons held up the 2T-1 for Ped's inspection. "What do you think?"

Ped regarded it with his hazel eyes wide. "You got it all done?"

"Yep. It's ready for some engine tests." The old man's brown eyes were still clear and piercing, his expression determined.

"Why don't you just wind it up and launch it?"

"Well, I'll tell you, Ped, I could do that, and we might see a glorious flight indeed, but there could also be a weakness in the rubber bands. If one of them snapped in midair and the craft plummeted to a tragic crash, we'd regret it."

The boy nodded in understanding. "So, we should test them first."

"Right. Here goes. I'll wind the propeller ten times. You count, and then we'll let the propellers wind down." Though he had only wisps of hair remaining, one strand kept falling into his eyes. The old man bushed it away with his surprisingly agile hand.

Persons wound and Ped counted ten revolutions. When the man released the propeller, it spun with a smooth whirring sound before it stopped.

"Okay, that sounded good. This time, count to twenty."

They continued to test in increments of ten until they reached two hundred. When Persons released the propeller with his right hand, he could barely hold on to the aeroplane with his left. "I think we're ready, don't you?"

"Yes, sir." Ped could barely contain his excitement.

The old man wound the rubber bands again, twirling the propeller with his finger. He set the model down on the hard prairie ground he had prepared for flight by removing the tumbleweeds and raking it flat. The aeroplane faced into the wind. "Are you ready?" he called.

"Yes." Ped held his breath.

The old man held the aeroplane down with an index finger of his left hand, held the propeller in check with the index finger of his right hand, and then, after a moment, he let go. The 2T-1 rolled quickly down the runway and jumped into the air with a suddenness that made Ped shout. It rose straight and steady to a height of about 25 feet above the ground before starting its descent. It flew a distance of 180 feet before settling into a perfect landing and staying up on its wheels.

"Wow!"

"Go get her, boy."

Ped leaped onto his bicycle and rode quickly to the landing site, scooped up the 2T-1, and rode it back. The pair continued to fly the model until late afternoon.

That evening, as Ped turned down his street, he saw that, dimly lit by the flattening sun on the Oklahoma horizon, his father's car stood accusingly in the driveway. Ped leaped off the bicycle and into the house in one motion.

"Perry Vancil," his father, Clifton, said.

"Yes, Papa." It was worse than he thought. The entire family sat at the table waiting for him.

"Wash your hands and come to dinner immediately."

"Yes, Papa." He ran to the bathroom and washed as quickly as he could, his hands filthy with the dust of Old Man Persons' model air field. He dried quickly and ran to the table. As soon as he planted his seat in the chair, he and the rest of his family bowed their heads in silent prayer. The several seconds passed too quickly. More silence followed as his mother, Georgia, picked up a platter of meatloaf and passed it to her husband. His older sister, Lois, a young woman of fourteen, already working at a department store in downtown Ponca City, picked up a bowl of mashed potatoes and helped herself to a spoonful before passing it to her younger sister. Helen, the baby of the family at eight, was the only person who dared look Perry in the eye. He knew he was in serious trouble.

The platters and bowls cycled around to their original resting places before finally, his father spoke.

"Perry, tell me about your day."

Does he already know I cut school, Perry wondered? *If he does, I'd better just fess up.* He looked into his father's stern face for a clue, but Clifton kept his eyes on his plate. A quick glance at his mother told him what he needed to know. He could always read what was in her mind.

"I went out to Old Man Persons' field and helped him test his new aeroplane model," he said.

There was no reaction from his parents at first, but Lois clucked her tongue involuntarily, and Helen rolled her eyes at him.

His father took a bite of meat, chewing it carefully and swallowing it before responding. "And what about school?"

"I didn't go."

His mother looked up at him. "Oh, Ped, honey," she said.

"I'm sorry, Mom. I knew Old Man Persons would be flying today when I saw the wind, and I—"

"And—" his father interrupted, "you chose to ignore your responsibilities and play hooky."

"I—yes, Papa."

Clifton lifted a bite of potatoes, but rather than put it in his mouth, he dangled it on the end of his fork and waggled it in Perry's general direction. "Young man, I work hard to put food on our table, do you realize that?"

"Yes, Papa."

"I do it so you and your sisters can go to school, get an education, not so you can go out and play."

"Yes, Papa."

"I appreciate your honesty when I asked what you had done, Perry. Perhaps you considered the fact that I had probably already had a conversation about it with your school. Nevertheless, I appreciate that you didn't lie to me."

Perry did not say anything. He sat with his hands folded in his lap.

"I want you to go to your room and think about what your punishment should be," Clifton said. "I'll be in after dinner, before bedtime."

Perry didn't move.

"Go on."

Perry left the table, his face burning with the tears he refused to cry. He walked—did not run—to his room and shut the door. He sat at his desk for a minute, wondering if his father would spank him or ground him, or both. After a minute he pulled out his scrapbook of aeroplane pictures he had clipped from magazines, and found a picture of the Great Lakes 2T-1 Sport Trainer.

8

The door banged against the wall, awakening Perry.

"Lieutenants Connors, Poythress, Worthington, and Row! Breakfast at oh two hundred! Briefing at oh three hundred!"

The lights in the hut snapped on and the voice slammed the door on its way out. Perry looked at his watch and saw that he had five minutes to get to the mess hall. Worthington already had his boots on.

"Come on, rookies, I'm your babysitter today," Worthington announced.

Perry dressed quickly and pushed open the door. A brace of wet English fog slapped him in the face as he turned toward the mess hall, Worthington and his co-pilot on one side of him and Billy on the other.

"Fresh eggs!" Worthington said, picking up a tray. "Learn to eat them before a mission, even though you can't imagine it right now."

Perry and Billy followed Worthington's advice and took two each when they were offered. The four men sat together eating, except Billy, who only drank his coffee.

"You'll regret that," Worthington said.

"I'll regret eating those eggs," Billy replied.

"Come on, Billy," Perry urged his co-pilot. "The man's had a dozen missions ahead of us. Do what he says."

Billy ate the eggs, despite wanting nothing to do with them, and stared when Worthington went back for seconds.

Bud and Boettcher came in half an hour later, skipped the eggs, and poured coffee for themselves. Perry didn't let them sit down.

"No, you'll have the eggs."

"Whatever you say, Captain," Bud said, returning to the counter.

Boettcher just stared at Perry.

"Get some for Boettcher, too."

"Okay."

At the Briefing Hall, Perry and his officers sat together, a row behind Worthington and his officers. On stage, a large black curtain hid what Perry knew to be a map of today's mission. The room filled up quickly before the base commander entered and walked the length of the center aisle and up the short staircase. Perry and a few other rookies started to stand at attention, but none of the veterans did, so he sat back down.

"Gentlemen, I know we haven't been up in a week, due to bad weather, so just to keep you in shape, today we've got a little milk run for you."

An assistant pulled back the curtain to reveal the target on the west coast of France, the airfield at Vannes-Meucon.

"Twenty-one airplanes, carrying two-hundred-fifty-two five-hundred pound general purpose bombs are going to neutralize this airfield, and by that I mean bomb the hell out of the runways so the enemy cannot land or take off. Also take out the storage areas located here," he pointed to the western edge of the airfield, "and get back safely. Any questions? Good."

Worthington turned around. "Everything clear?" he asked Perry.

"Fine," he said.

"Let's get out there."

After take-off, Perry spiraled up to his assigned position and waited for the group leader to give the signal. He felt as cool as ice, no worries or concerns whatsoever. As soon as the group formation departed, Perry took his place at the bottom of the low squadron and proceeded to fly in formation as he had been trained.

He reached into his bag and brought out the plastic doll Phyllis Marie had given him in Redmond. He found an inconspicuous place for it above his head and clipped it to the bulkhead.

"Well who's that?" Billy asked.

"Mickey," Perry said. "Our first son."

"You don't have children."

"We will."

Billy nodded.

An hour and a half later, after flying into the bomb run, he turned control of Phyllis Marie over to Bud, his bombardier, and sat back, watching, listening, and waiting.

"Bombs away," Bud stated rather matter-of-factly over the interphone as Perry and the rest of the Phyllis Marie crew felt the upsurge due to the sudden loss of three tons.

"Let's go home," Perry said, taking back control. He banked the airplane, following the course set for him by his group formation leader, maintaining position. *Easy does it,* he thought.

Suddenly, small bursts of black smoke appeared with red flashes ahead.

"Flak." Perry spoke into the interphone. He knew to just keep flying, that to attempt avoiding flak meant wasting fuel—or worse—flying right into a different burst than the one you were trying to miss. Still, he wished they were higher. As if in answer to his wish, the group formation began to climb.

Flak—*Fliegerabwehrkanone*—the 'flight defense cannons' of Germany, quickly became the American and British bomber crews' worst nightmares, since there was nothing anyone could do about them. Radar-directed, the heavy Flak shells exploded with little warning at pre-set altitudes.

Then a horrible sound, like muffled ripping, reverberated through Phyllis Marie.

"We're hit!" Perry recognized his Engineer's voice.

"How bad?"

A long silence followed.

"I repeat, how bad?"

"I don't actually see any damage, except some holes in the fuselage deck near the waist gunners, over."

"Injuries?"

"Negative."

"Keep your eyes open."

"Yes, sir."

Perry circled over the English countryside, awaiting his turn to enter the approach pattern and land at Framlingham. After landing, he taxied back to Phyllis Marie's technical site.

His face fell when he saw the ground crew chief, Sergeant Harold Blumberg, standing below, waiting for Perry to drop out of the front hatch. Blimp, as he was called, had already established a close working relationship with the green pilot in the week since the arrival of Phyllis Marie and this, her maiden voyage. The sergeant appreciated the fact that Perry spent so much time inspecting the airplane.

"You won't have time for this on combat mornings, you know, sir," he had said, "no matter what they taught you stateside. You're going to have to trust me to do it, and you can, sir."

As soon as Perry's feet hit the concrete, Blimp saluted and simultaneously started in on him. "Excuse me, sir, but what the hell did you do to my airplane?"

"Your airplane?"

"You didn't think it was yours, did you? It may be named after your grandmother or girlfriend, but—"

"Wife."

"Whatever, but this is my airplane, and I'm not happy to see these flak holes in it."

"No, I wasn't happy to get them, either. Is there any serious damage, Blimp? We couldn't find any."

"I don't think so. So far, I've found seven holes in the fuselage deck, but I'll let you know. I brought the paint, by the way."

"Paint?"

"It's a tradition here, that after your maiden voyage, you name the airplane—I know, Phyllis Marie—and we paint the nose art. What do you say?"

9

As the water rose, flooding a third of the width of the road, Edwin Stanton skimmed through, gently drifting the car away from the water, preventing it from slipping sideways. Water splashed up and into the car, soaking him and all of his passengers. The wall of water banged at the back tires again, one last insult, before the road turned right, away from the torrent, and the car climbed onto higher ground.

Edwin pulled the car over to the side of the road. The Stantons turned to see their horses and cows floating down over the fields with just their heads above water. Behind them, the flood continued to pour over the large levee like a waterfall, into the fields of the farms below.

The west house was gone, as was the east house. The Stantons' house listed to one side, then turned and rotated with an awful groan, pinned like a butterfly to the ground by its chimney. It continued to turn, back and forth, until the family heard a loud crack. The granary tower slowly toppled into the house with a crash and the house stopped turning.

"What are we to do?" Hazel asked.

Edwin put an arm around her. "There is an old shack up this way on high ground. Let us go up and have a look."

She smiled.

Putting the car in gear, he moved forward, turning off the main road onto a tractor path. After a few minutes, they arrived at the shack.

"I've been here before," Kenneth said, "last summer, when we were branding."

"Hazel, if thee would get everyone inside, I shall look around and see how bad it is."

Edwin took Kenneth with him and surveyed the surrounding area. They could see in all directions, and all they could see was water. They stood on an island in the middle of what appeared to be a new lake.

"I have a job for thee, son," Edwin said.

"Yes, Father?"

"Take all the rain slickers and some rope from the car. Tie up the sleeves and tie the slickers up between the tree and the porch to catch the rainwater. We are going to need it."

The heavy rain continued. In the afternoon, some of the livestock arrived, the horses and three of the cows, exhausted, in search of higher ground. Edwin tied them to the porch near one of the rain slickers of fresh water.

Hazel came outside to look around and found Edwin watching the surrounding water.

"It seems strange," she said, "to see buildings floating in flood waters."

"I think that is our chicken house over there," he said.

"They look like wood chips."

The shack contained exactly three pieces of furniture: one table, one bed and one chair. Thanks to the rain slickers, the refugees could drink fresh water, but there was no food. A cord of dry firewood stood next to the stove, but no one brought matches and they found none. They spent a miserable night, made more so because, in their haste to evacuate, they had brought no diapers for the baby.

By Sunday morning, the thundering waterfall had melted into a trickle, but the water stood high all around them. The rain continued lightly. There was nothing to do except milk the cows, providing some nourishment at least. The group waited and watched, hoping for a sign that the waters were starting to recede.

On Monday morning, they awoke to see that the water level had dropped.

"I think we may be able to make it back down to the house," he said, "but there won't be any fresh water."

"There are jars in the pantry and pans under the sink," Hazel said. "We can take some with us."

"I would suggest thee and the other women stay here with the children. The men shall go on a scouting expedition."

Edwin drove the car carefully, noting the high water mark

as they descended. "Had we waited any longer, we would have been caught in it." He dropped the men off near the ruins that had been their houses, arranging that he would return for them, before driving to his own.

The house still stood, or so it appeared from a distance. Edwin drove in and parked. Before leaving the car, he could see that when the granary collapsed, it had knocked the house off its foundation by more than a foot, tearing out the front porch and the west wall of the living room. When he walked in, he saw that the south side of the house, including the kitchen and back sleeping porch, had come apart from the rest of the house, except for a single two-by-four above what had been the upstairs. Water had stood above the floor of the second story throughout the house. Two feet of mud stood in some parts now. The fireplace, which had valiantly held the house together during the crisis, had since collapsed into a pile of bricks. In each room, or what was left of them, all the furniture stood in a jumble against one wall. The cedar chest, Edwin's wedding gift to Hazel, had been swept completely out of the house with all its contents. A sinkhole had sucked away part of the floor, and with it, the beds and mattresses. When the house re-settled, it had sucked yesterday morning's breakfast tablecloth under a wall, so the tablecloth stuck out on both sides, indoors and outdoors. Edwin's Morris chair stood upside down, covered in mud, in the garden.

Mother Hill will be worried, Hazel had said. Edwin had not pointed out to her that the Hills could have been flooded as badly or worse than they were, and he tried to call them on the telephone, which did not work. He searched the cabinet above the stove and found dry matches. Another search revealed some dry towels and clothes in a closet upstairs, including several diapers.

Outside, Edwin could barely walk without his feet coming out of his rubber boots, leaving the boots behind in the deep mud. He found some of Hazel's table linens wrapped around the windmill and stuffed them in his boots around his feet. Dead animals littered the entire area, including most of his prize-winning pigs. He counted fourteen. The unpleasant stench of death began to rise in his consciousness. This will need attention immediately, he thought, but it will have to wait until tomorrow. One lone hen wandered about, scratching at the mud. Edwin caught it and put it in the trunk of the car.

He drove back up to the muddy road. Both men waited for him there.

"Were you able to salvage anything?" one man asked.

"Matches, diapers, and a chicken," he said. "We've got to bury those animals tomorrow. Did you find many at your places?"

"Everywhere you look," the man from the east house answered.

"My place is nothing but mud," the other man said, "and there's a lake now by the levee, where my sorghum crop used to be."

"What does thee mean, a lake?"

"Just what I said. I don't know exactly how deep it is, but I'm guessing the surface is about four feet above the level of my fields."

The group spent their second day in the shack in less discomfort. Hazel lit a fire and washed the four children—her own and the neighbor boy—using hot water and rags, before passing out dry clothes. The other two women wrung the chicken's neck, and then plucked and dressed the bird. After Hazel bathed and changed, the men took their turns, and then Hazel took over cooking the bird while the other women bathed and changed. The mood lightened, despite the fact that one chicken did not go very far among nine people. Thanks to the cow, they could drink their fill of milk.

On Tuesday, the three men, along with Kenneth and the neighbor's boy, and the Outland farm hands who came to see how bad it was, spent the entire day burying the dead livestock on the Outland property and the farm to the east. While they were away, a car arrived at the shack, neighbors whose homes had been spared. They went away with a list of the things Hazel and the other women said they needed, and came back four hours later with double the requested amounts of everything, including another bed and mattress. For the first time since the flood, Hazel put her face in her hands and wept, overcome by the generosity and kindness of strangers.

On Wednesday, all the Stantons returned to what had been their home. The farm hands turned out in force. They all stood together in a group, surveying the damaged house. Edwin said, "Had it come in the night—"

"We would not have lived," Hazel finished his sentence.

"You're lucky to be alive," an older hand said. "The whole town of Pueblo was flooded under sixty feet."

"Sixty feet?" Edwin took off his hat and turned to look at the man.

"Yes, sir. They say more than seventy died. The lower part of the city is still under water. All the buildings there are gone. I heard one fellow say the damage was going to be in the millions. The army came yesterday. They already built a hospital on the high side. They're calling it the worst flood in the history of the state."

"What about Fowler?"

"I don't know," the older hand said.

"It's safe," someone called out. "The bridge is out, though. We can't get there yet, except by boat."

"Missus Stanton," one of the younger farm hands asked, "is there anything in particular you want us to look for?"

She hesitated, glancing at Edwin. "The flood happened so early."

Edwin looked at his wife. "If thee has something in mind, let the man know."

"There are two things," she said. "One is a cedar chest. It stands about knee high."

"That shouldn't be too hard to find." Edwin smiled at the young farm hand.

"The other is very small. It's ridiculous even to consider it."

"Her engagement ring," Edwin said.

"Yes." She smiled. "It was in my purse. How did thee know?"

"Thee was pulling so hard on thy finger I feared it would come away from thy hand."

The farm hands all laughed. "Missus, if I can find it, I will," the youngest said.

Edwin's largest sow returned, wheezing and coughing, looking for the entire world as if it had a very bad cold. The animal felt hot to the touch. Edwin made a dry place for it in what had been the barn. It wheezed and struggled for breath for another day before dying of pneumonia.

Meteorologists who studied the event reported that the flood was the result of a general rain system in the Upper Arkansas River Basin, and though there had been a great amount of rain, it was no greater than many other storms. An investigation into what came to be known as the Pueblo Flood revealed the true cause of the flood. The previous year, the Colorado State General Assembly had created the State Highway Department in response to the rapidly growing number of cars. Their construction of concrete highways on many of the well-traveled routes, without proper regard for drainage, had caused the destruction.

In the late summer light, two farm hands carried the waterlogged cedar chest up from the fields where they had found it. George Outland and Arthur Chilson arrived in George's car with word that the bridge to Fowler was open. The youngest farm hand came up behind Hazel and tapped her on the shoulder. She turned to look at his smiling face before looking down into his outstretched muddy hand. He held her purse, filled to the brim with mud. She dug into it, sifting the contents with her fingers, until she found her engagement ring.

10

While Blimp Blumberg painted the nose art—"Phyllis Marie," in a tall thin yellow script on the right side—Perry painted "Row's Rowdies," under the pilot's side window and Sergeant Kiss painted the words, "A Kiss in the Ass," obscenely encircling the tail gun. As if in mute approval, when he was finished with his primary task, Blimp painted "Crew Chief Sgt. Blumberg," in small white letters on the left side of the nose, followed by six little torpedoes.

"One for each ton of armaments you drop," he explained.

"It looks mighty fine," Billy drawled.

"It won't always be this easy," Blimp said, turning on the ladder and addressing the entire crew. "You weren't here for Regensberg."

"What happened at Regensberg?" Perry asked.

"We lost four planes in that one, plus a couple that had to ditch in the Mediterranean. It was only our third mission, and we sent twenty planes. The idea was to take out their Messerschmitt factory, which we did, and then fly on over to Telergma in Algeria. The only time we've tried that. We got 'em good, killing thirteen confirmed enemy aircraft, maybe three more, but they got us, too."

"One of those four was yours?"

"Yeah," Blimp said, "lost over the target area."

"Sorry to hear it."

"Yeah, well they dropped their bombs first, though. Listen hard, you guys, uh, sirs. You make it past five missions and you gain enough experience to get out of this thing in one piece, so, next time you go up, you take care of my airplane and get back here safe."

"Yes, sir," Perry said, putting a hand on Blimp's shoulder.

Blimp saluted quickly. "I'm sorry, sir."

"Nothing to apologize for," Perry assured him.

Two days passed without a combat assignment. On the third day, Perry and Billy rode their bicycles to mail call and received letters from their wives.

"Phyllis Marie writes that Nancy Davidson is pregnant," Perry said.

"Does she say where Everett ended up?"

"No." Perry cast his gaze far across the field. "Tomorrow's Sunday?"

"Yes."

"Want to go to church with me, if we don't get called out, I mean?"

"Sure," Billy said, without looking up from his letter.

Perry took a V-mail form from the box and wrote a quick note: 'Everett and Nancy have done in less than three months what we couldn't do in three years. Well, when I get back, I'll try to remedy that situation, darling (with your consent, of course).'

Perry and his officers received their expected promotions, along with the other rookie officers for whom Vannes-Meucon represented their first mission. That night at the hut Worthington approached Perry with his hand out.

"Nice going, old man," he said, shaking Perry's hand. "We'll make a first rate flyer out of you yet."

"Thanks," Perry said. "Can I ask you a question?" The shadow from Worthington's dim reading light cast an eerie image on the corrugated half-barrel roof of the Nissen hut.

"Anything."

"What happened over Regensberg?"

"You've heard about that, have you?"

"Just from my ground crew chief. He wasn't there."

"No." Worthington's eyes darkened and he frowned. "I wish I hadn't been. I lost some friends there." Without appearing to be aware of it, he pulled up a bare wooden chair and sat down backwards, arms folded across the backrest.

"How was it?"

"The funny thing is, it was no different from the milk run we took the other day. They've got us so well trained that we just put our butts in the seats and do what we're supposed to do when we're supposed to do it." He stared past Perry into his memories. "When it's all over, then there's time to remember feeling the heat from an explosion next to you, watching a plane go down, realizing whose plane it is, counting the chutes, not seeing enough—you can feel the heat right through the glass, you know that? That's what I remember being different, the heat, right through the glass."

After a moment, he stood and turned away, shutting off his light by his bunk. Perry undressed in the dark, climbed into his sack and slept.

The door banged against the wall, awakening Perry.

"Lieutenants Poythress, Connors, Worthington, and Row! Breakfast at oh two hundred! Briefing at oh three hundred!"

The lights in the hut snapped on and the voice slammed the door on its way out. Perry looked his watch and saw that he had five minutes to get to the mess hall. Worthington already had his boots on.

11

When the crew completed five missions, the brass gave them a three-day pass along with their Air Medals. Of course, Dix already had his because of the missions he had flown while Perry served his suspension, a fact he gloated over in jest. The truth was, Row's Rowdies, also known as Crew Seven, had become an early standout among the rookie crews, the earliest to complete five missions, and without serious injury or damage to the Phyllis Marie. Rumors began to circulate about lucky Crew Seven, how they led a charmed life under the protection of the airplane with the unique name, the pilot's wife's name.

As far as Perry was concerned, they were lucky all right, but not because of any superstition. They had simply drawn the milk run assignments. With the exception of the Citroen factory at Paris, where they couldn't drop their payloads because of weather, they had flown to their destinations, dropped their bombs and come home without incident.

Oh, sure, he casually wrote to Phyllis Marie in a letter, they had finally seen enemy aircraft, and Kiss had even shot one down over their second raid on Emden, although it wasn't confirmed, but the job was taking on such predictability that when the three-ninetieth dropped over five tons of incendiaries on a tire factory in Hanau, Perry entered in his diary only that they had crossed over five European countries in a single day.

"So, what shall we do with our three-day passes?" Billy asked.

"We're going to London," Perry said. "Worthington says the Princess Garden Club is the place to stay when you're trying to save and send money home."

"Do we need reservations?"

"I took care of it, along with train tickets."

They arrived in London and transferred directly to the

underground, but when they climbed the stairs out of the
station, the fog was so thick they could not see their own
feet. They heard a strange clicking sound, which turned out
to be the heels of the Londoners' shoes.

"It's the rubber shortage," Perry said. "They've all switched
to hard leather."

"Amazing," Billy said, "but I'm starved. Let's get some
food, preferably meat."

"That's a fine idea," Perry said, turning and pushing Billy
through the near doorway of the Little Vienna Café.

"Yes, gentlemen, two for lunch? I recommend the
hamburger steaks, a favorite of our American flying friends,
and two pints?"

"Fine," Perry said, understanding only every other word
of the waiter's thick British accent.

"Did you just order?" Billy asked.

"I think so." Perry sloughed off his overcoat, intending to
leave it on the chair behind him, but another waiter took it
with Billy's and hung them by the door.

The pints of beer arrived immediately and Billy took a
long sip before sitting back and looking around the place.
"Will you look at that?" he asked.

"What?"

"There is just about every kind in here."

Perry looked around and realized Billy meant nationalities,
represented by their military uniforms and civilian dress.

"Lots of Brits, of course," Billy continued, "and every
kind of American, but also Indians, American Indians, Latins,
Russians, Chinese, Irish, Negroes, Poles, Belgians, French,
Norwegians, Greeks, Arabians—"

"I've never seen such a—I don't what to call it," Perry
said.

"An array?"

"A cosmopolitan populace."

Billy laughed. "That's one way to say it."

"London is a big place, or so I've heard. Can't say I've
seen any of it yet, other than this place, but I guess there's

room for all kinds."

The food arrived and Perry dug in for a big forkful of hamburger steak. He looked at Billy and saw the same disappointment in his face that he felt on his own. "This is about three quarters bread," he said.

"Next time, let's order something whole," Billy said.

"At least the beer is good."

"It's warm."

"Well, yes," Perry agreed. "I heard they drink it this way."

"Do they serve the wine hot?"

Perry laughed at the thought. "We may be complaining, but we're not at the mess hall."

"True."

"Come on," Perry said. "Let's finish up and go find a place called Selfridges & Co. I want to get some things for Phyllis Marie."

After a long cab ride and a short explanation from a clerk at Selfridges—that without clothing rations, Perry could not buy a thing—the two men found their hotel and fell into their beds.

The following day, after buying two bottles of Canadian Club Whisky—"Let's get these for the crew for Christmas," they agreed—and a bottle of 1928 French Champagne for Phyllis Marie, they attended a movie theatre and watched "Heaven Can Wait," with Gene Tierney and Don Ameche, and then dropped in on the Paramount Dome Hall with its high round ceiling and broad hardwood dance floor, three times the size of a basketball court. A dance band played at one end while several bartenders served drinks at the long zinc bar at the opposite end.

"Have you ever seen anything like it?" Billy asked, watching the frenetic dancers.

"That's the jitterbug," Perry said. "I think it started in Harlem."

"I've seen the jitterbug before, but not like this!"

"Like what?"

"All these big burly blacks dancing with blond English girls, and English men dancing with black girls."

"I guess you'd better get used to it, Billy. That's the cosmopolitan populace at work again."

Billy smiled as he watched. "Oh, I don't mind it, I've just never seen it. All my life, the Negro population has been kept apart. I never understood it—well, I mean, I understood it, but, I didn't think it was right—so to see them mixing so easily here, it's shocking."

"Isn't that part of what this war is all about, Hitler's treatment of the Jews in Europe? I wonder what Hitler thinks of the Negro race?"

On their third and last day, after a walking tour of bomb-damaged London in bright sunlight, Perry and Billy found their way back to the appropriate station and caught the train to Ipswich.

12

After dinner Clifton sat in his big chair in the living room with the radio on, a letter in his hands from his oldest daughter, Corliss, who lived in California. He did not listen to the radio and did not read the letter. His mind wandered. His thirteen-year-old son deserved some sort of punishment for cutting school and flying model aeroplanes with Old Man Persons, but Clifton struggled with what his correct response should be. His mind wandered further, to his job with Jett & Wood Mercantile. Although his original position with the company as the head of the one-man print shop had been a satisfying one, it had not lasted. The decision had been made, without consulting him, to close the print shop after The Great War, and Clifton had been—*what was the word Mr. Pratt had used?* Clifton had been promoted, yes, promoted to the sales staff. It became his responsibility to keep a wider and wider range of southern Kansas and northern Oklahoma customers supplied with the goods they sold. The travel seemed glamorous, at first, as he always needed a good car, and he replaced his cars frequently, but that aspect paled quickly.

The truth was, he had become a traveling salesman for the company, and he had become dependent on the income from an unfulfilling job.

Clifton remembered the day in 1930 when Mr. Pratt asked him into his office.

"Mr. Row," Pratt said, "big things are happening in your territory, in Ponca City, do you know that?"

"Yes, sir, I do," Clifton answered. "There is a new oil rig gone in."

"Not just a new rig, man. The Three Sands Field produced more than 33 million barrels of high gravity crude oil last year alone."

"Yes, sir."

"We need a man to go down there, re-locate right where

the boom town is forming, if we want to capitalize on the situation."

"What is it you want me to do?"

"Get down there, man! Ponca City! Open an office there, and start sending in some orders!"

"Who is going to take the Wichita territory?"

"We're not asking you to give up Wichita, Mr. Row, we're asking you to keep your Wichita route, but manage it from Ponca City. There is money to be made there. Come on, man, let's get cracking!"

"Yes, sir."

And so the Rows had moved away from Wichita, away from family, friends, and church, to Ponca City, where the oil barons were building their mansions in the dust, gargantuan confluences of Spanish revival and art deco architecture, where hotels and restaurants sprang up overnight and needed every kind of supplies, where the Roaring Twenties nightclubs poured the new jazz and the bootleg champagne into people's glasses as fast as the oil companies poured the crude oil onto the red hardpan clay, where Clifton drove more dusty miles and wrote more orders for goods than he had ever imagined possible, all on a middling income, supplemented only by the smallest commission schedule. Clifton longed for the creative process, the fun he had as a poet, a printer, and a publisher, but it was not to be.

He rose from his living room chair and went to his son's room. Opening the door, he found the boy asleep on the bed, still in his clothes, with his aeroplane scrapbook across his chest. Clifton pulled the book from his sleeping child's hands without waking him and looked at the pictures for a few minutes. Finally, he knew what he had to do.

"Perry," he said. He shook the boy gently until his eyes widened. "Come on, son, you need to get into your pajamas."

The boy changed quickly and climbed in between the covers his father held for him. Clifton tucked him in and sat on the edge of the bed.

"Is there anything you enjoy more than aeroplanes?" he asked.

"No, not really."

Clifton smiled. "It's good to have something you really care about."

Perry sat up and gazed into his father's melancholy face, remembering that there was still a punishment to be announced.

"Of course, you have to keep your grades up if you ever hope to actually fly an aeroplane, you know. They don't let people that cut school fly."

The boy looked at him, imagining that he had caused the sadness he saw. "I'm sorry," he said.

Clifton stood up. "Get some sleep. You need to go to school tomorrow and find out everything you missed today. Come straight home and spend the afternoon catching up on your schoolwork."

"Yes, Papa."

Clifton walked to the door. "Good night."

"Good night, Papa." Perry was left staring after him, confused and full of guilt, but, at the same time, strangely relieved.

The following summer, on Clifton's next extended trip to Wichita, he loaded up the new 1933 Ford four-door and took his family with him. They rolled into Ernest and Lena Crow's driveway three hours later. The two boys, Jim and Ernie, and their neighbor friend, Toots, ran up to the car and jumped on the running boards before Clifton brought the car to a complete stop, sending Georgia into gales of laughter. "Oh, you boys! Get off there," she laughed and slapped at their hands.

As soon as they could, the three boys absconded with Perry, so they could show him Jim's new mechanical toy fire truck.

"Here it is," Jim said, leading the parade onto the porch.

"Let me see," Perry said, reaching for it.

"Wait, look how it runs."

"How does it work? That's what I want to know."

"Like this," Jim said, as he revved up the spring inside and then let it fly across the porch.

"No, I mean how does it work?" Perry ran and picked it up and saw that there were four Phillips screws on the bottom. He pulled his screwdriver out of his pocket, and before Jim, Ernie, or Toots could stop him, he removed the chassis from the frame.

"Hey!" Jim protested, but it did him no good. Perry started to pry the rear axle away from the frame when something popped.

"Oops," Perry said.

"What do you mean, 'Oops?' "

"I think I broke it."

"Well, fix it, Mr. Mechanical Genius!"

"No, I can't. I broke the metal piece that holds this assembly in place, see?" Perry held the broken toy out for Jim's inspection, as if that would make it all right.

Tears welled up in Jim's eyes. "I only had that for two days!"

"Yeah, I can see that it wasn't built very well."

"Hey, what's the big idea?" Toots, who had passively watched up to this point, reached out and slapped the back of Perry's head. Perry turned and pushed him. Suddenly the two boys erupted into a full-blown scuffle, each of them throwing punches at the other. The Crows' dog appeared out of nowhere and attached her jaws to Perry's backside. If Jim hadn't been upset already about his fire truck, he would have thought that was pretty funny, seeing that the dog usually bit Toots when he was beating up on Jim or Ernie, but here and now the dog was protecting the more familiar Toots.

"Here," Clifton said, striding up the porch steps. "What's the meaning of this?" Ernest followed a step behind and pulled the dog off Perry at the same time Clifton pulled Perry off Toots.

"He broke my fire truck!" Jim cried.

"Why did you do that, Toots?" Ernest asked.

"Not him," Jim protested, and then, pointing at his cousin, shouted, "him!"

It was not the last time Perry got in trouble for trying to see how things worked.

In 1934, Clifton noticed that orders for Jett & Wood declined. When he delivered some goods to the opulent homes on Grand Avenue, he inquired from the cooks and servants why their orders were so reduced.

"Why, Mr. Row, haven't you heard?" Lulu Belle Montague, a large black woman, cook and head of the servant staff for one of the richer mansions finally told him what he wanted to know.

"Heard what, Miss Lulu Belle?"

"The Three Sands Field, Mr. Row."

"What about it?"

"It's gone bust. Folks say they've been drilling again, hoping to find more, but it's been two weeks now and the thing is as dry as the sand it was named after."

Clifton drove home as fast as he could in his new Ford and ran inside. "We're going home," he said to Georgia.

"We are?"

"Yes."

"How—?"

"Three Sands Field has gone dry," he said as he picked up the earpiece of his desk telephone. "Long distance, please."

"What does that mean?"

"Hello, long distance? Get me Jett & Wood Mercantile in Wichita, Kansas. Yes, I'll wait. It means the boom in Ponca City is over. Hello, yes, Mr. Pratt, please. This is C. C. Row in Ponca—Yes, hello. Good to hear your voice, too. I need to speak to Mr.—Hello, Mr. Pratt? C. C. Row, here."

Georgia stood by listening to a very long silence while Mr. Pratt spoke. Perry and his two sisters came into the living room and watched their father.

"Yes, sir, that's why I'm calling. Yes, that's right, it's gone dry. Yes, sir, I knew you'd want to know as soon as I—Yes, sir. Yes, sir. Yes, sir. Yes, sir. Yes, good bye."

He hung the earpiece on the hook.

"What does that mean?"

"It means we're moving back to Wichita!"

The girls started jumping up and down, holding hands.

"Papa, yes!" Perry was the first to speak. "Air Capital of the World! Here we come!"

13

"All right, this is Mission Twenty, Bremen, Eight October, 1943, Crew Seven flying Shoot-A-Pound. Let's hear from the pilot first. Lieutenant Row?"

"Where do you want me to start, sir?"

"Let's start with enemy aircraft. How many did you see and when did you see them first?" The de-briefings took place in the mess hall, six crews at a time talking to six teams of officers and stenographers.

Perry took a sip of coffee before starting. "There were dozens as soon as we hit the Dutch coast, sir, swarming all over us. I've never seen so many."

"How many?"

"I'd have to guess five dozen, sir. They came right up, as soon as we hit landfall."

"What types of aircraft?"

"Me-109s and JU-88s, sir."

"More of one type that the other?"

"More Me-109s, sir."

"Were you hit?"

"Several times, sir. I'm surprised it wasn't worse than it was. Our Bombardier, Lieutenant Fitzsimmons, took something in the arm. He's over at the hospital now."

"Was that from enemy aircraft or Flak?"

"I don't know, sir."

"It was Flak, sir," E said.

"Very well. Before or after the bomb run, Lieutenant Row?"

"After, sir."

"And the plane?"

"It was badly crippled, sir, two engines knocked out, hundreds of Flak hits, in the nose, in the mid-section, in the left wing, and in the tail. The right wing was hit by fire from an Me-109. That's how we lost number three, sir. I was amazed the thing still flew. I'm glad it wasn't our regular airplane. I've never seen Flak this bad."

"How many missions have you flown, son?"

"This was my sixth, sir."

"Where's your regular airplane?"

"Maintenance rotation, sir."

"Any mechanical problems with the airplane from this mission?"

"Engine three didn't sound good an hour after the group formation departed."

"And when did the enemy aircraft break off their attack?"

"Not until we were back over the Channel, after the bomb run, sir. They stayed with us for a long time."

"Did you get the Bombardier's report before he went to the hospital?"

"Yes, sir, we delivered fifty hundred-pound incendiaries, within a hundred feet of the primary targets, the submarines at the northern shipyards, sir. He said to report that if he missed by any more than that, it was on the docks and not in the water, but smoke obscured more detailed results than that, sir."

"Okay, now what about our aircraft? What did you observe?"

"My element leader, Captain Serpte, they were hit hard. The Fort exploded, and I only saw one chute come out of it."

"I thought I saw two, sir," Billy interrupted.

"Very well. Were you the deputy element leader, Lieutenant Row?"

"No, sir," Perry said.

"Did the deputy element leader move into position quickly?"

"Yes, sir, immediately."

"Did you see any other planes get hit?"

"Yes, sir, two others, none I could identify."

"Where were they, relative to your position?"

"One in the high squadron, one in the lead squadron, sir."

"Anything else?"

"We downed some enemy aircraft, sir, but I'll let the gunners tell you the details."

"All right, Lieutenant Row, thank you. Gunners, what do you have to report?"

"I got one, sir, an Me-109, just as it was attacking an element above us," Byrne said.

"Can anyone confirm that?"

"Yes, sir, I saw it go down in flames," Kiss said.

"Any more?"

"Sir, I got three," Kiss said. "Two Me-109s and a JU-88."

"What were the circumstances?"

"The Me-109s were part of the same attack on the element above us. The JU-88 was just stupid and flew right into my range. That was on the way back, sir."

"Can anyone confirm these?"

"Yes, sir, I can confirm the two Me-109s," Byrne said.

"And I saw the JU-88, sir." Mack McCormick said. "It just flew in behind and followed us, like he was trying to decide whether to continue attacking or not, sir."

"I didn't wait for him to make up his mind, sir," Kiss said. "I continued without him."

After the de-briefing, Perry and his officers returned to the Nissen hut, finding Worthington and his officers already finished with their de-briefing. They were playing the new radio from London. The seven men changed out of their flying gear without speaking until Worthington went over to Perry. "Where's Bud?"

"Hospital," Perry said. "Took a Flak hit in his arm."

"Tough ride today."

"Yes, I'd say so."

"I'm glad you got an easy introduction. This was as bad as I've seen."

"I'm glad of that, at least."

The two men nodded to one another before Worthington returned to his side of the hut. Perry sat down and pulled his makeshift writing table up to his bunk, starting a letter to Phyllis Marie that glossed over the horrors of the recent mission:

'Phyllis Marie wasn't with us yesterday. Her sister was, and she is badly crippled now. Phyllis Marie is as fine as ever. Bud is up the line at a hospital where he had a piece of flak extracted from his arm. He now will get a Purple Heart award. The rest of us are okay.'

He reached into his footlocker for a Hershey bar, eating it before continuing.

'Now that I have been promoted to First Lieutenant, please send gum and candy for those boring days without flying. Sometimes the fog is too thick, and we spend the days reading by the fire. Strange thing about sending news home, we aren't supposed to write anything about our missions, but we can send clippings from Stars and Stripes, the military newspaper. The stories are censored, but they tell a true and fairly complete story.'

Still feeling empty, Perry took another Hershey bar, his last, and ate half of it.

'I am also enclosing some propaganda pamphlets the RAF has been dropping on the Germans. I don't know what they say. Worthington brought a radio from London, so now we hear most of the programs around. Some are in French. New song here, "I'm Gonna Get Lit Up When the Lights Go Up in London." '

He leaned back against the wall and ate the rest of his candy bar before writing his last line.

'I yearn for the peace and quiet of our Idaho home.'

Two days later, nineteen airplanes from the three-ninetieth participated in an air battle over the city of Münster, the most savage to date. Unlike previous missions, this one targeted the civilian population of the city as well as an industrial target—the railroad marshalling yards. Had it not been for a fire in engine one during the ascent to the formation area, Perry would have piloted the twentieth airplane in the group. Instead, he aborted the mission and returned to Framlingham.

Perry and his crew sat on the grass outside the Framlingham tower, waiting for the return of their comrades, enjoying the birdsong in the rare warmth of the afternoon sun in a blue October sky. Most of Perry's enlisted men were smokers, along with two of his officers, so the men smoked cigarettes and read magazines while waiting. Another twenty men from two other crews that had aborted the mission, and all the ground personnel, waited with them. To the average observer, they would have appeared bored, which was anything but the truth. Perry, at least, and probably the other flyers, felt somewhat guilty at being left behind.

Quietly, the wind shifted. Perry pulled his collar together and buttoned it. A haze drifted in, bringing a cool haze over the field, breaking the idyllic setting and sending the birds away in search of shelter.

A radio crackled from the tower. At the same time, the throbbing sound of unsynchronized engines began to beat the air.

"Mayday! Mayday! Injured on board!" the radio voice shrieked.

The ambulance drivers ran to their vehicles and positioned themselves along the runway.

"There it is!" someone shouted, pointing at the first visible aircraft, only two propellers turning and smoke trailing from one of the disabled engines. The airplane didn't land as much as crash gently, taxiing quickly to the side to leave room for the pilots behind him, before appearing to collapse in a heap.

Perry leaped to his feet. "Come on," he said to Billy, and started to run toward the crippled Fort. Billy and the rest of the crew followed quickly, as did the other flyers and ground crew men. By the time they reached the runway, another Fort appeared above the trees to their right. This one made an ordinary landing. As soon as Perry reached the first airplane, the men inside started passing their wounded out the rear entrance door. Perry and Billy carried a man fifteen feet to a waiting Medic with a stretcher, trying to ignore the gaping chest wound, before returning to the plane and helping another man down to the ground.

Five more B-17s arrived in the next twenty minutes, all carrying dead or wounded, which the Medics quickly evacuated to the base hospital, before returning to the runway.

"Where are the rest of them?" Billy asked.

Perry didn't answer.

The men on the field stood waiting, facing the trees at the end of the runway. Fifteen minutes ticked by, during which all chatter ceased.

In the distance, Perry thought he heard the distinctive sound of the Wright nine-cylinder engine. Others began to crane their necks, trying to locate the noise.

"There!" A shout went up all around as the crowd spotted another B-17. The two inboard engines continued to drive the airplane forward, while the feathered outboards circled lazily, cheering on their comrades. The Fort made a smooth and routine landing, belying the two dead and five injured crewmen it carried.

"Are you the last one in?" Perry asked the pilot as he dropped out of the front hatch.

"What?" The pilot gestured toward his ears, indicating that they remained closed after his high-altitude flying.

"Are you the last one in?"

"It was a mess up there," he shouted, stepping into the back of the jeep that would take him to de-briefing. "I've never seen so many enemy fighters at once. We must have shot down twenty of them. All you had to do was shoot and you were bound to hit something."

"Wait!" Perry shouted as the jeep started to pull away. "Where's Worthington?"

"They went down over the target," the pilot shouted back. "I only saw two chutes, and those went out the main entrance, so I figure they were the waist gunners."

Perry, Billy, Bud, and Boettcher stood in a circle on the airfield staring at one another in shock. Worthington dead? He couldn't be. But Perry knew in his gut that it was true. He could not face the idea of returning to the hut and facing the empty bunks of his fallen comrades.

"Let's go to the Officers' Club," he said. "I'm buying."

They took seats at the crowded bar and ordered black-and-tans, listening to the stories of the aircrews that had flown the mission.

"Those rockets were incredible, and we can't touch them if they stay out of range like that."

"Yeah, that's no fair."

"I lost over half my crew."

"We were like fish in a barrel."

"The way they concentrated their attack was amazing, coming in from twelve o'clock level."

"They just ignored us until they had creamed the hundredth."

"And then they creamed us."

"The whole town was on fire when we turned away."

"I don't see how we can go on another mission after this, unless we can get some better escort cover over the targets."

"Anyone know how many ships came back?"

"Ten of nineteen."

"Eleven. One had to land at another base. She had over seven hundred holes in her. The pilot got it in the leg, but stayed put and helped the co-pilot bring it in."

"How many did we get? How many confirmed?"

"Sixty two, seven probables, eight more claimed."

"Are you kidding?"

"Man, that's got to be some kind of record."

As if the events centered on Framlingham weren't bad enough, Perry saw a copy of Stars and Stripes sitting on the bar. A familiar name jumped out from a small article on the cover page.

'Davidson, Everett, 2 Lt., posthumously awarded the

Purple Heart today after he was reported KIA. His B-17F was shot down yesterday over the North Sea, fifty miles west of the Danish coast, sources said.'

Perry showed it to Billy.

"Oh dear," Billy said. "I wonder if Nancy knows."

Perry simply shook his head. There was nothing he could say.

14

"Is this the new farm?" Four-year-old Phyllis Marie stood on the floor of the passenger side of the car, between her mother's legs, staring out the driver side window at the largest building she had ever seen.

"No, dear," Hazel smiled, smoothing her daughter's hair against her head. "That's Friends University."

"It's so big! Look at that silo! When will we get to the farm?"

Edwin glanced in the rearview mirror at his other children, asleep in the back seat, cushioned by one another.

"Keep thy voice down, Phyllis Marie," he said. "Let the rest of them sleep."

She glanced into the back seat just in time to catch her brother's wink, then turned and looked at her father with enormous eyes.

"We aren't going to the farm just yet," he said. "We are going to your Uncle Irvin and Aunt Mary's home first, until arrangements can be made."

"What's 'rangements?' "

"Arrangements, dear. We still have some things to arrange with the people who own the farm."

"What people?"

"The Ekeland sisters."

"Are we related to them?"

"No, dear."

"Are we going to be?"

Edwin smiled at his inquisitive daughter: green-eyed, dark haired, always cheerful, always wanting to know more. "Not being possessed with the necessary information, I cannot inform you with that degree of accuracy becoming one of my station."

She looked questioningly at her mother's placid face before returning her view to the houses and empty lots going by.

Edwin slowed down, dropped into second gear, and turned onto a broad tree-lined street, and then stopped in front of one of the houses, setting the brake and shutting off the engine.

Kenneth and Virginia stretched and looked around. Kenneth opened the door facing the curb and put one leg out.

Mary emerged from the house first, her large bosom rising and falling as she plunked down the front stairs, shouting, "They're here, they're here!"

The girls, Marjorie and Lucile, twelve and seven years old, followed closely. Lucile ran past her sister, leaped onto the running board of the truck, and looked in at Phyllis Marie. "Hello," she said. Phyllis Marie buried her face in her mother's lap.

"Doesn't she remember me, Aunt Hazel?"

"She will, dear. It has been a very long drive and she hasn't slept today."

Finally, Irvin Stanton emerged, holding a newspaper in one hand, his tall frame erect, and stood on the porch. He waved wordlessly to his younger brother, who nodded in response. They stood watching as Hazel and Mary embraced at the curb. "How was the trip?"

"Hot and tiring," Hazel said. "How one can get so exhausted sitting and doing nothing, I do not know."

"Come in, come in," Mary said, full of hustle and bustle, gathering Hazel up in her arms and leading her toward the stairs. "I've put all four girls in the front room, so you and Edwin are to have the girls' room, and Kenneth can sleep on the back porch. I have lunch ready. Are you hungry?"

"I think Edwin is," Hazel replied, "but I don't know about the rest of us." The two women disappeared into the house.

Irvin swept his big left hand toward the cargo in the back of the truck. "Can I give you a hand unloading these things?"

Edwin flinched, hearing his brother abandon the plain speech of the Friends. "Let's eat first," he said. "Kenneth, are you hungry?"

"Yes, sir." The boy stepped out of the car, followed by his

sister.

"Fine," Irvin said. "Then after we've eaten, the three men will tackle the job. How's that, nephew?" He clapped the boy on the back.

"Fine, sir."

The four adults gathered around the large dining room table while the five children found their places at a smaller table set up for them in the front parlor. A hush fell over them as the Friends, accustomed to silent prayer, began their typical brief and personal communion with their Lord, but Mary, a Baptist, broke the silence. "Isn't anyone going to say Grace?"

Irvin glanced up at her and then started. "Heavenly Father, bless this reunion of family and this meal which you have provided. Amen."

"Amen," Mary responded.

Edwin looked up at his brother but said nothing. Irvin's conversion to the Baptist church had been many years ago.

"Well, go on," Mary chided. "You folks must be starved." The various platters and bowls began to circulate clockwise.

After taking a piece of chicken, Edwin spoke to his brother. "Have you heard from the Ekeland sisters?" Hazel noticed he had dropped the plain speech in favor of the colloquial English that belonged to the household.

"They're out of town," Mary said.

"They're in Kansas City," Irvin said, "but they left a letter and some instructions for you."

"And Mr. Livingston wants you to call," Mary said.

"I thought you were done with photography," Irvin said.

"I'd rather retire, sure," Edwin answered, "and just raise corn and pigs, but I have a family to raise. The studio needs someone; the pay is decent for part-time work, and it's only a mile in from the farm. I don't see how I can refuse."

Edwin opened the letter after lunch and scanned it quickly. From the look on his face, Hazel could see the news was not good.

"They are in Kansas City," he said. She waited patiently,

not understanding what Kansas City represented.

"Oh, no," he said. These were about the strongest words Edwin ever used when a disappointment or disaster struck.

We have survived the flood, Hazel thought. *We can survive anything.*

Finally, after reading the letter twice, Edwin dropped it into his lap.

"What troubles thee?" Hazel asked.

"We cannot move into the farm yet. The previous tenants have refused to leave."

"How can they refuse to leave?"

"Well, I do not know, but they have, and the Ekeland sisters have engaged an attorney to assist them in starting an eviction."

"What shall we do?" she asked. "Have we any money?"

"Not really."

15

The door banged against the wall, awakening Perry.

"Lieutenants Poythress and Row! Breakfast at oh two hundred! Briefing at oh three hundred!"

Why didn't he call Connors and Worthington, Perry wondered, envious that they didn't have to fly today. Then he remembered. He looked over at the four rolled-up mattresses that had been Worthington's and his officers' until the Münster raid four days ago.

All right, he thought, *this isn't the time to think about them.*

Detach. Automatic pilot.

Dress in layers now, in the clothes already laid out for this moment. Shave, because the oxygen mask is more comfortable after shaving. Walk to the Mess Hall; eat the fresh eggs if they're available; drink the coffee.

Attend the briefing; find out the name of the target—Schweinfurt, the ball bearing factories; determine the position within the group formation; learn the route; listen to the weather report—bad fog; listen to the comments about the German defenses.

Detach. Automatic pilot.

Ride out to the airplane in the jeep; determine the condition of the airplane; meet with the ground crew chief; meet with the officers; get started on the checklist. Start the engines. Get in line and wait for the fog to lift. Wait for the take-off.

Take off. Spiral up and into place. Wait for the group formation to finish. Get on the oxygen. Wait.

Set the course, follow the group formation, and fly. Observe the departure of the escorts—the P-47 Thunderbolts—as they reach the end of their range. Observe, also, the sudden arrival of the enemy aircraft that have been hovering, monitoring the group, waiting for their abandonment by the fighters.

Stay precisely in place, tucked in fifty feet back and fifty feet to the right of the element lead, maintaining the course. Watch and listen as the gunners do their jobs, calling out the bandits; stay on top of all the numbers, all the tasks, all the gauges. Watch as B-17s above and below explode and fall out of formation. Count the chutes. Move up into the vacant position. Watch as enemy airplanes charge in from twelve o'clock level, missing with their guns, exploding after fire from the top turret. Count the numbers and types of aircraft encountered.

Detach. Automatic pilot.

Begin the bomb run, turn over control to the bombardier, feel the jolt of the bombs as they are released; take control back; bank left; observe the damage on the ground; resume position within the group; fly; wait.

Observe the enemy fighters finally break off their attack at the arrival of the P-47 Thunderbolts as they fly out from England to greet the returning group formation. Note the time. Note the fact that it has been three full hours of sustained attack by the enemy fighters.

Fly. Land. Attend the de-briefing. Report. Dropped bombs. No damage to aircraft. No injuries to crew. Return to the hut. Undress. Sleep.

"Perry!" Billy's voice insisted. Perry preferred to remain in his unfinished dream of model airplanes in the fields of Kansas, far from Europe, far from war. "Perry!"

"What?" he said.

"Are you awake?"

"Now I am, yes." He looked past Billy to see that a rookie crew had taken over the bunks that had been Worthington's.

"You've been asleep for fourteen hours," Billy said. "I was getting worried."

"I'm fine." He sat up, rubbing his eyes to clear his vision.

"You haven't heard, have you?"

"Heard what?"

"About the raid on Schweinfurt yesterday." Billy's tone was harsh and insistent, like an angry bee.

"What about it?" Perry realized he was still not quite fully awake.

"They're calling it one of the worst disasters of the war."

"What? We sleepwalked through it. It was a milk run!"

"Not for the three-hundred-fifth," Billy said, turning his attention to a copy of Stars and Stripes. "Of the fifteen airplanes that formed up on the wrong combat wing, due to inclement weather, thirteen failed to return to base."

"Let me see that." Perry took the paper.

"It says we lost a total of sixty B-17s yesterday," he said. "Have you heard how many came out of the three-ninetieth?"

"One."

"It also says that as a result of this mission, there's to be a review of the Eighth Air Force in general, that it might cost the commander his job, and that they may re-evaluate our need for fighter escorts."

"They aren't thinking of taking them away are they?"

"No, no. They need more range. External fuel tanks would allow them to fly all the way with us. That's what's needed." Perry read further.

"Black Thursday."

"What's that?"

"They are calling yesterday's mission 'Black Thursday.' "

16

"Mr. Murdock?"

The acting Managing Editor of the Wichita Beacon finished scanning the article about the new bus service being established between Wichita and Hutchinson before looking up to see Irvin Stanton standing in his doorway in white shirtsleeves, summer sweat forming beads on his brow and upper lip. It was too hot for the gentlemen to wear their coats.

"I. J., come in," he said, motioning his employee to a chair.

"Mr. Murdock, I understand there is a need for some freelance photography work here. Is that correct?"

"It depends on the quality of the work, of course, but yes, we can use an extra hand now and again." He leaned back in his chair. "Is your brother back?"

"Yes, sir, and he is in a bit of a spot. He's—"

"Caught on at Livingston's, I hear?"

"Yes, sir, but there isn't enough work for him. He's supposed to take over a tenant farm north of town, but that deal has been put on hold for at least two months. If there was a way—"

"My wife swears she saw him behind the meat counter at Safeway last week. Did she?"

"Yes, sir, he's doing whatever he can to make ends meet, and the family is staying with us, but—"

"Tell him to get over to Riverside Park and get some good baby pictures. We need them for a story on the Wichita Fresh Air Baby Camp."

"Today, sir?"

"Most definitely today, the sooner the better."

"Very well, sir, thank you. What sort of arrangements—"

"Have him come see me as soon as he's got those photographs developed."

Irvin returned to his desk, picked up the earpiece of his

telephone, and blew into the mouthpiece.

"Yes, Mr. Stanton."

"Greta, ring my home, please."

"Yes, sir."

He hung the earpiece in its cradle and began reviewing a new article about the widening of Douglas Avenue between Hydraulic and Grove. The instrument on his desk rang, one short, one long, and he picked up the earpiece again.

"Mary?"

"Yes, dear," she shouted, her voice tinny.

"Is Edwin there? I'd like to speak to him."

"Yes, dear."

A moment passed before his brother's voice finally came over the wire. "Yes?"

"You have an assignment. Something of a trial run, I think."

"Let me get a pencil."

When he came back, Irvin gave him the details.

"I'm on my way now," Edwin said, "and thank you."

Edwin hung the earpiece on the cradle at the left of the telephone instrument mounted on the wall. After retrieving his camera, tripod, and case, he and took his hat from the stand by the door. Mary, stretched out on the parlor divan, called after him. "Good news?"

"An assignment from the Beacon. Tell Hazel, won't you?" He went through the screen door without waiting for an answer.

"I will. Good luck."

At the back of the house in the sleeping porch, Kenneth practiced his trumpet, playing "Canal Street Blues" from the Louis Armstrong with King Oliver's Creole Jazz Band Solo Book, which he had received for Christmas the previous year in Colorado. Sitting in the dining room, Hazel and Virginia wound yarn together, close enough to listen to Kenneth's practicing, but far enough away not to disturb him. Virginia would have preferred to read the book that she had recently checked out of the public library with her new card. Marjorie and Lucile played jacks on the kitchen floor.

Phyllis Marie, playing outside at the edge of the lawn near the house with a shoebox, stood and waved as Edwin strode to his car. "Goodbye, Father!"

"Goodbye, dear!" he called to her. "Mind your Aunt Mary as you would your mother!"

"I will," she said, dropping her box and running to the curb in time to be lifted and squeezed and kissed.

Unnoticed by anyone, Irvin's white cat, Portia—allegedly a direct descendant of Champion Lady Sophia herself, though no papers existed to prove it—crept around the corner and pressed her nose against the corner of the lid of Phyllis Marie's abandoned shoebox. The cat sniffed the air and then froze, her blue eyes staring at the box. A few seconds later, she reached out one tentative paw and batted lightly at the box. The lid came away at the corner and the head of a small garden snake emerged, just an inch at first, and flicked its tongue at the air.

Other than the pupils of her strange eyes dilating to black saucers, Portia kept still. Even her tail, which usually flitted back and forth in time with nothing perceptible, remained still and rigid.

The snake chose the wrong moment to decide the coast was clear and slithered from its former cage. This was only one of several pet snakes Phyllis Marie had been collecting in her first few weeks in Wichita, unbeknownst to anyone.

Portia pounced. Her jaws caught the snake perfectly at the midpoint between head and tail, puncturing the clean smooth skin without severing the body. She leaped in the air as the snake tried to bite back in self-defense.

There was nothing for the cat to do but present her fine catch to someone who would appreciate it, so she ran up the steps, batted at the screen door—which bounced open a few inches—slipped into the house and saw Mary dozing on the parlor divan. In a second, Portia leaped upon the large bosom of her drowsy mistress and gazed lovingly into Mary's face, the cherished prize dangling and writhing out both sides of her mouth.

Mary opened her eyes and screamed.

Every member of the household came running to see what was the matter. In the middle of the parlor stood Mary, holding the cat by the scruff of the neck at arm's length, the snake still writhing in its jaws. "Oh, what a fright!" Mary cried, huffing and puffing, trying to catch her breath.

Phyllis Marie burst into the room, carrying her now empty shoebox. "My snakes are missing!" she shouted. She looked up at the cat, broke into an enormous grin, and said, "There's one!"

One evening after supper a week later, Irvin and Edwin sat on the front screen porch sharing the newspaper in the fading sunlight. Kenneth had advanced to John Philip Sousa's latest opus, "The Gallant Seventh," with its rising chromatic crescendo in the opening section. He played it over and over. The women huddled in the kitchen, chatting and cleaning up after dinner, while Virginia and Marjorie prepared the four girls' beds in the front parlor. Phyllis Marie and Lucile sat on the floor in the dining room, playing with one of Mary's hairpins.

Irvin stood and pulled on the chain above his head, turning on the electric porch light, before speaking.

"Edwin, have you read this article in the Beacon, linking Prohibition and the resurgence of fundamental religion as reactions to the social revolution on today's campuses?"

"That seems backwards to me. Surely the excesses of the so-called Jazz Age are reactions against Prohibition, not the other way around, and I can't say that fundamental religion is experiencing a resurgence, unless you count Billy Sunday as representational of fundamental religion."

"Hardly."

"No, I think the younger generation is losing touch with the church."

Bzzt! The light went dark. Inside, Lucile screamed once and then continued to shriek in terror. Irvin and Edwin raced into the house to find the girl pointing at something in the darkness, something on the floor: the apparently lifeless form of Phyllis Marie.

Edwin dropped to his knees, took his daughter's hand in his two and started to rub. He rolled her over onto her back and searched her wrist for a pulse. Irvin carried his daughter Lucile away to the front porch.

The women and Kenneth exploded into the room in a single bang. "What happened?" the boy asked.

"Kenneth, do you remember which house is the doctor's?" Edwin asked breathlessly. "You met him a few days ago."

"The big green one on the corner."

"That's it. Go get him. Quickly, son."

"Oh my, what now?" Mary balled her hands into fists and clutched them to the cheeks of her face. The other girls huddled around her, jumping up and down.

Hazel, always calm in an emergency, kneeled on the other side of her daughter. She took Phyllis Marie's left hand and began patting and rubbing.

Edwin used his thumb to gently raise the girl's eyelids. "I can't find a pulse, but she seems to be alive."

"She's not breathing." Hazel leaned over, pressing her mouth against the child's, and puffed air into her until her little chest rose.

Mary brought a kerosene lamp from the kitchen and lit it. "Look there," she said, pointing.

Edwin followed her finger and retrieved a bent-open hairpin, scorched on the two open ends. He noticed the electrical outlet on the wall, also badly scorched.

"Why is it so dark in here?" the doctor asked, coming in through the front screen ahead of Kenneth.

"She's electrocuted herself," Hazel said, puffing another tiny lungful.

"Let me in there." The doctor searched her left wrist for a pulse before examining her right. "I don't see any kind of burn injury. Keep doing that, but faster," he said to Hazel. He slapped the girl's wrist and forearm hard.

"Ow!" Phyllis Marie cried out as she sat up, bumping

heads with her mother and pulling her hand away from the doctor at the same time. "That hurt!" She glared at him and then buried her face in her mother's dress, starting to cry. Hazel rocked her gently.

"Oh, what a fright!" Mary shouted. "When are those Ekeland sisters due back?"

The girls hugged Mary and continued jumping up and down, but at a slower tempo than before, with wide grins on their faces.

"I can't take much more of that child," Mary said.

Edwin stood, smiling and shaking hands with the doctor. Irvin and Kenneth joined in.

"But I didn't do anything," the doctor laughed. "Put her to bed, Hazel, and watch her, see that she stays calm and gets some rest. Call me if there's a change."

On his way out, he saw the hairpin in Edwin's hand and shook his head, astonished.

But his shock was nothing compared to Mary Stanton's.

17

Just like every Friday afternoon during the difficult war months of late 1943 through early 1944, Patsy the Blue Cairn Terrier ran up the sidewalk toward the Stanton's house in Caldwell, followed closely by her owner, twenty-three-year-old Trudy.

"Phyllis Marie!" Trudy called, "I came as fast as I could!"

Phyllis Marie opened the door and without missing a beat, Patsy leaped into her waiting arms. "My goodness, I'm glad to see you, too. Yes, I am," Phyllis Marie cooed as the dog licked her face.

"When you said you got a letter from Perry in England, I closed up the office, swung by my mother's, picked up Patsy, and here we are!"

"Not just a letter," Phyllis Marie said, "a clipping, too. He was in that big battle that was in the news last week."

"Really? The place where so many airplanes were lost, with all the ball bearing factories?"

"Yes, Schweinfurt, and he's okay."

"Thank goodness for that."

"Come on, the others are upstairs already. They're peeved at me because I insisted we wait for you."

"Oh, my, well let's go."

Patsy climbed the staircase first; she already knew the way. After all, the four girls—Phyllis Marie, Trudy, Ruby, and Jeannie—spent nearly every weekend together having a slumber party. The dog flew into the room and into Ruby's lap.

"Aren't you the sweetest thing," Ruby said, petting her, holding her close to settle her down. Patsy's tail went into double time.

"Come on, Phyllis Marie," Jeannie said, giggling with excitement. "Let's hear this letter."

Phyllis Marie joined the other girls on the floor of the living room of the upstairs apartment in Edwin and Hazel's house that she and Perry shared. It had become a weekend haven for the four girls whose husbands served overseas. Every letter home, from every husband, belonged to all four girls, except, of course, for the intimate parts.

Which do you want first, the clipping or the letter?"

"The clipping," they chorused, knowing that it would be more informative, and that the letter would make more sense afterwards. As soon as Trudy settled in, her back against the sofa, Phyllis Marie began:

"London, Consolidated Press—The little boy that had a giant firecracker boomerang on him has nothing on Lieutenant Perry V. Row of 216 South Topeka Avenue, Wichita, Kansas."

"Why Kansas?" Jeannie interrupted.

"I don't know," Phyllis Marie said. "That's his parents' address.

"Go on," Trudy said.

"Lieutenant Row was one of the pilots on yesterday's raid against Schweinfurt, Germany. The Nazis have a new rocket gun and they were firing it at Lieutenant Row. 'I saw a rocket just over our right wing,' says Lieutenant Row. 'We could see it coming a long way off and thought it would hit between the inboard engine and the cockpit, but it missed us. When it went by, it was just a big red brick.' "

"Is that all?"

Phyllis Marie nodded and handed the clipping to Ruby.

"Wow!" Jeannie said.

"Read the letter now," Trudy insisted.

"Okay." Phyllis Marie unfolded it carefully. She skipped the first part because it contained the code that told her he had been in the Schweinfurt raid. When he wrote the coded messages, they didn't make much sense otherwise, and she had promised not to tell anyone about the code.

"He writes, 'I got my sweets rations today and the two bars of chocolate are gone already. Back in the states, I never got hungry for candy like I do here. I guess it's because it is hard to get. A big box of candy would really taste good once in a while, so send one along, will you, huh? This morning we climbed to twenty-eight thousand feet in solid overcast and then a few clouds were above us, yet. That was the longest I ever flew in instrument conditions except on the trip over.' "

"Is that all he has to say about the mission?" Jeannie twisted her blonde hair into ringlets pensively.

"Yes, it is," Phyllis Marie replied. "He has to be careful about the censors, you know."

"The newspaper said they flew over seven hours," Trudy said in wonder.

Phyllis Marie continued.

"'I hope there is a lot of those hundred dollar money orders piling up at home during the next four or five months. I would like to see over a thousand in the bank so we can settle down comfortably sometime in the near future. Perhaps we can buy the studio and let the folks retire on their acreage.' "

"What acreage?" Ruby asked.

"There is no acreage, he's being silly." Phyllis Marie laughed before continuing.

" 'Gee, I'm hungry for a big box full of Hershey or Nestles. Candy is about the most welcome sight I could think of seeing come through. We toast bread slices from the mess hall on the pot-bellied stove and melt butter and chocolate bars on them before bed. I trade my cigarette rations to the smokers for their K ration chocolate bars, too. Wind is whistling cold tonight. It makes you want to cuddle closer to the stove and dream of the good old days when you could take a hot bath and go jump in a warm bed and cuddle. Now we come in wet and shivering until we get in a cold bed and after so much time it becomes comfortable. Phooey. I'd rather irrigate than live in a rainy, foggy country. I'll be home soon to take up that dangling end, and we will again start living as man and wife. That's worth fighting for. Love, Perry.' "

"Dangling end, huh? Whatever does he mean by that?" Jeannie asked, giggling.

"That man eats a lot of sweets," Ruby said.

"He didn't before he went into the service." Phyllis Marie frowned a little.

"Are you going to send him more candy?" Trudy leaned forward, her sandy brown hair falling into her eyes.

"Yes. You wouldn't believe the amount I've sent already, and he's only been there six weeks. He must be sharing it."

"Did you finish the photo album you were working on?" Trudy asked.

"Yes, here it is. See how it has all these pictures in it, just like President Roosevelt suggested, to remind him of what he's fighting for, what he has to look forward to when he comes home?" It was four inches by six, slim, containing a dozen photographs of Phyllis, posing in the familiar places of home.

"Apple pie, that's a nice touch," Jeannie said.

"Pretty wife waiting, that's the main thing," Trudy said, flipping through the black pages of the little booklet.

The four girls ate dinner with Hazel and Edwin before walking downtown to a movie. On Saturday morning, they visited the post office, but none of them found letters from their husbands—Perry in England, two in North Africa and one in the Pacific—so they played shuffleboard in the driveway for awhile, until it was time to check downtown for the afternoon post. When they found no letters again, Ruby slipped into one of her anxious moods. The other girls tried to cheer her up with music on the radio. Hazel prepared dinner and Edwin served it to the girls with a towel over his arm, pretending to be the Maitre D' at a fancy Boise hotel. Phyllis Marie brought out her latest sewing projects and they spent their time just like every weekend of the difficult war months of late 1943 and early 1944.

18

Finally in the late summer of 1924, the Ekeland sisters—with the assistance of two Deputies from the Sedgwick County Sheriff's Office—succeeded in evicting the family from their farm north of Wichita, allowing Edwin to remove his wife, three children, and truckload of furniture from his brother's home before any further disasters struck. He pulled his over-laden car away from the curb and pointed it east, away from Friends University and across the Arkansas River, until he could turn north and drive five miles out of town to 37th Street, where he turned back to the west and crossed over the Little Arkansas.

"How much longer?" Kenneth sat forward. "These roads are terrible out here."

"Complaining will not get thee home any faster," Edwin said.

"There is the turn," Hazel said, reading from a page of directions the Ekeland sisters had given her the night before.

"Help us watch for the walnut tree, Kenneth." Edwin had already been to the ranch, but he wanted to engage the boy in finding the way.

They drove on for another mile. Edwin spotted the tree but refrained from commenting.

"There!" Kenneth cried out from the back seat. "I see it! Dead ahead!"

As soon as the car stopped by the side of the house, the three children jumped out, shouting and running. Edwin and Hazel, on the other hand, made no such move. They sat in stunned silence.

The house looked as if a whirlwind had blown through it. Shutters tilted away from the window frames. Some windows appeared cracked, while others missed entire panes of glass. No one had painted the exterior in at least five years, and the steps leading up to the back porch sagged in several places.

"Well," Hazel said.

Edwin put on his most determined and cheerful expression. "She said it needed some work."

"The immigration laws need work. This is a disaster."

"Now, it's not that bad," he soothed. "We'll get things in order in no time."

Hazel heaved a deep sigh. "Well, let's see what we have inside."

A quick survey revealed only three bedrooms upstairs, not four, which meant fifteen-year-old Virginia would have to double up with five-year-old Phyllis Marie, leaving one bedroom for Hazel and Edwin and the third one for Kenneth.

"Edwin, come look," Hazel called.

Her husband entered the middle bedroom and saw that the tall windows opened onto the roof of the front porch.

"Do the other rooms have this same access?"

"No," Hazel said. "I wouldn't be able to sleep at night knowing that the children might come out here."

"Then we shall make this our room. All the better to see the stars at night." He took her in his arms and squeezed her tightly.

"Look up there! I want that room!" Kenneth shouted from the ground.

His sisters emerged from under the walnut tree.

"Too late," Edwin called back. "The room assignments have been made." He whispered into Hazel's ear, "We had better decide about the other two rooms quickly."

"It doesn't matter," she said. "They are the same."

"Which room is mine?" Kenneth shouted.

Still embracing, Hazel and Edwin each pointed in an opposite direction and shouted, laughing, "that one!"

Virginia laughed as well. "You two are a sight."

It took the rest of the day to unload the car and the furniture truck when it arrived and move the heavier pieces of furniture up to the porch, the lighter ones into the rooms, so no one noticed Phyllis Marie's discovery behind the house. She found a big cottonwood tree with nicely spaced knots and gnarls for handholds, perfect for climbing. With considerable effort throughout the afternoon and into the fading sunlight, she finally found her way up into the crook of the tree, about five feet off the ground. From there, she could see the peak of a roof stretching away from her.

She sat there studying her next objective, shivering a little as the earth cooled around her. The building was actually a chicken house, but she didn't know that, didn't even care. All she cared about was that if she could climb up that one big branch, then she could drop right down onto that peak.

"Phyllis Marie!"

She heard her mother's voice calling her inside. Weighing the possible consequences she might encounter if she delayed going into the house, she decided that further exploration would have to wait until another day. She jumped from the tree into a pile of leaves and ran and up the back steps into the kitchen, but her plan would be thwarted because, unbeknownst to her, the next day would bring something entirely new.

19

Perry and the crew settled into a dull blur of November boredom, rainy and flightless days around the hut, where reading Churchill's five-volume World in Crisis became Perry's favorite activity, since it was an easy way to induce a coma-like sleep.

Even a surprise pass to London, where Perry and Billy saw several stage shows, walked all over the town, and saw a million people, held no real interest for him. As he wrote in a letter to Phyllis Marie, he thought of his wife constantly and the fun they might have together were she along. Perhaps then the old town might have impressed him.

An occasional mission punctuated the routine, but ever since Schweinfurt, the missions lacked anything to hold the interest of the men of the three-ninetieth, or so they tried to project to the world and to each other. The gossip among the two-hundred men at Framlingham often centered on lucky crew seven, the men who came through every scrape untouched, as long as they flew together in the airplane named after the pilot's wife.

Crew seven participated in a milk run to Wilhelmshaven, a mission to Gelsenkirchen—where Flak again tore holes in their alternate airplane, Shoot a Pound, for eighteen minutes—and another mission in Phyllis Marie to Duren, where they dropped their bombs and flew home without damage or injury.

One bit of welcome excitement came in the form of a Stars and Stripes article, listing Worthington as a Prisoner of War. Perry nearly cried in front of his men but held it in.

Duren marked the tenth mission for most of the crew. They would receive their Oak Leaf cluster to the Air Medal Award. Not only that, word spread around the base that the Eighth Air Force had nominated the three-ninetieth for the Presidential Unit Citation for their "—conspicuous battle action and extraordinary heroism in connection with the highly successful bombing mission over Schweinfurt, Germany, October, 14, 1943."

It was just another mission, Perry thought to himself, but he was grateful for the awards, especially the Oak Leaf Cluster, because it meant that as a veteran crew, he and his comrades now possessed the experience that would help see them through this thing to the end.

The enlisted men of the crew pointed out to the officers that their eleventh mission, to Münster, flying the Anoxia Queen, had come on November eleven, Armistice Day, which celebrated the end of World War One, at the eleventh hour and the eleventh minute. It was another sign to them that crew seven was lucky. They were beginning to buy into it themselves.

Perry, however, wanted to dispel the lucky crew seven myth, so much so that when his feet had become frostbitten on the Münster raid, he had kept it to himself, seeing the doctor on the Q.T., rather than let word get around that again, when crew seven flew in an airplane that wasn't the Phyllis Marie, bad things happened. He couldn't argue with the statistics, though. The only times someone from crew seven had been injured—the time Bud Fitzsimmons caught Flak in his arm, and his own frostbite—were the times Perry flew a different airplane.

A striped kitten adopted the officers of the hut. Perry named it Tiger and attempted to feed it powdered milk without mixing in any water, an offering the cat rejected, but it seemed to be a natural born mouser, so the eight officers of the hut agreed to do whatever necessary to keep Tiger happy.

After another milk run to Bremen and a more difficult return to Gelsenkirchen, Perry wrote a letter to Phyllis Marie that unintentionally gave away too much of the horrors of war to her:

"I hope this gets through the censors. It is funny in a way. On a recent raid, an FW-190 attacked our ship head- on and had his sights on our number one engine. He came up a little from below so I didn't see him until he was almost fifty yards out and Bennett opened up on him with the top turret. Nose guns had been blasting away at him for some seconds. When I caught sight of him, I quit watching the formation and looked at him in fascination. In reality, I flew into him and it must have scared him so badly, he never did get a shot off at us. He was flaming when he went by my window, only about thirty yards or so away. When I looked back, I was nearly a hundred feet higher in the formation than I was supposed to be. Bennett claimed him, but it went as a probable."

When Phyllis Marie put the letter down, having read it to the girls, she saw the shock in their faces.

"I can't imagine what he must be going through," Phyllis Marie said, "to be so—inured. Is that the word?"

"Accustomed?" Trudy offered.

"Yes, to be so accustomed to what's going on around him, that he can write about this experience and consider it funny, is truly frightening to me."

"Think of the things they must see every day that he doesn't share with you," Trudy said.

Ruby buried her face in her hands and started to cry. The other three girls moved closer and wrapped their arms over and around her. No one could think of anything to say.

More bad weather led to another pass, this time for six days. Perry and Billy reluctantly went to London again, but this trip held more interest for them than the last one. They attended a live stage show, "Strike Up a New Note," the first Perry had ever seen, saw the Betty Grable movie "Sweet Rosie O'Grady," and ate at the four-story Lyon's Corner House, with two large dining halls—one with chamber music. There were also two cafeterias: one just a tea room with buns and biscuits, the other a 'one and four'—four dishes and a beverage for a schilling, four pence—plates with tiny sandwiches, salads, breads, and sweet apple sauce with cherry syrup, and a beverage choice of tea, coffee, or cocoa.

Perry enjoyed feeling the thickly-carpeted rooms, watching

the waiters buzzing around in stiff shirts and tails while the waitresses actually did all the work, hearing the musicians playing *In the Hall of the Mountain King* and observing the customers sipping their tea, but he thought the food was lousy, probably due to rationing restrictions.

Back in his hotel room, he read an article to Billy about the November Cairo Conference, in which Roosevelt, Churchill, and Chiang Kai-shek discussed their intentions to bring unrelenting pressure against their brutal enemies by sea, land, and air, to expel Japan from all territories she had taken by violence and greed, and to call for an independent Korea.

"Seems like they've got a war to win first," Billy said.

Upon returning to Framlingham, Perry and Billy dropped by the Phyllis Marie to inspect the new chin turret upgrade—fifty-caliber machine guns installed in the bombardier compartment, just like the new B-17Gs—but they encountered Blimp Blumberg making an additional modification to the pilot's compartment.

"What's this tube for, Blimp?"

"It's a pee tube, sir," Blimp said. "You attach this using a condom, see? Connect the tube to the condom with a rubber band first though."

"That's brilliant! Are you boys that bored?"

"I'm just trying to make you comfortable, sir."

On the way home from failing to bomb the next target, the Hispano-Suiza Aircraft Engine Plant in Paris, due to heavy Flak that turned away the three-ninetieth, Perry tried out the new modification, which, according to Billy, made the Phyllis Marie the first and only B-17P.

"It works great," Perry told his co-pilot. "If we can't drop the bombs, at least we can—"

"Perry!" Dix's voice said over the interphone.

"Go ahead."

"We have an unidentified leak coming from the fuselage of the plane."

"Say again?"

"We have an unidentified leak coming from the fuselage

and it is freezing over my window."

"December 10, 1943, Dear Phyllis Marie, Billy and me and several of us fellows took baths by candlelight when the electricity went out, as there was no reading to be done in the dark. One of them was an original pilot with the group, having trained in the states before the group landed here. He has twenty missions, just four more than I have, and his ship carries sixteen swastikas and a duck (for ditching, when they made a forced landing in the channel). They just promoted him to Captain. Two fellows finished their tours of operation today, the first two of the group, and they are already Captains. Phyllis Marie was in the shop for a new engine. We led an element today for the first time, and I saw the Pyrenees Mountains. Soon now, all the older crews will be leaving and crew seven will be leading a squadron! When we got back there was a big party at the Officer's Club, and one of the boys in our hut brought back a big chunk of cheese, salami, buns, and a big can of tomato juice.

"A bomber crewman could never give enough praise to our friends the P-47 pilots, who hover over us on the way in and the way out to ward off attacks by the enemy fighters.

"The Jerries are afraid of the Thunderbolts, so we are now generally unmolested, but they seem to be getting desperate and in spite of our heavy cover, they try hard to break up our formations. Perhaps they are sore because the RAF has hit Berlin.

"We've been mixing powdered milk and powdered eggs for Tiger the cat. Combined with the English mice he eats, it makes for a sleek cat. Thank you for the big box of Hershey's and Whitman's that arrived yesterday, and please don't worry about how much candy I eat. My clothes hang on me like sacks, and I eat all I want. In fact, please send more, especially that Almond Roca.

"I'm still trying to slog through Churchill's 'World in Crisis,' but it's a tough read, an old-fashioned writing style, very proper, very British, but very informative. I've read everything else on this airfield, and I devour the magazines and newspapers that come here immediately.

"We started for a mission the other day but weather forced us back, and the formation broke up, so we flew back from near enemy territory on the deck, just skimming the water, through rain. Some joker jettisoned his bombs near me and we felt the concussion at a thousand feet. If it had been closer, we would never have felt it.

"Today was a fun day, as Billy and I took Blimp and E up in the Phyllis Marie for a test hop to break in the new engine, had a lot of fun, and would have had more if we could have run the engine faster. We flew formation with P-47s but went so slow they couldn't stay back with us, flew in formation with a B-24 until he put his wheels down for a landing, and then tacked onto another B-17, running up and down the countryside buzzing airfields. We ran over the countryside looking at church steeples, castles, small farms, woods, flew over the old castle at Framlingham, high walls enclosing a courtyard, surrounded by a deep moat, quite well preserved, and apparently inhabited. We saw fishing boats with red sails, larger boats with barrage balloons, and found a sunken vessel with two masts sticking up before heading back. Love, Perry."

20

Phyllis Marie awoke to the sound of rain on the roof. She had not slept well anyway, because she was in a strange place. She never slept well in new and unfamiliar places.

Virginia stood between the beds, already dressed. "It's about time thee awakened, child," she said. "Doesn't thee know what day this is?"

"No, what day is it?"

"It's the first day of school and Father is taking us in the car because of the rain."

"School? It's cold," Phyllis Marie said, pulling the covers up under her chin. "I thought it was summer."

"Summer is over. Come on, thee."

"But I had plans for today."

Virginia did not respond. Rather, she started downstairs, one careful step at a time. Phyllis Marie thought even Virginia's footsteps were prim and proper, an old lady already at fifteen.

Virginia is wrong, Phyllis Marie thought. Virginia and Kenneth go to school, not me. That's how it had been in Fowler. If moving to Wichita meant she, too, had to go to school, then she wanted to go back to Colorado.

"Phyllis Marie! Get thee down here!"

The unmistakable earnestness of her mother's voice came all the way up the staircase and into the room. There was no denying that tone. Phyllis Marie leaped out of bed and dressed quickly before running down the back staircase two steps at a time and bouncing into the big kitchen. Virginia sat at the table eating. Hazel stood at the large stove cooking homemade sausages from the ground pork Edwin had brought home from the Safeway. "Sit down, honey," she said. "Virginia, get Phyllis Marie some oatmeal, please."

Edwin came in dripping wet from his rain slicker just as Phyllis Marie took a chair at the table. "That outhouse is going to need some work," he said.

"Edwin!"

"Oh, sorry. Where's Kenneth?" He hung his coat on the stand and took his place at the table.

"Still upstairs."

"Are you girls ready for school?"

"Yes," Virginia replied firmly.

"No." The younger girl sulked.

"Why not, Phyllis Marie?"

"I didn't know I had to go to school. I want to go back home."

"This is home now, honey," Edwin said, "and even if we could go back to Fowler, thee would have to start school there anyway."

Hazel turned toward her younger daughter and slid a pork sausage onto her plate. "What does thee think school is? Doesn't thee know how much fun it is?"

"I had plans for the day."

"What plans?"

"Secret plans."

"Oh," her mother said. "Well, whatever they are, they can wait, I'm sure."

Edwin went to the bottom of the rear stairs. "Kenneth, does thee wish to walk to school in the rain?"

"No!"

Phyllis Marie and Hazel giggled at the thought. Virginia cut a single bite of sausage with her knife in her right hand, set down the knife, transferred the fork to her right hand, stuck the bite with her fork and raised it to her mouth.

"Then I recommend thee comes down here soon."

After chewing for several moments, Virginia transferred the fork back to her left hand and picked up her knife with her right.

Phyllis Marie giggled again. "It's going to take you a long time to eat that thing like that."

"It's called etiquette," Virginia said, without looking up. "Thee might want to know about it thyself one day."

Kenneth slammed down the stairs and into the room with all the noise he could produce.

"Honestly!" Virginia said.

"What? Don't I have time for breakfast?"

"Yes, you do," Hazel said, sliding two sausages onto his plate.

Kenneth stabbed one with his fork and bit half of it away, chewed it three times and swallowed, before putting the rest of it in his mouth. Phyllis Marie stole a glance at Virginia to see her reaction, but the older girl pretended not to see.

"Come on," Edwin said. He stood and retrieved his rain slicker. "I have brought the car up close to the door."

When Kenneth took his second sausage in his hand and put on his raincoat, Phyllis Marie imitated him, leaving Virginia the only one still at the table with food on her plate. When no one was looking, she took the remaining half a sausage in her mouth and stood up. Edwin Stanton and his children trooped out to the car, leaving Hazel behind in the farmhouse kitchen on their first morning at the new place.

The brick schoolhouse of Pleasant Valley District 128 School consisted of two classrooms, two bathrooms, and an office for the principal—although all the students, from the first grade to the eighth, gathered in only one classroom. Outside, the swings, the monkey bars, and the teeter-totter in the big playground would have to wait until the first sunny day. After saying his goodbyes to his father and sister, Kenneth took Phyllis Marie by the hand and led her through the gate.

"Isn't Virginia coming to school?" Phyllis Marie watched as the car drove away in the rain.

"She's in high school," he answered. "Come on."

He led her into the classroom and seated her at one of the small desks on the left side, facing the teacher's desk, before finding a large desk for himself on the opposite side. A sea of children separated Phyllis Marie from her brother, some of them in small desks, some of them in middle-sized desks, and three boys, including Kenneth, in large desks. Phyllis Marie wanted to cry.

The other two eighth graders had known each other their
entire lives and took no notice of the new boy. Big farm
boys who stood nearly six feet already, Harold and Denton
jostled and punched one another in boyish fun bordering on
hostility—giggling like little children one moment, challenging
each other to greater feats of strength the next—as they traded
punches to the shoulder with their big calloused hands. Their
behavior proved infectious. All the children emulated them
by shouting and pushing one another, giggling and talking in
loud voices and with rapid motions.

The teacher, Ruth Pitty, had graduated from Friends
University with a teaching degree in the spring of 1924. She
wore a tiny bonnet over her tiny head and tiny shoes on
her tiny feet. At a height of four feet and eleven inches, she
stood shorter than a third of the children in this, her very first
classroom.

When she entered the room, no one noticed. She put down
her books and stood behind her desk the way she had been
taught, expecting the children to see her and quiet down, but
it didn't work. She wrote her name in big, bold strokes on the
blackboard, reaching up as high as she could, but the children
didn't notice. She announced her name as loudly as she could,
but no one heard her. Finally, out of desperation, she took the
yardstick down from the blackboard and slapped it on her
desk seven times, until there was silence.

"My name is Miss Pitty," she said. Before she could draw
another breath, Harold burst out laughing.

"I'm glad I'm not sitting too close!" All the other children
laughed at his coarse comment. To her discredit, Miss Pitty
did not get the joke.

"What's your name?" she asked.

"Harold, Miss Spitty," he answered, emphasizing his
pronunciation, to everyone's giggling glee. Now she heard
it, and in a horrible moment, wondered why it had never
occurred to her that this particular perversion of her name
could become a problem in a classroom. Certainly she had
considered that a student might refer to her as 'Miss Pitiful,'

but she had managed to matriculate without recognizing the potential for this dreadful comparison to a bodily function. She felt her ears turn red.

"Come up here, Harold." She brought her chair around to the side of the desk.

The classroom fell silent. Was this really to be the new teacher's first act, to spank the class bully? Did she really think she could get away with that?

Phyllis Marie's heart jumped into her throat. *What is she going to do? She's not going to strike him, is she? Is this what school is all about? If this teacher is starting with that big boy, how long will it be before she strikes Kenneth, before she strikes me?*

The boy knew what was expected of him and he gracefully leaned down, taking the back of the chair in his hands. Miss Pitty applied her yardstick to Harold's backside ten times, with as much force as she could muster, as much as she dared, without breaking the yardstick. When she was done, the boy stood up and faced her, towering over her.

"If you're done dusting my pants off for me, I'll go back to my desk."

The children howled, except for Phyllis Marie. She had felt the pain of every blow, the pain Harold had denied, and it was too much for her. She burst into tears, and worse, she wet her black bloomers. Within moments, Miss Pitty was standing in front of her, trying to console her, but Phyllis Marie wasn't about to be consoled by the woman who had just beaten another student right before her eyes. Kenneth came to her rescue.

"I'm her brother," he said. "I think I should take her home."

"Yes, you do that," she said. Kenneth took Phyllis Marie's hand and they left immediately. The rain stopped shortly after the children started walking.

When Hazel saw her children walking up the path from the road, she dried her hands but didn't leave the house. She waited for them to arrive.

"What happened?"

"Go change your clothes," Kenneth told his sister. "I'll tell her about it."

Phyllis Marie dashed up the back steps and into her room. She changed into a flannel shirt and her dungarees and came back downstairs, where she found her mother sitting at the table shelling walnuts with a hammer and a brick.

"Where is Kenneth?"

"He's gone back to school."

The girl looked at her mother, who did not look up from her work.

"Do I need to go back to school?"

"Yes, tomorrow."

"Am I in trouble?"

"Does thee think thee is in trouble?"

The child thought about that a long time.

"No."

"Good." Her mother looked up. "Would thee like to learn how to shell walnuts?"

21

The door banged against the wall, awakening Perry.

"Lieutenant Row! Breakfast at oh two hundred! Briefing at oh three hundred!"

"Hey, wait a second there," Billy called after the messenger. "Why didn't you call me?"

"Hey, shut up!" the new pilot in Worthington's bunk said.

"You've been bumped. Your crew is the Deputy Squadron Leader, so the Major is riding shotgun as Command Pilot."

"Aw, that stinks!"

The messenger went on down the road as Billy turned to Perry. "If I don't have the same number of missions as you, we won't get to go home together!"

"You should get dressed and come with me to the briefing. Maybe you can catch a ride somewhere. They're always asking for substitutes."

"Yeah!" Billy shouted.

"Oh come on, you guys," the other pilot said. "Give us a break."

Perry and Billy rode their bicycles to the Mess Hall so Billy could look for a sign-up sheet or talk to someone about getting on the mission.

"It just so happens," an officer with a clipboard said, "I need a tail gunner in the Squadron Leader. You'd have to pull double duty as Formation Observer, relay information about who needs to pull in tight, come up, that sort of thing. Have you ever done that?"

"Yes, sir," Billy lied.

"Okay, you're on."

Billy got his eggs and joined Perry at the table.

"If you're in the tail of the Squadron Leader, and I'm piloting the Deputy slot, we'll be eyeball to eyeball."

"Yeah, that's right, Perry, so watch out, because I'll be the guy giving orders, telling you to pull in closer."

"Yes, sir, Lieutenant Poythress, sir!" Perry grinned.

After take off and formation, Perry glanced forward and left at the tail of the Squadron Leader. He could make out Billy's familiar features, even behind the oxygen mask. When he waved, Billy waved back.

The major, the Command Pilot in Billy's co-pilot seat, took no notice. He studied his flight and battle plan, speaking to Perry only when his duties as co-pilot required it. On two previous raids to the port and shipyards of Emden, the three-ninetieth had met no resistance from the Luftwaffe, so they didn't expect any today either, but just as the forty-one Forts crossed landfall above the Dutch coast, six twin-engine enemy fighters attacked.

E saw them first from his top turret position. "Bogies at twelve o'clock coming out of the clouds!"

He and Bud Fitzsimmons on the new chin turret started firing their fifty calibers at the three lead fighters. Ignoring the Phyllis Marie, the fighter group aimed their entire firepower at the Squadron Leader. E ripped through the lead enemy fighter and it burst into flames just as Bud leveled at least a dozen shots into the number one engine and pilot compartment of another, but it was too late. Three of the other four fighters launched rockets into the American Squadron Leader. Before anyone could act, it exploded in flames, one wing separating completely from the fuselage.

Jump, Billy.

"I see two chutes," the major said.

"I confirm that," Perry responded, and thought, *but not from the tail.*

Billy, jump, damn it.

The burning debris that had been the Squadron Leader fell toward the earth.

Billy didn't jump.

As Deputy Squadron Leader, Perry didn't have time to think about Billy, to grieve for Billy. He flew forward, assuming the position of Squadron Leader.

"Kiss," Perry called.

"What's going on?" he answered.

"We're Squadron Leader now. You're the new Formation Observer"

"Got it," Kiss said, followed by, "Seven nine three, come up. Four two eight, come forward."

Thirty additional single engine enemy fighters attacked from the south, dropping four more B-17s in an extended battle that lasted an apparent eternity, until the three-ninetieth knocked about two dozen from the sky. Perry could hear Kiss's voice on the interphone, taking over what had been Billy's role, adjusting the airplanes in the group formation behind them.

"Bud," Perry called into the interphone.

"Yeah."

"You're the Group Bombardier now."

"Yeah."

"Are you all set?"

"Yeah. For Billy."

Gunners fired angrily at enemy fighters buzzing around Perry's ears as he adjusted his course and became the rock upon which the other pilots leaned.

"Bud," Perry said, "I'm starting the bomb run now."

"I show four minutes from drop."

"Four minutes."

Fly the airplane, Perry thought, *as accurately as I can, allowing no distractions.*

"I show three minutes," Bud said.

"Three minutes."

Pretty bad cloud cover, Perry thought. *He'll be able to drop, but we won't get accurate assessment, not today.*

"I show two minutes," Bud said.

"It's all yours," Perry answered, relinquishing control of the airplane.

"Got it."

Out of Perry's view, Bud looked through the bombsite for another hundred twenty seconds. Boettcher watched as Bud released the bombs and called "Bombs away!" The thirty-five surviving bombardiers in the remaining thirty-five Forts of the three-ninetieth released their bombs on Bud's cue.

Perry felt the familiar upward jolt as six tons of armaments fell from Phyllis Marie's bomb bay.

"It's all yours, Perry."

"Got it," Perry said, banking left and setting Boettcher's course for home, leaving Billy's remains behind in a field somewhere in the Netherlands.

The officers at the briefing hailed Perry and his crew as celebrities, conquering heroes, obligated to pose for photographs with the base commander and the Major who had been their Command Pilot, the man for whom Billy had been bumped. Word got around that the charm was still at work; it was true they had lost their co-pilot, but that was because he had ridden in another airplane. The men of the three-ninetieth mourned the loss of the Squadron Leader and his crew, but they celebrated Perry and his lucky crew seven and the Phyllis Marie, for they had led the show today.

Despite their new celebrity status, lucky crew seven did not feel jubilant. They wandered away from the festivities as soon as they could—the enlisted men to their quarters and the officers to their hut. Upon their return, his two surviving officers watched Perry as he opened Billy's foot locker and removed the fifth of Canadian Club Whisky that matched his own. They had bought the two bottles together on their first trip to London. Neither officer questioned him about it, although Perry could see the curious expressions on their faces. He chose not to explain.

On a three-day pass to London, given in appreciation of their role in the Emden raid, Perry and his two officers made the best of a bad situation. Bud already had a steady girl, whom Boettcher referred to as Bud's Irish Colleen.

"Say, Colleen," Boettcher said, "haven't you a couple of friends for my mates here? We could go dancing."

"Sure," she said, and arranged for the four of them to meet her friends at a local nightclub.

"This won't do," Perry said. "I'm married."

"To our airplane," Boettcher said, laughing.

"These are nice girls, Perry," Colleen said. "They just want to dance and have some fun."

The six got acquainted a bit, and when Boettcher asked one girl to dance, the other girl asked Perry.

"Go on," Bud said. "I'll order drinks all around."

"Oh, all right," Perry said reluctantly.

"I understand you lost a mate recently," the girl observed, but her thick Scottish brogue left Perry helpless.

"What did you say?"

"I said—don't worry about it. I love this song, don't you?"

Perry doubted she had said the same thing twice, but it didn't matter, since he didn't understand her either time. When he saw the drinks arrive at the table, he gestured that they return.

"Here you are, Captain," Bud said as Perry sat down, handing him a gin martini straight up.

Perry took a sip. "It tastes like gasoline."

"Eat the olive," Bud suggested.

He and his girl danced while the girl who had danced with Perry sulked a bit, but she drank her martini quickly and convinced Boettcher to dance with her. Perry followed her example and drained his glass.

"Another round," he called to the passing waiter.

Perry drank a second and then third martini. He watched his companions dance, and declined further invitations, forcing Boettcher to accommodate both girls, a task he didn't seem to mind. Unaccustomed to the steady and heavy drinking, and before he could wonder what a fourth martini might do to him, Perry passed out in a puddle of gin under the table.

The following morning, he awoke alone in an unknown room with the taste of rancid juniper in his mouth and a headache that he could not place, having never had one quite like it before. *Where is my wallet,* he asked himself, and sat up, locating it on the bed stand, complete with money and identification papers.

Where's Billy? Did he go to breakfast without me? He looked around at the unfamiliar wallpaper, the strange lamps on the bureau, and when memory came, before he could gather himself, before he could prevent it, he buried his face in his hands and wept uncontrollably, his deep sobs harsh against his throat.

22

"Mom?"

"Yes, Ped."

The nine-year-old boy sat up on one of the chairs at the kitchen table where Georgia prepared dinner. She read in his face that something weighed heavily on his mind, but she waited for him to figure out what he wanted to say. He was such a quiet child. She took every opportunity to encourage him to express himself.

"Why don't I have a brother?"

"A brother? Well, let me see." She thought he looked like he knew she was stalling, looking for an answer, so she'd better give him one. "I guess that's just the way it worked out," she said. "You have three sisters, two older ones and one younger one."

"Yes, I know that, but no brothers."

"No, that's right, no brothers." She waited to see what else he had to say, but he didn't seem to have anything to add. "Why do you ask?"

"Well, if I had a brother, then it would be easier to fly airplanes."

"Would it? How?"

"Well, I could throw one and he could catch it, and then he could throw it back to me."

"Oh, I see. Have you asked your sisters to play airplane with you?"

"I'm not talking about playing, Mom, I'm talking about flying, actually flying in the air, like one of Old Man Persons models, except—"

"Except what?"

"Except those models are too small. I want one I can get inside and actually fly, like—"

"Like Lindbergh."

"Yes," he said, a big grin crossing his face. "Do you think

I could fly someday?"

"Yes, I do. I think you have the ability to do whatever you want to do, whatever you decide to do, but Ped dear, it isn't just a matter of wanting it. If you plan to fly an airplane someday, you have to study hard. You have to learn things like science, mathematics, and physics."

"Yes," he said quietly. "I know." He played with one of the string beans from the table, holding the stem between his thumb and forefinger, spinning it. "I think having a brother would help, too."

23

Edwin Stanton was nearly forty and no stranger to pig farming. He had raised pigs off and on since childhood, despite his more urbane alternate career as a photographer. He was neither a poor man nor a rich one. He worked hard to earn enough to keep his family fed and clothed, and the work was never harder than when he took over the Ekeland farm.

No one had planted a sweet corn crop during the summer, so there was no harvest except for the feed corn. Fortunately he discovered an abundance of seed corn in the storage barn—the second of the three barns behind the house—so that was one issue he did not have to face.

The poultry shed—the outbuilding closest to the house— housed no chickens, no poultry of any kind, but he had a plan, which was to place fifteen-year-old Virginia in charge of raising poultry, both chickens and turkeys. He hoped that by the spring he would have enough money to get her started with several dozen of each.

This left the last and largest problem to overcome. There were no pigs in the pig barn. If he hoped to have something to take to market in late summer, he had to get started right away. He needed a boar, several sows, and a couple dozen weaned piglets, preferably gilts and barrows, although he found all the tools necessary for castration in the storage barn, so if it was necessary, he could buy uncastrated piglets. With the feed crops in the field, he could start looking right away, but first he began the difficult task of thoroughly cleaning the pig barn, something no one had done in over a year. When Hazel saw him putting on the long rubber hip boots and rubber gloves, she quietly joined him.

Meanwhile, Kenneth took Phyllis Marie to school each morning on his bicycle. She sat on the handlebars and leaned back against him, his body, swaying back and forth as he propelled them forward. If school means I get to ride on the bicycle with my big brother, maybe it isn't so bad after all, she thought.

As they passed a house along the way, a big brown neighbor dog came running at them, barking and snarling.

"Look out!" Phyllis Marie cried. The mutt nipped at her heels. "Ow! Get away!"

A smaller black and gray dog caught Kenneth's cuff and tore it.

"Hey, you!" he shouted. "I'll get you for that!"

Phyllis Marie started to cry as Kenneth pumped the pedals as hard as he could. Finally out of range of the dogs, which trotted back to their home, Kenneth turned the bicycle around and stopped.

"Are you all right?"

"He bit me," Phyllis Marie snuffled.

"Let me see."

She kicked off her shoe while he kept his eye on the retreating dogs.

After pulling her sock off for a quick inspection, he said, "He didn't break the skin."

"Are we going to have to come back this way?"

"Don't worry," he said, picking up her shoe. "I'll take care of those two."

They went on their way to school. At the lunch hour, Kenneth and the other two eighth graders took the horse and filled the hayrack with hard, dry dirt clods, and set off down the road. Whether the teacher noticed their departure or not didn't concern them. They were on an important mission.

As they approached, the two dogs came running at them, barking and snarling.

"Get them!" Kenneth shouted.

The boys immediately armed themselves, and as soon as their targets were in range, they started chucking their clods as hard as they could. The smaller dog turned tail immediately, but the big brown dog, the nasty one, kept coming. The boys kept up the barrage until finally, one of the clods hit the dog square in the mouth. He stopped and spat dirt.

"Hit him again!" Kenneth shouted, and the boys started running toward the dog, chucking clods lightly now, more as a threat and a reminder. The dog turned tail, joining his little friend behind the fence, and as soon as the boys got to the fence, they saw two old men sitting on the porch in rocking chairs. For the a moment, Kenneth worried he'd catch hell for what he had done, but then he looked at the men a little more closely. They were laughing.

After school, Kenneth shoved a few hard clods in his pockets. He didn't need them, though. When he and Phyllis Marie passed the house, the dogs stayed on the porch and hid behind their masters' chairs.

When they got home, Phyllis Marie ran inside to change clothes and ran out just as quickly. She made a beeline straight to what had become her secret tree. Within half an hour she was sitting in the crook, five feet above the ground, spying out her path to the roof of the poultry house. She was determined not only to reach it, but to walk it. She planned her route carefully, knowing that one slip meant a fall to the ground. Finally, when she thought she was ready, she lit off across the branch without any hesitation. She didn't stop until she was way out above the poultry house. By grasping the branch with her hands and swinging down, she could bring her feet within a one-foot drop to the roof. She waited for her body to stop swinging and then let go, landing perfectly on all fours, as gracefully as if she had practiced it a dozen times. She sat back against the branch and surveyed her realm like a queen.

Edwin found a pig farmer east of Wichita who was willing to sell him two boars and eight sows for a song.

"What's wrong with them?" Edwin asked.

"Nothing," the old man said. "I'm retiring and moving with my daughter to California. No more pigs for me."

The old man delivered the pigs the next day and suddenly, Edwin had a drove. He put one boar and four sows in one family pen and the rest in another, leaving two family pens open for farrowing and future expansion.

Hazel found a Victrola megaphone in the attic. She brought it downstairs and dusted it off, thinking it would come in handy for calling Edwin in from the fields. It showed its usefulness sooner than expected.

The following Saturday, Hazel offered to pay Phyllis Marie an allowance to shell walnuts for one penny per cup. The girl used the brick and hammer the way Hazel had shown her, working down in the root cellar, where the walnut harvest waited in burlap bags.

As she worked, a mouse emerged from a hole in the wall. "Hello," she said with polite curiosity.

The mouse rose up on its hind legs.

"Do you want some walnuts?"

Wanting to see the mouse more closely, Phyllis Marie picked it up by the tail, but it twisted and bit her on the thumb.

"Ow!" she screamed. "Let go!"

The mouse hung on with its jaws, so Phyllis Marie flung her hand with a snap, and the mouse went flying.

Hazel arrived at that moment to find her weeping daughter's thumb bleeding.

"What happened?"

She bundled Phyllis Marie up to the kitchen to wash and dress the wound, but she could not understand the girl's incomprehensible tale.

"Hold that in the hot water for a moment," she said, taking up the megaphone and stepping out onto the back porch. "Edwin! Yoo hoo!" She shouted into the cone until she saw him wave and start running toward the house.

"Come on, daughter," he said when he arrived. "Calm down and show us what happened."

Her thumb newly bandaged, Phyllis Marie led them down the steps of the root cellar and pointed to the worktable. The three of them saw it at once: a dead mouse lying on the brick, his little skull cracked open like one of the walnuts. Before anyone could react, a strange cat jumped up on the table, took the mouse in its mouth, and jumped down to the floor.

"Whose cat is that?" Edwin asked.

"Can we keep it?" Phyllis Marie countered.

"Well," Edwin said, his voice trailing away. The girl smiled.

When the cold Kansas winter settled in, Edwin made a discovery of his own: that there was a space behind the big wood stove in the kitchen that was large enough to stand and dress. It didn't take long until every member of the family waited eagerly to hear that it was his or her turn to occupy that space. The cat, which decided to stay, considered this a great imposition but allowed the invasion, knowing it would not last very long.

In the spring, Edwin came to the dinner table with an old book in his hands.

"Virginia, I need thy help."

"Yes, father?"

"I need thee to be in charge of the poultry, like thee was back in Colorado. We are going to raise both chickens and turkeys."

"Yes, father. I can do that."

"Good," he said. "I have a gift for thee. This was my father's book. It has everything thee needs to know about raising chickens. If you have questions or need help, just ask."

"Yes, father."

"Tomorrow, after school, thee and I shall take a look at the poultry house and see what it needs. I hope to buy some chicks on Saturday, and thee can come with me."

The next day Edwin built an elevated brooding box from an old washtub and some wide mesh screen, finishing it in time to show it to Virginia when she arrived after school. Together they placed it in the corner of the poultry house behind the small wood-burning stove.

"Thee shall need to keep this stove running day and night for at least six weeks," Edwin said. Kenneth and thy mother and I will help thee."

On Saturday, the two of them drove to another farm nearby and bought three-dozen chicks.

"When do we get the turkeys?" Virginia asked as they drove home.

"In a month we'll see how the chickens are doing. We need them to get established before we can start the turkey poults."

"Poults?"

"That's what turkey chicks are called."

Meanwhile, with Virginia and her father away, Phyllis Marie took the opportunity to try something she had been planning for a few days. She opened one of the double-doors of the poultry house and one of the double doors of the storage barn and sure enough, just as she thought, they met end to end in a straight line with only a few inches gap in-between. She ran back around to the near side of the poultry house and climbed the cottonwood tree, easily scrambling out onto the roof of the poultry house. Running to the far end of the building, she sat on the edge and lowered her feet to the upper edge of the poultry house door. It waggled dreadfully. If she was going to achieve her goal, she was going to have to stabilize that door.

She ran along the peak of the roof back to the cottonwood tree, scrambled down to the ground, and ran to the other side of the poultry house. She looked until she found four big rocks. She placed them on the ground, one on each side of the poultry house door and one on each side of the storage barn door, testing that both doors felt immobilized. The storage barn door did not, so she brought a ladder outside and leaned it against the door before running back to the other side of the poultry house, up the tree, out onto the roof, and back to the far side of the structure.

She sat down on the edge again, and lowered her feet to the poultry house door. It felt secure enough, so she stood up on it. In one fleet motion, she placed one foot in front of the other, step by step, crossed over to the storage barn door, and walked along the top of the door until she reached the storage barn. She hoisted herself up onto the roof, climbed to the higher peak of her newest conquest, and surveyed the scene, just in time to look over the house and see her father's truck coming up the road.

By the time Edwin stopped next to the poultry house and pulled the handbrake on the car, the poultry house and storage barn doors were closed and Phyllis Marie was jumping up and down next to the cargo door at the back of the car.

"Are those the new chicks? Can I see them? Can I hold them?"

Over the course of the year, Phyllis Marie extended her range, opening the door on the other side of the storage barn and running across that second chasm to the pig barn. At the far end of the pig barn stood a tall river birch tree with sweeping branches that reached across the peak of the building. Phyllis Marie climbed her secret cottonwood, ran across the poultry house and the storage barn to the roof of the pig barn and hid in the branches of the river birch, wishing there were more doors to prop open, more barns to conquer. From this secret vantage point, she could see her father and the men he had hired working in the corn and sorghum fields to the north and east.

Virginia raised a flock of chickens and when they started producing eggs, Edwin came home with two-dozen turkey poults. He and Virginia separated the two flocks in the poultry house, giving the new poults the wood-burning stove, and arranging a larger brooding box on the ground for them, instead of the elevated one they had used for the chickens. Virginia enlisted her younger sister's assistance in feeding the turkeys, which ate mashed, hard-boiled chicken eggs with a lot of pepper. Phyllis Marie peeled the eggs, Virginia mashed and peppered them, and by the end of the third year, she started to make a lot of money with her turkeys.

Edwin's pig business took off, too, and before long he had a large enough drove that he started selling pigs for meat through his butcher job at Safeway. He advertised and sold live piglets in the Wichita newspapers, and saw a reasonable profit. He invested in a wagon and two horses, which Phyllis Marie named Biddie and Browny, and made room in the storage barn for them. With the addition of the wagon, he could hurry the corn harvest, to the benefit of humans and pigs alike.

The Stantons attended the University Monthly Meeting of Friends every Sunday, as they had done twenty years earlier, before their departure to California. In 1925, construction began on a new building of their own, two blocks east of the University, at the corner of University and Glenn. On October 10, 1926, the group assembled in their accustomed basement for the beginning of worship, and then paraded down the street en masse to the newly completed structure, where the worship service ended.

All the family members attended: the blood uncles, aunts, and cousins, and the other uncles, aunts, and cousins. Both were held in the same esteem as far as the Stantons were concerned. Phyllis Marie knew no difference. The Carters and their sons, Bill and Tommy, the Mendenhalls, the Rows, with their three daughters, Corliss, Lois, and Helen, and their son Perry, and their cousins, Ernest and Betsy Crow, with their two sons, Jim and Ernie. The Chilsons did not attend, being away at their mission in Ruanda-Urundi.

Phyllis Marie wept as she walked, carrying her candle, separated from her family. She did not understand what was happening. When she arrived at the new home of the Meeting, she jumped for joy at finding them.

By the same time the following year, eight-year-old Phyllis Marie had conquered the outbuildings at the farm. Whenever Edwin and Virginia were away, and she could play her game without interference, she propped open all of the barn doors and anchored them with the nearby special rocks she kept. She flew up the cottonwood tree without a thought now, having done it so many times, and ran along the peaked roofs and doors at full speed until she reached the last run of the last barn. From there she leaped out into space as far as she could, catching the big birch branch just right, so that it swung her down to the ground and dropped her as gracefully on her feet as a swan flying in and landing on a pond. Without pausing, she ran to the other end and climbed the cottonwood, repeating the circuit.

Hazel worked at the kitchen sink, watching out the back window, marveling at the imagination of her daughter, praying that caution would see her through to the end of the game without a fall, remembering the Robert Frost poem she had read recently in a magazine.

One could do worse than be a swinger of birches.

When Phyllis Marie wasn't running her aerial course, she was playing tea-party hostess to her three pet ducks, Ike, Mike, and Pike, who followed her around like she was their mother. They waited for her at the base of the cottonwood tree, eternally quacking surprise when she came running back from the other end of her course.

Phyllis Marie always kept ducks for pets, dressing them in little baby bonnets She particularly enjoyed taking them for rides on her tire swing in the river birch, and watching them bob and weave back and forth in a fruitless effort to keep their heads in one place. She always had a box or two of snakes she had gathered in the fields or along the riverbeds, but she had to take care that the cats, ducks, and chickens didn't get to them.

In late October of 1927, it began to rain.

"Edwin, wake up," Hazel said, sitting up on the edge of the bed and placing her feet on the floor.

"I hear rain."

"Yes." Her husband raised himself on his elbow. "It has been raining hard for three hours. Is thee worried?"

Hazel nodded, her blue eyes wide. "I feel as if something terrible is going to happen."

"I can understand."

"Is thee not worried?"

"Not from only three hours, no." Running his hand sleepily through his hair, Edwin stifled a yawn. "It does remind me of the flood, though."

"Yes."

"Now, thee must remember we are on higher ground here."

"I know."

"Even if the Little Arkansas overflows its banks and floods the bridge, we will still be quite safe."

She did not respond.

"Come back to bed," he said with a plea in his voice. "It's cold without thee."

Hazel tried not to smile, but one corner of her mouth quirked up in spite of her determination.

"That's better," her husband observed.

She moved close to him and pulled the covers over their heads.

24

Hard rain fell throughout the following three days and nights. The ground turned to mush, so that Edwin lost a shoe when he visited the pig barn, but upon his return, he reported that everything was safe, that there were no concerns with any of the livestock. The family stayed indoors and waited out the storm.

During the fourth night, the house was rocked by thunder and lightning. One bolt struck so close that they heard the electrical sizzle of it at the same time they saw the blinding light, followed immediately by thunder.

"I think it hit the walnut tree," Edwin said.

Finally, after five days of hard steady rain, the storm abated, and Edwin went out again to inspect the crops and the bridge. Not daring to take the car, he hitched the hayrack to the two horses, Biddie and Browny, and came back two hours later with the report that, indeed, the Little Arkansas had overflowed its banks and covered the bridge to town.

"The walnut tree has been split in two," he said. "Several acres of corn are under water, and the cabin down there by the river is flooded."

"So is the root cellar," Hazel said, "and Irvin called. He wants to bring supplies, but he already knows the bridge is under water."

"That's all right, we can get them across in the hayrack."

"Will thee call him?"

"Yes." Edwin shrugged off his wet rain slicker and kicked off his boots in the kitchen before walking through the dining room and living room to the front hall. He took the telephone earpiece in his left hand and turned the crank several times with his right.

"Good morning to you, too," he said, responding to the operator.

"Yes, we're all fine out here, and you?"

"Good, I'm glad to hear it."

"Yes, thank you. Would you ring my brother, please?"

Then, after a pause, he said, "Yes, it's me. I understand thee is in need of a water taxi service."

"Yes—"

"Yes—"

"All right, I'll meet thee at the bridge in two hours."

"Yes—"

"Yes—Goodbye."

Hazel stood behind him. "He's bringing someone?"

"Everyone, like it was a picnic."

"Oh, dear. I had best get some food ready."

"No, they are bringing the picnic, and a lot of other supplies."

"Oh."

"They're worried about us, since this is our second major catastrophe in a decade, but guess what, Hazel?"

"What?"

"We're just fine."

"Are we?"

"Yes, we are."

Edwin and the family took Biddie and Browny and the hayrack down to the riverbank. The rain had stopped and the sun struggled to lay claim to Kansas once again, but it had not yet succeeded. Hazel and the children got out when they saw Irvin's car pull up on the other side of the river. Edwin slapped the reins and encouraged the two horses into the water. A week ago they could have walked across, but today they could no longer touch the riverbed and they began to swim. The wagon floated along behind them like a boat with Edwin onboard, constantly re-directing the horses upstream, away from the bridge, to compensate for the ground they lost due to the current. When they got to the other side, Edwin drove them up on the bank and around in a great circle so they faced the river again. Mary and Lucile climbed in, while Irvin and Edwin loaded box after box and bag after bag into the back.

Finally, with Irvin's car secured against any further rain, they started back across, Biddie and Browny paddling as fast as they could go. They reached the near bank and gathered the Stanton family in for the ride home.

When they got to the farm, Hazel was the first to dismount. "Edwin, the root cellar is flooded. We've lost a lot of food, but the canned goods, they can be saved, can't they?"

"Yes," he said. "With some special talent, I think they can." He turned to the wagon and lifted first Lucile and then Phyllis Marie down to the soggy ground. "Girls, I have a special job for you."

"I'll get a hot bath ready for them," Hazel said. "Come on, Mary, Virginia, we have work to do."

Edwin led the girls to the root cellar, with Irvin and Kenneth following.

"We need you two girls to go in there and rescue every can and jar you can reach. Are you able?"

"Yes, father," Phyllis Marie said. "Come on, Lucile."

The two girls went down the stairs and into the cold murky water up to their waists. Kenneth stood on the stairs, receiving the cans and jars from the girls and passing them up to the two men, who loaded them into a wheelbarrow and took them in batches to the kitchen.

When the girls gave up, partly because they could not see any more cans to retrieve and partly out of cold and exhaustion, Edwin and Irvin carried them into the house and the waiting arms of their mothers, who bathed them, fed them hot soup, and put them to bed.

More families came with carloads of supplies—all their friends from the Friends Meeting. With each telephone call, Edwin drove Biddie and Browny down to the river to pick up the new arrivals: the Chilsons and their two daughters, Rachel and Esther; the Carters and their sons, Bill and Tommy; the Mendenhalls; the Gidleys; and the Crows, with their two sons.

Kenneth brought out the canoe, so he and Bill Carter could take it to the fields and use it to paddle up and down the rows of corn, salvaging as much as they could. The families feasted on roasted corn and butter that night, so much of it and so delightful that most of them could not remember that Hazel had prepared her famous pork chops and red gravy, too.

Families slept everywhere, in the parlor, in the living room, in the dining room, and no one complained. A part of the Friends Meeting was the gathering together of family during crisis, whether the family ties were held together by bloodlines or not. Phyllis Marie grew up in an atmosphere of family where every adult man was an uncle, every adult woman an aunt.

The next day, Kenneth and Bill left early with the canoe. Everyone assumed the boys had headed for the cornfield, but they assumed wrong.

"Bill, wake up," Kenneth had whispered in the darkness. The boys had dressed quietly and left before anyone could challenge their plans.

They drove the hayrack across the Little Arkansas and up to Sullivan's Dam.

Shouting, Kenneth could barely make himself heard against the sound of rushing water. "Look at that!"

"Are you sure this is a good idea?" Bill shouted back.

"Sure! It's a once-in-a-lifetime chance! When else are we going to be able to shoot the chutes with water this high?"

"Where can we put in?"

"Over here," Kenneth said, picking up one end of the canoe.

Bill picked up the other end and they climbed to a spot above the dam.

The city fathers had built the chutes in the late nineteenth century as part of a recreation center with picnicking and ice cream and lemonade. When built in 1897, the chutes were one hundred fifty feet long but not intended for use in white water like Kenneth and Bill were seeing today.

They put the canoe in the water and climbed in. As they paddled into the stream they picked up speed until there was no point in paddling. The only thing to do was hold on tight as they approached the chutes.

Bang!

They hit the rapids with a force neither of them had imagined. They sped along at a dizzying speed, as the water buffeted them from side to side. Suddenly the canoe pulled left, then right, then left again, and over it went, spilling the two boys upside down into the water. For a few moments, Kenneth couldn't get his bearings and found himself scrabbling at the wooden planks of the chutes, thinking he had been swimming toward the surface. He righted himself and came to the surface in a huge gasp for air, just as the thrill ride ended and he spilled into the river.

"Bill!"

Kenneth couldn't see him.

"Bill!"

Kenneth swam to the bank and scrambled up onto a large rock. From there, he saw the inverted canoe, held against the planks of the chutes by the strong currents, which were pinning Bill's body against the interior of the canoe. Kenneth jumped feet first into the water above the chutes and allowed the current to guide him into the canoe, which broke loose at his kick. Once in the relative calm of the river, Kenneth reached the boy and turned him over so his face was out of the water, but he was unconscious. Kenneth swam hard, dragging him back to the water's edge and up onto the muddy bank. He flopped him over onto his belly and squeezed a pint of water out of him before he started to sputter and cough.

"Bill!"

Bill hacked and coughed for several minutes before sitting up under his own power.

"I must be crazy," he said.

"Yeah, me too," Kenneth answered. "Shall we go again?"

Bill looked around. "Where's the canoe?"

"I don't know."

They found the canoe washed up on the opposite bank of the river. By the time they retrieved it and hiked back up to the top of the chutes, they were both exhausted and secretly pleased that they didn't have to try again because of it. They loaded the canoe into the hayrack and headed the horses home.

The boys made light of their adventure that day, but Edwin and Hazel and Bill's parents were not happy. The six of them sat around the kitchen table, the boys, wrapped in blankets, sitting closest to the stove.

"I knew something terrible was going to happen," Hazel said, reminding Edwin of her premonition the first night of the flood. "You two are lucky that one of you didn't drown."

The boys said nothing. What good would it do to tell them that one of them had nearly done so?

The telephone rang and Edwin left the kitchen to answer it.

Hazel stood and paced up and down. "That canoe is going away in the attic, and thee is not to use it again until next summer, is that understood?"

"Yes, ma'am," Kenneth said.

"That goes for both of you."

"Yes, ma'am," Bill echoed.

Edwin came back into the kitchen, his face white, his eyes focused on his wife. He brought Hazel's sister, Edna Chilson, with him from the front room where she had been chatting.

"What is it?" Hazel asked.

"That was Western Union."

"Oh, no."

"It's from George Outland."

"Josephine," she said. "She's gone."

"Yes."

25

Perry had been curled up in his bunk all day. When he awoke at nine, he accepted another officer's offer of coffee and toast made on the hut stove, but he kept to himself, reading Churchill's "World in Crisis", the second volume, which he had promised himself he would complete by the New Year. It didn't look as if he would make it.

Perry ignored Bud and Boettcher, sitting on the edge of Bud's bunk—the men had rearranged the furniture after Billy's death two weeks ago—until finally Bud spoke.

"Are you just going to stay in bed all day?"

"That was my plan, yes," Perry answered without looking up.

"Come with us," Boettcher said. "We're going to help put up the decorations for the party tonight."

"It's Christmas Eve," Bud said, reaching across and patting Perry on the knee. Perry pulled away, turning himself and his book toward the wall.

"You go ahead. I want to read."

The door banged against the wall, startling the three men.

"Captain Row! Lieutenants Boettcher and Fitzsimmons! Consider yourselves on Stand By! Captain Row! Report at once to the base commander's office," the messenger said before pulling the door shut and bicycling down the lane.

"I wonder what that's all about," Bud said.

"I'll go find out." Perry swung his legs off the bed and reached for his pants.

"You don't suppose we have a mission now, do you?" Boettcher asked. "It's three o'clock in the afternoon."

"On Christmas Eve," Bud said.

"You go on to the mess hall and I'll catch up with you there," Perry said, pulling on his boots.

At the commander's office, the door stood open and the

empty desk outside sat in mute testimony to the holiday. Perry knocked.

"Come in, Captain Row."

Perry's promotion had been the only bright spot in the past week. The Eighth Air Force might have listed Billy as Missing In Action, but everyone on board the Phyllis Marie that day knew better. Perry felt relief at the fact that he had received his Captain's bars in time for his first face-to-face meeting with the commander. Stepping into the office and saluting, Perry realized this was not to be a face-to-face meeting however. A British officer sat with his back to Perry, facing the commander, who returned Perry's salute and offered him a chair.

"Major, this is the man I've been telling you about, Captain Row, Perry V. He has completed twenty missions for us, the last three as one of our Squadron Leaders. Captain, this is Major Haskins, Nigel, British Special Detachment to the three-ninetieth."

"My pleasure, sir," Perry said, shaking hands with the man seated next to him.

"Captain," the British Officer said cordially before rising from his seat and leaving the office, closing the door behind him.

"He'll be back," the commander said, "after we've had a chance to chat."

"Yes, sir."

"How's it going, Perry? I know you had a rough go of it after losing Lieutenant Poythress. I want you to be frank with me."

Perry considered carefully before answering. "Yes, sir, it hasn't been easy. I've had a different co-pilot for each mission since I lost Billy, some better than others—"

"But none of them Billy."

"Yes, sir."

"One of those co-pilots rotated out after flying with you. It was his twenty-fifth mission."

"I didn't know that, sir."

"No, I know you didn't know. He told me you were one of the best pilots on the base, but he also said you gave him nothing, no opportunity to get to know you, no conversation, not even a 'well done,' after the mission. Why was that, Captain?"

Perry sat quietly, thinking about it.

"If you don't know the answer, I can guess at it."

"Sir?"

"You don't want to get hurt again."

"Yes, sir, I suppose that's true. I miss Billy terribly."

"Tell me about him."

"He was a better pilot than me, sir, but just a boy really, very naïve, from North Carolina. Up there and on the ground, too, he knew what I was going to do before I did. Until the Emden mission, I had never had another co-pilot. He was like a brother, sir."

"Yes, I see. I'm going to get you someone steady for your last five missions."

"That would be a big help, sir."

"What about the rest of your time?"

"Sir?"

"Are you sleeping?"

"Sometimes," Perry said, "but with sleep comes the nightmare."

"Just one nightmare?"

"Yes, sir, seeing the Squadron Leader going down."

"Yes, I understand, Captain. You know, I lost two friends in that same airplane, both the pilot and the command pilot."

"Yes, sir, I know."

"How are things back home?"

"I'm married, sir, for a little over three and a half years."

"Children?"

"Not yet, sir."

"So you plan on them when you get home then."

"Yes, sir." Perry almost let the subject go at that, but then to his own surprise, he continued. "Phyllis Marie gave me this toy, this plastic doll."

"So, you named that plane after your wife."

"Yes, sir."

"Go on about the toy."

"She named it Mickey, the name we chose for our first son, and told me to bring him home safe to her."

"That's nice. We need reminders of why we're here."

"Yes, sir."

"I see you got your Captain's bars."

"Yes, sir."

"And your other officers—Boettcher and Fitzsimmons—have they gotten their First Lieutenant bars yet?"

"Yes, sir."

"Good. I'm going to need you veteran flyers during your last five missions. I have five rookie crews starting after the first of the year, and I'm counting on you to show them how it's done."

"Yes, sir."

Perry waited to see what topic the commander would like to cover next. He was certain that he had not summoned Perry for a nice little chat, but so far—

"Captain, I'm having the Phyllis Marie outfitted for a special mission. I thought you might like to know about it."

"Sir, yes I would."

"I've added a few seats so the airplane can transport some VIPs, very secret, very hush-hush, and I've ordered extra fuel tanks in the bomb bay. I've also installed one of the toilets from an older B-17."

"Where is it going?"

"Oh, well I can only give that information to the crew that's volunteering for the mission, Captain."

Why must they always play such games, Perry wondered? He could feel steam rising from the back of his neck. "Do you already have someone in mind, sir? Because if you don't, then I volunteer my crew, sir."

"Ah, splendid!" The commander stood and opened the door, addressing Major Haskins. "I believe we have a volunteer crew for your mission, Major. Come in."

As Haskins returned and settled back in his seat, the commander drew open a curtain to reveal something quite different from the usual mission map. The red line stretched west across the British Isles into the Atlantic Ocean, south around the Iberian Peninsula of Spain and Portugal, east into Gibraltar at the mouth of the Mediterranean Sea, and then southeast to the city of Tunis on the northern coast of Africa.

"Re-fueling in Gibraltar?" Perry asked.

"Or the Canary Islands if necessary," Haskins replied. "Hence the additional fuel capacity."

"How many VIPs?"

"Three."

"Who are they?"

The Major did not hesitate. "Their code names are Mr. Mann, Mrs. Warden, and Mrs. Graham. That's all you need to know until we reach Tunis."

"We, sir?"

"Yes, Captain," the commander said. "Major Haskins is to accompany you as your co-pilot, if you don't have any objections."

"Have you piloted a B-17 before, sir?"

"Yes," Haskins said, "about two hundred hours, Captain."

"Two of the passengers are women, sir?"

"Yes."

"Are you Mr. Mann, sir?"

"No." Haskins spoke briskly, "there are three passengers, plus yours truly."

Perry got up from his seat. "May I, sir?"

"By all means."

He went to examine the locations of Gibraltar and the Canary Islands. "Long flight," he observed.

The Major nodded.

"What about the return, sir?"

"We haven't quite worked out the details," the commander

said. "It's urgent to get these VIPs to their destination as soon as we can, within a margin of safety."

Perry studied the map for a few more seconds. "Where are the VIPs now?"

"In my quarters," the commander said.

"Is the airplane ready?"

"It should be by now."

"I need to notify my crew and change into my flying gear. And you, sir," he asked Haskins. "Have you got your flying gear here?"

"Back at your commander's quarters."

"Very well, sir," Perry said, saluting. "No time like the present."

"I've sent messengers to your officers and crew."

"My officers are at the Mess Hall, sir."

"Yes, I know."

Bud and Boettcher met Perry at the hut. By the time they arrived at the flight deck, the enlisted men were waiting, and Blimp had completed the ground check, but no one was inside the airplane.

"What are you standing around for, a salute?"

"Captain," Kiss said, "we wanted to see who the bigwigs are."

"They're Zulu tribesmen for all I know. Get on board. Byrne, Mack, you two see that our guests are all tucked into their special seats."

"Yes, sir," they answered, just as a jeep arrived carrying Major Haskins, along with the VIPs. They appeared to be a British couple, perhaps thirty-five, he in an overcoat, carrying the distinctive black bag of a doctor, and she in a cloth coat. They won't be warm enough in that, Perry thought. An older woman accompanied them, perhaps in her late fifties, wearing a full-length fur coat. She's too young to be his mother-in-law, Perry speculated, but at least she'll be warm enough. Among the civilian luggage the soldiers loaded from the jeep into the Phyllis Marie, Perry saw several heavy blankets. Good, he thought. Someone has thought this through a bit.

The long flight to Gibraltar lasted over four hours and the re-fueling took another hour. Haskins did not permit the VIPs to disembark from the airplane, but he did ask the crew members to leave, allowing the two women some measure of privacy to use the exposed toilet in the bomb bay. Later, Haskins approached Perry as he inspected the rudder of the Phyllis Marie.

"Captain, would you mind? Mrs. Warden would like to speak with you. I put her in the co-pilot's seat."

Perry returned to the pilot seat, tipping his cap to the woman as he sat down.

"Captain," she said, "I wanted to thank you for taking us on this dreadful adventure."

"I'm sorry, ma'am, has it been dreadful? Are you warm enough?"

"Oh, no, excuse me, your piloting, everything about the trip has been splendid. It's the reason for the trip that's dreadful."

"I'm sorry, Mrs. Warden, I don't know the reason."

"Oh, you dear man," she said. "My name isn't Warden, it's Churchill." Perry thought she would burst into tears. "They tell me my husband may be dying. I'm bringing a doctor, a specialist in heart and lung disorders."

"I'm sorry, ma'am."

"You really don't know who I am, do you?"

"I'm sorry, ma'am, but no."

"It's really quite refreshing. For security reasons, I can't go anywhere anymore because of my husband's position, as if the Nazis would care where I have lunch."

All at once a possibility struck him. "Mrs. Churchill? Mrs. Winston Churchill?"

"Yes, my husband was returning from Tehran and Cairo when he came down with a dreadful pneumonia, and his ship had to stop in Tunisia."

Perry's jaw dropped.

"Oh, dear," she said. "Have I said too much? Nigel is always telling me I'm a security risk."

"No, it's not that," he said. "It's just that I've been reading his book for the last several weeks. I brought it along with me."

"Really? He'll be so pleased to hear that. Which one?"

" 'World in Crisis' ", he said.

"Oh, dear, that old thing? I never could finish it, I'm afraid." She laughed.

"Then the couple you're traveling with," Perry asked. "Are they—?"

"Couple?" She thought a moment, turning her head involuntarily toward the rear of the airplane, as if trying to visualize her companions. "Oh, dear me, no. He's the doctor, the lung specialist, you know. I've never met him before. The woman is my secretary."

Haskins pushed his head up through the opening in the floor between them. "Time to go, madam," he said.

"Yes, very well, Nigel. After we get in, and if Mr. Warden is well enough, do bring this young man around to see him won't you?"

"Yes, madam."

"Bring along your book," she said to Perry as she descended from the pilot's compartment. "He won't believe me if I tell him."

"Yes, ma'am."

From Gibraltar, Perry flew the Phyllis Marie an additional three and a half hours, landing in darkness on Christmas morning in Tunis, near the old section of Carthage, about nine hours after departing London.

Perry and his crew, except for Major Haskins, were escorted to a large empty barracks, where together, officers and enlisted men, they fell onto the nearest bunks and slept.

26

The smell of strong coffee invaded the barracks, gently awakening Perry and his crew. Upon opening his eyes, Perry saw Major Haskins wheeling in a service cart with two pots and a basket of breads and biscuits.

"If any of you Yanks want tea, let me know and I'll go back for it." Haskins poured a cup and turned toward Perry. "How do you take yours?"

"Black," Perry croaked, trying to find his morning voice.

Once the others had their cups, Haskins returned to Perry. "Get your pants on, old man. You've been granted an audience in fifteen minutes."

"Can't I shave first?"

"Don't worry. The Warden is still in his nightshirt."

As Perry rode with Haskins and his driver to a building on the other side of the airfield, he noticed a very large presence of British military police; they were stationed every hundred yards or so along the road and fence perimeter.

"He gets first class treatment, doesn't he?"

"He doesn't usually. In fact he insists on traveling incognito whenever possible, but there are some others here that require more stringent arrangements."

"Who?"

"Ah, that would be telling, now wouldn't it?"

Despite Haskins attempt at secrecy, however, as soon as the jeep pulled up at the entrance to the building, behind a vehicle with four-star flags at the front, Perry recognized the general as he stepped out.

"Eisenhower's here?"

"Did I say that? Driver, linger back here a bit will you, until the other vehicle pulls away."

Perry watched as two British officers followed Eisenhower into the building and disappeared.

"All right, driver, pull up now."

Haskins escorted Perry inside. As he entered, he had a strong sense that the VIPs occupied the room to the right, but Haskins opened the door to the left, and there sat Churchill, barefoot and in his nightshirt, as promised, sitting in a plush chair and eating breakfast from a rolled up tray.

"Is this the fellow?"

"Yes, sir."

"So, Captain, I gather you're the one."

"The one, sir?"

"Yes, the other person who has read my book—other than myself, that is."

Perry let out a nervous laugh. "Yes, sir," he said.

"Did you bring it?"

"Yes, sir." Perry took the book out from under his leather bomber jacket. He handed it to Churchill, who took it and autographed it.

"Thank you for bringing my wife and doctor in my hour of need, Captain. Keep them flying."

"Yes, sir. Thank you, sir," he said, retrieving the book from Churchill's outstretched chubby hand.

The Major touched Perry on the back, his signal that the audience was over. As he followed Haskins, Perry saw two soldiers entering the room across the hall, carrying a large pasteboard map of southern Italy with the name of one coastal town highlighted: Anzio.

That afternoon, the British served Christmas dinner to the American B-17 crew in their barracks, after which Haskins returned, pulling a chair up to the table. The crew listened as he talked.

"I've been trying to work out the details of your return, but we've hit a bit of a stick," he said. "There's no petrol for your aircraft. We're trying to get you some, but it's looking as if you gentlemen will be our guests for a few days."

"What about you?" Perry asked. "Aren't you coming with us? What about the three VIPs?"

"We're all staying with Mr. Warden," he said.

After he left, Perry walked over to his bunk and to the

amazement of his crew, returned with two unopened fifths of Canadian Club Whisky. He poured an inch into each man's glass before lifting his own and saying, "Boys, this is the way Billy would have wanted it." After a quiet cheer to Billy, they drank in silence.

Each day Perry checked in with the British airfield offices, and each day he heard the same answer: no petrol. The Warden party and all their guests departed in secret on the third day, leaving nearly the entire place to Perry and his crew. They washed their clothes, having brought only one change. Finally, on the sixth day, the British Operations Officer showed up at the barracks, looking for Perry.

"Sir," he said, "I have good news and I have bad news."

"Go on."

"We have a shipment of petrol coming by truck," he said. "That's the good news."

"But it's not enough," Perry guessed.

"No, that's not it."

"Please, just tell me."

"We can fill you up, auxiliary tanks and all, and it's plenty to take back to Framlingham, sir, with quite a bit to spare, if you go directly across Europe, which you will have to do, because there is a battle going on at Gibraltar, and Las Palmas in the Canary Islands is closed due to a nasty storm."

"Boettcher!" Perry bellowed.

"Have you got a course set for Framlingham, direct?"

"Of course."

"Along the Pyrenees, like we discussed?"

"Yes, sir."

"Bud, you're set to co-pilot?"

"Yes, Captain."

Perry turned back to the British Operations Officer. "I don't see a problem. We'll fly above the Flak, at an altitude we couldn't fly with the VIPs on board, and we'll be fine. When can you be ready?"

"We've begun re-fueling already. I'd say you could leave tomorrow morning.

At sunrise, against the beginning shimmer of heat from the desert, the lone B-17 lifted off the airstrip and started its slow banking turn toward the north. Perry climbed steeply, achieving ten thousand feet and switching to oxygen over the Mediterranean. He climbed to thirty thousand feet as they reached landfall west of Marseilles. They were flying without incident, running parallel with the Pyrenees Mountains far below, when suddenly, as they approached the North Atlantic coast, four Messerschmitt Me-109s attacked out of nowhere. One of them rapid-fired its guns as it flew under the Phyllis Marie. Eight crewmembers shouted positions into the interphone at once.

"Bandit going away at eleven o'clock low!"

"Another at one o'clock level!"

"What's that sound?"

"Where'd it go?"

"We're hit!"

"There's fuel leaking from below number two engine!"

"Bandit coming around on your side!"

"I see it!"

"Quiet!" Perry shouted. "Radio!"

"Here!"

"Try to raise some fighter escorts!"

Perry feathered the number-two engine and hit the fire extinguishers as the gunners opened up in every direction on the enemy aircraft.

"Did you hear me?"

"Working on it."

"You should see it now!"

"I see it!"

"Flak bursts below us!"

"Don't worry about them!"

"Bandit at four o'clock level!"

"Here we go!"

"Smoke coming out of number-four engine!"

"Number-four engine is on fire!"

"Perry, should I sound Mayday?"

"Negative!" he shouted. He feathered number-four and hit the fire extinguishers before leaning forward to see the burning engine. At that moment, machine gun fire tore through the bulkhead where his head had been. *I do NOT want to ditch on New Year's Day,* he thought. Aloud he shouted, "Where are those escorts?"

The plastic doll—Mickey—rattled above his head with a new sound. The gunfire had damaged the toy. Perry remembered the promise he had made to bring it home safe. With only two engines running, his chances were looking worse and worse. If they lost another, they would have trouble maintaining altitude. Perry scanned the horizon, estimating the distance to the English Channel—the distance to safety—wishing he had Thunderbolt protection on this flight. I wish Billy were here, he thought.

"We're leaking fuel and losing altitude," the navigator called.

"I see it. If the—"

More gunfire tore through the empty Bombardier compartment at the front of the airplane, drowning out the navigator's answer. Bud, sitting in the co-pilot seat, whistled low.

"Say again, Navigator!"

A pair of Me-109s emerged from the fogbank above and opened up on the B-17, aiming at the number three engine, missing high.

Fog, he thought. If only I could climb into it.

"If the fuel loss continues at the current rate, that is, if it doesn't get any worse, we can just clear the cliffs with a course change of seven degrees port, but I cannot guarantee you a place to set her down."

Suddenly, Perry heard a terrible gnashing sound rumble through the airplane, a metal-on-metal groaning that made his teeth ache. Two thick arms of fog reached out and snatched his ship, engulfing his crew and himself with it.

27

Hazel felt her ankles turn to water. She thought she would topple right over onto the kitchen floor. Her sister Edna moved quickly to her side and supported her while Edwin moved the rocking chair from its place near the big baseburner stove. Hazel melted into the chair, completely undone by the news of Josephine's passing.

Although shocking, her oldest sister's 1927 death did not come as a surprise. Josephine's health had continued to deteriorate after the surgery in Kansas City. The family thought that the cancer on her spine had returned.

The Carters slipped out of the kitchen quietly, leaving the family to mourn in private. Of the six girls born to John and Elizabeth Hill, only half of them survived now: Niota, the second girl, living in California, Edna, the fourth girl, who spent most of her adult life in Africa, and Hazel, the sixth and youngest. She wept openly, stung by the horrible reality. She began to shiver. Edwin brought a blanket and wrapped it around his grieving wife.

Over the course of the next several days, Hazel remained in the chair almost exclusively. Phyllis Marie became terrified at what she saw: her mother, inconsolable and unable to stop crying. Edwin comforted the child and kept her occupied away from the kitchen as much as possible.

"Hazel?" Edna finally said. The news had shocked Hazel four days ago. She had not noticed that the floodwaters had receded, the friends and families had gone home, the children had returned to school.

"Hazel," she repeated. "Talk to me, dear."

Hazel's raised her head a bit and gazed at her sister.

"Please, dear, I'm worried about thee. Thy family is worried, too."

"Yes," Hazel said. "I can't believe she's gone."

"I know, dear, but she is gone, and it is time for thee to

start thinking about going on without her."

"Yes, I know."

"We have to decide about Mother, dear. She needs us now."

"Yes, I suppose that's right."

Edna placed a cup of hot coffee into Hazel's hands. "Drink this, dear."

"Yes."

"I have an idea about Mother," she said.

"Yes?"

"We are planning a four-year furlough from the mission in Ruanda-Urundi, as you know, in order to give the girls a stable home while they go to Friends University."

"Yes."

"I think Mother is worried about where she will stay."

"She can stay here."

"She can stay with us, too. In fact, I propose we share her, six months each. We shall keep the house in Wichita during our coming year in Africa."

"Yes, that's good," Hazel said, her glassy eyes clearing as she started to think about the necessary details. "It would be warmer for her at thy house in the winter."

"And she would enjoy living here at the farm in the summer, I think." Edna stood, smiling at the change in her sister. "And where does thee propose she sleep?"

"We'll make up a place for her in the front parlor," Hazel said, smiling for the first time in four days. "She shan't need to climb the stairs that way."

Edna took her sister's hand. "Welcome back, dear."

"Have I been away?"

"We thought so, yes."

The following week, Elizabeth Hill arrived on the train and settled into her new winter home with her daughter, Edna, while Hazel recovered her equilibrium.

Around that time, Kenneth decided he wanted a car. His trumpet playing had improved to the point that he was starting to get some gigs around Wichita, even though he was only fourteen. He formed a little dance band and played for the local high schools and sock hops. He also sneaked out to the nightclub on the west side and listened to the jazz played by the local coloreds. They never would have been tolerated in any of the downtown clubs, but they tolerated this white boy with the trumpet. Without a car, Kenneth found it difficult to go where he needed to go.

Salvation came from an unexpected direction.

"Father, I spoke to Miss Ekeland yesterday," Kenneth said at dinner one evening.

"Did thee? And what was the topic?"

"She says she can get me a job at the insurance company."

"Doing what?"

"Delivering mail around the office in the morning and picking up mail in the afternoon."

Edwin looked over at Hazel.

"When would thee go to school?"

"In between," he said. "I could work in the morning from 7 until 8:30, go to school, then go back after school."

Edwin looked at Hazel again.

"I could save the money and buy that car we talked about."

His father did not speak.

"I could save the money I'm making from the dance band, too."

Edwin took another long glance at his wife.

"Does thee have any objections to thy son's plan?" He waited for Hazel to express any concerns she might have.

"What about the pigs?" she asked.

"I'll feed them when I get home."

"And homework?"

"After dinner."

"And sleep?"

"I'll sleep after homework."

"And practice?"

Kenneth looked down at the table. "Before the insurance

company."

"And how will thee get there?"

"Bicycle."

Edwin leaned on his elbows. "It sounds like a lot of work and a lot of responsibility."

"I can manage it," the boy said. "I need the car to be able to go to the dances, and we have more dances coming up on the east side."

Edwin caught one more look at Hazel to make sure she agreed with what he was about to say. They had already discussed the issue. She nodded.

"If thy grades suffer, thee shall have to give it up."

"Thank you, Father, Mother! Can I call her?"

"Yes, go ahead."

Kenneth worked this grueling schedule for two years, saving every penny from his insurance company job, his dance band gigs, and his allowance from his work around the farm. To everyone's amazement, he arrived at the farm one evening driving a big blue Hupmobile—a convertible with a rumble seat, an unusual combination. Hazel and her mother, Elizabeth, saw him arrive and came out the back door. Edwin came running in from the fields, and Virginia arrived from the poultry barn.

"Where did thee get this?" Edwin asked.

"A man across town."

"How much did thee pay?"

"Not very much. It's not new. It's used."

Phyllis Marie came running from the direction of the pig barn, followed by her vast menagerie of ducks, chickens, dogs, cats, and her newest, her pet goat. Before anyone could foresee or prevent it, the goat leaped up onto the hood of the Hupmobile.

"Hey!" Kenneth shouted. "Get down from there!"

The animal left several scratches in the paint job. Phyllis Marie looked up into the faces of her parents and siblings. When none of them had anything to say, her Grandmother Hill leaned down and waggled a crooked finger in her face.

"Thee little you, thee!"

In 1928, East High School boasted an excellent concert and marching band, comprised of seventy-five musicians, including sixteen-year-old Kenneth Stanton. That was the same year that John Philip Sousa toured eight states to promote the very first recordings and radio broadcasts of the Sousa Band. The high school students, like the rest of the city of Wichita, eagerly anticipated their arrival.

One day at the beginning of rehearsal, the band director, Mr. Hanson said, "Students, how would you like to go down and meet John Philip Sousa's train?"

"Could we?"

"Yes!"

"Wonderful idea!"

Hanson took his group to the train station the following week, their uniforms pressed, shoes shined, instruments polished and shako hats combed and brushed. A large crowd, which included the Stanton family, had already formed, and they applauded when the East High Band marched in and took its place. Within minutes the train whistle sounded in the distance.

"Washington Post March," Hanson shouted. "One, two, three, four!"

The train stopped and the musicians of the Sousa Band stepped off to the music of their own leader. Kenneth watched as they stood listening, smiling, pleased at the reception. When the old man stepped off the train, no one recognized him at first, because he wore a light blue seersucker suit, red necktie, and a slouch hat, rather than his traditional scarlet tunic and gold braids. It wasn't until he approached the band and stopped quite close to Mr. Hanson that Kenneth realized it was Sousa who stood listening until the end of the march.

"Thank you, sir," he said. "Most gratifying."

"Mr. Sousa," Hanson said, shaking hands, "the honor is mine. Won't you conduct one of your pieces?" Hanson tried to place his baton in the March King's hands.

A man in the crowd called out, "Play 'Stars and Stripes!' "

Others took up the call for Sousa's most famous piece.

"Do they know it, sir?"

"From memory, Mr. Sousa."

"Sir," Sousa shouted, taking the baton and turning to the man in the crowd, "I wrote that piece, and the name is 'The Stars and Stripes Forever!'" He turned to face the band, gave them one preparatory measure, and conducted them through the entire march. Upon its conclusion, the crowd burst into applause. Sousa handed the baton back to Mr. Hanson and walked on down the platform with his musicians all waving to the crowd. Kenneth grinned from ear to ear.

The concert that night sold out completely, with standing room only in the back of the auditorium.

The next year, Virginia started Friends University at about the same time as her cousins Esther and Rachel Chilson, home on the pre-arranged four-year furlough. Esther and Virginia knew a couple of boys, Ralph Choate and Howard Roberts, students at the University. Howard lived as a boarder at the home of Ernest and Betsy Crow, and spent time with their two boys, Jim and Ernie.

One evening, Virginia expected Howard to come calling. When she entered her room, she found it was a mess. Phyllis Marie's clothes were thrown in every corner and the girl was playing with a rabbit on her bed. The sisters had always shared a room, and Virginia usually tolerated the child ten years her junior, but not on this occasion. "Mother!" she called.

"What is it, dear?"

"I don't know what to do with her! How am I supposed to get ready for Howard's visit in a room like this?"

"Phyllis Marie, take that rabbit and go find thy father," Hazel said.

"And do what?"

"And do nothing. Thy sister has an important guest tonight."

"Who, Howard? He comes here all the time!" She laughed and bounced out of the room.

"Mother, can't we please have the living room to ourselves

this evening?"

"Of course, dear," Hazel said, picking up her youngest child's things and putting them away. "Kenneth is gone already, to a dance with his band. We'll keep Phyllis Marie occupied while thee entertains Howard."

"She hasn't eaten all the cookies I baked, has she?"

"No, dear, they are safe."

"Can thee help me into this dress?"

"This is what thee is wearing?"

"Yes, why?"

"Isn't it a bit too dressy?"

"No, not for tonight it isn't."

Hazel regarded her daughter curiously. "Why, what's special about tonight?"

"Mother, please!"

"Yes, yes, turn around so I can get to the zipper."

The doorbell rang.

"Oh no," Virginia said. "He's early."

"I'll take care of it. Finish dressing and come down stairs."

Hazel bustled down the stairs.

"Edwin, take thy younger daughter upstairs, please."

"Why?"

"Go on, please, ask questions later."

"Come on, girl." Edwin motioned to his younger daughter. "We have things to do elsewhere."

"What things?" Phyllis Marie asked, climbing onto her father's back.

"I don't know yet."

Hazel opened the door as soon as Edwin disappeared up the stairs.

"Good evening, Mr. Roberts! Won't you come in, please?"

"Good evening, Mrs. Stanton," he said, stepping across the threshold, towering over Hazel as he twisted his straw hat in his hands.

"Sit down, please, anywhere. I'll just get some refreshments from the kitchen."

Hazel reappeared in what seemed to Howard like only a heartbeat or two. "Virginia will be down in just a minute."

"Here I am," she said, drifting down the stairs in her lavender dress, her hair combed back behind her ears.

Howard stood still. "Don't you look—" He paused in search of a word he never found.

"Thank you," Virginia murmured.

"Here, I'll take that." Hazel took his hat. "If you'll excuse me." She dropped his hat on the chair in the front hall on her way up the stairs.

Her husband and daughter stood at the top of the stairs looking down. "Get away from there," she said, waving the back of her hand in the general direction of Phyllis Marie. "How long has it been since thee actually went to bed on time?"

"Who, me?"

"Yes, thee. Tonight, thee is going to bed early to make up for all the other times!"

"Why?"

"Go on, get in there. I'll be in shortly to tuck thee in."

"Mother!"

"Get!"

Phyllis Marie went to her room and changed into her pajamas. She climbed into the bed and pretended to read, but she tried to hear what was going on downstairs instead.

Hazel came in and tucked her in. "Lights out, young lady. I don't want to hear a peep out of thee tonight."

"But, Mother, what's going on?"

"Not one peep!" She turned off the light and left the room. "Good night, dear." She pulled the door completely shut and latched it.

"Well," Phyllis Marie said, just above a whisper. "Well," she repeated, just a tiny bit louder. She heard no response. Slowly, she crept out of bed and crawled to the door. Looking through the keyhole, she decided that her mother had shut her parents' door, and that the light she could see was coming from the living room.

She turned the doorknob slowly until it stopped, pulled the door toward her, just one inch, and peered out. As she thought, her parents' door was closed. She slipped out into the hallway, and closed the door behind her as quietly as she had opened it. She crept down the stairs, avoiding the squeaky steps, and sat at the bottom listening.

"Virginia, will you marry me?" Howard said.

Phyllis Marie caught her breath. Before her sister had time to discover the eavesdropper, the girl climbed the stairs quickly and quietly, opened her bedroom door, closed it behind her, leaped into bed in the dark, and pretended to be asleep. The door opened slightly, but Phyllis Marie did not look to see who it was.

The next morning she learned that her sister had accepted.

One night a year later Phyllis Marie, now a girl of twelve, awoke to the sound of whining. She recognized that it was coming from her dog, Patsy, a little black and white spotted dog of dubious breed. She looked outside but did not see her. Dressing quietly, so as not to awaken her older sister, she crept out of the room and down the stairs, taking care to avoid the squeaky steps, placing her feet in the silent places she had memorized.

In the yard, she found a trail of blood leading to the fields. She followed it easily in the moonlight until she found a large area, wet with blood, but she did not find Patsy.

Returning to the house, she heard the whining again, and realized that the trail of blood led from the fields to the house, not the other way around. It led under the back porch stairs and into the crawlspace under the house. There she found Patsy, along with four brand new pups.

As dawn crept in, Phyllis Marie crawled out to prepare food and water for the dog and the pups, but Patsy followed her. Phyllis Marie intended to keep the birth a secret, fearing her parents would send the pups away.

"Go back, Patsy," she said. "I'll bring it to you."

The kitchen door opened. Hazel and Edwin stood there in their robes, staring at their youngest child and the dog, covered in mud.

"Did Patsy have her pups?" Hazel asked.

"How did you know?"

Hazel smiled. Edwin's reaction was something less positive. He found himself growing less and less comfortable with his younger daughter's precocity.

Later that summer, Edwin walked into the pig barn to discover Phyllis Marie standing by a corral fence, watching, as a sow farrowed her seventh piglet.

"What are you doing?"

"Watching pigs get born," she said. "Isn't it amazing?"

Edwin turned and stomped into the house. "Hazel!"

"I'm in here," she called from the living room. "What's wrong?" She came bustling in, wiping her hands on her apron.

"Hazel, we brought the children here to see nature, but I did not expect thee to let Phyllis Marie stand there and watch pigs be born!"

The Stantons' farm life drew to an immediate end.

28

Friends University required a responsible couple to guide the students at the East Hall for Men. In his capacity as President of the University, William Orville Mendenhall felt that no one suited that requirement better than his good friends Edwin and Hazel Stanton, so in the summer of 1931, when he learned that they wanted a new home in town, he saw to it that they received the assignment. When Edwin balked at the idea, Mendenhall arranged a contract for Edwin to handle the photographic needs of the University, and that clinched the deal.

In the autumn, the Stantons took possession of the house, a sprawling two-story with a basement. Edwin put his new photography studio in the front room, on the same side as the family residence. The front left room remained the men's living room and lounge, complete with a very large library table and several pieces of stuffed furniture, chairs, sofas, and divans. A door opened from the back of that room to the sizeable dining room, with a pass-through partition from the substantial kitchen.

Virginia continued to live with the family after she graduated from Friends University and started teaching school. The first room off the front hall became her and Phyllis Marie's room. Edwin and Hazel could get to their rooms from the front hallway or the kitchen. They created a combination bedroom and sitting room, with a spacious walk-through closet that they shared with their daughters. If they emerged from their suite in the other direction, they found themselves in a hall leading to the kitchen, the dining room, or the back porch.

Kenneth, now a student at Friends himself, stayed upstairs with the men. They had small study cubicles located around the stairway in the center of the second floor, and beds in the large wrap-around sleeping porches.

The basement contained a ping pong table, a phonograph

and more lounge space for the men, but twelve-year-old Phyllis Marie soon learned that she could go from her room to the bathroom, pretend to return to her room, and slip down to the basement, where the college boys interested her far more than the animals on the farm had.

Phyllis Marie had never imagined working at her young age, but one day at S. & H. Kress and Company, her cousin Lucile, who worked behind the notions counter, convinced her to apply for a part-time job selling seasonal goods and greeting cards. She got the job and made twelve dollars and fifty cents a week. The college boys from East Hall became frequent customers and visited her often at the seasonal counter.

Virginia and her fiancé, Howard Roberts, spent a lot of time with the two Crow boys, Jim and Ernie. One day at Sunday School Phyllis Marie came up to the boys.

"Are you coming to my sister's wedding? I got a big new floppy hat to wear."

"I suppose so," Ernie said. "When is it?"

"Next Wednesday. I'm the maid of honor."

"Don't you have to be married to be the maid of honor?"

"No, silly. If you're married then you're the matron of honor."

As they giggled together, another boy came up. "Hello," he said.

"Hello," she answered.

The boy turned and walked across the room to Betsy Crow. He stood behind her chair and shyly surveyed the room.

"Who's that boy with your mother?" she asked Ernie.

"That's my cousin, Perry. You remember him, don't you, Aunt Georgia and Uncle Clifton's boy? They moved to Oklahoma a few years ago, but they've come back to Wichita."

"That's Perry? He's taller than he was. He was in Sunday School with us before they moved away."

"We used to play together all the time before they moved. He comes to church with us a lot, and he's going to be at

Allison in the fall. Your father knew Uncle Clifton and Aunt Georgia in school in Oklahoma, when they were kids."

Phyllis Marie scratched the toe of her shoe against the floor and stole a glance at the boy. "Yes," she said. "I remember."

If Hazel had been there to see the look in her daughter's eye, she would have wanted to warn young Perry Row.

29

Phyllis Marie unlocked the door to her parents half of the Idaho duplex they shared. *Where are Father and Mother,* she wondered as the telephone began to ring again? *They ought to be home from the studio by now. It's after five. Maybe they needed to stay longer,* she thought as she pulled off an earring and dropped gracefully onto the divan, picking up the receiver.

"Stanton residence," she smiled.

"Honey, this is Mom Row."

"Howdy!" She greeted her cheerily. "Has it started snowing in Wichita?"

There was a chilly silence on the line. Finally Georgia responded, "Dad's on the extension. Are you there?"

"I'm here," a man's voice stated quietly.

Phyllis Marie could barely recognize it as Clifton's. Her fingers tightened around the cold receiver as she visualized her parents-in-law: Georgia standing in the kitchen and Clifton, sitting in his big chair by the radio in the living room.

"What's wrong?" she asked.

"Honey," Georgia said, her voice trailing off.

"You're scaring me now."

"Honey, I don't know why this didn't come to you instead of me, but I got a telegram today."

Phyllis Marie grew rigid and held her breath. *No,* she thought. *No!* "What does it say?"

"It says that Ped is missing, honey."

"Missing?" Phyllis Marie drew in a sharp breath. "Read it to me, will you? What exactly does it say?"

Another chilly silence crackled through the earpiece.

"Mom?"

"Papa has the telegram," Georgia said. Phyllis Marie thought it sounded as if Georgia had muffled the phone with her apron.

"Yes," he said. "I have it."

Phyllis Marie could hear the brittle paper unfold in the Wichita living room, thirteen hundred miles away.

"It says, 'I regret to inform you that report received states your son First Lieutenant Perry V. Row missing in action in Europe since December 1943. If further details or other information are received you will be promptly notified.' "

Tears fell from her eyes but she paid them no mind. She sat very still, stunned by the news, wanting very much for time to stand still, just for a few minutes, so she could gather her thoughts.

"They got his rank wrong," Phyllis Marie said. "He's a Captain now. Maybe they got the name wrong, too." She knew she was clutching at straws, but she had to do something. "It doesn't give a day?" Her stomach clenched and she bent to protect it, but she couldn't protect her thoughts.

"No," Clifton said.

"It doesn't give a country?"

"No, just 'Europe.' "

"Why did it come to us?" Georgia asked. "She's his wife."

"I know, honey," Clifton said. "I don't understand either. Phyllis Marie, are Edwin and Hazel there?"

"No," she managed to whisper. "They haven't come home from the studio yet. I just got in myself. Did you try to call before?" She didn't know why she was asking; it didn't' really matter. Nothing did—except Perry.

"Yes, honey," Georgia said. "We've been trying your phone upstairs and this one for about an hour."

He's all right, she told herself. *It's a mistake. He's safe; he has to be.* "You'll let me know if you hear anything new, won't you?"

"Or course," Clifton said. "Be strong, now. You know we love you."

"Yes, I will. I love you, too." She hung up the receiver and stared through wet green eyes at the pattern of the wallpaper.

Dad has the telegram—

It says that Ped is missing—

We regret to inform you—

First Lieutenant Perry V. Row is missing in action—

December 1943—

Europe—

She's his wife—

I don't understand either—

Be strong, now. You know we love you.

Yes, I will. I love you, too.

"What did you say?"

"I said that since she loves me, and I love her, and we've been engaged since August of 1938—"

"That's eighteen months, Father," Phyllis Marie said. "After all, this is 1940!"

"Yes, that's right," Perry continued, "this is February of 1940, and the apartment upstairs is standing empty, waiting for us. I don't see any reason to wait for a June wedding!"

"No, I don't either," Phyllis Marie added. "You two would have more room and so would I, and Perry wouldn't have to live in your photography studio anymore, and, well, Mother, what do you think?"

"It doesn't leave us much time to plan a wedding, dear," Hazel said. "What will thee wear?"

"And the date you've chosen," Edwin said, "March seventeen, that's St. Patrick's Day."

"Yes, but it's Palm Sunday, too," Phyllis Marie said, "and Perry's sister, Corliss, will be here from California. Besides, we have a plan for the wedding that doesn't need much preparation."

"It's a good thing I've already signed up to provide the church flowers that day," Edwin said so matter-of-factly that his daughter and future son-in-law missed the point.

"Besides, the idea of spending hundreds of dollars for a dress I'm only going to wear once is ridiculous!" Phyllis Marie continued.

"Oh?" Hazel turned to her husband. "What flowers has

thee ordered?"

"Didn't I tell thee? I found some lovely bouquets of poinsettias, milk thistles, and poison ivy."

"Oh! You two!" Phyllis Marie jumped to her feet.

Hazel rose from the living room divan into Phyllis Marie's waiting embrace. "I love thee, daughter. God's blessings on thee."

The next day Perry met Edwin in downtown Caldwell at noon. They walked from the Stanton Photography Studio to the large department store at the end of the next block and took two seats at the lunch counter.

"Who did you say we were meeting?" Perry asked.

"His name is Jim and he's a friend of mine from Rotary Club. He's a department manager here, and he needs a salesman. If thee is going to marry, thee will need a better job than painting billboards and water towers. Here he is."

The two men stood up and shook hands with introductions all around.

"Edwin tells me you're a pretty bright boy," Jim said, after they had ordered.

"Well, I'm glad he thinks so," Perry said somewhat sheepishly, but with a big grin nonetheless.

"And you're getting married."

"Yes, sir."

"You've got some work experience, have you?"

"I've been working as an outdoor painting contractor," he exaggerated, "and parking cars, and soda jerking."

"And you think you're ready to take on a sales position?"

"Yes, sir."

The plates arrived and the three men ate in silence. Perry's face glowed red with embarrassment. He was certain the interview had gone badly. Perhaps he should have had a résumé to give the man, who had probably seen right through that 'outdoor painting contractor' crack.

When the check arrived, Edwin reached for it, but Jim was faster. He turned it over and signed it before handing it back to the counter man.

"Can you start tomorrow?" he asked.

Perry blinked in surprise. "Yes, sir."

"Edwin's word is good enough for me. I'll see you at nine o'clock in the Personnel Office."

"Yes, sir," Perry said. "Thank you, sir."

"Thank you, Jim," Edwin said, standing and shaking his hand. Perry noticed that his father-in-law did not use the plain speech.

The next morning, Perry sat nervously in the hall outside the Personnel Office. He wore his best shirt, a new pair of trousers his mother had sent him for his birthday, and a tie he had borrowed from Edwin. Jim arrived and ushered him through the necessary paperwork before taking him downstairs to the men's shoe department.

"This is the stockroom," Jim said, "and these are the stocking slips. Returns go over there. We don't keep all the sizes and colors of all the styles out on the floor. There just isn't room to do that, so we keep a representative variety out there. Try to get a feel for what the gentleman is interested in, find out his size, or measure for it, and then inquire about color. Got that? Style first, then size, then color."

"Yes, sir."

"Have you ever measured a foot?"

"No, sir."

"But you've seen one of these," he said, pointing at the black and silver metal tool on the floor.

"Yes, sir, every time I've bought a pair of shoes."

"This is a Brannock Scientific Foot Measuring Device," Jim said, kicking off his right shoe and sitting in the chair at the one desk. "First, make sure the customer's heel is back in the device, then adjust the heel-to-ball measurement, and last the heel-to-toe. You try it." He pushed the thing toward Perry. Perry got down on his knees and measured Jim's foot as demonstrated.

"Any questions?"

"No, I don't think so."

"Okay, Tiger, go get 'em, and if you do well in men's shoes, we'll move you up to women's shoes."

"Yes, sir."

Perry arrived at the Stanton's for dinner, exhausted from bending over, measuring feet, running back and forth from the showroom to the stockroom, climbing ladders, and wrapping up shoe boxes all day. He collapsed onto the divan in a heap.

"Tough day?" Edwin asked without looking up from his paper.

"Yes," Perry said. "Who would have thought that selling shoes would be so tiring?"

"That's why it's a young man's job," Edwin said. "Does thee want to see part of the paper?"

"No, thanks. I'll just rest until dinner."

When Phyllis Marie came in five minutes later, Edwin held a finger up to his lips. "Thy future husband is learning the wicked ways of the world."

Perry slept through the meal.

The following day proceeded as the first had. Perry found himself running between the stockroom and showroom and decided he needed to slow down a little bit. After lunch, he tried to pace himself, making it a bit less stressful.

On the morning of the third day, Perry walked into the storeroom and found Jim sitting at the desk.

"Good morning, sir," Perry said.

"Is it?" Jim regarded him in silence for a moment. "Tell me, son, do you know how many pairs of shoes you've sold in the last two days?"

"No, sir, but I'll bet it's a lot!" Perry smiled at him.

"You bet it's a lot," Jim repeated. "The fact that you don't know is not a good thing, son."

"What's wrong?"

"What's wrong is that you didn't fill out any stocking slips! How are we supposed to re-order the shoes you sold if you don't fill out any stocking slips?"

"I don't understand." Perry stood erect, facing his

supervisor. "I didn't sell any stockings."

"What?"

"Nothing, sir," Perry said, realizing his mistake.

"Do you know what this means?"

"No."

"It means I have to go back through all the sales slips to re-create the missing stocking slips. It will take me all weekend."

"Is that something I can help you with?" Perry asked.

"Well, it would be, if you weren't fired. The Personnel Office has a pay envelope waiting for you. Don't spend it all in one place."

Well, now what? Perry asked himself. He picked up his pay and walked out of the store. *I suppose I could whine and complain,* he thought. *The man never told me what to do with stocking slips. No, but you could have taken a little initiative, you could have looked at the forms and figured out what they were for. He did point them out to you, after all. All right, enough whining.*

He stepped into a phone booth at the drug store around the corner from Stanton Photography and dialed a number.

"Mr. Potter? Is that job still open, painting that oil tank out west of town? Yes, sir, I'll see you in the morning."

As far as anyone outside of the two families knew, Palm Sunday at the Caldwell Presbyterian Church—there being no Monthly Meeting of the Friends in town—looked like any other Palm Sunday, except perhaps that the flowers were somewhat more extravagant, and the out-of-town guests appeared more elegantly dressed than the locals might have expected. The service was the usual Presbyterian program of alternating hymns and scriptures followed by a sermon— somewhat different from Monthly Meeting, but not outside the experience of the tolerant and amenable Friends.

"May the Lord bless you and keep you," the minister said in Benediction. "May He lift up His countenance upon you and give you peace. May the Lord make His face to shine upon you and be gracious unto you."

Members of the congregation were surprised to hear the organist begin to play 'O Promise Me.' Some of the congregation sat, others stood, confused, before returning to their seats.

The door to the minister's left opened and Perry stepped out, wearing a new suit. Instinctively, the congregation turned to the back of the church, but instead of seeing a bride in white coming down the aisle, they saw Phyllis Marie in a tailored burgundy suit and matching hat, and her father in his Sunday best, rise from the congregation and walk down the aisle, stopping before the minister as the music ended.

"Who presents this woman to be married to this man?"

"Her mother and I do," Edwin said, and stepped away.

Perry and Phyllis Marie placed their hands together and faced the minister.

"The union you are about to enter," he said, "is the closest into which human beings can come. It is a union founded upon mutual respect and affection. Your paths will be parallel, your responsibilities will increase, but your joy will be multiplied if you are sincere and earnest with one another."

"Perry," he continued, "will you have this woman to be your wedded wife, to love her, comfort her, honor and keep her, and forsaking all others, keep you only unto her, for so long as you both shall live?"

Perry nodded. "I will."

"Phyllis Marie, will you have this man to be your wedded husband, to love him, comfort him, honor and keep him, and forsaking all others, keep you only unto him, so long as you both shall live?"

"I will," Phyllis Marie said as she stared through wet eyes across the darkened room at the pattern of the wallpaper. An entire hour had passed since the phone call from Mom Row.

The kitchen door opened. Edwin and Hazel burst in, laughing about something.

"It's dark enough in here," Edwin said, turning on the overhead kitchen light.

"Phyllis Marie, is thee here?" Hazel called out in her

cheery voice as she shut the door.

Her daughter reached above her head and switched on the lamp by the divan.

Edwin shook his winter coat off. "Thee has been crying," he said.

"Mom Row called," Phyllis Marie said. "She got a telegram."

"What's happened?" Hazel called from behind her husband. Edwin sat on the divan and took his daughter's hand in hers.

"It says Perry is missing in action."

30

Phyllis Marie looked up from the divan to see that her mother had thrown off her coat and pulled up a chair.

"It doesn't give a day?" Hazel asked.

"No, not according to Dad Row," Phyllis Marie answered. "It just says December, 1943."

"It doesn't even give a country?"

"Just Europe."

"But thee is his wife," Hazel said. " I thought that as his wife, thee would be his next of kin. Isn't that what thee would expect, Edwin?"

"Yes, it is," he said.

"I know," Phyllis Marie said. "Mom and Dad Row didn't understand it either. I don't know what to do. Isn't there someone I can call? The War Department? Our Congressman? The President?"

"I'll drop over to the draft board in Boise," Edwin said. They may have some ideas." He took his hat in his hand and walked out the door.

"There is someone," Hazel said.

"Who?"

"Thee can call silently upon God."

Hazel closed her eyes, lowered her chin, and gently squeezed her daughter's hand.

Phyllis Marie allowed herself to remember the ninth grade, when fifteen-year-old Perry had walked into his new classroom at Allison School to find six giggling girls huddled together in the front of the room. Although he had been born in Wichita and felt that he knew Wichita as his own, she knew he had felt shy and embarrassed on that day, starting at a new school as if he were in a new city. Had he raised his head enough to actually look at the girls and the other students around him, he would have recognized most of them from church or from the school he had attended before moving to

Ponca City. Instead, he quickly found a seat in the back of the classroom, opened the first book that was handy and started to read.

The six giggling girls were Phyllis Marie Stanton and her new friends: the group that soon called itself the Laugh-a-Lot club and paraded down University Avenue in pajamas in the middle of the hot Kansas summer nights, plucked their eyebrows at slumber parties at Phyllis Marie's house—the East Hall for Men—and flirted over ping pong with the college boys. The girls traded left shoes with one another, so that each girl wore one green shoe and one brown, for example. They danced for the talent show in diaphanous, cheesecloth costumes that neither parents nor teachers realized would expose their innocent and naked little bodies underneath—like a half a dozen Vestal Virgins—when lit with the bright lights of the stage.

Phyllis Marie remembered that Perry had watched the classroom fill up with strangers who were not strangers, children he knew but did not know, and that he had wondered what it would be like to fly.

She also remembered the story he had told her that on Saturdays, he rode his bicycle out to the airfield where one day he had seen two men working on an airplane. They and a third man took no notice of him at first as they stood together with their hands on their chins, facing their new prototype, discussing a problem they were having. Perry stood quietly at a distance.

When they chose a course of action, one man climbed into the cockpit and another climbed a stepladder and reached into the engine. The third man, standing by and watching, noticed Perry. "Do you like airplanes?"

"Yes, I do," Perry said. "What's this one called? I've never seen one like it, and I've never seen a picture of it in the magazines."

"No, you won't see this in a magazine, at least, not yet," he said. "This is the Cessna C-34, which my nephews there built."

"It's a beaut'." The boy couldn't hide his enthusiasm.

"Yes, it is."

Perry frowned. "I thought Cessna Aircraft closed after the old man lost control of the company and his best friend crashed the CR-2 racer."

The man stood there for a moment without speaking. He rubbed his nose with his fingers. "You really know a lot about airplanes, don't you?"

"Yes, sir."

"Well, these boys are going to re-open Cessna with this airplane, and they think it's going to be a big seller."

"Have they flown it yet?"

"No, not yet. Maybe another week or two."

"Well, I'll come back then. Maybe I'll be able to see it fly." He was full of hope and optimism.

"Maybe so, son." The man put his hand out for Perry to shake. "It's been good to meet you. What's your name?"

"Perry Row, sir."

"I'm Clyde Cessna. Call me Clyde. Oh, and Perry?"

"Yes, sir?"

"I'm not that old."

The hour was very late by the time Phyllis Marie and her parents went to bed that night, but the contents of the misdirected telegram kept them all awake. Phyllis Marie gave up pretending to sleep around three in the morning and moved to the sofa with her blankets and pillow. She remembered more stories about Perry and his family.

Perry had returned home from the Wichita airfield one day to find his sister Lois and her boyfriend Bill sitting on the porch swing. Bill was four years older than Perry, but despite the age difference, they had become friends.

"Perry, with all these sisters, you need someone to show you the man's point of view," he said. "There's a job down at the tire store where I work and I think I could arrange for you to have it if you wanted."

"You bet I want it." Perry leaned his bicycle against the house and came up the steps.

"Can you meet me there after school tomorrow? I'll introduce you to the boss."

All day at Allison School, Perry could think of nothing but the possibility of working—a real job with money in his pocket—at a time in America when there were no jobs. Within seconds of the last bell, he jumped on his bicycle and headed downtown.

Wearing grimy coveralls, Bill stood in the driveway entrance to the shop area, his face streaked with sweat and stained black from the tires.

"Hello, Perry," he said. "Come on over here and meet the boss."

They walked toward the office, but before they got there, the boss stepped out of the doorway.

"Hey, boss," Bill said. "This is Perry, the young man I told you about."

"How old are you, son?"

"Fifteen, sir."

"Have you ever worked before?"

"Yes, sir, I had a paper route and I've been mowing lawns."

"Let me see your hands." He reached out and pulled the boy's hands toward him, turning them over. "Not much callous." Glancing at Bill, he said. "You'd better make sure he wears gloves."

"Yes, boss."

"He's your responsibility. Show him the ropes."

"Yes, boss."

Bill turned away. "Come on."

"Did I get the job?"

"You got the job."

In the late summer of 1935, as soon as they turned eighteen, Bill and Lois married, and they had a son in 1936. Perry, now a junior at North High School, became an uncle. He continued working in the tire store with Bill until a stack of tractor tires fell on him, injuring his back. The injury placed any work plans on hold until he could recover. Once he was up and around again, he found an easier job at Dale Drug, working behind the ice cream counter. All he had to learn was how to operate the milk shake mixer, which his cousin Jim was happy to show him.

With the money he earned from his new job, Perry bought a car. He drove Bill's sister, Gracie, to high school every day, and he drove out to the field where Clyde Cessna's nephews continued to build airplanes. One day, he thought, as he watched them testing one model, he, too, would fly.

Until that day arrived, he contented himself with riding his bicycle down the few hills available to him in Wichita so he could feel the lift, or he and Bill drove his car fast on the roads outside of town so he could feel the thrust.

On Sunday evenings, Perry attended Christian Endeavor, an event he looked forward to each week, because he could see Phyllis Marie Stanton there. If he arrived early enough, he could talk to her alone and even steal a kiss in the window seat, before anyone else arrived. The high school kids ended the meeting by driving to Nu-Way, the hamburger joint, and ordering the locally famous sandwiches with a root beer, before going their separate ways.

Then one day at North High, Perry discovered something. He participated in some track and field events. What he discovered was that he didn't care about the hurdles or the javelin or any of those other events, but when he ran, he could feel the speed and it felt good, like flying.

Soon, with training and practice, he qualified for the track and field team, along with his cousin, Ernie Crow. Perry trained until he could run seventy-five yards in nine point one seconds, one hundred fifty yards in seventeen point eight seconds. He lettered in his senior year, a varsity runner. He could almost fly.

After graduation, he enrolled at Friends University and his life changed forever.

31

In the summer of 1937, Phyllis Marie and Lucille spent their free time—what little they had away from their jobs at Kress & Company—listening to records on the Victrola and playing ping-pong with some of the college boys in the basement of East Hall for Men.

"How does it feel to be a high school graduate, Phyllis Marie?" one of the men asked. "Didn't you finish a year early?"

Bip bap, bip, the ball said, bouncing on the hard green table. Billie Holliday sang "Moanin' Low" in the background.

"It feels great," she answered. "Fifteen-four."

"What kind of classes are you going to take at Friends?"

Bip bap, bip bap, bip.

"Sixteen four. Your serve. Languages," she said. "I want to join the Diplomatic Corps."

"Is your father going to let you do that?"

Bip bap, bip bap.

"Seventeen four. Why not?"

"Go easy, child! Can't you let an older man win?"

Bip bap, bip.

"Seventeen five, gramps, feel better?"

Lucille laughed, standing at the Victrola.

Bip bap, bip bap, bip bap.

"Eighteen five. Why wouldn't he let me?"

"Hmm, let's see. You're a girl, for one, and the world isn't a safe place for girls or boys these days, or haven't you noticed?"

Bip bap.

"Nineteen five. Seems just dandy to me."

Hazel's clear voice called out from the top of the basement stairs. "Phyllis Marie, is thee down there?"

Bip bap.

"Yes, Mother, I'm about to beat an old man at a game of

ping pong. Five twenty. My serve."

"Well, get up here quick. The Freshman Orientation Reception starts in an hour and thy date will be here soon!"

"Who's taking you to the shindig, kid?"

Bip bap, bip.

"No one you know, gramps. Five twenty-one: game, set, and match! Come on, Lucille!"

Actually, her date was someone the college man would have known. All the men in the dorm kept their eye out for Phyllis Marie Stanton as if she were their own little sister. Her brother Kenneth, away at the Eastman School of Music, wouldn't have it any other way, so they all looked after her like she was family and they all knew she had been dating Carter Thompson off and on since she was a ninth-grader at Allison.

Phyllis Marie was the kind of girl Carter's mother approved, due to her regular attendance at Monthly Meeting on Sunday mornings and Christian Endeavor Sunday evenings. Even if they weren't that serious, they had fun together, and Carter could even get the family car once in a while. He took Phyllis Marie to the movies on the occasional Friday night, double dating with Lucille and her beau.

Hazel knocked on her daughter's door just as Lucille tied Phyllis Marie's belt in the back. "Is thee in thy dress yet? He's coming up the front walk," she hissed in a half-whisper.

"Yes, I'm ready." Phyllis Marie called out, unconcerned about whether Carter heard her or not.

Downstairs, Edwin opened the door. "Come in, Carter," he greeted the boy. "Come right in." Edwin grimaced a bit, but tried not to let the scowl show on his face. What is that smell, he wondered?

"Here she is," Hazel said, chirping gaily into the front room.

Phyllis Marie followed behind her, pretty in her dress and smile.

"Good evening, Phyllis Marie," Carter said.

"Good evening, Carter. Do you like my—what on earth is

that dreadful smell? It smells like—shoe polish."

"Oh," Carter stammered.

"Oh," Edwin echoed.

"Oh," Phyllis Marie said. "You polished your shoes, didn't you? For me? How sweet."

The boy's face puckered pink and Hazel thought for a moment that he would simply melt into the front room carpet, but he gathered himself up and said, "Shall we be going?"

"Yes," Phyllis Marie said, "thank you."

They walked the short distance to the University and entered the Recreation Hall just five wordless minutes later.

"Would you like some punch, Phyllis Marie?"

"Certainly, thank you."

"I'll be right back."

She stood and watched as the children she had known for the last four years of attending school and church, entered the room and started milling about one another, asking the ordinary questions. Who teaches the science classes, she heard one say. Are you taking any math classes? I hear that professor grades on a curve. It all seemed rather dull until she noticed Perry Row and Gracie Belle Aley walk into the room.

Her mind started to spin. Gracie Belle's brother Bill is married to Perry's sister Lois. Does that make them in-laws? For some reason, while she pondered this question, Perry looked all the way across the room right at her.

"Here's your punch, Phyllis Marie," Carter said. "They have a nice assortment of cookies, too."

"Do they?" She never took her eyes from Perry.

"I considered bringing you some, but I didn't know what kind you'd like."

"Anything but macaroons, Carter."

"Okay, I'll be right back again."

Perry excused himself from Gracie Belle and walked over to Phyllis Marie in quick steps, never taking his eyes from her.

"Hello," he said, his eyes twinkling to match his smile.

"Hello."

"Are you having a good time?"

"Actually, I'm not."

"I thought not. Hello, Carter."

"Hello, Perry," Carter replied, feeling decidedly disadvantaged as he arrived from the refreshment table with bundles of cookies in napkins.

"Carter, would you mind very much if I took Phyllis Marie home? She's not having a good time. Would that be all right with you, Phyllis Marie?" He offered his arm.

"That would be fine," she said, taking his elbow, "if it's all right with Carter."

"Don't you want the punch and cookies I brought?"

"No, I really don't, Carter. You can have them."

Carter's shoulders sagged. "Well, okay, then. See you tomorrow."

"See you tomorrow."

Perry led her back across the room toward Gracie Belle, who stood laughing with a small crowd.

"Will you be alright to get home?"

She took one look at the couple and broke out in a big smile. "Sure, Ped, whatever you say."

"Good night, then." Perry and Phyllis Marie turned as one and headed for the door.

"Where are we going?" she asked.

"How about Dale Drug? I've got my mind set on something sweet." He placed his hand gently across the small of her back while they walked, as if to emphasize that the something sweet of which he spoke had nothing to do with Dale Drug.

She felt the hair on the back of her neck rise. *He's being pretty forward,* she thought. This was something new from Perry, who had always appeared a bit shy, even awkward around her, despite the occasional kiss before Christian Endeavor on Sundays. They had known each other since she moved to Wichita, seeing each other here and there, church and school, but somehow, this was different.

They walked along quietly until they reached the drug

store. He reached out and took the door, allowing her to enter first. His cousin, Ernie, sat at a table in the back with his girlfriend, Bertie, but if Perry saw them waving, he pretended that he did not, steering Phyllis Marie to a booth up front.

"What will you have?" he asked.

"Chocolate soda."

"Make it two," Perry said loudly, waving at the boy behind the ice cream counter, "and put them on my tab."

"Do you work here?"

"Yes."

"I don't remember seeing you here, but then I don't come here that often."

"No, what with your job at Kress & Company and school, you don't have time."

Phyllis Marie was surprised. "Do you have my schedule memorized?"

"No, not yet." His eyes and smile twinkled again. He leaned forward to kiss her and she met him halfway. Neither of them wanted to pull away.

32

Within a week of the beginning of school, Phyllis Marie settled into her new routine. Leaving home fifteen minutes before her eight o'clock class, with her books, sack lunch, and work uniform, she attended Archery and French, or World Civilization and English on alternate days until noon, when she ran for the downtown bus.

She ate her sack lunch on the bus and arrived at Kress & Company in time for her one o'clock shift, working four hours a day, Monday through Friday and a full shift every Saturday.

Meanwhile, Perry—his goal, as always, to fly—took a much tougher schedule, with English, World Civilization, Drafting, Calculus, Chemistry, and Track and Field classes during the day. He held down a job on occasional afternoons behind the ice cream counter at Dale Drug, and a part-time evening job parking cars and selling eggs on commission downtown, since the family that owned the parking lot owned a poultry farm as well.

The Saturday a week after the Freshman Orientation Reception, when Phyllis Marie got off work, she found Perry sitting on the curb waiting for her.

"Hello," she said. "So, now you really do have my schedule memorized." She watched carefully as he unfolded his six-foot frame and stood to his full height.

"I thought we might walk," he answered. "We could buy some milk and donuts."

"Donuts?"

"Yeah, there's a good place right up the street."

"Okay, let's go."

"Can I carry your books?"

"Sure." She passed her burden over to him, sensing the strength in his arms as he took it.

After visiting the donut shop, she asked, "If you could do

anything in the world, what would it be?"

"Fly." His eyes took on a gleam.

"Just like that. One word."

"Yep."

"What do you mean, in an airplane or like a bird or Peter Pan?"

"Any of those would do," he grinned, "but since it's unlikely I'll grow wings any time soon, I hope to learn how to fly airplanes."

"Isn't that dangerous?"

"Sure. Life is dangerous." He took a donut from the bag she carried and bit almost half of it away. "What about you?" he asked through his mouthful.

"I want to travel. No, wait. That's too selfish. I want my sister to get well."

"Your sister? Is she still having trouble with her eyes?"

"It's not her eyes. That's what one doctor thought, but it's more than that. She can't walk straight. She loses the feeling in her hands and arms and then it comes back."

"What do they think it is?"

"They don't know."

They walked along quietly, her shoulder pressed against his arm.

"What was the selfish thing you said? Oh, travel. Is that why you talk about joining the diplomatic corps?"

"Yes, I want to see the world, maybe make a difference in it."

"Maybe I could fly you there."

"Maybe."

With their donuts and milk in hand, they walked west to Perry's house. He led her in the back door and through the kitchen to where his mother, Georgia, stood in the living room at the ironing board, her back to them.

"Hi, Ped, honey, how was work?"

"I brought a friend home." He tickled his mother gently along her spine. A shiver ran up Phyllis Marie's back at the sight of his affection toward his mother. "Want a donut?"

"Oh! No, thank you!" She set the iron on the board and turned, wiping her hands in her gathered up apron. "Phyllis Marie Stanton! How nice to see you."

"Hello, Mrs. Row," Phyllis Marie said.

"We'll be in my room," he called over his shoulder.

"All right, dear. Dinner at seven! Can you stay, Phyllis Marie?"

"I'll call home and see about that."

"Don't eat too many donuts, children."

Perry led her to his room, actually a sleeping porch off the back of the house. Model airplanes hung on strings from the rafters and posters of airplanes covered the walls.

"You call this a room?"

"Sure," he said, climbing up on the bed, stretching his lean body to its fullest length.

"Doesn't it get too cold in the winter?"

"I have enough covers."

"You sure know how to show a girl a good time, don't you?" She grinned at him as she climbed up on the bed next to him. "Hand me a donut."

From that day forward, people understood that Perry and Phyllis Marie had become a couple. Perry's sister, Helen, still in high school, begged her brother to take her along on Friday nights when he took Phyllis Marie to the movies for ten cents each, but no dice, he would tell her. Friday night was the only night the two of them had alone together, except when they double-dated with Ernie and Bertie, or with Perry's friend and one of his girlfriends. Helen would have been a fifth wheel.

One Saturday evening after the weekly donuts and milk ritual, Clifton sat in his chair in the living room, listening to the radio while Georgia ironed. Perry and Phyllis Marie held hands on the sofa while Helen—stretched out full length on the floor—pretended to do her homework.

Phyllis Marie stood up and went over to Clifton's chair. Before anyone could stop her, she plunked herself down in his lap, as she was accustomed to doing with her own father.

"Oh!" he said.

Ignoring his exclamation, she reached up and twirled a lock of his wavy hair in her finger. "I don't think 'Papa' suits you," she said, almost absent-mindedly. Clifton's family froze breathlessly, waiting to see what his reaction would be to this overly familiar gesture.

"No?"

"No, I think I'm going to call you 'Dad!' "

Perry grinned while Georgia stifled a laugh in her apron.

Helen sat up straight. "No one calls him 'Dad,' " she protested. "His name is 'Papa!' "

"I'm going to," Phyllis Marie said.

"Child," Clifton said, trying to suppress the grin blooming on his face, "if you want to call me 'Dad,' then you can call me 'Dad.' "

One day, Perry met Phyllis Marie coming out of the Chapel, the same Chapel where they attended weekly services on Mondays, but this was not a Monday and Phyllis Marie looked strange to him.

"What's wrong?" he asked.

"I'm not supposed to tell."

"Oh." He looked at his shoes. "Sorority initiation, I suppose."

"How did you know?"

"I just went through my initiation, too. Everyone's involved in it this week."

"Not much of a secret, I guess."

"No. What did they make you do?"

"It was disgusting." A shiver ran down her spine at the thought of the rite they had made her perform. "They tied an oyster to a string and made me swallow it, and then they pulled it back up."

"It could have been worse."

"How?"

"I was blindfolded and made to eat mush that tasted—well, let's just say, it smelled like—nothing you'd want to eat."

"Ridiculous," she said. "Why do people go through this every year?"

"Beats me." He looked her in the eye. "Did you get in?"

"Yes."

"Me, too."

They held each other close, not wanting to let the embrace end.

That evening at home, Phyllis Marie sat down to dinner with her parents in their private apartment in the dormitory, but the mood was different. Phyllis Marie could sense it.

"What's the matter with you two?"

Edwin and Hazel looked at each other. Edwin put his fork down. "We wanted to talk to thee about this notion of joining the diplomatic corps."

"Notion? It's not a notion, it's a career choice."

"It's not a choice we are happy about," he told her. "We have an offer, well, a possibility, of a photography studio for sale in Caldwell, and we—"

"Caldwell? Where's that?"

"Idaho, near thy Uncle Alva and Aunt Gertrude. They want us to buy it and come live close to them, and with the three of us working in the studio, we think we can make a go of it."

"The three of us?" Phyllis Marie's shoulders sagged as her appetite flew out the window. She put her fork down, too. "We're moving to Idaho?"

"Not right away," Hazel pointed out.

"No, that's right," Edwin continued. "We won't go until the beginning of summer, and when we do, that is, when thy mother and I go, we'll leave you in the care of thy Aunt Blanche for a little while—"

"Just a few months, dear."

"Yes, that's right, just a few months, until we can arrange a place to live, and then—"

"Well, where will you and Mother live for those few months?"

"In the studio," he said. "We think that we can save money that way while we get the business back on a firm basis, and then when we have a place for us to live, we will send for thee."

"I'm not hungry," Phyllis Marie said. "May I go to my room?"

"Of course, dear," Hazel said. "I know this is something of a shock. We'll talk more later."

Phyllis Marie rose from the table and left the room.

Before Archery class the next day, Phyllis Marie met Perry outside his Calculus class.

"What are you doing here?" he asked. His eyes drilled into her, as he noticed her distress.

"Something awful has happened," she said. "We're moving to Idaho."

"When?"

"They're leaving at the beginning of summer. They expect me to join them later."

"So, you'll be staying in Wichita for a while, is that right? How long?"

"I don't know."

The bell rang. He kissed her and the electricity of his touch thrilled her. He turned and entered his classroom. She ran down the hall to the elevator, fighting back tears, and made her way to the roof section where the Archery instructor had set up straw bales and targets.

Her friend Mildred waved her over, smiling, but her smile faded when she saw Phyllis Marie's face. "Have you been crying?"

"I hate crying," Phyllis Marie answered. "It gives me a headache."

When it was her turn, Phyllis Marie put her toe to the line, nocked her arrow, drew it back and let it fly. The arrow completely missed the target, the straw bale, and the wall. It flew out into west Wichita, never to be seen again, at least, so she hoped.

That night at dinner, Phyllis Marie made an announcement of her own.

"I'm going to change my major." When neither of her parents reacted, she continued. "I'm going to take pre-nursing courses and start nursing school in the fall."

"No, Phyllis Marie," her father said, without looking up. "It's too dangerous, the work is very difficult, and thee would see all those men's bodies."

Edwin looked across at his daughter's disappointment, her face pointing down into her lap.

"You are going to come work in our photography studio and become a professional photographer. I don't want to hear another word about it."

Phyllis Marie sat motionless.

"Now eat thy dinner."

He waited for her to pick up her fork.

"Yes, Father," she said miserably.

33

Phyllis Marie Stanton Row continued her review of memories for two sleepless nights, stopping for little else, until she had resolved that there was nothing to do. *Maybe when the war is over,* she thought, *I'll be able to learn the truth of what happened, but until then, I have to start accepting the fact that he is dead, or a prisoner somewhere. As much as I'd like to believe he is hiding in some barn in the French countryside, or—*

"Phyllis Marie," a voice hissed in the dark. "Wake up."

"I'm awake," she said. "Come in." She propped herself up on the sofa and turned on a light. Hazel and Edwin, both in robes and slippers, came padding into their daughter's half of the shared duplex.

"Can't sleep?" Hazel asked.

"No, not since the telegram."

"I thought not, so when it came, I told thy father we should just come up."

"When what came?"

"This," Edwin said, producing a yellow envelope from his robe pocket.

"Another telegram?" Phyllis Marie sat up with a jolt. "When did this come? Why didn't you give it to me sooner?"

"It just came a moment ago," he said.

"At this hour?"

"It's marked 'Urgent.' "

"Open it," Hazel said.

Phyllis Marie looked at the envelope first. "It isn't from the government, it's from England."

"Open it."

"Open it."

She feared its contents, didn't want to know what she thought it said, but finally, curiosity won out.

She scanned it quickly, smiled, then read aloud:

IT IS NOT TRUE STOP
MY PARTY CANCELLED STOP
IT SEEMS MIRACULOUS STOP
BUT WHAT ELSE STOP
YOU I MICKEY SAFE STOP
I CANNOT SAY MORE STOP
THIS HAPPY NEW YEAR STOP
LOVE PERRY

"He's alive!" she shouted. "He's back in England and he's safe!"

She gave the telegram to Edwin, who read it, but only understood part of it.

"The code," she said. "Remember the code? He's back in Ipswich, back at his airfield."

"What code?" Hazel asked, taking the telegram.

"Who's Mickey?" Edwin asked.

"Oh, it's a very long story, but he's going to be your grandson!" She wrapped her arms around him and hugged him tightly before transferring her affection to her mother.

34

Perry looked over his left shoulder at the source of the terrible gnashing sound, the sound of a Nazi rocket shredding his number one engine from the inside out, leaving only a gaping hole in his dead wing. He felt the airplane sag as the weight of the entire craft re-centered on the one surviving engine.

"E! Move that fuel to the right wing! Now!"

He thought about the fog for a moment, wondered how long it would last, as he switched over to instrument flying. The fog hid him from the enemy fighters but made it harder to find his way to safety. He needed to maintain altitude if possible.

"Can we clear the cliffs?"

"We've got to lighten the load."

"Jettison everything! The empty fuel tanks! All the guns! All the ammo!"

After E completed the fuel transfer, Phyllis Marie flew a little better, but she was still a pig on wheels with just one engine. He and the gunners started working on dropping the auxiliary tanks through the open bomb bay doors, but there was a problem. The first tank in the bomb rack stuck, for no reason they could see. E took a screwdriver and stepped out on the catwalk.

"Put your parachute on," Matt called to him.

"No time," E said. He pried up the safety catch on one side that the ground crew had installed, but he saw that both of them had to be pried up at once.

"Matt!" he called. "Get a screwdriver! Pry up that other one on your end!

Working together—neither man wearing parachutes over the open bomb bay doors—the two men pried the safety catch up and over the bar holding it in place and the first auxiliary tank flew out from under them. E nearly lost his balance, but he caught himself against the bomb rack. The remaining three auxiliary tanks followed, and they watched as the tanks splashed into the English Channel below.

'What was that?" Perry shouted.

"The auxiliary tanks being jettisoned." Bud watched as the two men came back to safety off the catwalk.

"Bud," Perry said.

"Yes."

"I need altitude readings compared to the elevation of the cliffs we're approaching. I need to know whether to try a crash on land or in the water."

"I can give you that, hold on."

"Sooner than later, please."

Bud examined the instruments for a few moments before answering. "You've gotten margin of safety right now of—"

Perry held to his course, waiting to hear.

"A hundred feet."

"Landing gear up," Perry said.

"Landing gear up."

"Holding steady at a hundred feet."

"Thirty seconds to landfall at ninety feet," Bud said.

"Pilot to crew, assume crash positions."

"Twenty seconds to landfall at eighty feet."

Perry could see texture ahead: the cliffs rising up, and the trees of a farmer's windbreak.

"Ten seconds to landfall at seventy feet."

"I need a nice soft lettuce patch," Perry said.

"Landfall, sixty feet."

"Some of these trees are sixty feet."

"There!" Bud pointed to a patch of green in the distance.

Perry counted down. "Five four three two one—"

The Flying Fortress bellied into the green crop and brown soil beneath, tipping to the right because of the weight imbalance. Perry pulled lightly left, keeping her right wingtip from touching as long as possible, until finally she ground-looped to a stop.

"Everyone all right?"

The loud cheering drowned out Perry's question.

Half a dozen men came running toward them, all carrying pitchforks and other farm-implement weapons, but as soon as they were close enough to see that the Phyllis Marie wasn't a Nazi aircraft, they relaxed their warrior-like attitude.

"Are you hurt?" one farmer asked as Perry dropped out of the forward hatch.

"No, I think we're all fine, except for the plane. Is there a telephone I can use? I need to make arrangements to get it out of your field."

"I haven't got a phone. All that will have to wait. There's a blackout," he said. "All the lines are down. Nazis are bombing London. We thought you were them."

"Sorry about your field," Perry said.

"Don't worry your head," the man smiled. "It's a cover crop. I'll be plowing it under in a week or two."

"I need to get these men back to base."

"I can drive you part way in my truck, but not until after the blackout. Can I offer you gentlemen some tea?"

Between the frequent blackouts and the fact that none of the crew had any money or identification other than their dog tags, it took them two days to return to Framlingham. They climbed out of yet another farmer's truck in front of the airfield and headed straight for the mess hall, where the staff fed them leftovers and sent a messenger to the base commander.

"You boys are a sight for sore eyes," the commander said, storming through the door. "Where's my airplane?"

"Somewhere south, in a field between Dover and Deal, sir."

"Got a bit off course?" he grinned.

"Just a bit."

"Now, gentlemen, I'll be working day and night to rectify this thing for you, so don't worry about it. Just relax for a few days, and we'll get it taken care of."

"What thing is that, sir?"

"Oh, well, you've been declared MIA, mission in action,

and unfortunately, Uncle Sam does make things a bit uncomfortable for guys like you who make it back."

"How so, sir?"

"Well, your pay has been stopped, for one thing, your families notified, your possessions gathered up and placed in storage, but we'll get it all straightened out. Who would like to send a telegram home, courtesy of the Eighth Air Force?"

35

"March 8, 1944, Dear Phyllis Marie, it has been six months since last I could write a letter to you in confidence that it would not be censored. Although I will be seeing you soon, I have so much to tell you, and so much free time now, that I will take advantage of both. You've asked about the mission where I was declared missing, and there really is little more I can add that I haven't already told you. It was a secret mission and I transported VIPs to a secret location. The return flight was bad, the worst I have seen in this war, with one exception, the day I lost Billy. To this day, I still have nightmares about that moment, seeing Billy's plane break into a fireball and drop like a stone. I wake up, and I'm certain I have been yelling 'jump' out loud. Anyway, after the secret mission, the brass put us out to pasture a bit. Perhaps they could not assign us while we were still listed as MIA, or they thought we were shattered by the experience, or they just wanted to give the green crews enough rookie experience that they could benefit from having a veteran crew around, I don't know. Finally, when they let us fly again, we had to fly another airplane, a worthy enough ship, Rovin' Ramona, while they made extensive repairs to Phyllis Marie. They kept promising to have Phyllis Marie ready for our last mission, but it just wasn't in the cards. Another crew will get her, and I hope she serves them as well as she did us. Our first mission back, to Heuringhem, France, was an easy one, and because he had flown so many extra missions at the beginning of our tour, Bud Fitzsimmons rotated out. Dix decided to stay and marry the Irish girl, so I don't know what will become of him. He might go back in for another rotation. I read the article about Wallace Balckman's crash. What irony, to have died while training a crew, after his decision not to pursue a combat career. If you write to Eve, please convey my condolences to her. I could not write to you about an accident

I had, or rather, didn't have, involving my crew. We were required to attend an armaments lecture, despite our twenty-some missions, and the instructor did something wrong, I still don't know what. The bomb exploded, sending fragments in every direction, and even though I sat in the front row, right in front of this joker, I was not touched, but Boettcher, Mack, and Kiss were all injured, Mack the worst of it. It was just wrong-headed to require veteran crewmembers to attend such a thing. Now Mack must stay behind to complete his missions after he recuperates. The rest of us finished our last two missions in late January and early February, both in Rovin' Ramona, both to Frankfurt-am-Main, and both without incident. Except for Mack and the replacement co-pilot I had for the end, we all finished up. The co-pilot will have to catch rides with other crews now. E, Eric Bennett, got word he has a new daughter, just before we all shipped out in several different directions. Bud went on 10-day detached service giving Public Relations talks in London. Biehl stayed behind to provide some training. Kiss signed on for another tour of duty. Byrne, Boettcher and I spent two weeks at the CCRC, Combat Crew Replacement Center, including my birthday, but they were re-located and I was still waiting. Statistics show I am a man of some twenty-six years of age, now. I feel like a kid of nineteen, but I have to admit I am getting older. I begrudge giving this part of our life to this unholy business, though it may be better to be separated now than to have to be separated later when our children are growing up. As it is now, we can have the pleasure of raising them together. One never knows what might have happened had events occurred otherwise. I spent a lot of time playing blackjack with some other bored officers, listening to Tommy Dorsey on the radio, and eating fine meals on tablecloths. Finally, I departed for Liverpool on a troop truck and boarded US Army transport ship Edmund B. Alexander, anchored in Liverpool harbor, where I ate steak and white bread for the first time in 6 months. The crossing has taken seven days, and now, as I write to you, I can just make out the growing skyline of New York City. Tomorrow I will disembark, drop this in the mail, and send you a telegram, which you will have already gotten by the time you see this. I hope to see you on or before our St. Patrick's Day Wedding Anniversary. Love, Perry."

MARCH 11 1944 IN NEW YORK WILL BE HOME SOON PERRY

MARCH 13 1944 MEET ME UTAH HOTEL SALT LAKE TUESDAY 14 RESERVATIONS MADE PERRY

MARCH 14 1944 PHYLLIS MARIE DARLING DELAYED ENROUTE SEE YOU ABOUT NOON THE FIFTEENTH UTAH HOTEL

Phyllis Marie stood in the lobby of the Utah Hotel reading the newspaper, or trying to read it, attempting to contain her excitement. She wore the same burgundy suit she had worn on her wedding day four years earlier, and refrained from sitting to avoid unsightly creases across her lap. She glanced out the window at every passing soldier, wondering, *is that him? Will I even recognize him after all the things he has been through, or will he look the same?*

After another glance at the paper and one out the window, she looked up at the desk—and there he was, his uniform hanging on him, easily two sizes too large. She heard him ask for her by name and as she started to walk toward him, the clerk looked at her over Perry's shoulder, a look Perry caught and followed. He turned, took two steps toward her and caught her in his arms. As they kissed, guests in the lobby and patrons in the hotel restaurant watched the handsome embracing couple, each of them projecting their own thoughts and circumstances regarding love, the war, or their own loved ones away at the front. Perry and Phyllis Marie paid them no heed, lost in their embrace, as they turned and entered the elevator. The bellman stood by with Perry's duffel.

"Three," Phyllis Marie told the elevator operator, without taking her eyes from her husband's face.

They stepped into their room, holding or touching in some way, whatever was possible, comfortable, never allowing their contact to break.

"You're here," she said finally as the bellman closed the door behind him.

"I'm here," he replied.

They undressed quickly, embracing again, touching every pore of skin that they could. She pulled him gently onto the bed, which she had already turned down, smoothing out the sheets in the morning after she had awakened.

Hours later, he unpacked and placed the bottle of 1928 champagne on ice. They celebrated his return with a turkey dinner served by room service.

He brought something else out of his duffel.

"Here," he said. "I promised to bring him home safely, but he didn't fare quite as well as I did." Perry handed Phyllis Marie the plastic Mickey doll, his abdomen punctured. "I found this—" he handed her a fragment of metal, about the size of a bottle cap, "—wedged between my boot and pants leg, after the same flight. I think this is what hit him."

"What is it?"

"Flak."

Phyllis Marie kissed the little toy. "Then if it hadn't hit him, it would have hit you. Maybe he even saved your life."

"Maybe." Perry smiled into her luminous green eyes. "Because something sure did."

Back home a few weeks later, at a celebration of his return from the war, Perry insisted on sitting at a table in the restaurant where he could keep his back to a corner and his eyes on the patrons and staff, making people very uncomfortable. Phyllis Marie recognized for the first time the extent that her husband's experiences had changed him.

He suffered from nightmares nearly every night, punctuated with horrible moans and groans of agony. He thrashed about so much that Phyllis Marie had to flee their bed on several occasions, or risk getting an inadvertent slam or kick. Photographs taken after the war showed a much more sober countenance than those of the carefree boy in his scarlet and gray letterman's sweater.

Word came from Arthur Dix, still in England, that the rookie crew assigned to the fully renovated Phyllis Marie promptly lost her on their first mission, a bombing raid to Berlin. Some of the crew parachuted, but one man was too wounded to jump, so the pilot made a forced landing in the damaged airplane behind enemy lines. Without lucky crew seven, Dix wrote, the ship had lost its magic. The Phyllis Marie spent the remainder of the war in the Luftwaffe KG 200 as a Nazi decoy ship.

Perry spent the remainder of the war in relative comfort, ferrying B-29s from manufacturing plants to airfields, enjoying the sheer joy of flying without combat, and yet when the war ended and he received his honorary discharge, he announced to Phyllis Marie and his family that he was through with piloting.

Perry was not through with flight, though. He used his GI bill to major in Aeronautical Engineering, and when he got his degree, there was a job waiting for him with Boeing in Wichita.

Shortly after their return to Kansas, in the autumn of 1946, Perry and Phyllis Marie fulfilled one of their promises to one another by giving birth to their son, Michael. They called him Mickey.

Epilogue

"Hello?" Michael answered the phone in the dark.

"It's your mother," Phyllis Marie said. "I need your help."

"What time is it?"

"It's late. I don't know. It's late. I can't get your father off the toilet."

"What do you mean?"

"He's too weak to stand up. He nearly fell, and now I can't get him back to bed."

"I'll be right there." He hung up the phone.

Michael turned on a lamp and looked at his reflection in the mirror. At fifty-one, he resembled his late grandfather Clifton more than either parent, but at this moment, he searched unconsciously for any resemblance he could find to his father, Perry. Finding it—in the way he held his head and shoulders—he threw on a shirt and some pants before stepping into a pair of sandals and driving the ten minutes to his parents' apartment.

"Can you put your arms around me?" he asked his father. "No, over my shoulders like—yeah, let's try that."

He half carried and half dragged Perry from the bathroom and backed him up against the bed, flopping him down as gently as possible. Phyllis Marie caught his feet and swung them up onto the mattress. Perry seemed to fall asleep within seconds of having the covers pulled over him.

Slumped at the dining room table, she looked more distraught and more exhausted than Michael had ever seen her. He sat down next to her.

"What am I going to do?" she asked. "He's a lot weaker and I can't do this alone anymore."

"I know."

"I called your brother earlier and told him about the appointment with the doctor today. He asked if it was time for him to take a leave of absence from work and I told him no."

"But I think it is time," he said. "Just like we've been planning."

She looked into her son's eyes. She could see from his face that he was right, but admitting it seemed like giving up somehow. She didn't like the idea.

Michael stood up and walked toward the study.

"Where are you going?"

"To call him."

Her younger son Terry arrived the following morning in time for a meeting with the doctor.

"Perry's wish is to die at home," Phyllis Marie said. "He doesn't want to be attached to any machines or to have his life extended artificially in any way. Is there any reason we can't honor that wish?"

"No," the doctor replied. "I can recommend a hospice nurse who can come in for an hour each morning if you want."

"Fellers," she asked, "are you with me on this?"

"Yes," Michael said. "We can work in shifts so there are always two of us available and one resting."

The doctor called around and found a hospice nurse who had an opening starting in six days, on Monday. Phyllis Marie and her sons agreed that they could take care of Perry without her for the remainder of the week.

"Do you need help making any kind of final arrangements?" the doctor asked.

"You mean funeral arrangements," she replied. "We are both to be cremated and our ashes scattered at sea. It has all been paid for, long ago."

"That's good," he said. "Nothing to worry about, then. Remember, when the end comes, it doesn't constitute an emergency. You don't need to call 911. Just call the hospice and they will arrange transportation."

"I understand," Phyllis Marie said through the tears she tried to hold back. "I hate crying. It gives me a headache."

"I know this is hard," the doctor said, taking her hand. "When that time comes, I recommend that you don't call them right away. Take a little time and allow yourself some time alone to grieve."

"Yes, I will."

The doctor installed a catheter before he left—to prevent any more dangerous midnight trips to the bathroom—and he arranged for the local pharmacy to send over a prescription of morphine tablets.

In spite of the cool November temperatures, Perry wanted only a sheet over him. Whether that was because of the cancer, they didn't know, but they removed the blanket and bedspread after he kept kicking them away. Phyllis Marie and her sons took turns sitting with him, holding his hand, looking after his needs, but he said very little until the second afternoon.

"Phyllis Marie?" he asked.

"I'm here," she said, squeezing his hand and turning her face away to hide her tears.

"Listen to me," he said gently. "This very important to me." He waited until she turned back to him. "If I don't come back, don't waste your money on a funeral."

"What are you talking about? We've already paid for our cremations."

He continued. "Take the money and go to Wichita. Spend it on a party with our families and friends. Spend it on a celebration of what my life meant. Promise me you won't waste your time crying."

"Yes," she said, remembering the night before he flew out of Scott Field. "I promise." She wiped at the corner of her eye with her sleeve.

On Thursday, he responded very little. Phyllis Marie put her mouth to his ear and spoke loudly, saying, "Perry!"

"Mm-hmm." He opened his eyes briefly.

"Are you warm enough?"

"Mm-hmm."

Later that day, he seemed asleep, but his face twisted into

a contorted grimace.

"Perry!"

"Mm-hmm."

"Are you in pain?"

"Mm-hmm."

"Let's give him another pill," she said. "He shouldn't have to suffer any pain."

By Friday, he could no longer take pills or drink water from a straw. Phyllis Marie called the doctor who arranged a delivery of liquid sublingual morphine.

"Shouldn't we arrange for some kind of intra-venous drip, now that he's not able to drink water?"

"That depends on whether you want to prolong his life artificially," the doctor said.

"No. We agreed on that before."

"His organs are shutting down now," he explained. "It's a natural part of the process. Keep him comfortable and free of pain. That's the best we can do now."

Late Friday night, his breathing slowed.

Twenty minutes after midnight on early Saturday morning, he took one last heavy breath and died.

"Shouldn't we call someone?" Terry asked.

"Not yet," she said. "Let's take a few minutes alone with him first. Would you turn on some music? Michael, will you turn the lights down low? I'll make a pot of coffee."

They sat together for a couple of hours, the three of them, around Perry's bed, stroking his shoulder, patting his hand and witnessing the event.

Phyllis Marie held Perry's hand and rubbed his forearm. "He told me that when he died, he wanted me to throw a big party for the family," she said through her tears. "I want to go to Wichita. Will you take me?"

"Yes," her sons answered.

Her sons made the arrangements just as she wished. They held a celebration of his life in the basement of University Friends Church, where Perry and Phyllis Marie had attended Sunday school, where they had first kissed.

Over two hundred people attended—sisters and brothers and in-laws and cousins and nieces and nephews from every branch of the four families—so many people that they had to draw back the room dividers and set up additional chairs for the overflow crowd. Phyllis Marie spoke first, followed by each of her sons.

Phyllis Marie held back her tears and smiled at her large extended family, telling stories about her life with Perry, taking enormous comfort from the knowledge that she had honored his last wishes.

The End

ALSO BY TERRY ROW
FICTION / LITERARY

SUMMER CAPRICORN

The late-afternoon shadows lengthened into a mid-August evening. Ravens flitted among the redwood treetops, as Adam went into the corral to replenish feed and water, and to shovel manure to the compost heaps. The playful kids came up to him and butted him, and he clapped their sides, producing lovely thumping sounds on their broad abdomens. One of them turned and reared up on his hind legs and butted Adam in the upper thigh, the force nearly knocking him over. He hadn't noticed, but over the course of a few weeks, they had become much bigger.

"It won't be long now." Bill's voice from the fence surprised Adam as much as this new appreciation for the size and strength of the kids.

"He almost knocked me over."

"They've had a big growth spurt. What's the yield?"

"Barely eight quarts a day."

"We can make it go back up for a while if we separate them from their mothers. But they'll keep us awake at night if we do."

Adam looked at Bill. Bill stared vacantly across the corral toward the river.

"What do you want to do?"

Bill answered by shaking his head and looking up into the trees.

Clifton Edwin Publishing
3463 State St., PMB 244
Santa Barbara, CA 93105
805 344 1431
www.CliftonEdwin.com

ORDER BLANK

TITLE	PRICE	QTY	EXT. PRICE
Summer Capricorn *by Terry Row*	$15.95 x	____	_____
Untarnished Reputation *by Terry Row*	$14.95 x	____	_____
Phyllis Marie	$17.95 x	____	_____

SUB-TOTAL   _____

SALES TAX (CA RESIDENTS)   x 0.0875

SUB-TOTAL   _____

SHP./HND. ($1.95 PER BOOK)   +   _____

TOTAL   _____

Send check with this order blank to:

> Clifton Edwin Publishing
> 3463 State St., PMB 244
> Santa Barbara, CA 93105

Or order online at:

> www.CliftonEdwin.com

Or call:

> 805 344 1431

ALSO BY TERRY ROW

HISTORICAL FICTION

UNTARNISHED REPUTATION

"*I say, sir,*" *I said, rather tactlessly, nearly shouting to him at a distance of only a few feet. "Are you Doc Holliday of Tombstone?" I extended my right hand toward him.*

The clerk dropped to the floor behind the front desk while everyone else in the room, including Sheriff Johnson, took several steps back. Doc Holliday dropped his right hand to within an inch of his sidearm and fixed me with a stare that chilled my marrow.

"*I am, sir,*" *he said, slowly, "although I no longer claim that town for my home address." After a moment, I dropped my hand, too, and he grinned at me. "Please forgive me if I do not shake hands with you. I shake hands with no one." His skin drew so tightly I could see the outline of his skull beneath his gaunt features.*

"*Theodore Roosevelt, New York and the Dakotas,*" *I continued, introducing myself to him for a second time. "I beg your pardon, sir. I'm often told I speak too freely. I meant no offense or embarrassment.*"

Clifton Edwin Publishing
3463 State St., PMB 244
Santa Barbara, CA 93105
805 344 1431
www.CliftonEdwin.com

ORDER BLANK

TITLE	PRICE	QTY	EXT. PRICE
Summer Capricorn *by Terry Row*	$15.95 x	____	_____
Untarnished Reputation *by Terry Row*	$14.95 x	____	_____
Phyllis Marie	$17.95 x	____	_____

SUB-TOTAL _____

SALES TAX (CA RESIDENTS) x 0.0875

SUB-TOTAL _____

SHP./HND. ($1.95 PER BOOK) + _____

TOTAL _____

Send check with this order blank to:

Clifton Edwin Publishing
3463 State St., PMB 244
Santa Barbara, CA 93105

Or order online at:

www.CliftonEdwin.com

Or call:

805 344 1431